# *The* Summer *That* Shaped Us

# *The* Summer *That* Shaped Us

### A Novel

## LORI WILDE

AVON

*An Imprint of HarperCollinsPublishers*

THE SUMMER THAT SHAPED US. Copyright © 2025 by Laurie Vanzura. All rights reserved. Printed in the United States of America. No part of this book may be used or reproduced in any manner whatsoever without written permission except in the case of brief quotations embodied in critical articles and reviews. For information, address HarperCollins Publishers, 195 Broadway, New York, NY 10007.

HarperCollins books may be purchased for educational, business, or sales promotional use. For information, please email the Special Markets Department at SPsales@harpercollins.com.

Avon, Avon & logo, and Avon Books & logo are registered trademarks of HarperCollins Publishers in the United States of America and other countries.

FIRST EDITION

Interior text design by Diahann Sturge-Campbell

Title page and chapter opener art © Danussa/Shutterstock.com

Library of Congress Cataloging-in-Publication Data has been applied for.

ISBN 978-0-06-335215-5

25 26 27 28 29 LBC 5 4 3 2 1

*This book is dedicated to all the little girls who had mothers they couldn't trust. I see you, honor your strength, and send love for your healing.*

# *The* Summer *That* Shaped Us

# Chapter 1
## *Eloisa*

*"A challenge is nothing more than opportunity in disguise."*
—*Eloisa Hobby*

Each sunrise, for the last fifteen years since she created Hobby Island, Eloisa dined on a breakfast of fresh berries, homemade scones, clotted cream, and peppermint tea. She fed her sweet calico, Felena; donned a festive hat that often didn't match her outfit; detoured into the flower garden; and plucked a bright bloom and stuck it in her hatband. She would gather her needlework, mount her unicycle, and pedal through the cobblestone streets of Crafters' Corner, her knitting needles clacking.

"Halloo!" she called to everyone she met and nodded as she purled and pedaled. "Good morning to you."

"Good morning. Halloo!" they'd echo, raising hands and sending sunny smiles in greeting.

"Great day to be alive!" She would give a merry laugh and cycle on, a tail of colorful yarn flying out behind her.

But not today.

Today was different.

Today was troubled.

In all honesty, today stunk like Auntie Dot's salves and poultices.

Not that Dot's pungent home remedies weren't helpful, for they were, but the liniments and tinctures reeked to high heaven.

On this sun-kissed dawn in early May, the island's sole security officer, Paul Chance, knocked on her front door while Eloisa was still in her terry-cloth bathrobe. Felena weaved around her ankles, mewing, as Eloisa let Paul inside.

"Good morning, Paul." Her smile was cheery as ever, but the look in his eyes and his unannounced arrival on her doorstep suggested this was not a happy visit. "Come in, come in. Would you like some peppermint tea?"

"No, ma'am." He doffed his sun-faded Tilley hat and held it clutched in one hand. Bits of dewy grass clung to the cuffs of his work pants, and garden shears protruded from his back pocket. "I have unpleasant news."

Eloisa suspected as much.

Paul was a striking man of forty. Dark hair. Straight white teeth. Tall. Strong. Handsome. Julie, his late wife, had been Eloisa's ex-husband's niece. And Paul was like a nephew to her.

She had built the resort for crafters around the same time Paul became a single father. Circumstances pushed him to leave his cybersecurity work for the navy, and that's when Eloisa stepped in, offering him a job and a free, safe place to raise his little girl.

It had been Paul's idea to pose as the island's gardener. A discreet way to observe the guests and circumvent problems before they started. Win-win for Eloisa to have a security officer and an accomplished gardener wrapped up into one excellent employee. She couldn't run the place without him.

Eloisa smoothed her bedhead hair, tightened the sash on her robe, and led the way into her tidy office. She eased down onto the vibrant green settee and patted the cushion beside her as the pastel fingers of dawn slipped across the room and Felena hopped into her lap.

Paul settled in, resting his Tilley hat on his knee. He smelled of springtime dew, jacaranda blossoms, and cedar mulch, an earthy, steadfast scent.

"What's brought you here on this fine day?" Eloisa met Paul's intense blue eyes.

"The algorithm I created for your private quilters' group"—Paul's voice was even, but Eloisa heard tension running through it—"flags unusual activity, things like rapid private message exchanges or repeated contact with multiple members."

Eloisa nodded. Her understanding of technology was limited, but her grasp of human nature was profound.

"And what has your algorithm discovered?" She scratched the calico behind her ears.

"It's identified a pattern consistent with online scammers, targeting members of your quilting circle. A user has been catfishing other group members by pretending to be a love interest." Paul paused, allowing the gravity of the situation to sink in.

"My goodness, a sweetheart scam." Eloisa bit her bottom lip as Felena's soft paws kneaded her lap. "That's dreadful, but how can we be certain? I don't want to accuse anyone without solid evidence."

"The algorithm picked up a cluster of complaints from the members, along with unusual account activity. One member, in particular, Jeanie Montgomery, seems to have been hit the hardest. There's evidence suggesting she's lost a significant sum of money, perhaps even her life savings." Paul pressed his lips together, pity in his eyes.

"Oh dear." Eloisa placed a palm to her heart. "I feel so responsible."

"It's not your fault. We had every safeguard in place, but scammers do what scammers do. Don't worry. We'll nip this in the bud. That's why you've got me . . ." His gaze sought hers. "There's something else you should know."

Eloisa tilted her head and peered into his trustworthy eyes. "And what is that, my dear?"

"I'm acquainted with Jeanie Montgomery."

"What a strange coincidence!"

"Not that strange. Jeanie's a seamstress by trade and an avid quilter. You run one of the biggest online quilting forums in the world. It's just unfortunate that another member of the group targeted her."

Was this a conflict of interest for Paul? Eloisa searched his body language for clues. He wasn't a secretive man, but he was self-contained. "What's your association with Jeanie?"

"Back in high school, I dated Jeanie's daughter, Luna."

"Ahh, blast from your past."

"It's stirred a memory or two." He gave an amused smile, but the look in his eyes signaled her to leave the topic alone. Eloisa could see that this Luna woman was a painful wound, even after two decades.

She wondered what had happened, but she was far too polite to ask. "All right."

"I'm just being up-front. Full disclosure."

"I appreciate that. As for the scammer, do we have any idea who it is?"

"From the interactions and patterns," he said, keeping his explanation simple for her, "I've narrowed it down to three group members. All have displayed similar red-flag behaviors."

"Three suspects. That's impressive, Paul, that you weeded out so many others. We have over six hundred thousand members on the forum."

"I did work for the NSA for six months," he reminded her. "They taught me skills many don't have. I just wish I could pinpoint the culprit."

Eloisa let out a soft sigh. Well, this news put a crimp in her day. "We must act, Paul. We can't allow deceit, manipulation, and theft to harm our sacred space."

"I agree."

"Any suggestions?"

"I propose we invite Jeanie and the three suspects here for the quilting competition this summer. Send out those coveted golden tickets of yours, all expenses paid. Who could turn down a gratis vacation to Hobby Island?"

"Excellent idea."

"We'll watch the suspects when they get here and uncover who the real scammer is so we can confront them in person." Paul rested his palms flat against his thighs.

"What if one or more of them doesn't accept the invitation?"

"We'll observe those who do come and either rule them in or out and whoever is left . . ." He trailed off.

"Hmm, it just might work. And we'll give the culprit an opportunity to make amends once we've identified the scammer."

"I knew you were going to say that." A rueful shake of his head along with an affectionate laugh. "That's where it gets sticky. If the scammer doesn't confess when confronted with the evidence, we'll have no choice but to notify the authorities."

Eloisa considered this. "Or we create such an atmosphere of love and acceptance, the wrongdoer is eager to unburden themselves and receive forgiveness for their misdeeds."

"That's your way, Auntie Eloisa. Leading with kindness and compassion," Paul said. "Trouble is, not everyone is redeemable."

She understood that truth far more than Paul realized. Eloisa thought of the wealthy megachurch preacher her religious-zealot parents had forced her to marry when she was seventeen. She snapped her fingers and shut off the memories. *Poof!* Not letting that man live rent free in her head.

"Not everyone, no," she said. "But many people, and I'd hazard to say most, are capable of change."

"I'm here to do whatever you need."

Eloisa panned the landscape outside the window with a sweeping hand and giggled. "We'll send out golden tickets to Jeanie and the three potential scammers. They can each bring two family members or friends with them so they will feel at ease. And Hobby Island shall be the stage where this mystery unravels."

"That's the spirit." Paul got to his feet.

Cradling Felena in her arms, Eloisa showed Paul to the door, wished him good day, and assumed her morning routine, but the startling news had thrown her off-kilter. In the kitchen, she burned the scones and put too much sugar in her tea, and when she picked up her knitting, she discovered she dropped a stitch several rows back.

"Fiddlesticks." Frowning, Eloisa examined the dropped stitch, her mind still whirling with the unfolding online drama.

She needed to rebalance herself.

Eloisa got dressed, squared her shoulders, lifted her chin, and straightened her hat. Time to take her own advice.

"Challenges are just opportunities in disguise," she said to Felena, who watched her from the middle of the patchwork quilt.

Outside on her unicycle, Eloisa took several deep, calming breaths, the scent of the sea mingling with the floral fragrances of the island. Today might have brought unexpected news, but it also brought a chance to right a wrong and protect her cherished community.

And wasn't that the purpose of Hobby Island? A place where challenges turned into triumphs, and stitches, in fabric or in life, could be mended with tender loving care.

Resolute, she pulled her knitting from her pocket, went to work on the dropped stitch, and cycled on.

# Chapter 2
## *Luna*

*"Even the most tangled yarn can be unknotted."*
—*Eloisa Hobby*

L una Montgomery Boudreaux was six years old when she first realized she couldn't trust her mother.

Middle of the night. Stormy winds lashing the panes. Thunder growling throughout the hollow. Stark lightning electric bright. Jeanie's eyes wide, hair wild. Shaking Luna from sleep. Dragging her off the bare mattress. Snatching up Luna's clothes from the floor and stuffing them in a black garbage bag.

"Come on, honey, wake up. We gotta get out of here. Our last chance."

Luna confused, yawning, stumbling into threadbare sneakers and the hand-me-down jacket that was two sizes too big. It wasn't the first midnight awakening, and it wouldn't be the last. Jeanie's urgent murmuring to "*hurry, hurry, hurry.*"

"Where we goin'?" Luna asked, rubbing the sleep from her eyes.

"Shh, shh, don't wake the others."

"Why?"

"No questions. Just do as I say."

Mad dash from the derelict house in the drenching rain without an umbrella, trash bag bouncing against Jeanie's side. Jumping into the Bondo jalopy. Shivering on the cold seat as Mom popped the clutch. They shot from the driveway, tires squealing.

Careening down the pothole-filled dirt road, making a clean getaway, but then a figure stepped from the shadows in front of the car, blocking their escape.

*Daddy.*

Rain-soaked and furious, Jack carried a bottle of Wild Turkey by the neck between two fingers.

Mom gunned the engine and for one horrifying second, Luna thought she would run him over. She cringed, brought her knees to her chest, curled her icy fingers into fists, swallowed a whimper, and braced for impact.

But Jeanie slammed on the brakes just in time, coming within inches of hitting Luna's swaying father. He hunched his shoulders and lowered his head like a bull ready to charge, nostrils flaring, eyes black as the night.

He bellowed louder than the howling wind. *"Jeanie!"*

Jack and Jeanie stared at each other through the windshield, and it was as if a strange, hypnotic spell wove over her mother.

Dad flung the whiskey bottle into the ditch. Mom tumbled from the car, leaving the door hanging wide open and rain blowing in.

Jeanie ran to him.

He caught her in his arms, spun her around, and covered her face in kisses, rain falling in sheets, wipers squeaking across the glass as Luna bit her fingernails and feared another vehicle would come around the curve and hit them.

Dad, smelling of whiskey, climbed in behind the wheel. Mom wrapped her hand around Luna's wrist, putting her into the back seat with a capricious promise whispered against her ear, "Everything will be all right now."

Now, thirty-four years later, on this sunny spring day in early

June, Jeanie wrapped her arm around Luna's wrist again and whispered in her ear, "Everything will be all right now."

The old memory whipped through her and the hairs on Luna's nape lifted. To her those words were code. *Your world is about to collapse.*

But despite that unnerving warning, things weren't bad. Far better than they'd been in a long time.

It was Saturday, June 1, and Luna, her mother, and Luna's fifteen-year-old daughter, Artemis, stood on the wharf in the Gulf Coast village of Everly, where the limo driver, who'd driven them two hundred miles from their hometown of Julep, Texas, had just deposited them in this charming seaside setting.

The weather was mild, and the water was calm. Birds chirped. Fluffy white clouds drifted by. Honeysuckle scented the breeze. By all accounts, a pleasant day.

Last week, Jeanie had received the golden ticket, inviting her to a summer stay on Hobby Island—all expenses paid—plus entry into the coveted quilting contest that carried a one-hundred-thousand-dollar grand prize.

Keen on winning the competition, Jeanie had been in an excited dither ever since. To her chest she clutched the best quilt she ever made wrapped in butcher paper and slipped inside a cloth covering, positive that she would snag that grand prize.

Luna loved her mother with all her heart, and Jeanie was an excellent seamstress. In fact, she was the best Luna had ever seen, but creative design was not her mother's strength. Luna wasn't sure if Jeanie's expert sewing skills could make up for the quilt's uninspired composition.

But she would never tell her mother that. Jeanie took everything to heart, and the last thing Luna wanted was to hurt Mom's feelings.

Besides, if she counted her mother's shortcomings, that meant

Artie got to catalog Luna's. Jeanie had done her absolute best, and Luna didn't doubt it. Although sometimes her best simply hadn't been quite good enough.

Did Artie feel the same way about her?

Considering what happened with Herc, most likely. Maybe this stint on Hobby Island would bring them all closer.

*Or pull you further apart.*

Luna nibbled her lip and looked around for her daughter. Spied Artie feeding money into the vending machine, never mind that Luna had packed plenty of snacks. They had to watch every penny, and she wondered where Artie had gotten the money. From Jeanie?

Artie punched the button, and then leaned down to claim her overpriced Cheez-Its.

Her daughter had inherited Herc's mahogany brown hair, chocolate brown eyes, and olive complexion. Luna was glad Artie hadn't gotten her dishwater blond hair, blah hazel eyes, and pale skin that burned to a crisp instead of tanning.

Luna also admired Artie's fearlessness. Even though Artie's bravery often caused her trouble. Luna's sweet-natured son, Beck, had skipped second grade because he was so very smart and therefore graduated high school at seventeen and was now, at eighteen, enrolled in his freshman year at the University of Oklahoma on a baseball scholarship. He had been an easygoing child, giving her not an ounce of grief. Raising Beck had been a breeze and Luna cakewalked through early motherhood.

Then three years later, along came Artemis. Her daughter charged through life like a general executing a battle plan, full of courage and zeal, mowing over everything in her path.

Perhaps it was Luna's fault for naming her daughter after the Greek goddess of the hunt, but she didn't regret giving her child a noble identity.

Beside her, Jeanie shifted the quilt in her arms to check her watch. "The ferry should be here any minute."

"Mom, you don't have to carry that quilt. Why don't you put it with the luggage." Luna nodded at the suitcases the limo driver had stacked on the pier.

"Got to make sure nothing happens to it. This quilt is worth one hundred thousand dollars."

"All right." Luna let it go. If Mom wanted to lug the quilt around with her, let her lug it.

They were still finding the shape of their relationship after Luna and Artie had moved in with Jeanie just two short weeks ago. They were living in the run-down Victorian house that had been in Jeanie's family for four generations. And while there was plenty of room, it hadn't been an easy adjustment.

Returning to Julep had been humbling, but Luna was ready for stability. Stability was not a quality she associated with her mother, but what Jeanie lacked in grit, she more than made up for in comfort.

Her mother was the kind of mom who threw back the covers and invited her to snuggle in the bed with her. She adored Hallmark movies, baking cookies, and hot chocolate with little marshmallows. She kissed Luna's skinned knees, braided flowers in her hair, and would often burst into song to lighten dark moods.

And for now, Luna relished her mother's simple comforts.

She had lost a lot over the course of the past thirteen months when the hospital called her at two in the morning and broke the news that Herc had gotten hit in the cross fire between two rival gang members he'd been patching up in the ER.

"But he's okay," she said, her grasp on reality slipping. "He's fine, right?"

"I'm so sorry. We did all we could, but Dr. Boudreaux didn't make it."

Long ago, Herc had chosen the high-pressure world of emergency medicine over private practice. He claimed the specialty better suited his ADHD, but Luna believed an addiction to the life-and-death drama was a much more likely motivation. His high-octane personality was part of what attracted her to him. Herc brought to the relationship what she lacked—excitement, charisma, and supreme self-confidence.

She thought grieving her husband of nineteen years was the worst of it, but she'd been wrong.

A month after the funeral, Herc's best friend and lawyer informed her that her late husband had left behind a staggering amount of gambling debt, and she was almost penniless.

No life insurance policy because Herc had stopped making payments when he got in deep to his bookie. He drained their savings, 401(k), and brokerage accounts, leaving her with just a few thousand dollars in checking. Nor had he been paying their taxes for the past three years and the IRS wanted their share ASAP. The only thing he hadn't touched were the kids' college funds. She supposed she should be grateful for that.

She liquidated their assets in an estate sale, sold off Herc's Porsche and her Tesla, keeping their sixteen-year-old minivan. The proceeds had been just enough to live on until she sold the house and paid off the government.

Their marriage had been conventional. Herc took care of the finances, Luna raised the kids. She liked the traditional roles, and it was an honor raising decent human beings while Herc provided the means for her to do so. She thought she made a solid choice in a life partner. She'd thought by marrying him she would never suffer the financial struggles her parents went through. But Herc had a gambling problem he hid for years.

Did he hide it? Or had she just turned a blind eye?

Yeah. That last part.

She shouldered as much responsibility for the situation as Herc. She checked out of their marriage long before his death, focusing on the kids and ignoring the holes in her and Herc's relationship. Time to stop blaming Herc and move on.

Questions popped inside her head. The same questions that had been percolating since she arrived in Julep two weeks ago. What now? Where did she go from here? What did she want from life? Who was she? Because he had graduated a year earlier, Beck was out of the nest and Artie not far behind. What was next for Luna?

Then Jeanie got the golden ticket. An impromptu vacation seemed the perfect way to sort herself out. So here Luna was, lost and confused, but riding the wave life threw at her. Not much different from when she was a kid.

Maybe this was her best chance at reconnecting with her mother, righting past wrongs and forming a closer bond with her daughter.

For the next two months, this was Luna's simple goal.

# Chapter 3
## *Jeanie*

*"Scissors cut, but they also shape. Choose your cuts wisely."*
—*Eloisa Hobby*

Jeanie bobbled on her way up the gangplank of the Hobby Island Ferry.

"Mom, watch your step." Luna reached for her arm.

"Oops, I'm so sorry." Jeanie's heart skipped.

"No need to apologize, just be careful, please. Falling overboard is not an option," Luna said, but her admonishment was gentle and compassionate, not the scolding Jeanie deserved for her woolgathering.

"Hey." Artie ran up to them. "There's no cars on this ferry. How come?"

"It's a passenger ferry." Luna put her arm around her daughter's waist, bringing her closer, until the three of them huddled at the railing.

*Gathering her chick.* Jeanie smiled. Luna was such a mother hen.

"But how do cars get to the island?" Artie bounced on the balls of her feet encased in Doc Martens moto boots. She wore cutoff blue jeans, which in Jeanie's estimation were far too short, but she wouldn't comment on her granddaughter's attire. Times had changed, and she didn't want to sound like an old fuddy-duddy.

"No cars allowed," a female voice behind them said.

They turned in unison to see who'd spoken. A woman near Jeanie's own age with a Jamie Lee Curtis pixie haircut and an effervescent smile. She strolled over to put an empty paper cup into the recycle bin.

The woman wore a silky azure blouse tucked into tailored white trousers. Her skin glowed with bronzer, and her lively blue eyes sparkled. A beaded necklace and matching earrings glittered when they caught the sunlight, accentuating her graceful neck and delicate features.

Her full lips curved upward in a warm, inviting smile and her unlined forehead seemed to belie her age, as though she were in her early fifties rather than in her midsixties like Jeanie, but the dark spots on her hands gave her away.

She was gorgeous and beside her, Jeanie felt like a dull brown wren in her pale pink, paisley-print maxi sundress and Birkenstocks.

"Apologies for butting in," the woman said. "But heads up, there's no cars on Hobby Island, just golf carts, scooters, and bikes. And there's a lot of walking." The woman extended her hand to Jeanie. "I'm Sharon, by the way. Sharon Rooney. It's nice to meet you."

"I'm Jeanie, and this is my daughter, Luna, and my granddaughter, Artemis. We call her Artie for short."

"You've been to Hobby Island before?" Luna eyed Sharon.

"Yes, last year," Sharon said. "Which one of you scored the golden ticket?"

Jeanie held up her hand. "Me."

"So *you're* the crafter." Sharon's friendliness drew Jeanie. "We're going to be fast friends, Jeanie. I can tell already."

Luna tensed. Jeanie's daughter distrusted people who were too chummy-chummy. Then again, Luna distrusted everyone until they'd proven themselves over weeks, months, and years.

"What's your craft?" Sharon asked.

"Quilting."

"Oh, oh, me too! Are you entering the contest?"

"That's what's inside here." Jeanie clutched her quilt tighter.

"Hmm. I don't think that's how it works." Sharon shook her head. "But I could be wrong. Last year we sewed the quilt while we were on the island."

"I can't enter this?" Jeanie's spirits nose-dived. She couldn't sew an entire quilt in a few weeks. Not without her Singer sewing machine.

"Don't listen to me." Sharon waved a hand as if shooing off a fly. "I could be off base."

The boat surged forward, leaving the Everly dock. Jeanie almost lost her balance. If Luna wasn't standing close enough to grab her arm, she might have fallen.

"Here we go!" Artie hollered, jumping on the bottom rung of the railing, and leaning over. The wind whipped her long dark hair and billowed her loose-fitting top around her. She looked so free and brave it touched Jeanie's heart.

"I'm the Queen of the World!" Artie flung her arms wide.

"Get down." Luna snapped her fingers.

Artie tossed her head, ignoring her mother. Luna's irritability was understandable, given her tough circumstances, but Artie was also struggling.

Jeanie touched Luna's arm. "Loosen the reins a little?"

"Mom, she could fall off the ferry."

"I know, it's . . . don't get mad at her, okay? She's just so full of life." Jeanie glanced over her shoulder at Sharon. "And we're in public."

"Oh yes, we should always consider the opinions of others." Luna might be mad, but she heeded Jeanie's advice, stepping closer to Artie and tugging her from the railing. "Come on, kiddo, get down."

"So," Sharon said to Jeanie. "This is Nanette . . ."

A busty redhead dressed in black leggings, a turquoise tunic, and black ballet flats, and who put Jeanie in mind of Blanche from *The Golden Girls*, wriggled her fingers. "Howdy!" she said in a throaty Texas drawl. "Nice to meetcha."

"And this is Isabelle." Sharon waved at a petite woman in a yellow boho romper with matching espadrilles. Isabelle looked a decade younger than Sharon and Nanette. Her smile was lopsided but genuine, quirking up on the left side, and her well-groomed eyebrows were thick and lush. "We three met on the island last summer and we're so excited to be invited back."

"I entered the jewelry-making contest last year." Nanette jangled the numerous bracelets at her wrists. "I made these m'self. This year, I'm entering the quilting contest, but I'm a novice quilter so I have no aspirations of winning. It's just fun to compete. Also, I'm eager to see the butterfly hatchery. I missed it last time."

"Butterfly hatchery?" Artie asked.

"Oh yes. Didn't you get the brochure? You should read the brochure," Sharon said. "It's got all the details about the island events."

"We didn't get a brochure." Jeanie shook her head.

"Sure, you did. It came in the box with your golden ticket."

"Did it? I'll have to check when we get to our room," Jeanie said.

"Oh no," Sharon said. "If you don't have the golden ticket in hand when we dock at Marshmallow Landing, the ferryman won't allow you off the boat. Security is priority one at Hobby Island. So you better get it out now."

"Thanks for the advice, Sharon. I sure am glad we ran into you ladies." Jeanie dabbed perspiration from her forehead with her fingertips.

"We should go get your ticket." Luna steered her away from the trio of women and over toward the luggage rack. When they were out of earshot, her daughter said, "You don't have to make friends with every person you meet."

"What do you mean? You don't like Sharon?"

"I don't *know* Sharon. That's the point. The woman seems nosy to me. You don't have to obey her."

"No, no, you're wrong. She's just being helpful." Jeanie set down her quilt, accepted the suitcase Luna passed to her, and squatted to open it. "She's been to Hobby Island before, and she knows what she's talking about. I think she just wants us to appreciate her knowledge, which I do."

"Just curb your enthusiasm, okay?"

Jeanie searched the contents of the suitcase and found the bejeweled wooden box with the golden ticket inside and a glossy pamphlet. "See, she was right about the brochure."

"Just don't become insta-friends. No harm in taking your time."

Luna was wary and kept up her guard. Jeanie didn't know where her daughter had gotten that from. Both Jeanie and Jack were open and accepting . . .

*Being open and accepting to any and everyone is why you're in this pickle.*

The thought blazed like a neon sign in her mind. A blistering heat that had nothing to do with the bright sunshine burning her cheeks.

"Mom! Gran! You can see the island from here! Come look. You gotta see this. The island is *purple*!" Artie waved them over.

Jeanie and Luna exchanged glances and smiled at each other.

Jeanie zipped up the suitcase and tucked the box under her arm. Together, she and Luna moved toward the bow, where Sharon, Isabelle, and Nanette also stood.

"It's magical." Artie exhaled a happy squeal the way she had as a four-year-old when Jeanie and Jack accompanied Luna and her family to Disney World.

Indeed, the island lay straight ahead, and it was bathed in various shades of purple, from lavender to lilac to rich indigo.

"How is it so purple?" Luna marveled.

"The jacaranda trees." Sharon gestured. "They grow over sixty feet tall, and they're planted along the road leading to the village."

As the ferry approached the beautiful island, Jeanie's pulse quickened and her throat squeezed tight, as if she gobbled her food too fast and it wouldn't go down.

"It's gorgeous!" Artie clapped. "I love it. It's like a fantasy."

"Fantasy Island," Jeanie murmured, thinking of the old TV show that had aired on Saturday nights when she was a teenager.

"You're going to love it here," Isabelle said. "After visiting last year, I changed so very much. I was fifty pounds heavier but something about Hobby Island helped me get a handle on my eating. I lost fifteen pounds in two months while I was here, and then when I went home, I just kept losing until I got to my goal weight. I struggled with my weight my entire life—emotional eating—but now, the battle is gone."

"It's true," Sharon said. "And you look fabulous, by the way. I almost didn't recognize you when you arrived at the ferry."

"Thank you," Isabelle said and tossed her head. "This time around, I'm hoping to kick my vape habit."

"Good luck," Nanette said. "I have heard tales of other miraculous things happening on Hobby Island."

The six of them watched in silence as the ferry drew closer and for one shining moment, Jeanie forgot her problems and why she had come to Hobby Island. The sweet scent of jacaranda blooms reached her nose. The island smelled like tranquility. Jeanie closed her eyes for a second and took a deep breath, letting the fragrance fill her lungs. The island seemed as if it was putting on a show just for them.

Up ahead a large white wooden sign spelled out *Marshmallow Landing* in glossy red script. The ferryman collected their golden tickets and went back to driving the boat. As they neared, he blasted the ferry whistle, signaling their arrival.

The honking startled a flock of great white birds resting in the jacaranda trees. They launched into the air, their flight splitting open the purple canopy and showering lavender petals onto the deck of the ferry, painting a dazzling scene right before everyone's eyes.

The ferryman, a grin crossing his weather-beaten face, tapped a button on his console. The harsh alarm subsided, leaving in its wake the natural chorus of the island, the whisper of the wind, the rhythm of the waves, the distant cry of the departing birds.

A lavender blanket covered the water around the boat. Artie and Luna reached out, faces upturned, to catch the falling petals, both laughing out loud in wonder.

Watching her daughter and granddaughter laughing together shifted something within Jeanie, a softening, an opening, a gentle welcoming of the unknown.

The island was within their reach. It sat quiet and deserted, but it pulsed with an enigmatic energy that whispered of the thrilling adventures that lay ahead. The mystery of Hobby Island beckoned them closer, and in its inviting silence, Jeanie found a radiant beacon of hope.

But then her cell phone dinged in her pocket, breaking the spell the island had woven over her. Blinking, she pulled out her phone and looked at the screen.

The text was from Julep Bank: Urgent! You must call now . . .

The rest of the text wouldn't be visible until she opened the text messaging app, but Jeanie didn't need to open it to know what the rest of the text said.

"What's that about?" Luna asked, peering over Jeanie's shoulder.

"Nothing. Robo text." Feeling panicky, Jeanie jammed the phone into her pocket.

"Then why did you go pale?"

"Did I?" Jeanie pressed the back of her hand against her forehead. "It must be the heat."

"It's in the low seventies."

"What's with the third degree?" Jeanie heard edginess creep into her voice.

Oh dear, she didn't want to cause a scene. She needed to chill out, or she'd give herself away. If she couldn't come up with one hundred thousand dollars by the end of the next month, the bank would start foreclosure proceedings. She was reluctant to tell Luna they were on the verge of losing the house. Not after all her daughter had been through.

Jeanie was so embarrassed she'd gotten herself into this terrible fix.

*No fool like an old fool*, said Jack's teasing voice in her head.

At the thought of her late husband, she pressed a knuckle against her eye. No more grieving. It had been three years since she lost him. Time to let go. But Jack had been part of her life since she was younger than Artie. He'd been her heart, her soul, her everything.

Her twin flame.

His death had left her so lonely she fell victim to an online sweetheart scam. Jeanie knew she needed to tell Luna the truth, but she couldn't seem to force the words. There was still hope she could fix this situation without Luna ever needing to know.

Once she got to the island, she would call the bank and beg for more time. And if she could just win the grand prize money, it would solve all her problems.

And if she couldn't?

Jeanie shivered.

The idea of losing her home and selling all she owned churned her stomach. How many times had she put on garage sales and watched people paw through her cherished possessions and low-ball her on the price? Three dozen at least. Well, she'd be doing it three dozen and one if she didn't win this contest.

She was starting over from scratch, just like Luna, but unlike her daughter, this was her own foolish fault. She hugged herself hard, cast an eye to the bucolic blue sky, and whispered, *"Please."*

# Chapter 4
## *Luna*

*"Sometimes the best way to find yourself is to get lost in a labyrinth of colors."*

—*Eloisa Hobby*

Ten minutes later, the six travelers disembarked with their luggage. The ferryman tooted the horn and chugged back to Everly, leaving them alone on Marshmallow Landing.

The early-afternoon sun glinted off the water, casting them in golden halos. They were pilgrims, embarking on an unknown journey, and the moment seemed weighted with meaning somehow. The sweet scent of the jacaranda trees rode the air, and purple petals stained the cobblestone pathway stretching before them.

Luna fixed her gaze on the dreamy landscape straight from the fairy-tale mural she painted in the kids' playroom when Beck and Artie were small. She dreamed it as a portal into an enchanted realm, and that's what this was like.

How could it be that her imaginative haven from thirteen years ago was an actual place? Her pulse skittered and an odd excitement churned in her belly.

To Luna's surprise her fairy-tale mural design had ended up on the cover of a glossy Dallas magazine. It happened after a reporter came to their house to interview Herc. Her husband had saved the life of a local celebrity after everyone else was certain the man would die.

The reporter saw the mural, fell in love with it, and returned the next month to do a story on Luna. After the feature ran, several people encouraged her to enter her design into a lofty art contest for muralists. Based on such an enthusiastic response, she gathered up her courage and submitted her artwork.

And she won! A thousand-dollar prize and a blue ribbon she put in a scrapbook. And she received offers from people to paint murals in their homes.

It was the most exciting thing that had ever happened to her. Even after all her drastic downsizing, she held on to five copies of the magazine. Whenever she looked at the cover, she got that same feeling of pride and accomplishment just for creating a beguiling space for her children.

It was the first—and last—time she felt like a genuine artist.

She thought about doing something more with her design skills after that success, but Herc pooh-poohed her desire to go to art school, saying the children needed her and they were her priority.

Luna agreed and packed away her art supplies, but she couldn't stop herself from noticing shapes and colors, shades and hues, negative space and perspective. She saw the world through a visual lens and used her insights to interpret emotions.

It was just how her mind worked.

And this island world was incredible—the palette intoxicating, the composition balanced and unified, the contrast of colors both warm and cool pleasing her sense of aesthetics.

Awed, Luna stared at the appealing beauty all around them. An urge to grab a sketchbook and start drawing overwhelmed her. But she hadn't created art in years, and she threw all her sketchbooks away when she liquidated her possessions and sold her home to pay off Herc's gambling debts.

"What now?" Luna whispered, not knowing why, but reverence seemed appropriate somehow.

"We wait." Sharon perched on her huge suitcase like a perky sparrow, unruffled by the uncertainty that lay ahead. Isabelle and Nanette sat down together on the edge of the dock kicking their feet back and forth over the purple-hued water.

"Wait for what?" Jeanie asked, her voice vibrating in the stillness.

"A ride?" Artie guessed.

"Patience." Sharon aimed her cryptic smile at Luna.

The woman's perfect smile gave her the willies. She didn't trust a dazzling smile. Luna shot Sharon the side-eye.

"Mom! Mom!" Artie stormed over, cheeks puffed, lips pursed. "Something's wrong with my cell phone. I can't get on social media!"

"Oh." Sharon tapped a manicured index finger against the tip of her nose. "I forgot to tell you. Cell reception is spotty on the island, depending on your carrier, and they don't have wi-fi here either. The staff use landlines or satellite phones."

Artie gasped and clutched her phone to her chest. "What? No! Mom! Fix this! Fix this now!"

"Honey, I'm not in control of the island's internet service. It is what it is."

"I can't believe this! This is the worst." Artie gurgled like she was being strangled.

Luna had to pick her battles. "It's a minor inconvenience. You'll be so busy on vacation that you won't miss social media. I promise."

"Gak! You brought me to this godforsaken hellhole to shrivel up and die of boredom!" Artie stomped across the deck.

"Aah," Isabelle said. "The drama of youth."

"She's been under a lot of stress this last year." Luna sighed, feeling like the worst mother in the natural universe. Not because of the internet thing. It would be healthy for Artie to stay off her phone for the summer, but for the fallout from losing her dad. Grief widened like ripples on the water, touching everything.

"I have a way with teenagers." Sharon canted her head and offered a smile. "Do you mind if I give her a pep talk?"

That would go over like sour pickles. Sharon had no idea what she was getting herself into with Artie, and Luna wasn't clueing her in. She waved toward her angry kid. "If you're not afraid of having your head bitten off, be my guest."

Confidently, Sharon hopped off her luggage, delicate as a wicked pixie, without knocking it over and sauntered toward Artie.

Her daughter plopped down underneath the *Marshmallow Landing* sign, scowling, her arms crossed over her chest in a pugilistic way.

Luna had to give the woman props: Sharon was at least sixty, and she drifted down into a cross-legged position next to Artie with the grace of a yogi.

Sharon spoke to her for a few minutes in a hushed tone, and Luna couldn't hear a word she said.

Artie glowered at Luna.

Sharon kept talking.

Artie shook her head.

Sharon put a hand on Artie's shoulder.

The clench in Luna's belly, which had anchored there the day she learned Herc had gambled away their future, tightened, and Luna continued fretting. Except now, she was thinking about the text message that flashed across Jeanie's phone. The text from Julep Bank.

Urgent! You must call now . . .

Was Mom in financial trouble?

Jeanie had seemed distracted ever since she and Artie moved in, often so caught up in her thoughts that she bumped into furniture and mumbled apologies to chairs, dressers, and side tables. Luna put down Mom's clumsiness to having her space invaded by her daughter and granddaughter. Besides, Jeanie had always been absent-minded and since Luna had so much going on herself, she kept her mouth shut.

But now, she was alarmed.

Throughout Luna's childhood, her parents struggled financially. While they always had enough to eat, there had been many times when they didn't have a place to live. Couch surfing, staying at campgrounds, or living out of a van for weeks at a time. Jeanie pretended it was a grand adventure, but Luna noticed the fear in her eyes, and the way she took in extra sewing. Dad's get-rich-quick dreams landed them in a crisis more times than Luna could count.

Unsettled, Luna shifted her gaze back to Artie and Sharon.

A bright smile broke across Artie's face. She bobbed her head. How had Sharon accomplished *that* miracle?

And then something unexpected happened.

Artie jumped up and rushed over to her. "Mom, I owe you an apology for acting like a brat."

Unable to hide her shock, Luna blinked, flabbergasted. "I . . . uh . . . that's all right, sweetheart." What had Sharon whispered to Artie in those precious few moments they'd chatted? "Everyone has bad days."

Artie caught Luna in a bear hug that almost sent her toppling. "Thanks, Mom."

"For what?"

"Taking me on this trip."

Luna righted herself. "Well, honey, thank your grandmother. She was the one who won the golden ticket. If it weren't for her, we'd be stuck in Julep all summer."

Artie pivoted and swooped in to hug her grandmother. "Thanks for winning the golden ticket, Gran. This vacation is gonna be epic!"

Across the deck, Luna caught Jeanie's eyes. Her mother wore the same expression of disbelief. They shared a silent moment of I-didn't-see-that-coming-but-I'm-not-complaining.

*Thank you*, Luna mouthed to Sharon, who nodded and beamed.

"I'll get our luggage," Artie said and skipped to the pile of suitcases the ferryman had stacked on the dock.

Nanette and Isabelle followed Artie to collect their own suitcases while Sharon strolled over to Luna and Jeanie.

"What did you say to her?" Luna asked Sharon, perplexed and amazed by the instant change in her daughter's attitude and more than a little jealous of the other woman's sway with Artie.

A Cheshire cat smile slipped across Sharon's face. "I revealed the secrets of Hobby Island."

"Which are?"

Sharon seemed smug, but she had reversed a truculent teen in a matter of minutes, so Luna wasn't judging.

"Well . . ." Sharon swept a hand at the beautiful landscape around them. "You're about to find out."

Just then, a steady clicking noise drew everyone's attention back to the cobblestone path.

*Click, click, click.*

From the thicket of jacaranda trees, a woman appeared. She was a senior citizen, her silver hair turning from artful charcoal to monochrome poetry curled beneath a dashing gray fedora. A vivid sunflower peeked from the brim, a bright splash of jovial yellow playful against the solemn gray. Her clothes were lilac and deep aubergine, with a silky lavender top offsetting a flared skirt of darker, regal purple, and, most surprising of all . . .

. . . the woman was riding a unicycle.

While knitting.

What in the world?

The skirt, an apt symbol of the woman's outrageous character, swished in the rhythm of her cycling and knitting, exuding an audacious elegance and crinkly sound.

Was she seeing this? Luna blinked twice.

*Click, click, click* went the knitting needles flying along as they knotted together the flamingo-pink yarn dangling down the sides of the woman's hands. In an amazing display of grace and coordination, she handled the knitting needles with the flourish of an expert conductor leading an orchestra, and the vibrant yarn danced between her fingers.

Luna watched, mesmerized. The lulling click of the needles echoed the island's pulse beat, every knit and purl creating a story from yarn. The woman's eyes twinkled with a mischievous glint as she held up her creation, radiant in the afternoon sun, and revealed she was knitting a map of the island.

"Well, now . . ." The woman's voice was as warm as summer itself. "Aren't we having a jolly good time?" Her words, spoken in a playful tone, swirled in the air light as dandelion seeds on a breezy day.

She laughed, a high genuine laugh full of energy and verve. "Welcome, welcome, my dear friends, to the island! I'm Eloisa Hobby, your host, and I'm so very thrilled you are all here!"

# Chapter 5

## *Artemis*

*"Be the quirk in the quilt. Stand out."*

—*Eloisa Hobby*

A rtie eyed the knitting woman perched atop the unicycle. She was small but wiry, with half-moon reading glasses resting on the end of her upturned nose. The knitting needles clacked, punctuated by the squeaking of the pedals as she wheeled back and forth to keep her balance.

"You must be Jeanie," Eloisa addressed Gran without missing a beat, finishing the stitch, then tucking her knitting into the large front pocket of her skirt and holding out her hand to Gran.

Gran shook hands with the woman and gave a little curtsy as if she was meeting royalty. "Thank you for inviting us to your island. It's a great honor to be here."

"Oh, no, *I'm* the one who is honored. To have someone of your quilting stature travel all this way to take part in our modest contest. Why, it's *my* privilege."

Her grandmother blushed and lowered her head. "You're too kind."

Artie resisted an eye roll. Good grief, grown-ups, and their formalities. Truth be told, she was überpissed to get dragged along on this dumb excursion to an old lady quilting convention or whatever.

Right now, she should have been in Italy with her dad and Beck. The month before Dad got murdered, they'd started planning a Roman holiday just for the three of them while Mom took a girls' trip with her friends to some fancy spa in Arizona.

At the thought of her dad, Artie tamped down her grief and iced it over with a layer of I-don't-give-a-shit. She missed him like crazy, but if she let herself think about it too much, she'd lose it.

Mom hadn't coped well, and Artie wanted to be the exact opposite of Luna. Especially after Artie found out about Dad gambling away everything. It had come as a jolting shock and Artie was ticked at her father for putting Mom in this position—having to live with Gran in a worn-out oil field town like Julep.

Maybe that's what would keep Artie busy this summer—planning her future and deciding who she wanted to be when she grew up.

A low chirring noise drew everyone's attention back to the path just as a six-person, Day-Glo-green golf cart wrapped with a map of Hobby Island motored into view. Behind the wheel sat a tall, sturdy-looking older woman dressed in vibrant red. With a booming laugh, she goosed the electric engine and zoomed closer.

Artie beamed. Maybe this old lady island wouldn't be as boring as she feared.

"Cheers!" the driver called, cheery as sunshine after a May rain shower. The woman had a booming British accent, and she sounded the way butterscotch tasted, rich and sweet. "Your chariot has arrived, dear guests!"

Mom shot the driver a skeptical look as the woman parked the elongated golf cart alongside Eloisa Hobby. Her mom distrusted everyone, but she distrusted flamboyant people most of all.

Artie was intrigued.

Her grandpa Jack had been flamboyant. Grandpa hadn't been afraid of anything or anyone, and she missed him with a passion. He told dirty jokes, sang naughty songs, and *did* things—he drove stock cars, water-skied, and went bungee jumping.

Once, when he was supposed to be babysitting them—while Gran had surgery and Mom sat at the hospital with her—he took Artie and Beck to a nightclub, slipping them in through the back door.

They glimpsed a jiggly woman with no clothes on, and Grandpa Jack let them have a sip of his beer. It tasted awful, but Artie pretended to enjoy it to impress him. Beck spat it out, and Grandpa Jack poked fun at her brother.

Mom nearly had a stroke when she found out and, after that, refused to leave her and Beck alone with Grandpa Jack ever again.

The driver unfurled from behind the wheel, smoothed down her red pinafore, and patted her steel-gray hair mussed wild from the golf cart ride. The woman's knobby elbows stuck out like oak tree knots, and her hands were as big as Frisbees and speckled with dark spots. She wore ribbed red knee socks and scuffed Doc Martens boots, just like Artie's.

The woman tromped over and stuck out a palm. "You must be Artemis."

How did she know?

Speechless, Artie bobbed her head and shook the woman's hand.

"My name is Dorothy Higginbottom, originally from Manchester, England. These days I'm Hobby Island's artist in residence and you may call me Dot."

"Hi, Dot. Please call me Artie."

"Oh, I like that. Artie the artist."

"I'm not an artist."

"Everyone's an artist. They just don't always know it yet." Dot let go of Artie's hand. "And you're *mine*."

"Y-yours?" Artie stammered, irritated at being thrown off her game. "What does that mean?"

"Eloisa assigned me to look after you while you're here."

"Assigned?"

Eloisa pedaled over on the unicycle. She was knitting again, fingers flying, needles clacking. "All our guests under eighteen get an auntie to look after them. Dot's yours."

"What's an auntie?" Artie asked Eloisa. "I mean besides the obvious definition."

"An auntie acts as your guide to the island," Eloisa said. "She sees to your every need and keeps you safe."

"*Every* need?" Artie arched an eyebrow.

"Within reason, of course." Eloisa's smile was cryptic.

Artie whipped out her cell phone. "Hey, Dot, can you hook me up with cell service?"

"Happily, no." Dot shook her head and waved at the hilly peak rising from the middle of the island. "Trouble Ridge blocks the cell towers from the mainland."

"Trouble Ridge?" Mom asked, scanning the area. "That sounds ominous."

"Happily?" Artie scowled and clenched her cell phone.

"Dot's a Luddite," Eloisa said. "But don't worry. She'll keep you so entertained you'll never miss your phone."

"I seriously doubt that's true." Artie snorted.

"Trouble Ridge?" her mother said again. "I don't like that name. This island is supposed to be peaceful and idyllic. That's what the brochure says."

Artie groaned and slapped her forehead with her palm. "Mom, it's just a name. It means nothing. Roll with it."

"Dot sometimes looks on the shady side of life. It's one of her quirks, and we do love her for it. She keeps us grounded," Eloisa said. "But she's the only one who calls it Trouble Ridge. To the rest of us it's Opportunity Ridge."

"That's a significant difference," Mom said, "between trouble and opportunity."

"Yes, exactly." Eloisa beamed as if Luna was a straight-A student. "It's all in your perspective. Life can be a trouble or an opportunity. It's your choice how you see things."

"As if it's that easy," Mom mumbled, "turning your thinking 'off and on' like a light switch."

Eloisa sent Mom a look of such kindness that Artie liked her even more. "Every challenge we're presented with can be a gateway to either trouble or opportunity. Like half a glass of water. Is it half full or half empty?"

Nanette fluffed her striking red hair and joined in the conversation. "It's like choosing a lens through which to view the world."

"Precisely." Eloisa nodded. "The universe doesn't label events as good or bad. It simply presents them to us. It's our mind that creates heaven or hell right here on Earth."

Mom swung her attention to Dot. "What do *you* think about the glass of water?"

"I question if it's even water." Dot chuckled. "It's dangerous to assume."

Mom grinned at the extraordinarily tall woman. "I think you just might be my spirit animal."

"We'll get along swimmingly." Dot laughed and stuck out her hand to Luna.

"Interesting." Eloisa pulled a notebook from her pocket and jotted down something.

Artie itched to know what she wrote.

"Load up, mates. We have a schedule to keep." Dot waved an index finger over her head in a circle.

"Indeed," Eloisa said. "Everyone, go along in the golf cart with Dot. I'll take a shortcut through the glen and meet you in Crafters' Corner for orientation at four. See you there!"

With that, their enigmatic host cycled off through the jacaranda trees.

"What about our luggage?" Artie asked Dot. She didn't like leaving her things behind even if the island was as safe as could be.

"No worries. Orion will pick up your suitcases and deliver them to your rooms," Dot said.

Orion?

"Who is Orion?" she asked.

"The gardener's kid."

Kid? Did that mean Orion was a teenager? God, she'd kill to have someone her own age around here. With her luck, the guy was probably twelve.

Artie's pulse quickened. In Greek mythology, Orion and Artemis had quite a tragic love story. Artie had never met another person named for a character from Greek mythology and she was curious. Who was this Orion? Could he possibly be near her own age?

She pictured him with tousled hair, windblown by the ocean. And his eyes? Oh, perhaps a lively blue, like the midmorning sky when not a cloud dared show its face.

Maybe he was tall and lanky, with shoulder-length curls and a mischievous grin. Or perhaps he was short and stocky, with close-cropped brown hair and deep gray eyes that sparkled whenever he smiled. Would he wear a baseball cap and say "Morning, miss!" in a chipper voice? Or perhaps he was more the shy, nose-in-a-book type? It'd be fun if he knew about the whole Artemis-Orion bit from mythology. They could laugh about it together.

Artie giggled to herself, thinking of their first meetup. She'd probably end up tripping over her own two feet or saying something goofy like *Hello! Fancy being named after a constellation, eh?*

The merry laughter of her mother, grandmother, Sharon, Isabelle, and Nanette climbing into the golf cart brought Artie back from her daydreams. It was good to hear Mom laugh.

Everyone else settled into the back seats while Artie took shotgun beside Dot. The large woman gave the cart some juice, and they bulleted down the cobblestone pathway to their destination.

Behind her, Mom, Gran, and the other ladies discussed crafts and hobbies and Artie tuned out their conversation.

Dot swerved to miss a squirrel when the little fella darted across the path. Nanette shrieked as the golf cart bounced and the wheels left the ground for a second. Artie laughed her ass off.

"Hold on tight!" Dot hollered over her shoulder.

Artie clutched her seat and peeked out at the scenery. Everything around them was as vibrant as a dreamscape—bright green grass, lush purple trees, pink seashells along the shore, and endless azure ocean that stretched for miles in either direction. Now and then, they'd pass through a field of wildflowers—a mix of pinks, purples, yellows, and oranges so bright it hurt to look at them.

Dot pointed out interesting sights as they drove through the countryside. She showed them the road that led to the turtle preserve and butterfly hatchery, then directed their attention to sailboat rentals and a lighthouse open to guests.

The golf cart coasted down the small incline toward the quaint little village by the sea.

"We have one main street in Crafters' Corner," Dot said. "But we've got everything you need."

"Except for the internet," Artie said.

"Give us a month," Dot said. "We'll make a Luddite of you yet."

"Over my dead body."

Dot laughed. "You won't miss that phone at all. You'll see."

The cobblestone pathway forked just before they reached the shops and restaurants. Dot veered left away from the village and headed toward a row of ten Victorian-style houses, all with B&B signs on the front lawn.

"When you come out of your B&B, you'll walk straight up Main Street to Crafters' Corner." Dot waved in that direction. "We'll meet in the quad for orientation at four."

Dot guided the golf cart up the winding drive of the last B&B in the uniform line of houses.

The B&B was a majestic blue two-story with gables and shutters painted a soft cream color. It looked a lot like Gran's house in Julep, except in better shape. A wraparound porch issued an invitation for guests to sit on the white rocking chairs and enjoy the potted plants and sea view.

"Welcome to the Nestled Inn!" Dot said as they got out.

Dot showed them around the grounds and explained the history of the Nestled Inn.

Inside, the house smelled like someone was baking sugar cookies. The aroma of vanilla and cinnamon drifted into the hallway. Artie wanted to eat the delicious air with a knife and fork. She licked her lips, anticipating.

"Yoo-hoo! Vivi!" Dot called. "We're here!"

"Right on time!" A vivacious older woman whose voice was as smooth as silk pajamas appeared in the foyer. "Hello, I'm Vivian Faraday. Welcome, welcome to the Nestled Inn."

Vivian was retro in a cornflower blue headscarf and dramatic wide-framed glasses. She had on a sleeveless, short-hemmed Barbie-pink sundress, matching designer stilettos, and deep crimson lipstick. She was as spindly legged as a thoroughbred horse with ample cleavage spilling from the plunging V neckline. Their hostess radiated goodness at them, her big blue eyes shining, and a wide gap between her two front teeth punctuated her smile and gave her a strange innocence.

"Come on in." Vivian ushered them into the living area.

The women in this place were wacky AF, and Artie loved it.

Through the panoramic window, Artie spied the idyllic ocean, an endless vista of waves, aqua blue and white caps, rolling onto shore as if to say, *Come on in.* Umbrellas, sun worshippers, and surfers dotted the pristine beach. The nautical theme ran across the floor, ceilings, and walls. The wall color was a soft shade of sea blue, the floor a beachy brown, and the furniture a dark aqua, decorated with beige and white throw pillows. The room made Artie feel peaceful just standing in it.

"Jeanie, Luna, Sharon, Nanette, and Isabelle," Dot said. "Vivian will show you each to your rooms while I get Artie settled in."

"We're not sharing a room?" Gran interlaced her fingers the way she did whenever she was nervous.

"No, you each have your private space." Dot smiled.

Luna met Artie's eyes. "Will you be okay on your own?"

"*Pfft.* I'm fine." Artie waved a hand. Mom was so freaking overprotective.

"Let's get settled in and then meet here in the foyer at three forty-five." Mom smiled and Artie loved seeing her in a cheerful mood. "We'll walk to Crafters' Corner together for orientation."

Vivian took the adults in the opposite direction on the first floor.

Divide and conquer? Artie scratched her chin and slid up her guard. Just like Mom, suspicious and assuming the worst. *Dammit*.

"Artie?" Dot hovered on the bottom step of the staircase. "You with me?"

"Yes, yes." Artie nodded. "I'm coming."

With that, she left her family behind.

# Chapter 6
## *Luna*

*"Life's a tapestry. You can't dodge the snags, but if you weave with courage, you'll find a community to stitch alongside you through every twist and knot."*

—*Eloisa Hobby*

*O*rion.

The name Dot had spoken at Marshmallow Landing pulled Luna down a tunnel of memories she couldn't shake. She dropped onto the mattress in her room at the Nestled Inn and took a deep breath as memories flooded her.

Artemis and Orion.

Characters from the Greek mythology she studied at Julep High School in her junior year with her study partner, Paul Chance. Artemis, the goddess, and Orion, a handsome mortal who hunted with her by the light of the full moon.

Luna and Paul, like the mythological Artemis and Orion, had started out as simply good friends.

They took astronomy together as well as their AP class in World Lit, and they bonded over their love of books and stars. Paul pointed out Luna's name meant moon, and he dubbed her Moonbeam because—in his words—she had a smile that lit up the night.

Their relationship grew into something stronger, richer, and they fell in love. By their senior year, Luna and Paul were planning their future together. On long summer nights, they drove into the countryside in Paul's pickup, lay on a blanket in the truck bed, gazed at the stars, and discussed their escape from Julep.

"Wouldn't Orion and Artemis be cool names for our kids?" he asked.

"What if we have two boys or two girls?"

"The names could work for any gender."

"Let's do it. Let's name our kids Artemis and Orion."

"Deal." They shook on it and laughed.

She recalled that special night. The last time they ever made love. A week later, everything fell apart, and she never saw Paul again.

But she hadn't forgotten their vow.

When Beck was born, she wanted to name him Orion, but Herc put the kibosh on it, asking to name his firstborn son after his father, and she liked the name Beck, so she agreed.

But she dug in her heels on Artemis, knowing they would only have two children, and Herc gave in. She never told Herc about her pact with Paul. Why bring that up? Luna adored the name Artemis, and not just because it reminded her of Paul, but because she wanted to name her daughter after a goddess who was strong, brave, and daring.

Luna couldn't help wondering if Paul kept his promise and named his child Orion. Silly to think he might have upheld his end of the bargain and that by some wild stretch of the imagination, he was here on Hobby Island with his child.

While not common names, Orion and Artemis weren't *that* unusual. She and Paul didn't own Greek mythology. The odds that this Orion was Paul's child were one in a million. But her foolish heart wondered, *What if?*

Ridiculous. Even if Paul was on Hobby Island, he was most likely married. Goodness, what was wrong with her spinning fantasies?

But Luna couldn't stop thinking about him.

Paul Chance.

Her first love. The guy whose heart she broke. He'd been the high school basketball star, and she'd been the editor of the school newspaper. They dated for two years until it all fell apart one dark summer night.

Guilt burned her throat. How might things have been different if she'd chosen Paul over Herc? If she'd been more forgiving, and less judgmental?

Those old memories assaulted her, and in her mind's eye, she saw again the decrepit roller rink where Paul kissed her for the first time. She recalled he'd tasted like the cinnamon Altoid he'd popped, his mouth warm and eager. She remembered the Dairy Queen, offering a Hunger Buster half-priced meal deal, nostalgia dumping images of her and Paul sharing a banana split in a back booth. He had whipped cream on his bottom lip, and she licked it off.

And the Julep water tower . . .

At some point, most teens in town scaled and defaced the water tower as a rite of passage. Luna offered her virginity to Paul on that creaky metal scaffolding despite her fear of heights. They used their clothes as a blanket and made love beneath the graffiti of PAUL LOVES LUNA in crimson spray paint for the entire world to see. The earnest message was long gone, the graffiti painted over each year by the town council, but the bittersweet memories remained.

Paul joined the navy after she dumped him. Luna went off to college, started dating Herc, and that was that. Over the years, she never bothered looking Paul up on social media. The past should stay buried and besides, no good could come of tripping down memory lane.

But now she was single . . .

Luna stretched out on the bed and covered her face with a pillow. *Ack.* Her life was a train wreck.

*Snap out of it.* She closed her eyes and sighed. *Relax.* She was on vacation. *Be in the moment and just breathe.*

* * *

Luna woke, disoriented. She sat straight up in bed and blinked at her surroundings. The late-afternoon sunlight streamed in through the sheer curtains, illuminating dust motes spinning in the air and drifting across the polished wood floor. Her head filled with cotton-candy dreams, sweet and airy. She squinted at her surroundings, unsure of where she was.

It took a second to remember.

She was in an incredibly plush bed, in a darling B&B, on a secluded island oasis, and it scared the living bejeebers out of her. How many times over her childhood had she awakened in a strange place?

More times than she could count, and she hated that vulnerable feeling.

She glanced around her room, taking in the details—the breezy white wicker furniture, the brass bedstead, the original seascape artwork on the walls, and on the nightstand, a green ceramic vase filled with fresh-cut sunflowers. A cheery reminder that she was at a resort.

That's when Luna noticed her luggage on the floor just inside the door. Someone had come into the room while she slept! Alarmed, she jumped up.

Good grief, she hadn't even roused.

She hadn't intended on napping. She'd simply fallen backward onto the bed, exhausted from the trip, and daydreaming about Paul Chance, and found herself enveloped in the deep, soft mattress. To be honest, she hadn't slept so hard in years. Luna looked for a clock but didn't see one so grabbed her purse and dug out her cell phone.

Four o'clock. She conked out for two hours. Why hadn't anyone awakened her? She started a group text between herself, her mother, and Artie.

Where R U?

It wasn't until she got the red exclamation mark in the message box, which told her the text went unsent, that Luna remembered the cell service on the island was unpredictable.

Because of Trouble Ridge.

How annoying. There was no way of contacting Artie or her mother.

Irritated with herself, Luna went to the bathroom, combed her hair, applied lip gloss and fresh sunscreen, slung her purse strap over her shoulder, and left the room. She locked the door behind her with the old-fashioned skeleton key Vivian had given her.

In the hallway, her sneakers creaked against the waxed floor. She forgot to ask the room numbers of her mother and daughter. How could she have been so lax?

The house was silent. Was she the only one here?

"Hello?" she called out softly.

No answer.

Luna continued down the hallway, past a few other doors, until she reached the living room. In an armchair by the window Vivian sat with her nose in a book. Luna longed to ask what her hostess was reading. She loved books. Reading had gotten her through many troubling times as a kid, and it was still her refuge when life got rough. She read almost two hundred books in the last thirteen months since Herc died.

Slinking out of view, Luna weighed the cost versus benefit of enlisting Vivian's help in getting to Crafters' Corner. The cost if she didn't? She'd have to search on her own to locate her mother and Artie. The benefit? She didn't have to rely on someone else.

She stood in the hall, dithering.

*Go. Leave. Hide.* Her instincts. They hadn't always served her well. Maybe she shouldn't trust her gut. Luna stayed rooted. Wanting to reach out but battling her internal resistance.

"Good afternoon! I thought I heard someone." Vivian closed her book and tucked it underneath her arm. She came down the hallway toward Luna, taking quick mincing steps. She changed from her sundress, and now wore pink feathered mules with kitten heels and a straight pencil skirt, also in pink, which limited her stride. The woman's whimsical clothing brought a smile to Luna's lips. She looked like senior citizen Barbie.

"Has everyone gone?" she asked.

"Yes, they popped off to Crafters' Corner."

"Without me?"

"They didn't want to wake you. You seemed to need the rest. They said they could fill you in later on whatever you missed in orientation."

"Were you the one who left my luggage in my room?"

"I did. I thought you'd want your things with you as soon as possible. I knocked on the door, and when you didn't answer, I assumed you'd left. I apologize if I overstepped."

"It's all right." Luna nodded. "But please don't enter my room again without permission."

"I won't. I do apologize." Vivian looked wretched.

*Don't be a jerk.* "Your heart was in the right place, and I do appreciate you bringing my luggage to me."

Vivian set her book on a wall shelf in the hallway. Luna sneaked a peek at the title. *The Alchemist* by Paulo Coelho. She read it in high school but remembered little about it.

"Are you ready to head out?" Vivian radiated goodness.

"You're coming along?"

"I serve at your pleasure. I'm here to guide you on your journey."

"Journey?"

"Figure of speech." Her compassionate eyes took Luna aback. "We're all on some kind of journey, right?"

"I suppose. And if I don't want guidance?"

"I'll step aside. I'm here to meet your needs, whatever they might be. And if you want to be alone, say, 'Beat it, Vivian.'"

Luna wasn't so sure she wanted Vivian tagging along, but she didn't want to seem unfriendly. She did like the effervescent woman.

"Okay, let's head to Crafters' Corner," Luna said.

"Great! We'll take the scooters." Vivian crooked a finger. She led Luna into a mudroom at the back of the house. Bike helmets hung on the wall in an assortment of sizes and styles.

Vivian took down a pink helmet to match her outfit. "Please, help yourself."

Luna picked a simple black helmet and strapped it on. She couldn't remember the last time she'd worn a helmet. Probably when she rode on the back of Herc's Ducati that he owned when they first married. He loved that bike so much, but sold it when she got pregnant with Beck. The tender memory touched her heart. Overall, Herc could be a pretty selfish guy, but he'd had his shining moments.

They stepped outside. Behind the house, colorful scooters sat parked in a line, ready to ride.

"Wow," Luna said. "The scooters are beautiful."

"Thank you for the compliment. They're all hand-painted by moi." Vivian put a palm to her chest and raised her chin at a prideful tilt. "The Nestled Inn scooters stand out from all the others in town."

"They're too pretty to ride."

"Oh no, they *love* being useful. It's their raison d'être." The French phrase, rolling off her southern accent, came off both frisky and charming. Vivian ran her fingers along the handlebars of her vibrant pink scooter. "They also appreciate it when you call them by name."

"Um . . . okay." Luna didn't know what else to say.

"My scooter is Barbie."

Of course that was her name. *Her?* Good grief, she was losing it.

"I don't mind lending her out if you want to borrow Barbie. On Hobby Island, we share and share alike. No need for possessiveness."

Luna just stared at her.

Vivian gazed back. "This is all strange to you, isn't it?"

"Honestly? I feel like I've fallen down a rabbit hole."

Vivian's laugh mingled with the sound of wind chimes clinking in the gentle breeze. "You'll get used to us soon enough. The place grows on you."

*Like barnacles?*

"Pick out a scooter." Vivian extended her arm in a Vanna White wave.

Luna hesitated. She didn't know which one to pick. "Which one is Ken?"

"There is no Ken, sweetie. Go for Harvey. He'll give you a gentle ride."

"Which one is Harvey?"

"The aqua scooter with dolphins. Go on, introduce yourself."

Luna walked over to the aqua scooter. Anthropomorphizing

inanimate objects seemed silly but was harmless enough. And a little fun. She rolled with it.

"Hello, Harvey," Luna said. "How are you?"

Harvey, it appeared, was the strong silent type.

"Now that you're good friends, hop on!" Vivian jumped on Barbie and off she went.

Giggling, Luna mounted Harvey—gosh, that sounded dirty—and followed the older woman down the driveway.

# Chapter 7
## *Jeanie*

*"Crafting is about delighting your own creative soul."*
—*Eloisa Hobby*

The cute town square of Crafters' Corner was filled with crafting stores, quaint curio shops, and aromatic restaurants. The yeasty fragrance of fresh baked goods wafted from Breaking Bread, the cozy little bakery on the corner. At a charming outdoor bistro, colorful umbrellas covered patio tables, and a chalkboard sandwich sign listed a menu of seafood dishes. Gorgeous flowers bloomed in planter boxes. Overhead, string lights crisscrossed the village—they would look so magical in the evening—setting an idyllic mood.

A temporary stage with a podium graced the quad, with rows of folding chairs arranged in front of it. Amid the festive atmosphere, crafters migrated to the seating as music played over the outdoor speakers. Jeanie strained to hear the song above the buzz of conversations. It took her a minute to identify Ricky Nelson's "Garden Party," and she helplessly hummed along.

Artie walked beside her, scanning the quad. "I don't see anyone here remotely my age."

"I'm sure you're not the only teenager on the island," Jeanie said, cradling her finest quilt in her arms. Perhaps she shouldn't have brought the quilt, but she was protective of her creation. Despite what Sharon had told her on the boat, she hoped this quilt could win her one hundred thousand dollars and save her home from foreclosure.

"I better not be!" Artie's eyebrows shot up in alarm.

"Where shall we sit?" Jeanie shifted the quilt into her right arm and looped her left elbow through Artie's, hoping to reassure her granddaughter that everything was all right.

"In the back so we can bounce if it's Boresville."

Jeanie shook her head, amused by her granddaughter. "Lead the way."

Artie paused and glanced over her shoulder down Main Street. "Should we save a seat for Mom?"

"She might still be napping, but I suppose it won't hurt to put my purse on an empty chair in case she shows up." Jeanie crinkled her nose. "Unless they run out of seats, and someone needs the spot. We don't want to inconvenience anyone."

"Gran, you worry too much about inconveniencing others. They can sit on the planter wall if needed."

"I don't want anyone getting cross with us."

Artie let out a sigh. "You also worry too much about other people's moods."

That was true, and she couldn't argue. Conflict didn't bother Artie; in fact she seemed to relish it. The girl was a lot like her grandpa Jack in that regard. Jeanie admired her devil-may-care attitude even as she was jealous of it. Jeanie worried about what people thought of her.

A lot.

"Okay, fine, we won't save Mom a seat. If the place fills up and Mom shows, she can have my chair and I'll sit on the planter wall. How's that?"

"Thank you. Can we sit in the front? I can hear and see better from there."

"Only for you, Gran." Artie slipped her arm around Jeanie's waist, giving her a side hug. "Only for you."

Just as they settled into the front row, Jeanie resting the quilt on her lap, Eloisa Hobby exited the yarn store, charmingly called The Yarnery, and crossed the quad to the stage. She wore a gauzy white-and-blue dress that fluttered about her like the ocean breeze, giving her an ethereal, otherworldly appearance. On her head perched an ultramarine homburg with a white peony peeking jauntily from the hatband.

Eloisa picked up the microphone, waved at the crowd, and gave a little giggle. "Good afternoon, everyone. Welcome to your first day on Hobby Island!"

The crowd cheered.

Eloisa doffed her hat, gave an elegant bow, and then settled the hat back on her head. "Hobby Island is a place where creativity is not only embraced but exalted. Here, we consider arts and crafts as therapy and for those of you looking to escape the rat race, you've found your home away from home for the next two months."

Someone tapped Jeanie's shoulder, and she glanced up to see Luna standing there. Artie hopped up.

"Sit here, Mom." Artie gave up her seat and darted to an empty chair in the last row.

Smiling, Luna sat down beside Jeanie. It was good to see her daughter looking so well rested.

Eloisa let Luna settle in before continuing. "Some of you won a golden ticket and are here for the competitions. Others of you are family or friends who've come along to support your loved ones in their endeavors. No matter who you are or where your talents lie, you'll find something here for you to enjoy."

Clouds thickened, casting cool shadows over the assembly. Jeanie eyed the sky. Oh dear, it might rain.

"On Sundays we have nondenominational services in our little island chapel, just right over there, with ceremonies at both nine and eleven a.m." Eloisa pointed to the white stucco building with a terra-cotta roof and majestic bell tower several yards behind the stage.

Eloisa did a bit of housekeeping about the island and the logistics of getting around, then she described the various classes and activities available, everything from quilting to knitting to woodworking to jewelry making to paper crafts to pottery-throwing. The list went on and on.

The crowd murmured, excited.

"But that's not all!" Eloisa walked as she talked, pacing the stage with the microphone. "We have nightly events, including concerts, stage plays, and movies on the beach."

That was right up Jeanie's alley. What a lovely place. How had she gotten so lucky as to snag a golden ticket?

"This place seems almost too perfect," Luna murmured. "With its vibrant colors, peaceful atmosphere, and cheerful faces. I wonder if something darker lurks beneath the surface, waiting to be uncovered."

Goodness, but Luna could be so pessimistic and guarded sometimes. Then again, if Jeanie had been more cautious, she wouldn't have ended up in the fix she was in. Grasping at straws to win a quilting contest to save her ancestral home from foreclosure.

"There are currently one hundred guests on the island," Eloisa said. "And seventy-five staff members besides myself, most of whom live on the mainland in Everly. The island is a year-round home to only seven of us. So we're quite a close-knit group, and now you are part of our community too. We're so incredibly happy that fate has brought you all here."

"What's fate got to do with it? She's the one who sent out the tickets," Luna mumbled.

Jeanie slanted a look at her daughter. Luna had been edgy since Herc died and that was understandable. She'd been hurt and betrayed, and she was justified in her feelings, but if she didn't open her heart, she could end up bitter. For all her own flaws and mistakes, bitter was one thing Jeanie refused to be. She prayed this vacation might help her only child relax and start healing.

"Do please have the time of your lives. Hobby Island is built for peace and happiness. Just remember," Eloisa said, "the island gives you back what you bring to it. Bring joy, and it gives you joy in return."

Eloisa didn't elaborate. Jeanie peered at Luna again, who had her arms folded and her head tilted, sizing up the island owner.

Their hostess beamed from the podium. "There will be individual meet and greets at each of our seven craft shops. Pick the store that most piques your interest and dig into all that it offers. Or you can shop-hop to get a broad overview of our artistic offerings. In each craft store, the contest rules for that craft are posted."

For a moment, the late-afternoon sun broke through the gathering clouds, casting Eloisa in a golden glow. A dove cooed from a nearby tree. The woman looked radiant. Happy.

Jeanie wished she could bottle the other woman's peaceful contentment and drink it up like a healthy smoothie.

"The seven contests will be held at Prism Pavilion on the Saturday before everyone leaves the island. There is a five-thousand-dollar first prize for each category and a one-hundred-thousand-dollar grand prize winner!"

Jeanie had no idea how many people might enter the quilting contest, but if there were a hundred guests on the island, she had to assume her odds were far better than one in a hundred. Some people were here purely for vacation and had no interest in competing.

"If you have any questions or needs, just ask an employee. We're all here to help," Eloisa said. "And now I'll let you enjoy your evening. Have fun at the craft shops and don't forget to grab your list of contest rules if you're entering."

Eloisa turned an eye to the sky bunched with gray clouds. "Looks like we better hurry before the rain begins. But don't worry, our afternoon rainstorms never last for long."

The crowd hopped to their feet. Luna said, "I'm going after Artie, we'll be right back," and she took off.

A raindrop plopped on top of Jeanie's head as the skies darkened. She hunched over her quilt to protect it from the rain. The cover she wrapped it in wasn't waterproof and she glanced around for her daughter and granddaughter.

But the quadrangle was empty, everyone fleeing for shelter. "Jeanie!"

She whipped her head around and saw Sharon waving to her from the doorway of the quilt shop, A Stitch in Time. "Come in! You'll get soaked."

Jeanie froze, the wind whipping her skirt around her legs. Where were Luna and Artie? She'd been terrified of storms since the night Jack wrapped his pickup truck around an oak tree. The memory added to her feeling of inadequacy and defeat.

The sky unzipped and dumped water on the village.

Drenched, Jeanie hurried to the side door of the quilting shop where Isabelle, Nanette, and Sharon all rallied around her. Breathless and exhilarated by her escape from the storm, she crossed the threshold and entered a delightful world of quilted comfort.

*  *  *

A round-faced woman with curly gray hair styled higher than Jeanie thought gravity would allow greeted her at the door. She had on a royal blue pinafore, which matched the red one that Dot had worn, and cat-eye, tortoiseshell glasses perched on the end of her nose. "Hello, I'm Clare, the owner."

"I'm Jeanie."

"Welcome, welcome, Jeanie. Come on in and let's get you dried off." Clare produced a towel from behind the counter, pushed it into Jeanie's hand, and ushered her toward a small seating area by the window that looked out onto the street.

Sharon, Nanette, and Isabelle migrated deeper inside the store and were oohing and aahing over bolts of fabric.

Jeanie looked around the quilt shop, taking in the colorful fabrics and patterns that adorned the shelves and tables, breathing in the scent of fabric softener, cotton, and spray starch. Artistic quilts hung on the walls, many of them Hobby Island seascapes. They were all so beautiful. Far more beautiful than the quilt Jeanie clutched in her arms.

Where were Luna and Artie? She sank onto the camelback sofa. A kitten-themed quilt was spread across the back. It stirred memories of a kitten quilt her grandmother had made her, and homesick nostalgia curled inside Jeanie.

Other people came through the front door, laughing and talking and closing umbrellas. Clare sat on the sofa beside Jeanie.

"Thank you, Clare," Jeanie said, patting her wet hair dry with the towel.

"You're so welcome. I'm sorry I didn't call to you sooner. You're drenched."

"It's just water. I won't melt."

"Indeed." Clare laughed. "You're quite practical at heart, aren't you?"

Jeanie lifted her shoulders to her ears. "Honestly? I don't know who I am anymore."

"Well, even better." Clare grinned as if being lost was an excellent thing. "You have the joy of figuring it out. Hobby Island is the perfect place for that."

Joy wasn't quite the emotion Jeanie would slap on it, but okay.

"What's that you've got there?" Clare cocked her inquisitive head and nodded at the quilt in Jeanie's lap.

Jeanie's cheeks heated. "Nothing."

"It's something." The woman's eyebrows leaped up like acrobats. "Is it a quilt?"

Jeanie pressed a hand to her forehead. "Uh-huh."

"You brought it to enter the contest." Clare was astute.

"I did, but on the ferry ride over, Sharon told me we have to make the quilts here. I feel like such a dummy."

"Goodness, but how could you have known?" Clare asked.

"I should have called for clarification."

"Well, no worries, you have this lovely quilt to fire your inspiration for the contest. Let me get you a list of the rules."

Clare got up, went to the counter, and returned with a flyer detailing the rules for the quilting contest. Handing it to Jeanie, she sat back down again. With a sinking heart, Jeanie read the rules written in calligraphy.

## Quilting Contest Rules

1. Quilts must be hand quilted, no machine quilting allowed.
2. Quilts shall be 36" x 36" in size.
3. Quilt design must depict an aspect of island life (flora, fauna, activities).
4. Quilts are to be made of 100% cotton fabric.

5. *The color palette is restricted to coastal hues (blues, greens, tans).*
6. *Quilt design must be the entrant's original work, not copying popular patterns.*
7. *Quilts will be judged on creativity, interpretation of theme, workmanship, and visual impact.*
8. *Quilt top, batting, and backing must be created on the island during the contest period.*
9. *No use of embellishments (beads, sequins, etc.). Fabric and thread only.*
10. *Quilts must be finished and submitted by the contest deadline of July 27th.*

"Jeanie?" Clare put a hand to her wrist. "Are you all right?"

"Yes, yes, of course," Jeanie said, her mind whirling from the implications of the contest rules. They seemed impossible to follow in the time allowed.

"You're very pale, and your skin is cold."

"It's . . ." Jeanie rested both hands on the flyer lying atop the quilt in her lap. The paper soaked up water from the damp quilt.

"Challenging." Clare nodded. "I understand completely. While Eloisa's contests are quite fun, they are never easy, but it *is* doable. We've had a winner every year for the past fifteen years."

Doubt seized Jeanie. What if she just gave up? Waved the white flag. Surrendered. Left the island? Accepted that through her own foolishness, she lost her house? Winning this contest was nothing more than a pipe dream.

But how could she just walk away? Losing her ancestral home didn't just affect her. Luna and Artie would be homeless right along with her.

And worst of all? Either way, whether she stayed to compete

or turned tail and ran, she had no choice but to tell Luna the truth.

Jeanie let out a shuddering sigh as reality sank in.

For there was no way she could win the contest without her daughter's help. Absolutely none. While Jeanie was an expert seamstress and her workmanship impeccable, she had no eye for design, and that element counted for three out of the four points of judging criteria.

Distraught, Jeanie jumped to her feet, only to be hit by a wave of dizziness.

The next thing she knew, she was lying on the floor, looking up at Clare, Sharon, Isabelle, and Nanette.

# Chapter 8
## *Luna*

*"When life hands out scraps, make a quilt."*

—*Eloisa Hobby*

It had taken Luna a hot minute to locate Artie, whom she found peering in the window of the art supply store, Palette, directly across the quad from the stage assembly. As she caught up with her daughter, the rain hit, and they'd ducked inside just as Jeanie sprinted for the shelter of the quilt shop.

They browsed the art shop for a few minutes and Luna, feeling inspired, bought the only general-purpose sketchbook the store carried and a box of drawing pencils. When the rain ebbed, they dashed to the quilting shop and discovered Jeanie sitting on the floor, surrounded by a circle of concerned women.

"Mom!" Luna shoved her bag of art supplies at Artie and sprang to Jeanie's side, the others scattering to let Luna near her mother. "What's happened?"

"Nothing, nothing. I just got up too quickly and my blood pressure must have bottomed out. It's happened before, nothing to fret about." Jeanie stuck out her hand. "Give me a boost up, sweetheart."

Luna tugged her mother to her feet and bent to brush lint off her backside. Once Jeanie was righted, Luna picked up her mother's quilt and the bright yellow flyer on the floor beside it marked Quilting Contest Rules.

"Thank you all so much." Jeanie pressed her palms together in prayer hands and bobbed her head to the women who'd helped her. "Thank you, thank you."

Sharon, Nanette, and Isabelle murmured, "You're welcome," and the older woman in a blue pinafore rubbed Jeanie's arm and said, "You've got this. I believe in you. May I recommend a lavender bath tonight? It's very soothing after a long day of traveling."

"Thank you, yes, that's a lovely suggestion, Clare," Jeanie said.

"Vivian keeps lavender at the Nestled Inn. Just ask, and she'll hook you up," Clare said.

Luna took Jeanie's wrist. "C'mon, Mom, let's head back to the B&B."

"But aren't we going to dinner?" Jeanie asked.

Luna couldn't shake the feeling her mother was hiding something from her. "We can send Artie to pick up something to go. We've had a long day and should get to bed early. That lavender bath sounds like a great idea. We've got two whole months to explore the island's offerings."

"I suppose you're right." Jeanie fiddled with her necklace.

"We have sandwiches in the quilting room from Breaking Bread for the meet and greet. I could send some with you," Clare said.

"That would be so nice." Luna smiled at the older woman. "Thank you for your kindness."

Clare crooked a finger at Artie. "Come with me, and I'll get you fixed up."

Artie followed Clare to the back of the store, and Luna turned to Jeanie. "You're sure you're all right?"

"Yes, yes. I feel so silly."

Luna studied her. What was going on? "Do you feel like walking back? We can put Artie on my scooter. Or do we need a golf cart?"

"Yes, a walk will do us good if it's not raining."

"The sun is already coming out." Sharon opened the curtains wider to let in more light.

Artie came back with Clare, a brown paper bakery bag clutched in her hand, her eyes wide. "They have gobs of sandwiches! I got ham and cheese for Gran, turkey club for you, Mom, and two PB&J for me."

"Thank you again," Luna said to Clare. "How much do we owe you?"

"Nothing at all." Clare waved a hand. "The sandwiches are a welcome to Hobby Island for the quilters. You folks enjoy."

Outside the store, Luna pointed out Harvey to Artie and told her to take the scooter on back to the B&B and they'd catch up with her. It was a ten-minute walk, and she hoped the fresh air would clear their heads.

Luna tucked the flyer into her purse and Jeanie's quilt under her arm. They followed Artie, who zoomed ahead with their dinner and Luna's art supplies in the scooter's basket. The gray clouds had blown away, and as the sun slipped toward the horizon, it cast a dazzling glow over the island.

Jeanie cleared her throat.

Luna waited, sensing her mother wanted to speak. The jacaranda blooms on the ground released a sweet scent beneath their footsteps. The quilt was heavy and made Luna feel lopsided. She repositioned it in front of her, holding the quilt with both hands.

Jeanie sighed.

"What is it?" Luna asked, angling her a sidelong glance.

Her mother had changed from the dress she'd worn on the ferry to a sage-green skirt and white peasant blouse, but she still had on her beloved Birkenstocks. A hippie child who came of age in the 1970s, Jeanie wore Birkenstocks for most any occasion, owning every style and color the brand made. Her kind blue eyes had dark circles beneath them, and she had plaited her soft honey-brown hair, which was laced with gray, into battle braids. She was still quite beautiful at sixty-five. Luna hoped she'd inherited her mother's youthful genes.

"There's something I've got to tell you . . ." Jeanie paused. "And you won't be happy with me."

Luna exhaled. "Does this have anything to do with you passing out in the quilt store?"

"I didn't pass out, I just got weak in the knees." A defensive tone crept into her voice. "But yes."

"*Ooo*-kay." Luna braced herself for what might come next.

"What Sharon said on the ferry is true. That quilt"—she nodded at the quilt in Luna's arms—"isn't acceptable for the contest."

Luna said, "So you'll sew a new one."

"I can't win."

"Why do you say that?"

"Because sewing mastery is only one small part of the contest. Design, thematic vision, and creativity are weighted more in the scoring, and we both know innovation is not my strength."

Luna figured as much, but she wouldn't say that. "Well, just do your best. Who knows? The island might give you inspiration."

"You don't understand. I *must* win the grand prize." Her mother's tone turned insistent, and she stopped walking. They were standing in front of a Second Empire Victorian B&B painted vivid lime green with white trim named Sweetest of Dreams.

"Are you having financial trouble?" The idea alarmed Luna because she was in no position to help her mother. She barely had enough to make it through the next two months, and getting a job was at the top of her list. In fact, she spent the two weeks she and Artie had been in Julep sending out résumés and making contacts. It was hard when you had no job skills beyond mother, housewife, PTA volunteer, and occasional mural painter. If this vacation hadn't been completely free, no way could she and Artie have come along.

"It's more than that." Jeanie hiccuped.

Luna transferred the quilt again, moving it to the crook of her left arm and cocking her hip to help support the weight. She met her mother's gaze, but Jeanie couldn't hold it. Luna's stomach sank. When Jeanie got shifty-eyed, Luna worried.

"Just say it," Luna said. "I can take the truth. What I can't take are lies and deception."

"I've never lied to you!"

Luna shot her a cold hard stare, but Jeanie refused to look up. "Let me rephrase. I can't take the lies that you've convinced yourself are truths. Don't give me abstract theory. Give me the details. What's happened?"

Jeanie wrung her hands, then clasped them and brought them to the center of her chest.

"Mom?" The hairs on Luna's neck raised, and an icy chill ran through her. She had a terrible feeling about this.

Jeanie took a shuddering breath. The setting sun sent a shaft of light through the tree leaves, dappling her face with shadows and intensifying Luna's growing dread. "I . . . um . . . last year, I joined an online dating app for people over sixty."

Icicles tumbled down Luna's spine.

"It's called Now or Never."

"I don't require *that* much detail." Luna shifted the quilt back to her other arm. She didn't know if the middle of the street was the best place to have this conversation, but she needed information, and she needed it now. "Cut to the chase."

"It was exciting at first. A whole new world to explore. All these lovely silver foxes."

Luna held her breath and waited for her mother to continue, dismay mounting with every passing second.

"There was this one man, Rex Rhinehart. In his profile picture, he was drop-dead gorgeous and an architect from some famous firm. Or at least that's what he claimed."

Her mind leaped to the worst-case scenario. Luna couldn't have moved if there'd been an earthquake. Couldn't speak. Her heart pounded hard and shoved fiery blood over her eardrums. She could barely hear. Sweat broke out all over her body.

"We started texting each other . . ." Jeanie ducked her head, cheeks turning pink, and whispered: "Sexting."

"Oh, Mom."

"I know, I know. I'm so embarrassed." Jeanie covered her face with her palms.

Memories of childhood swept through Luna's mind as she recalled the times her mother had disappointed her. Not purposefully, but simply because Jeanie had been so codependent with Luna's father that she couldn't see outside the bubble of their dysfunctional relationship.

In her own marriage, Luna had overcorrected, desperate to avoid being helplessly attached to any one person, and she kept Herc at arm's length emotionally, terrified of enmeshment.

Jeanie took a deep breath and hugged herself. "Rex and I corresponded for weeks. I tried to get him to meet me in person—"

"But he always made an excuse not to meet," Luna guessed.

"Yes."

"Red flag."

Jeanie bobbed her head. "It was, but sadly I didn't see it. He kept telling me he couldn't wait to meet me in person, and I believed him."

"You fell for it, hook, line, and sinker," Luna said.

"I did." Jeanie went on, detailing what had happened to her. "He texted me morning, noon, and night. He told me how I'd become his world in such a brief time and that it's a sign from God we were meant to be together. That we were fated, soulmates—"

"I thought Dad was your soulmate." Luna tightened her lips. For so many years, Mom had used the soulmate excuse for why she tolerated unacceptable behavior from Jack.

"You can have more than one soulmate, Luna." Jeanie tossed her head, saying it as if soulmates were as much a fact as gravity.

"Okay, so he knew the magic word. What did he do?"

Jeanie winced. "He asked for money. He was in a financial bind with his business. It was a small amount at first, a few hundred dollars, so of course I sent it to him."

"Mom, no." Nausea rose in Luna's stomach.

"He had a good excuse and told me as soon as his finances were squared away, we would live happily ever after."

Luna let out a long-held breath.

"I was hooked. Locked into the idea if I broke things off with him, I'd be alone for the rest of my life. He asked for more money and then a little more—"

"How. Much. Did. He. Take. From. You?" Luna clutched the damp quilt to her chest. It was hard to breathe, much less speak. The shadows grew longer as the sun sank lower.

"Everything," Jeanie whispered. "All my savings—"

"Dear heavens, Mother!"

"I know, I know." Jeanie wailed and wrung her hands. "Believe me, I know, but that's not all."

"There's more?" Luna thought she might vomit.

"He asked me for a hundred thousand dollars. When I told him I didn't have any money left, he suggested I take out a lien on the house."

"Please tell me you didn't do that."

Soft tears were slipping down her mother's cheeks and dribbling over her chin. "I'm so sorry, Luna."

"The text message you got from your bank when we were on the ferry."

"Yes."

"Are you in foreclosure?"

"If I don't come up with a hundred thousand dollars by August 1, I will be." Jeanie whimpered.

"That's why you're so desperate to win the grand prize."

Jeanie swiped at her tears with both hands. "Yes, but there's no chance I can win it. Not when creativity and artistic design trump sewing skills."

"You'll lose the house if you don't win this," Luna said, flashing back to learning she would lose her own house.

Desperation clawed her as loneliness bit down hard on her hopes. Honestly, she was still sorting herself out from it. She moved in with Jeanie because she needed stability for Artie while she figured out her next steps. Now, she didn't even have that.

"Yes. I'm so sorry."

"It's not your fault. He scammed you."

"But I was an old fool—"

"You were vulnerable and in pain over losing Dad. Don't beat yourself up. What's done is done. We'll figure this out together."

Jeanie looked relieved. "So you'll help me win the quilting contest? I can't do it without you. You're the creative one. The artist."

Luna sighed. What choice did she have?

"Yes, Mom, I'll help." Luna handed Jeanie the quilt she carried. "But I need a little space from you right now. Go on back to the B&B and have sandwiches with Artie. I'll see you later."

With that, Luna turned and walked back to Crafters' Corner.

# Chapter 9

## *Artemis*

*"Be a loom, weave friendships."*

—*Eloisa Hobby*

After she had sandwiches with Gran in the dining alcove at the Nestled Inn, Artie asked her grandmother if she could go to Crafters' Corner for the welcome bonfire on the beach. Artie was desperate to find someone her age to hang out with, and she kept thinking about Orion, the gardener's son.

Yeah, she was building a fantasy. The guy might be nowhere near her age, or he might have a girlfriend, but she didn't care. All she wanted was someone under twenty to spend time with, and if Orion had a girlfriend, well, bring her along too. The more, the merrier.

"I don't know," Gran said. "Your mother might not approve."

News flash! Her mother hardly approved of anything. "Auntie Dot will be there. It's perfectly safe. And who knows, maybe Mom will show up too."

"I don't think so. She needs time for herself."

Artie eyed her grandmother. "Did you guys have a fight?"

"Not a fight, no." Gran slowly shredded a paper napkin over the plate she used for her sandwich. "We just have some things to sort through."

"Do you want to come with me to the bonfire?" Artie asked out of politeness.

She hated for Gran to spend her first night on the island all by herself, but Artie *really* wanted to go alone. It would be harder to meet new people with Gran tagging along.

"No." Gran shook her head. "You go on without me. I'm going to take a lavender bath and try to relax."

*Yay.*

"But . . ." Gran looked at her watch. "Please be back by nine."

"Aww, man, but it's almost seven thirty now. They don't even light the bonfire until it's full dark."

"Either stay in and play board games with me or go to the bonfire for an hour and a half. Take it or leave it."

"Fine. I'll take it." Artie took off, darting out of the B&B and heading toward Crafters' Corner.

\* \* \*

Ten minutes of tromping around the village looking for kids her age and Artie explored the entire place. So far, she came up empty. Seriously, where were all the teenagers?

The shops were less crowded now compared to the bistros and restaurants. Music filled the air along with the smell of woodsmoke. They must have lit the bonfire. That's when Artie spied a small passageway between the bookstore and the bakery. Why hadn't she seen it before? The alley was lit with twinkling lights, inviting her to explore.

Curious, Artie pushed forward, her Doc Martens scuffing against the cobblestones. The narrow alley seemed to stretch on forever.

Lining either side of the path were the back entrances of the buildings, with stained-glass windows and bright doorways, which housed the craft shops and restaurants. The smell of cooking food and aromatic spices filled the confines. Artie noted the back entrance of the bookstore, an apothecary, and a small café.

Someone had done some serious cleaning in the alleyway. The cobblestones were immaculate. Many odds and ends lay bundled in neat piles against the buildings. On a long folding table, Artie spied an array of jewelry, glass trinkets, combs and brushes, books, even musical instruments. Had someone set up their own pop-up shop in this forgotten corner of Hobby Island?

In the shadows, near the far end of the long table, movement caught her eye. Squinting in the dim light, she realized it was a young woman about her own age—*halle-freaking-lujah*—sorting items on the table while humming to herself. The tune was familiar, almost like a lullaby, but Artie couldn't place it.

The girl had short shaggy hair dyed a cool shade of purple. She wore torn jeans tucked into rubber boots and a black Brandi Carlile T-shirt. She moved with a simple grace that stirred Artie's envy.

She must have heard Artie's approach, because she looked up with striking gray eyes flecked with shimmering gold.

Eyes that left Artie feeling breathless and vulnerable.

Those eyes held secrets and mysteries untold. Secrets Artie had a desperate urge to unravel. A shiver ran through her, and goose bumps popped up on her arm.

The girl smiled. "Hello."

"Hi."

Artie closed the distance until they were a few steps apart. The girl gestured for Artie to come nearer to see the items she was arranging. The trinkets the girl crafted with loving care stoked Artie's awe. Some were made from metal and glass while others were crafted from driftwood, plastic, or cloth.

"You made all these?"

"My collections from the sea," the girl said. "I've been living on the island since I was a kid. I scour the beach for lost treasures, clean them up, recycle, repurpose, and sell to the guests who visit the island."

"You're an amazing artist. These are beautiful!"

"Thanks."

Wow, this kindhearted, quirky soul lived her life according to whimsy—just like Hobby Island itself.

The girl glanced up, an amused twinkle in her fantastic gray eyes, as if reading Artie's mind, laughed, and pointed to a sign propped on the table that read WHIMSY ENCOURAGED HERE.

"I'm Artemis," Artie said.

"I know."

"How?"

"I charge up the golf carts for the guests' arrival and bring in the luggage. Your name was on the list. You're staying at the Nestled Inn with your mother, Luna, and grandmother Jeanie, right?"

Wow, the girl did know a lot about her. Artie was at a disadvantage. "Yeah, that's right. By the way, everyone calls me Artie."

The girl's grin widened as she stuck out her hand. "Nice to meet you, Artie. Welcome to Hobby Island. I'm Orion."

# Chapter 10
## *Luna*

*"Even a single stitch can alter the entire fabric of your life."*
—*Eloisa Hobby*

Luna's childhood insecurities dogged her as she strolled the beach. Farther up the sand, the bonfire welcome-to-the-island event was starting, but she had no interest in joining the revelry.

Once again, Jeanie had let her down.

But honestly, didn't the real problem lie with Luna and her unrealistic expectations of her mother? Jeanie was who she was. A person who craved creature comforts. Jeanie didn't do well alone; she needed people around.

Perhaps, when she got right down to it, Luna was the reason Jeanie had gotten tangled up in a sweetheart scam. Luna had been so consumed by her own situation she hadn't been there for her mother.

Well, sulking wouldn't change things. Nothing to do but put her mind to it and come up with a spectacular quilt design that would put the other quilters to shame. Not that Luna knew anything about quilting, but that's where Jeanie's skills would come in. If they had any hope of saving the family home, they must team up.

Maybe it would be fun. Maybe this was a chance for her and Jeanie to connect in a meaningful way.

Luna's stomach grumbled, reminding her she hadn't eaten since breakfast. She strolled from the beach into Crafters' Corner. Although all the retail stores were closed, the restaurants were still open, but she didn't feel like a sit-down dinner alone. Her best bet was the tiki bar on the beach.

From the welcome party half a mile down the beach, she could hear raucous laughter, but here, the night was still and silent. The only sound was the gentle lapping of waves against the shoreline and a guitarist at the tiki bar covering the Rod Stewart song "I Don't Want to Talk About It."

Up ahead of her, a lamplighter lit tiki torches, sending flicking orange flames into the darkness and throwing long shadows over the sand. The air smelled of coconut and gardenias. A few people sat in the beach chairs that circled the inlet, their conversations low and muted.

Romantic.

From her peripheral vision, Luna saw one couple smooching up a storm. She was so busy staring and walking that she didn't see the man step off the wooden deck and onto the sand until she plowed straight into him.

He wore a white long-sleeved shirt with the sleeves rolled up to the elbows, khaki cargo shorts, and beach sandals. His shirt, untucked, rippled in the billowing wind. He reached out a hand to steady her.

Embarrassed, she jumped back without looking up. "Oops! I'm so sorry!"

"No, no, my fault. I walked right in front of you."

*That voice!*

Even without seeing his face, Luna knew him. He smelled the same. Like the cologne he favored so long ago, Paco Rabanne, and the bittersweet notes of grapefruit mixed with the zing of peppermint. Zesty.

*Paul.*

Her heart surged.

Twenty-two years later and he was still just as handsome. Maybe even more so. His hair was longer, curling at his collar and sprinkled with gray among the jet-black strands. Same chiseled features, same powerful jaw. Had he gotten taller? Or had she forgotten what a compelling figure he cut?

He stepped back, a look of surprise that she supposed mirrored her own creeping across his face. "Why, hello there, Moonbeam. Long time no see."

Eighteen again, and it was as if twenty-two years simply vanished. She stared at Paul, unable to speak, unable to do anything except gape and peer into his gorgeous blue eyes lit shiny by the tiki torch reflection.

Paul Chance, the love of her life, stood before her on Hobby Island. What were the odds? Astronomical.

The scariest part? The whispering voice in her head posed nonsensical questions. What if Paul still loved her? What if they rekindled their romance? What if . . .

Nope, no stupid, foolish hope. Old feelings aside, a relationship between her and Paul was untenable. She had lost a husband, her money, her home, and she tottered on the verge of losing yet another place to live, all within thirteen short months.

Her life was a hot mess. Falling in love again? Not an option, especially with the guy whose heart she'd shattered.

To even think that thought was sheer nuttiness. And yet, her heart melted as sweet memories swamped her.

Paul didn't seem to hold a grudge. The man exuded relaxed, easygoing self-confidence. Jealousy for his peace of mind whapped her in the shins and she teetered.

"Luna?" Her name fell from his lips as gentle as jacaranda blossoms drifting to the ground on a soft sea breeze. "Is it really you? Or am I having the best dream ever?"

When Dot told them someone named Orion would pick up their luggage, Luna's imagination had conjured up Paul, but she never actually believed he was on the island. Or that Orion might be his child. Jolted by the possibilities, her giddy heart galloped.

"It's me." Her voice quivered. "I'm here."

"It's so good to see you." An empty phrase people used when they hadn't seen you in a couple of decades. "You look amazing."

A strange silence passed between them, awkward and uncertain.

Then, as if pulled by invisible strings, Paul opened his arms wide. A welcomed invitation. Luna flung herself headlong into his embrace, as if they were still together and madly in love.

"You're trembling," he said.

"You are too."

"So I am." He released her and stepped back, locking gazes with her. "I can't believe it's you. I thought we'd never meet again."

"I believed the same."

"Can I have another hug?" he asked, eager as a golden retriever.

She nodded and moved closer, hungry to feel his arms around her again.

He squeezed her tight, and she hugged him back, soaking up the moment. She closed her eyes and ignored the passing of time. He picked her up off her feet and spun her around in a circle, laughing, as if she weighed nothing more than a sack of feathers. She'd forgotten just how good it felt to be in his powerful arms.

Reunited with the love of her life.

A dream she never dared dream.

Oh, how fast she raced ahead of reality. *Come back to earth, Luna.* Paul set her down, and when her feet touched the sand, she landed in the present moment. No longer teenagers, but two strangers, having led entire adult lives without each other.

"What—"

"How—"

They both laughed.

"You go first," he said.

"No, you."

"Would you like to grab a bite to eat?" He waved toward the tiki bar. "Have a conversation?"

She wanted that more than anything! It might not be sane, but she wanted it. "I was headed that direction when we collided."

"Well, then . . . it's fated." He held out his arm to her. "Shall we?"

"Lead on." Pulse leaping, she draped her arm around his and his big bicep bunched. Another sweet jolt. Another electrical thrill.

He found an empty bistro table at the tiki bar and took a seat on the wicker chair. Luna parked herself across from him and stacked her hands on the table in front of her.

The server scooted over. "What'll ya have?"

Paul gave Luna the rakish grin she remembered oh so well. That grin once coaxed off her panties on a water tower. "Something to drink?"

"Just iced tea for me."

"Nothing stronger?"

"I don't drink."

"Makes sense." He nodded. She didn't drink alcohol because of her father, but he didn't need to say that. It was understood.

"Don't let me stop you," she said. "If you want to drink, get something."

"No, I'm good." To the server, he said, "Two iced teas, Jim."

"Do you know your food order?" Jim asked.

"They have great tacos here." Paul winked, and it brought back the memory of a little hole-in-the-wall taqueria they once frequented in Julep called Orgasmic Tacos.

"Tacos sound . . . orgasmic." She bit the inside of her cheek to keep from blushing.

"Two taco plates." Grinning, Paul raised two fingers.

"On it." Jim drifted away.

Silence dropped between them, and Luna racked her brain for something witty to say, but her dazzled mind came up empty.

"So," he said. "Tell me about yourself."

"I'm here with Mom and Artie. Mom is entering the quilting contest."

"Artie?" An enigmatic expression crossed his face.

"My daughter," she said. "Artemis is fifteen and I have a son too, Beck. He's eighteen, almost nineteen, and a first-year student at OU on a baseball scholarship. He wants to go into sports medicine."

"Sounds like you've got some terrific kids. And you named your daughter Artemis." Humor tinged his words.

"Does Orion belong to you?"

"Yes." Paul nodded, his gaze never leaving Luna's face. "She's sixteen going on forty."

"Same with Artie. She thinks she knows everything. So, a daughter named Orion and not a son?"

"It's a gender-neutral name, and it just suited her."

"You're the gardener here?"

"I am." He nodded. "I also maintain the golf carts and scooters."

"That's what makes the island flowers so beautiful. *You.*"

"Orion helps with the gardening too. It's not all me."

"How are your mother and stepdad?" she asked. "I heard they left Julep some time ago."

"They're divorced, thank god," he said. "I never thought

Mom would leave Rick, but she finally did. She is living near her sister in Phoenix."

"I'm glad she's doing well."

"Are you and Herc still together?" he asked.

"You knew I married Herc Boudreaux?"

"I got the Julep newspaper online during my stint in the military," Paul said. "Your wedding was front-page news. Just the kind of story to set Julep buzzing."

Did he sound a little sarcastic? She studied his face, but he seemed sincere. After she'd broken up with Paul, he'd joined the navy. She learned that from his friends, not Paul. He never told her, but why would he? She had already sent him packing.

"Herc worked as an emergency department physician. He tended gang members at the county hospital in Dallas and got killed in a shoot-out last year."

Paul's expression remained neutral, unruffled. She couldn't tell whether the news of her husband's death affected him or not.

He reached across the table to lay his hand over hers. The warmth of his palm seeped through her skin. "I'm so deeply sorry for your loss, Luna. I hadn't heard about Herc. Here on the island, I'm out of touch with my old life."

He didn't know the half of what she'd been through, but Luna didn't need his pity and she wouldn't spill her guts about how Herc gambled away everything they owned. That was too much, too soon. He didn't need to know about Jeanie's financial troubles either.

"Thank you. What about you? Are you and Orion's mother—"

"My wife, Julie, passed away from a brain aneurysm while in labor with Orion."

Her heartstrings jerked. "Oh, Paul! That's so tragic for you and your girl."

"We had a tough go of it for a while. Raising an infant alone?" He shook his head. "Not for the faint of heart."

"Your poor daughter, losing her mother like that."

"Orion has no memory of Julie. It's not as hard for her as it must be for your Artemis. Losing your dad when you're a teenager has got to be the toughest."

"She's resilient," Luna said. "But I do worry."

"You wouldn't be my Moonbeam if you didn't worry."

*My Moonbeam*. Luna couldn't draw in a full breath.

Kind eyes accompanied his smile. His hand remained on hers and she didn't pull away.

"I'm sorry," she whispered.

"For what?" His eyebrows lifted, and he seemed genuinely surprised.

"For hurting you the way I did. I'm glad we've met again, so I can apologize. I was young, hurt, confused."

He hadn't deserved the punishment she doled out. Yes, he had been wrong, but she'd been too quick to judgment and even quicker to abandon him. Shame burned from her belly to the tops of her ears.

His eyes turned tender. "Water under the bridge, Moonbeam. Life's too short to hold grudges."

"Oh, Paul." She held his gaze. "That is so kind. You have every right to blame me."

He looked puzzled. "For what?"

"For giving up on us so easily."

"You were well within your rights. I gave you plenty of cause."

Their order arrived and between bites of scrumptious tacos, their conversation shifted to safer topics—Hobby Island, plant cultivation, parenting challenges.

"Oh my gosh, these tacos are—"

"Orgasmic?" He chuckled.

"Yes, yes, they are." She joined in his laughter. "Best tacos *ever*."

"That's high praise coming from a taco connoisseur, but you'll find food on Hobby Island leans toward the extraordinary."

"How did you end up on the island?" she asked.

"It's a little convoluted," Paul said. "My wife, Julie, was the niece of Eloisa's ex-husband, Charles. Eloisa helped raised Julie after her mother got deep into an opioid addiction following a back injury. Julie even lived with Eloisa and Charles for a time before they divorced. I've heard Charles was pretty abusive, but Eloisa doesn't talk about her past, so it's not fair for me to discuss it either."

Luna liked that he didn't gossip.

"Anyway, when Julie died, I left the navy and moved to Everly with Orion to be near Julie's family. Finding gainful employment in a small coastal town is difficult. Eloisa had just inherited Hobby Island from her parents, and she wanted to start a crafters' paradise, so she hired me to help her get it going."

"You've been here from the beginning?"

"I have." He finished the last bite of taco and dabbed his fingers on a napkin. "It's been a wonderful place for Orion to grow up. Not only is the island safe and peaceful but she's got Eloisa and the aunties who act as surrogate mothers. Accepting Eloisa's help was the best thing I ever did for my daughter."

"Where does Orion go to school?"

"Everly. She takes the ferry every day during the school year. I'm so proud of her. She's a straight-A student." The love in his eyes when Paul spoke of his daughter tugged at Luna's heartstrings. He'd given up his military career in exchange for a better life for his child.

"Is Eloisa as kind as she seems?"

"Even more so," Paul said, his voice filling with warmth and admiration. "She's an angel in human form. She's quite unique and she's helped so many people on their path to healing."

"How's that?"

"Mostly by providing a safe place for people to explore and learn about themselves through crafts and community, but she's also a fantastic listener."

His enthusiastic endorsement of Eloisa eased some of Luna's concerns about the woman and Hobby Island. The place seemed too magical, too perfect. But maybe it was just that simple. By spreading love and kindness, Eloisa attracted more love and kindness into her life until she just vibrated goodness. A circle loop of positive energy.

Luna so wanted to believe that, but her old wary doubts whispered, *It's not okay to feel too safe. Question everything and everyone.*

"You're doing it," Paul said.

"What?" Startled, Luna blinked.

"Fretting."

"How do you know?"

"You still have the tell."

"Huh?"

"You caress the back of your knuckles when you're worried about something. What's worrying you, Luna?"

"This place is surreal. I don't trust it."

"Ahh," he said, and then nothing else. A moment passed. Then two.

"Ahh, what?"

"You're still there." His tone was soft, his eyes compassionate.

That irritated her. "I'm still *where?*"

"Afraid to let down your guard." He held up his palms. "But no judgment. We've all got our own timelines for letting go of fear. Some of us never get there. That's okay too. People get to be who they are."

"I let down my guard with you and look how that ended." The

words blew right through her mind and shot from her mouth before she could stop them, blurting what was in her heart.

Paul winced as if he'd been gut-punched and exhaled audibly. "You've been through a lot."

"I have."

"I don't want to add to your suffering."

Luna cocked her head and studied him, trying to cipher what thoughts churned in his handsome head. "What are you talking about?"

"There's another story you know nothing about," he said.

"Another story?"

"My side of it. The story I couldn't tell you back then but now . . ." He drew in a breath. "Maybe it's time."

"Last call," Jim, the bartender, announced to the patio. "We close in fifteen minutes, folks."

"Let me walk you back to your B&B," Paul said.

"Don't we need to pay?" Luna asked.

"Orion and I get free meals as part of my employment."

"That's a nice perk, but I need to pay my share."

"I've got it covered, Luna."

What should she do? She wanted to prove a point, what point she wasn't sure, but she also needed to watch every penny.

"I'll leave the tip," she said.

He pulled a twenty-dollar bill from his wallet and left it on the table. Overtipping, but he'd always been generous; it came from them both having worked in food service when they were in high school. "I've got that too."

"Thank you for dinner."

"My pleasure." He offered his arm and smiled.

She slipped her hand around his elbow, and they walked up the beach toward Crafters' Corner and the row of B&Bs beyond.

Most everyone had left the area. A couple walked on the beach holding hands. Two men fished off a nearby dock. A golden half-moon hung in the night sky and Luna's blood flowed thick with feelings, a hard knot of emotions pressing against her chest.

Luna kept sneaking sidelong glances at Paul.

The breeze tousled his lush, wavy hair. He was still good-looking, and his incredible sex appeal knocked her sideways. His angular jaw sported two days' growth of beard stubble, just the right amount of scruff, enhanced by full, chiseled lips. Her heart fluttered and her cheeks burned.

"It feels like yesterday," he said.

Yes, twenty-two years disappeared in an instant, as her yearning for him grew stronger than ever. How badly she wanted to kiss this man! How much she wanted to taste him. Crazy, irrational notions and so dangerous, this heady rush of hormones coursing through her system.

Was she losing her mind? Her best friend in Dallas, Becca Derling, had told her it was time for her to get laid. But Luna wasn't free with her body. She did not willy-nilly follow her sexual impulses. Not thoughtful, methodical, careful Luna Montgomery Boudreaux.

Except around Paul, the bad boy. But he was no longer a boy, and he had never really been all that bad, just daring, and rebellious, until that horrible night . . .

"We're here." She stopped outside the wrought-iron gates and turned to face him. "The Nestled Inn."

"Quick trip."

His eyes fascinated her. She couldn't get enough of peering into them. "Too quick."

He stared back, enrapt.

"Good night." Shyly, she smiled at Paul, lowering her lashes to half-mast. "Thank you for walking with me."

"You're welcome." His tone as soothing as a cat's soft purr.

Neither of them moved. She ached for him to touch her, to kiss her. She willed it so.

"It's been a pleasure seeing you again." He sounded formal now, the intimacy of their walk ebbing. He took a step back.

Her hopes for a good-night kiss crashed on rocky shoals. Gracious! What was wrong with her? She wasn't eighteen and she stopped believing in fairy-tale magic long ago.

Once, this gorgeous man rocked her world. Now he was a stranger. A stranger she still had tender feelings for. How was that possible? The pulse in the hollow of her throat throbbed.

The lamplight delineated his features, emphasizing the tiny lines etched at the corners of his eyes. No denying the passage of time. She had facial lines of her own. Absent-mindedly, she ironed the wrinkle between her eyebrows with an index finger. She could rub all she wanted, there was no erasing the past.

He was not the same impetuous boy she'd known, and she wasn't that same infatuated girl. She was a mother, a widow.

Paul stepped closer and lowered his head and for one wild moment she thought her bizarre wish might come true and he would indeed kiss her. "I've enjoyed this."

"Me too." She puckered her lips. His lovely scent filled her nose.

"Would you like to go on a picnic with me tomorrow?" he asked.

"I would love that."

"That's great. Meet me in the quad at noon and we'll have lunch on the beach."

"Sounds like fun."

"It's a date. Good night, Luna." His voice poured over her as rich and sweet as melted caramel. She wanted to gobble him up.

"Good night, Paul." She closed the remaining few inches between them. "So nice to see you again."

"You too."

She touched her tongue to her upper lip. Waited. Silently inviting him to kiss her, but he did not. Instead, he half turned toward the street.

Disappointed, she exhaled. "Before you go . . ."

"Yes?"

"Tell me what else happened that awful night. What is it I don't know?"

He waved. "Forget it. I shouldn't have brought it up."

"Please, just tell me. I can't stand not knowing." It bothered her that a secret had lurked between them all this time.

"It's not my place. If you really want to know, ask your mother." Then he left her standing bewildered beneath the porch light, wondering what else had happened on that miserable night.

# Chapter 11
## *Jeanie*

*"Glue might stick things together, but it's love that keeps them that way."*

—*Eloisa Hobby*

On her second day in paradise, Jeanie awoke with a song in her heart. It was Jack's favorite, "Three Little Birds." The tune had been playing in Crafters' Corner yesterday, and it fell into her brain groove and looped the entire night.

But even so, she slept wonderfully. Better than she had in, well . . . had she ever slept so well? Jeanie didn't think so.

"Don't worry," she sang as she got dressed and braided her hair in one long side braid. She chose to believe it. Maybe everything would be all right. Here's hoping, Bob Marley.

Luna had taken the news about Jeanie being on the verge of foreclosure with grace and kindness. Most of all, she agreed to help Jeanie win the contest. With Luna on her side, how could they fail? Optimism pushed her forward.

Jeanie rubbed her palms together. They needed to get started. She dropped by Luna's room and knocked on her door but got no answer. Maybe her daughter was already at breakfast.

She went to the kitchen where Vivian stood at the omelet

station, making omelets for the guests lining up. Luna wasn't among them.

"Do you need help?" Jeanie bustled over to the inn owner.

"Oh my, no, things are going swimmingly." Vivian winked.

"That's good to hear."

Today, Vivian wore a vintage pink poodle skirt and saddle shoes as she dished up a Denver omelet for Isabelle, who was waiting patiently with her plate extended. Vivian had styled her hair in an Audrey Hepburn *Breakfast at Tiffany's* French twist, and she looked like an elegant bobby-soxer ready to hop to the Big Bopper.

Nostalgia washed over Jeanie for an idealized bygone era that had never really existed.

"Omelet, Jeanie?" Vivian waved a neon pink spatula.

"No, thank you. I'll just have coffee and some of those yummy pastries. If that's okay with you."

"Go for it." Vivian smiled. "You don't need my permission. You're on vacation and calories don't count."

"Have you seen my daughter this morning?" Jeanie poured herself a cup of coffee from the pot on the beverage cart and dribbled in a generous dollop of half-and-half.

"Luna went jogging." Vivian cracked an egg against the counter with a deft hand. "She left about twenty minutes ago. The weather is perfect for it, but then again, the weather is always perfect on Hobby Island." Vivian's ebullient laughter filled the room.

Guests were seated in every chair around the dining table so Jeanie decided to take her breakfast on the cozy front porch veranda. Just as she settled into one of the rocking chairs, Luna came bounding up the driveway of the Nestled Inn in her workout clothes and running shoes, glistening with sweat.

"Whoa, Mom." Luna clutched her chest and staggered backward. "You scared me. I didn't see you sitting there."

"I'm sorry to startle you, sweetheart. I suppose the sun must have blinded you as it came through the jacaranda trees."

"Yeah. Forgot my sunglasses." Luna dabbed the sweat from her forehead with a white hand towel she pulled from her back pocket and dropped into the rocking chair beside Jeanie.

"How was your run?"

"Fantastic. I did five miles in an hour."

"That's good, right?"

"It is for me." Luna paused, then sat forward in her rocker. "You'll never in a million years guess who lives on the island."

"Oh?" The hairs on her arm lifted at the intense expression on her daughter's face and an odd feeling of dread passed through her. "Who?"

Luna raised her head to meet Jeanie's gaze. "Paul."

Jeanie's heart clutched the way it did whenever Luna mentioned her old boyfriend, which thankfully hadn't been in years. "P-Paul Chance?"

"Yeah." Luna nodded, her eyes sparkling with an effervescent light that stirred Jeanie's worry. "Get this, he's got a daughter a few months older than Artie and her name is Orion."

Jeanie heard a soft gasp and realized it came from her mouth. *Calm down, old lady. You'll give yourself away.* "No kidding?"

"Mom?" Luna frowned. "Are you okay?"

"F-fine. Why wouldn't I be? It's unexpected, isn't it? Running into Paul Chance after so many years, and here on Hobby Island of all places."

"Small world, right?"

"Right," Jeanie echoed, her throat constricting.

Luna's entire face glowed in the morning sunlight. She

looked . . . *transformed*. "Paul is widowed and raising Orion on his own."

"I hate to hear that he lost his wife." Jeanie took a sip of coffee. "And so sad for his little girl."

"Paul and I had tacos at the tiki bar and talked until midnight, then he walked me back to the inn." Luna locked eyes with her. "It was as if twenty-two years passed in the blink of an eye. The old feelings returned like magic."

Jeanie gulped. "Oh my."

"Yeah." Luna bobbed her head. "We're having a picnic lunch."

"Today?"

"Yes."

"Wow, that's fast."

"I know, I know." Luna held up her palms, warding off Jeanie's criticism. "But the spark is still there, Mom."

Jeanie's pulse pounded so loudly in her head she could barely hear Luna.

"You know what else?"

"No."

"Paul said I needed to know the truth about *that* night."

"What night?" Jeanie feigned ignorance.

"You know what night. The night of Dad's accident. The night I broke up with Paul."

"Huh." Jeanie's voice came out high and reedy, like she was trying to speak through a whistle trapped in her throat. "Wh-what did he say?"

"He said . . ." Luna drilled her with a hard stare. "To ask *you* what really happened."

"Did he?"

"You have no idea what he's talking about?"

"No, no. I remember little about that night. Except for the sheriff arresting Paul for drunk driving. I was too upset about your dad's injuries to absorb much else. My memory isn't what it used to be."

"You remember nothing else?"

Jeanie widened her eyes, going for the innocent, doddering old woman and hoping to pull it off. "No. I don't know what he's talking about."

"You sure?" Luna's wary gaze raked over her.

"Do you think I'm lying to you?"

Luna shook her head and got up from the rocker. "You didn't tell me about getting scammed."

"That was omission, not a lie."

Luna studied her for a long moment. "All right then. I'm off to the shower."

Her daughter went inside the B&B, leaving Jeanie's knees quaking. Because her three little birds had finally come home to roost.

# Chapter 12
## *Luna*

*"Sometimes you need to unravel to find your true pattern."*
—*Eloisa Hobby*

Confounded by the conversation with her mother, Luna stood in the shower, shampooing her hair and turning things over in her mind.

What else could have happened that horrible summer night that neither Paul nor her mother wanted to talk about? How much worse could it have been? She couldn't imagine. What secrets were they keeping from her?

And why?

Her mind flashed back, transporting her to the wretched evening that had changed the entire trajectory of her life.

She and Jeanie were coming back from Tyler where they'd driven to buy Luna's prom dress and had gotten caught in an unexpected downpour. Torrential rain lashed the windshield of their ancient sedan, and the wiper blades—long past the point of needing replacing—dragged and squeaked, barely clearing away any water.

It took her back to another rainstorm when she was six years old, and in the middle of the night her mother spirited her from the hippie commune where they'd been living. Shoulders hunched, face grim, Jeanie clutched the steering wheel, her gaze trained on the slick road ahead.

"I can't trust your father to do the simplest thing," she muttered. "Can he put new wiper blades on the car after I asked him multiple times? No! No!"

Luna stared at her. Jeanie rarely said anything negative about Jack, but she was angry that night because her credit card had been rejected at the store. Jeanie didn't have the full purchase amount in cash, but she negotiated a deal to do free alteration for the dress shop owner's customers for the balance.

In the passenger seat, Luna sat clutching the gorgeous dress wrapped in blue tissue paper, feeling awful about the whole thing. Jeanie would have made Luna's prom dress herself, but she'd been so busy doing alterations for all the other girls in town, she didn't have time.

Luna tried to tell her mother it was okay, that she could just wear her Sunday dress to the prom, but Jeanie got a determined look on her face.

"You're a Vincent as much as a Montgomery, so you'll dress like it. Our family might have lost their fortune but not our dignity. You'll be the prettiest girl at the prom in that frock."

*Frock.* What a weird word. Luna's stomach knotted with dread. Everything was wrong and terrible—the rejected credit card, the storm, the useless wiper blades.

Bad omens.

On the outskirts of Julep, they passed by the Vista Verde mobile home park where Paul lived. He was home studying for finals, like Luna should have been. Their car rattled over the railroad tracks and rounded the steep curve. Through the rain-slick windshield, the mangled wreckage came into view.

Jeanie slowed.

Luna's heart jumped out of her chest. There, wrapped around

an enormous oak tree, was her father's rust-colored pickup truck, steaming and hissing.

She screamed. "Dad!"

Jeanie slammed the brakes, hydroplaning on the wet road, and wrestled the sedan to a stop in the bar ditch. The two of them burst from the car, running into the fierce storm. Rain drenched them instantly as lightning streaked across the sky. Luna sprinted for the wreck, her sneakers slipping in the mud.

She stumbled. Fell to her knees. Hopped up again.

*Please let my daddy be okay.*

How often had she recited that prayer? Dozens of times. Hundreds even. Whenever she found Jack passed out on the couch or face down on the front lawn. She reached the car ahead of Jeanie, and when Luna peered inside, her heart shattered.

Dad lay slumped unconscious in the passenger seat, his head covered in blood. She wrenched open the passenger-side door, and an empty whiskey bottle rolled across the floorboard and dropped out onto the ground.

"Dad!" She shook him, panic rising.

Jack didn't respond. He was out cold. Was he dead?

"No!" Jeanie shrieked, her face white with shock, and she dropped to the mud. "No! No!"

Luna put two fingers at her father's throat and a faint pulse flickered. "He's alive!"

"What's he doing in the passenger seat?" Jeanie asked. "Who was driving?"

A low moan, beneath the raging storm, caught Luna's attention. She slipped and slid her way around the smashed truck to the driver's side.

Paul lay sprawled on the ground outside the driver's door, drenched in mud, blood, and rain. An overturned whiskey bottle poured out its contents beside his limp hand.

Wh-what? She stared, stunned, unable to believe her eyes. "P-Paul?"

No, this couldn't be. Paul didn't drink. He knew her views on alcohol. It couldn't be Paul's bottle. It had to be her dad's. Nothing else made sense. Why was Paul in the truck with her dad? Why was he driving? Jack didn't let anyone drive his truck.

*Ever.*

Paul's gaze met hers. "Luna . . ."

He struggled to his feet, looked dazed and disoriented. The reek of alcohol hit her. Paul *had* been drinking. He'd been drinking and driving with her father in the vehicle, and he'd wrecked Jack's beloved truck.

Rage filled, she flew at Paul, pounding his chest, anguish eating her alive. "You bastard! How could you?"

Paul feebly tried to stop her blows. In that instant, the boy she loved was gone, replaced by this . . . this . . . *monster.*

"We're through. I never want to see you again!"

"Luna." He reached for her.

But she turned away, bile rising in her throat as the wreckage of her life lay before her. Paul had done this, and nothing could repair the ragged hole torn through her heart.

Sirens wailed in the night. Jeanie appeared beside her, taking in Paul, sizing him up. "Luna, go back to the car. Now!"

"But Dad . . ."

"I'll handle it." Jeanie sounded strangely calm and in control. "I'm the mother and you're the child. Return to the car and stay put."

Distraught, Luna obeyed, taking refuge in the sedan. Drawing her knees to her chest, hugging herself and sobbing as she rocked on the seat.

Her gaze fell on the stupid prom dress. The dress she bought to look good for Paul. None of it mattered now. Not the prom.

Not the dress. Not their relationship. She yanked the dress from the wrapping, opened the door, threw it on the ground, and viciously stomped it into the mud.

Luna couldn't think straight. She couldn't believe what was happening. Her dad might die, and it was all Paul's fault. He knew she hated alcohol and yet he'd gotten drunk with her dad. No way could she ever forgive him.

The emergency vehicles appeared, strobing lights cutting through the darkness. The paramedics worked on Jack and then loaded him on a stretcher and whisked him off to the hospital, while the state trooper arrested Paul and stuck him in the back of the cruiser. He sent her an anguished look as they drove away.

Luna and Jeanie collapsed into each other's arms, finally letting the crushing grief wash over them, and Luna's world was never the same again.

The days following the accident passed in a numb haze. Her father underwent emergency surgery to remove his ruptured spleen and repair his lacerated liver. The doctors placed him on a ventilator in the ICU and kept him sedated.

For three days, Jeanie stayed at the hospital around the clock. She refused to leave Jack's side. Luna brought her changes of clothes and food from home. When her father regained consciousness, Jeanie was there to inform him that Paul had been driving. Jack didn't remember the accident, much less that Paul had been behind the wheel.

Following the vehicle crash, Luna moved through each moment on automatic pilot, not speaking, barely eating. The intense tears from the first night dried up, but her grief grew. During the last days of her senior year, the cacophony of teenage voices in the hallways set Luna on edge. She couldn't concentrate, couldn't smile, couldn't pretend everything was normal. Her friends tried to offer words of comfort, but their sympathy highlighted just how alone Luna was in her despair.

She withdrew further into herself each day. She sat in the back during class, head down, speaking to no one. She ate lunch alone in an empty classroom, choking down each bite until she thought she might vomit.

At night, she lay awake until the early hours, mind racing with flashbacks of tender moments with Paul that now seemed tainted. Their Saturday night movie dates, their lazy Sunday mornings laughing over pancakes at the Waffle House, their stargazing sessions in the bed of his truck. These sweet memories were now agonizing reminders of what used to be.

She ignored Paul's calls. Just seeing his name on the caller ID pierced her heart, but she would not bend, and she refused to let him back in her life. Luna was unlike her mother. She had no tolerance for addicts.

That night, Paul was booked and then arraigned the following morning. The judge sentenced him to a hundred hours of community service, a thousand-dollar fine, and suspended his driver's license for three months. After his sentence was completed, he joined the navy and left Julep for good.

It didn't seem like punishment enough to Luna, but because it was his first offense, he got off easy.

The life and love she once knew was irrevocably shattered, leaving her utterly adrift and alone. Until she left for the University of Texas at Tyler. Most kids from their town went to that college. Hercule Boudreaux, class president, captain of the football team, straight-A student, and son of the richest man in Julep, took an interest in Luna and asked her out.

Jeanie championed Herc and encouraged the relationship. Herc could provide lavishly for Luna, and her mother told her to

forget about Paul and so Luna banished him to the basement of
her mind.

But then all the old love flooded back when they'd reconnected
last night, and her heart was torn in half.

* * *

In the Crafters' Corner town square at noon, Luna found Paul
waiting for her with a picnic basket handle looped over his arm.
Seeing him now, after her vivid flashback in the shower, was so
disorienting, she stopped before reaching him.

Last night had been magical. A wonderful reunion, as if none
of the awful stuff from their history had happened, but the flashback flung her hard into the past and gave a stark reminder of
their demise.

But that was twenty-two years ago. Paul had created a good,
solid life for himself and his daughter. Jack was long gone. And
her feelings for Paul were filled with regret and yearning. Could
she finally forgive him? Could he forgive her? Could she forgive
herself?

Or was there simply too much hurt between them?

"Hi, Moonbeam." He grinned as if everything was hunky-
dory in his world. "How are you today?"

She had once loved this man with all her heart and then hated
him just as fiercely. Swirled in emotional whiplash, her knees
wobbled.

He held up the picnic basket. "I hope you're hungry."

Fifteen minutes later, Paul unfolded a soft, woven blanket with
intricate designs, setting it on a lush patch of grass above the
beach with an expansive view of the ocean.

The sea stretched endlessly, its surface shimmering under the
touch of the noonday sun, casting hues of orange and pink across
the sky. The sound of gentle waves crashing against the rocks

below mingled with the distant cry of seagulls. The salty tang of the ocean and the faint scent of wildflowers dotting the surrounding landscape filled the air. It was the perfect romantic backdrop, isolated and intimate, with the vast, majestic ocean as their witness.

Paul sank onto the blanket and patted the spot next to him. "Have a seat."

"What's in the basket?" she said, struggling to keep things light. She had so many questions that needed answering.

"Sandwiches. Chicken salad, your favorite."

"You remembered!" she said, a warm feeling filling her heart. "Where did you pick up the takeout?"

"Not takeout. Made it myself. Just the way you like it. With red grapes and Granny Smith apples."

"You can cook?" she said, touched beyond measure, and her heart softened.

"Well, it is chicken salad." He gave her an endearing, lopsided grin. "Not exactly haute cuisine. As a single dad, I had to learn to cook so Orion wouldn't starve."

"I thought you might make use of the island's aunties. You're not playing this right. You should never have to cook with your gardening skills and that gorgeous smile."

"What? This little old thing?" He turned his grin on her full force.

Heated from the inside out, Luna felt her face flush. Oh, she was in over her head.

He opened the picnic basket and took out the chicken salad sandwiches on sourdough bread, which were cut into triangles. Paul passed one to her, along with a napkin and a bag of ruffled potato chips.

"Nah. I gotta do the cooking. It would be too easy to take advantage of all the help I receive from Eloisa and the aunties. I need to stay strong and on my toes raising a teenage girl. Can't let my parenting skills slip."

"I see your point," Luna said. "I'm already feeling beholden moving in with Mom, even though she never makes me feel that way. I think she really loves having me and Artie there."

"It's a fine balance to walk between independence and interdependence."

"What scares *me* is codependence."

"You don't want to be like your mother."

Laughing, Luna pointed a finger at Paul. "Ding, ding, ding. Nailed it."

"Unless you've changed a lot, you don't have to worry about that. You go in the opposite direction from Jeanie. You don't let just anyone in. You build walls and keep them high."

The chicken salad was delicious, but her throat suddenly tightened, and she couldn't swallow another bite. She set down the sandwich on the wax paper wrapping, dusted the crumbs from her fingers, and looked Paul in the eyes.

"I talked to my mother this morning. She claims to remember nothing about that night."

Paul exhaled and put down his sandwich too. "I want to be transparent with you, Luna."

"Please do."

"Seeing you again and being with you last night . . ." His eyes went shiny in the sun. "Well, it reminded me of what I threw away. Of everything we lost."

"Oh, Paul." Her hands were shaking. "I feel the same. But there's—"

"Too much dark history?"

She nodded, unable to continue.

"We've got to clear the air before we can move forward." He paused. "*If* you want to move forward."

"I-I'm—"

"Scared?"

"Uh-huh."

"Me too." He spoke into the wind, and she could barely hear him. "But I can't ignore my heart. Being with you again, it feels right. It feels good."

She put up both palms. "This is too much, too soon. I have feelings for you too, but—" She bit down on her bottom lip.

"One night, twenty-two years ago, I became the enemy, and that's the way you've seen me ever since, no matter all the good times that came before it."

"I was too hard on you. I had you on a pedestal, and when you fell off, I couldn't forgive you. I see now that my youth and fear made me harsh and intractable. I'm sorry for the pain I caused," she said.

"You thought I was driving drunk and severely hurt your father in a vehicle crash. I understood." His jaw tightened, and he glanced away, staring out at the ocean.

"You *were* driving drunk."

He shook his head, drew up one leg, and draped his arm over his knee. "I was hoping Jeanie would tell you the truth. This should really come from her."

"Well, she didn't." Luna kept her tone neutral, matter-of-fact. "It's up to you."

Paul met her gaze head-on and held it. Luna saw conflict in his eyes. This was painful for him. "I wasn't in the truck with your father that night."

She stared at him, not comprehending his words.

"I wasn't drunk."

Luna recoiled. Why was he lying? "I saw you. I saw the whiskey bottle. You staggered and slurred your words."

"I was pretending to have a head injury. Pretending I'd been driving. And there were liquor bottles everywhere falling out of that truck."

"But why would you do that?"

"To protect you."

"No. No." Luna shook her head and backed up, slid off the blanket. "That makes no sense. The sheriff said your blood alcohol was well above the legal limits and the lab tests confirmed it."

"Yes, but that's because your mother asked me to guzzle enough whiskey to fail the sobriety test once she realized what I'd done."

Luna let out a keening noise. Her chest so tight she could hardly breathe. "What. Did. You. Do?"

Paul looked weary and his blue eyes sad. "I was at home, in my mom and stepdad's trailer at Vista Verde. They were out for the evening, and I was studying for finals."

She owed it to him to listen, but she didn't really want to hear this. The repercussions were already too much to bear. If he hadn't been drinking, that meant she made him a scapegoat. Ruined them for no good reason.

"I heard the crash. I tried to convince myself it was just the thunder, but I went outside and saw your dad's truck wrapped around the tree. I called 911 and then ran to help him. When I saw the whiskey bottles, I knew he was blitzed. I also knew this would be his third DUI, and he'd go to prison."

"What did you do?" she whispered, already knowing.

"I considered the impact on you and your mother and reacted impulsively. I tugged Jack into the passenger seat and decided to tell the cops I'd been driving. I pretended I was behind the wheel and dazed from the accident. That's when you and Jeanie showed up. I didn't expect that."

Luna felt all the blood drain from her face and pool into her feet. Was it true? Bile rose in her throat, and she fought hard not to vomit.

"Your mom figured it out right away. She knew Jack would never let anyone else drive his truck. She also knew if the cops looked too hard at the accident, they'd figure out Jack was driving, and she knew we needed a distraction to take the focus off him. If I was drunk, they'd put the focus on me, and as a first-time offender, I would get off without major consequences. That's when she sent you to the car."

Luna put her hand to her mouth. She couldn't hear more of this. She knew her mother had enabled her father's addiction, but she had no idea how far it went.

"She grabbed a flask from the glove compartment and told me to drink it down. And I did." His eyes drilled into hers. "And then Jeanie swore me to secrecy. I kept my word all this time. Stayed silent. But twenty-two years have passed, Jack is gone, and it's time you knew what actually happened."

Her brain reeled. She flashed to that horrific night again. Her furious rage and desperate grief over Paul driving drunk and nearly killing her dad. Everything she believed about that night was a lie.

Anguish grabbed Luna. Why had she been so willing to believe the worst about Paul? The one person she had loved like no other.

Tears streamed down her cheeks in the cheery sunlight, the calming water in direct contrast to her turbulent emotions. The boy she loved had sacrificed *everything*—for her. The fog of that night finally lifted, and for the first time, she clearly saw the truth.

"You loved me that much?"

Relief washed over Paul's face. "More than you can ever know."

"How can you ever forgive me for the way I treated you?"

"It wasn't your fault. You didn't know. I would have made the same choice in your position."

"Oh, Paul, I am so very sorry." She was crying so hard she couldn't see.

"Shh, shh. Nothing to be sorry for." He pulled her close and cradled her head against his chest. The decades melted away and she was his girl again.

"Forgive me, please forgive me."

"There's nothing to forgive, Moonbeam. Everything's okay. We've reconnected, and that's all that matters."

They held each other tight as the surf pounded around them and for the first time in twenty-two years, Luna felt whole.

# Chapter 13
## *Jeanie*

*"Never underestimate the power of a well-placed apology."*
—*Eloisa Hobby*

Jeanie paced the cobblestone alley behind the Nestled Inn, moving back and forth in front of the row of gleaming scooters. Several guests had exited, claimed a scooter, and zoomed away.

They greeted her, and she greeted them back as if nothing was out of the ordinary. As if her mind and body weren't a terrible jumble of fear, worry, regret, and shame.

Luna's question about the night of Jack's accident had thrown her into a tailspin and Jeanie had lied to buy herself time. She prowled the B&B, unable to settle on a course of action, knowing whatever she said or did that this would end badly.

Should she come clean to her daughter? What if Paul kept quiet about Jeanie's actions that night? Then there would be no need to confess.

*Oh no, ma'am. That's no excuse.*

She couldn't count on Paul's continued silence and even if Paul didn't tell Luna, she and her daughter could never have open, honest communication as long as Jeanie continued to be deceptive. More than anything else, Jeanie longed for a genuine relationship with her daughter, longed for it more than winning the quilt contest or saving the house.

There was only one path to reach that goal: tell the truth and accept the consequences.

But what if Luna couldn't forgive her? What if she turned her back on Jeanie forever? She would certainly deserve it. Jeanie clutched her chest, felt pain stab her heart.

Oh dear, oh dear.

She reached the end of the alley and retraced her steps. The slap of her Birkenstocks echoed in the air. Her arms flapped lifelessly at her sides. She didn't possess the emotional energy to swing them as she walked.

Jeanie couldn't keep waiting for the other shoe to drop. She had to be proactive. Had to get this confrontation over with or they'd never move on.

Before she lost her courage, Jeanie headed to Crafters' Corner.

Her frayed nerves razor-honed her senses. The sun shone too brightly, despite her sunglasses and the covering of fluffy white clouds overhead. The flowering jacaranda trees she found so refreshing and sweet now smelled heavy and cloying. The music from the speakers in the quadrangle no longer soothed and today it jangled her nerves. The coppery taste of fear filled her mouth, sharp and caustic.

A flashy red scooter zipped past, coming scarily close to running her over. Jeanie jumped, pulse racing.

Up ahead lay the bookstore, A New Chapter. If only this trip could mark a fresh chapter in their lives. If they could just turn the page and start fresh. Embrace the future with Luna and Artie and let go of the past.

*If wishes were horses, beggars would ride.*

The adage her mother loved to throw at her streaked across Jeanie's frazzled mind. It always came back to her messed-up childhood, didn't it? The origins of the gaping wounds that she unintentionally used to hurt others. The abuse wasn't her fault, but healing her destructive behavior patterns was her responsibility. She could stay a victim, or she could change. She struggled with the damage for sixty-five years.

If she didn't change now, she never would.

That's when she spied Paul and Luna walking up from the beach. Her daughter's head rested on Paul's shoulder, and he had an arm around her waist as his head bent to Luna's. In his other hand, Paul carried a festive picnic basket.

They looked as if they'd just survived something awful.

*He's told her.*

Terror constricted Jeanie's stomach, and nausea overwhelmed her. She couldn't let them see her. Not now. Not like this. She was unprepared.

Yearning to escape, Jeanie glanced around for the quickest refuge. To her left, on the same side of the quad as Paul and Luna, lay the bookstore, behind her the B&Bs, ahead of her the beach.

She dodged right, darting toward the nearest building, the Hobby Island chapel. She raced inside.

The door whispered closed behind her.

Inside, the chapel was empty and silent. Stained-glass windows cast kaleidoscopic splendor across driftwood pews. An altar peeked out like a shy creature, adorned with scented candles that flickered like butterfly wings and bowls brimming with island flowers spilling their perfume.

Above her, the bell tower pushed skyward, waiting to send its sonorous voice winging over the island. The walls told tales in wood carvings—birds fluttered along the windows, fish schooled across the beams, shells and coral added glints of treasure. It was a sanctuary alive with the island's spirit; sunlight, sea breeze, and birdsong filtered in, sending Jeanie's thoughts aloft.

How easily prayers and daydreams could take flight in such a sacred space! The chapel restored the soul with its simplicity and connection to the island's beauty. Here, one could meditate on life's daily miracles that so often slipped past unnoticed. A quiet hallelujah to the gifts of peace, nature, and joyful rejuvenation.

The chapel gave her rash hope.

Jeanie stepped to the altar, her footsteps echoing loudly in the still asylum, disturbing the peace. She cringed and quieted her gait.

At the altar, she kneeled and brought her hands up to pray.

But once in position, Jeanie didn't know what to pray for. Forgiveness for sure, but it seemed inadequate. Grace? She certainly wanted that. Mercy. Yes. That was the one. She needed mercy.

She pressed her palms together, lined up her fingertips, and moistened her lips. Before she could pray, the chapel door creaked open, and a shaft of light fell over her.

Jeanie didn't have to glance over her shoulder. She knew who stood there.

If this were a western movie, right now, the outdoor speakers would be playing the theme song from *The Good, the Bad and the Ugly* instead of the beachy stylings of Jack Johnson's "Better Together."

"*Mother.*"

The word was frost in the air. Footsteps came closer, rattling the pine floors behind Jeanie. She didn't dare look back.

Her soul quivered. She had it coming. She avoided this moment for twenty-two years and believed she had escaped retribution. But no. The time had come. She bowed her head.

"What did you do?" The steely blade in Luna's voice thrust deep.

Knifing Jeanie right in the gut. She dropped the prayer hands and clutched her belly.

Luna stalked closer to the altar. "You think God will save you? Is that it?"

Oh dear. This was much worse than she imagined! *You can't ditzy hippie-chick your way out of this one, Jeanie Vincent Montgomery.* No? Rats. It was her go-to.

Time to own up.

Or risk losing Luna forever.

Her heart was thumping so hard and fast, Jeanie feared she might pass out. *Take your lumps, take your lumps. This is it. No more hiding.*

Drawing in a breath so deep it pushed a gulping shudder down her spine, Jeanie stood tall and slowly turned to face her daughter.

It took every ounce of bravery she could muster. Her knees knocked and mouth went dry. She dug her fingernails into her palms and braced herself for the hardest conversation of her life.

The light from the open door behind her daughter cast Luna in silhouette. Hands on her hips, she stepped forward, facing Jeanie down like an Old West gunslinger. Luna's piercing hazel eyes seared her, their usual warmth replaced by icy betrayal that cut straight to Jeanie's core.

Her stomach roiled and she wilted under her daughter's accusatory glare.

The sun-dappled interior of the chapel, normally an oasis of tranquility, now felt jarringly incongruous—a cruel irony—as dark emotions churned within her. The island paradise had become her own personal hell.

"You *knew*." Luna's voice quavered, her lower lip trembling.

Jeanie wanted to reach out and touch Luna's face, but the look in her daughter's eyes stopped her. She stood rooted to the spot beneath the bell tower, terrified that if she moved, she'd topple over.

"You *knew* Dad was driving drunk that night. You *knew* Paul pretended to be driving and dazed from a head injury to save Dad from prison."

Jeanie opened her mouth but could think of no words to defend herself. What she'd done was indefensible.

"You hid the truth from me." Luna crossed her arms, chin raised in defiance, as if bracing for a blow. A blow that Jeanie had already inflicted through her lies. "You encouraged Paul's lie and abetted him in deceiving law enforcement."

A choked sob escaped Jeanie's lips. The crushing weight of her lies—over two decades of accumulated deception—pinned her down and stole air from her lungs. Even the tropical birdsongs sounded like accusations in her ears.

*Liar, traitor, deceiver.*

Luna inhaled sharply, a single tear carving a trail down her flushed cheek.

"Sweetheart—"

"How could you, Mother?" She spat out the sentence with heated venom that pierced Jeanie's heart. "You let me believe Paul was drunk and caused the accident! Your lies broke us apart and left him with a false DUI conviction!"

The knot in her throat tightened brutally at the anger in Luna's eyes—anger Jeanie fully deserved. Luna was right—her deceit had destroyed Luna and Paul's relationship and damaged Paul's life forever.

She blinked back scalding tears.

"Dad was an alcoholic, and you knew it." Luna clenched her fists at her sides. "Not only knew it, but you enabled him."

Defensiveness grabbed Jeanie. "I loved your father, and he loved me."

"Mom, you were trauma bonded to an addict. Your relationship was so codependent, it could be in the *DSM*. You were an enmeshed enabler."

A heated flush of shame started at the bottom of Jeanie's feet and rolled up her legs to her solar plexus, burning a forest fire straight to her heart. She didn't know what the *DSM* was, but it sounded bad.

"Do you remember that wretched book you used to read to me?" Luna asked.

"Wh-what book is that?"

"The book you *loved* so much. The one that made me cry every single time you read it. Even so, you kept reading it. I should have known then how messed up you were."

"I don't know what book you mean."

"*The Giving Tree.* The story about a tree that gives and gives and gives to the little boy and the boy never even thanks the tree. And then he grows up, cuts her down, and builds a house out of her and at the end, as an old man, he has the audacity to sit on her stump."

"I *loved* that story. It reminded me of a mother's love for her child."

"I know you loved it. But it has nothing to do with your love for me. It's the story of you and Dad. He took and took and took and you gave and gave and gave. Mom, stop giving yourself away before you're nothing but an old stump!"

Jeanie couldn't have been more stunned if Luna had slapped her hard across the face. Was that really the way she saw things?

"You met Dad when you were thirteen years old. You married him at seventeen. You dated no one else. You told yourself some fantastical story about your fairy-tale romance, but it wasn't true love. It was just a toxic pattern. It was a codependent dance."

Luna's words held up a mirror to Jeanie's marriage. A mirror she spent half a century avoiding looking at.

"For years, you denied Dad's issues. You probably still can't face the truth. I can say that because I lied to myself plenty about my own dysfunctional marriage, ignoring Herc's gambling addiction, sweeping it under the rug, when I knew in my heart that things were bad. But I didn't want to look. Couldn't see it."

Yes, maybe her marriage hadn't been as wonderful as Jeanie liked to pretend, but she *had* loved Jack, and he had loved her to the best of his ability.

"What you say is true. I've refused to acknowledge it for a long time. It was easier to pretend everything was fine than to face the reality of your father's addiction. But he loved you, Luna. So much."

"I know that, Mom, but it wasn't enough." Luna hardened her chin. "When I was a kid, I had no security. No safe place to land. Not until my grandparents died, and you inherited the house. The Victorian was my only stable home growing up, and now we're about to lose it too, because you are so desperate for another fairy tale."

Luna's words pummeled her because they were on point. Jeanie winced, and her heart thudded painfully in her chest. "I had an idealistic view of love, but I tried my best. I know better now, and I'm sorry."

Luna didn't speak, just stared at her hard.

It was too little, too late. Jeanie knew it. What a mess she made!

Her daughter stepped toward Jeanie with her eyes narrowed. "You covered it up. You made excuses for Dad. I thought you were blind to his spiral into addiction, but you saw it, didn't you? And you didn't care because all that mattered was keeping the status quo."

Jeanie *had* enabled Jack's drinking for so long, sweeping away the debris while turning a blind eye as he worsened each year. She was complicit. What kind of mother chose a lie over her own daughter's well-being?

Jeanie's own mother, that was who, and Jeanie was no better than Francine. Maybe even worse because at least her mother had been open about who she was—cruel, invalidating, manipulative, unempathetic. Francine Vincent embraced her role as a controlling authoritarian and never pretended to be anything else.

But that night, on the rain-slick road, Jeanie realized she would lose Jack if not for Paul. And Jeanie had acted like her mother. What she'd done to Paul showed her dark side that she inherited from Francine.

She herself had used an innocent and sacrificed not just her daughter but Paul as well to serve her own selfish needs. If she was ever to be redeemed, she had to face how she had so greatly impacted Paul's life for her own. She was the villain here and there was no way around it. Paul was the victim and she the perpetrator.

Oh, she told herself a different story that night. She told herself she had no choice. Jack's third DUI meant prison, and it would devastate Luna to lose her dad. So she gave Paul the whiskey and told him to guzzle it to protect Jeanie from more pain and to keep their fractured family intact.

And Paul had done it because he loved Luna, and Jeanie had let him take the fall without any concern for how her lies would affect his life.

But in the darkest depths of her heart, she knew preserving Jack's secret meant keeping her greatest shame hidden—her inability to stop him from drinking. Her love was powerless against his addiction. She couldn't face that, couldn't admit that booze meant more to him than she did. That his addiction overpowered her. Hiding from it had seemed the only option and, in her cowardice, she selfishly put her own self-interests first.

"Well? What do you have to say for yourself?" Luna scowled.

Jeanie wouldn't deny it, wouldn't double down as Francine would have done. In the same scenario, her mother would have deftly spun things around. Francine would first deny, then attack, and if Jeanie still stood strong—which, granted, was rare—Francine would play the victim, accusing Jeanie of awful things to justify her own terrible actions. But Jeanie would not do that to Luna.

"I have my reasons," she said, "but it's no excuse. None at all."

Luna blinked. "Damn straight."

"I thought I was protecting you. I didn't want you to lose your dad. Instead, I destroyed Paul to save Jack." Her voice cracked as her throat spasmed. "I'm so sorry, baby . . ."

But even as Jeanie spoke the words, she knew they were hollow, empty platitudes that could never undo the damage she wrought. She failed her daughter in the most fundamental way a mother could fail her child.

She had put her own needs first.

Luna plunked down in a pew then, as if her legs would no longer hold her aloft. She dropped her head into her hands, her back rigid, shoulders shaking with quiet, convulsive sobs.

Aching over her daughter's grief, Jeanie wrapped her arms around herself, feeling small, alone, and adrift in a storm of her own making. She didn't deserve an ounce of pity.

The full impact of two decades of lies hit her in that agonizing moment. She saw how one deception bred so many more, a cancerous web steadily spreading, silently contaminating everything it touched.

Each small lie intended to shield Luna had ultimately hurt her more. Cut deeper. Robbed her of trust and innocence.

And now, the damage was irreparable.

Luna's youthful relationship with Paul, her implicit belief in their family, her sense of stability and home—all had been utterly shattered the night Jeanie protected Jack and convinced Paul to drink alcohol so he would fail the sobriety test. A wound so deep and jagged it couldn't heal easily.

If at all. She saw now how evil her actions had been.

With trembling fingers, she stepped toward Luna, yearning to comfort her, to make amends, though knowing, deep down, that she lost that privilege long ago.

"Please . . . You deserved the truth. I should have told you before." Squeezing her eyes shut, Jeanie prayed her daughter could somehow grant her the redemption she wasn't worthy of. "Can you ever forgive me?"

Luna didn't respond, just kept her head down.

Jeanie held her breath. She was close enough to touch her now, but she didn't dare.

After an eternity, Luna raised her head and met Jeanie's gaze, eyes bloodshot but her posture softening. Could Luna forgive her?

"I don't know how to forgive this betrayal. Maybe I can't. Maybe that possibility died the night you chose a lie over Paul's well-being."

Her words sliced into Jeanie, each syllable a new cut, laying bare the gravity of her failures. Luna was correct.

"You're right," Jeanie said through quavering lips. "What I did . . . it's unforgivable. I betrayed your trust in the most profound way, and I treated Paul horribly. I took advantage of his love for you. I did that. I was far more than wrong. I was selfish to the core, and it is the deepest regret of my life."

"I don't understand how you could lie to me all this time." Luna's small, broken tone speared Jeanie's heart.

Her fragility threatened to shred Jeanie's last sinew. "I—"

"You know how much I loved Paul. What he meant to me. Why? Why did you let me kill that love? Why did you let us break apart? And why did you push me to marry Herc?"

"May I sit down?" Jeanie lowered her voice.

Without a word, Luna nodded and scooted over, leaving Jeanie space in the pew beside her.

Jeanie perched on the edge of the bench seat, unable to relax. She crossed her legs at the knee and angled them toward Luna.

Her daughter shifted away from her.

Letting out a soft sigh, Jeanie blinked back tears. She had no right to cry. She caused all this. "I was wrong. So wrong." Her voice caught in her throat. "I thought I was protecting our family . . . but I destroyed your trust. I'm so deeply sorry."

The silence swelled between them until Jeanie thought she might break beneath its immense weight.

"Sorry doesn't cut it. If I had known the truth, I wouldn't have married Herc. Why did you champion that relationship, Mom? Was it simply because Herc was a Boudreaux and came from money?"

"That was part of it, yes," Jeanie said. She was done fudging the truth. "I lived the struggle of being married to a man who couldn't support his family. My wish was a different life for you. Paul—"

"Paul came from Vista Verde," Luna said. "That's another reason you didn't tell me the truth. Admit it. You solved two problems by having Paul take the fall for Dad's DUI. It kept Dad out of prison and got me away from Paul."

Startled by Luna's statement, Jeanie started to deny it, but had she? "If I did, it was unintentional."

"But maybe subconsciously?"

She saw the truth in Luna's eyes. Forgiveness would not come easily or quickly after such profound betrayal. The devastation was too raw, too vast. Jeanie had no right to expect instant absolution.

"It pains me to say, but it's possible. I told myself I was protecting you. Keeping you safe from my mistakes. I didn't expect the world to change so quickly. In my generation and all those that came before mine, a woman's greatest aspiration was a successful marriage. It's all our society let us have."

"Mother, I wouldn't have married Herc if I'd known Paul wasn't driving that night, if he wasn't drunk."

"I know."

"I did my best, but I couldn't love Herc the way he deserved to be loved, because I'd given my heart to Paul long before. God knows I tried, but deep down, Herc realized he was my second choice. Here's the big irony, Mom. Your lie convinced me to marry a man you thought would provide for me, but Herc left me penniless." Luna gave a harsh, humorless laugh.

"You can't regret marrying Herc. You wouldn't have Beck and Artie without him."

"That's true and I can't blame you for everything that happened," Luna said. "*I* went through with the marriage. *I* stayed for nineteen years when I should have gotten out. That's on me."

"You would never have abandoned Paul if you'd known the truth. It *is* on me. All of it," Jeanie said.

"That might be the case, but I can't beat you up over it. Not if we want to heal. Hanging on to a grudge will not make our family whole."

Jeanie could hardly believe Luna was ready to forgive her. She was unworthy of such kindness and compassion. "Do you mean it? Can you overlook the terrible thing I did? Can Paul forgive me?"

"Paul is the one who told me to go easy on you."

Jeanie couldn't hold back the tears any longer as her eyes sprang leaks. She was a sad, foolish old woman who'd caused her own suffering. "Did he?"

"Paul's a good man. He always has been."

Jeanie felt so horrible about all the heartache she caused. "I know."

Luna held her arms out, and Jeanie sank into her daughter's embrace. They hugged each other and sobbed together. Despite everything, it seemed Luna believed Jeanie had some kernel of good inside her. She clung to her daughter, her only port in this storm of her own making.

They stayed locked in the embrace for a long time before Luna leaned back to look at Jeanie. The encouraging expression on her dear face belied her bone-deep exhaustion.

"I don't know if I can ever fully forgive you, but if I let this destroy the goodness inside of me . . . you'll have taken everything."

Jeanie reached up to cradle Luna's face in her hands, both remorse and gratitude swelling within her. Her wise daughter had found the courage that Jeanie hadn't.

"We'll take it one day at a time," Jeanie vowed, her voice hushed yet fierce. "However long it takes. You lead, and I will follow."

Luna stared into her eyes, as if confirming Jeanie's sincerity. Then she gave the faintest nod before pulling Jeanie close once more.

Their journey to healing would be long and fraught with setbacks. They both knew words could not instantly mend the fractured foundation between them, but it was a start. They could walk forward together, slowly finding their way back to each other.

If Luna could summon even an ounce of grace for her now, perhaps, in time, full redemption would come.

"You do know you're not off the hook, right?" Luna said.

"Yes, I will do my absolute best to make amends to you, my dear daughter. No matter what it takes. I am committed to change."

"No, not to me, Mother. You need to apologize to Paul."

# Chapter 14
## *Luna*

*"Clay remembers the hands that shape it. So does the heart."*
—*Eloisa Hobby*

Like a trooper, Luna dried her eyes, squared her shoulders, and forgave her mother. What else could she do? She was stuck with Mom on this island for the next two months and they had a quilting contest to win if they had any hope of saving their home.

Holding a grudge served nothing. What was done was done. But she was angry and that was okay.

She left Jeanie in the chapel and stepped out into the bright sunshine of the quad. Blinking, she glanced around but saw no sign of Paul. She hadn't really expected to see him. He'd told her he had to get back to work tending the island's foliage.

But she wished he were here to give her another comforting hug.

Sharon, Isabelle, and Nanette passed by on their way to the beach decked out in swimwear, flip-flops, and sun hats. They waved to her. She waved back as if nothing had happened, not letting on that her world had turned topsy-turvy in many ways. Her mother had been deceiving her for twenty-plus years and Paul Chance was back in her life.

The trio veered over to Luna's side of the quadrangle.

"Hi," Isabelle said. "Are you and your mom coming to the opening quilting circle tonight?"

"Um . . ." Luna had no idea. Her mind was still reeling.

"You've got to come." Nanette rubbed sunscreen over her arms. "We heard Clare is giving tips and hacks for winning the quilting contest."

"Then yes," Luna said. "We'll be there for sure. Have a wonderful time."

"See you at seven." Sharon shifted her beach tote to the opposite arm and led the way to the beach.

"Please do bring your mother," Isabelle said. "She's lovely."

"I will." Luna wriggled her fingers in goodbye. Turning, she took a deep breath, trying to decide what to do next, then saw Artie and a teenage girl zipping toward her on scooters.

"Mom! Meet my new bestie, Orion!" Artie hollered as they rolled up.

Luna took in the pretty, purple-haired girl with familiar eyes. This was Paul's daughter. "Oh, um, hi, Orion. Nice to meet you."

Orion hopped off her scooter and extended her hand. She was dressed much like Artie, in denim shorts and a graphic T-shirt. "Nice to meet you, ma'am."

Paul's child, a walking reminder of the man she loved and lost so many years ago and now they were unexpectedly brought back together. The girl could have easily been Luna's child if her mother hadn't forever altered fate with her deception.

"Please, call me Luna." She shook the girl's hand. Orion's palm was warm and firm. A young woman confident in herself. She was impressed with the self-assured way the girl made direct eye contact.

"Luna." Orion's grin was a carbon copy of her father's.

A strange feeling brewed in Luna's stomach. A sensation she

couldn't quite identify. A sense of loss, for sure, but there was something more beneath it. Should she say something about having known Orion's father when they were teenagers? But that felt out of place, and she didn't want to make such an announcement out of context without Paul around for backup. And yet, she didn't want to hide vital information from the girls. She did not want to be like Jeanie.

Luna searched the crowd, looking around the quad, hoping to see Paul watering flowers or pulling weeds.

". . . so can I go midnight beachcombing with Orion?" Artie was pleading, palms pressed together. *"Pleeease?"*

Huh? Oh dear, she hadn't been listening.

"Midnight?" Luna said, sounding sterner than she intended. Artie needed a strong hand, yes, but the girl had been through a lot, and she tended to act out when she was hurt. "Certainly not. You have a ten p.m. bedtime."

"Mom, we're on summer vacation! Chill."

"Artemis, do not speak to me in that tone." Luna scowled. Paul let his daughter run around at midnight? She did not approve.

"Why do you have to be so mean?" Artie huffed.

Luna kept her voice even, firm. This motherhood gig wasn't easy. Knowing when to stay the course and when to give a little leeway was a skill in progress. "You can go beachcombing at a normal hour."

"Don't you know *anything* about beachcombing? You have to go at low tide," Artie said.

As much as she wanted to make her daughter happy, the idea of Artie out late with a girl she just met—even if it was Paul's daughter—sparked anxiety.

"I'll look after her," Orion promised.

Slowly, Luna shook her head.

Orion smiled kindly and all Luna saw was Paul shining through. She wanted to trust those heartfelt eyes, but simply couldn't. She might be Paul's daughter, but Orion was a complete stranger.

"Not tonight," Luna said, hedging. "We're still settling in. Maybe another time."

Artie's crestfallen face almost broke Luna's resolve, but she had to hold firm. Good parenting meant making tough choices, even if it was unpopular.

"Aww, man, you never let me have any fun."

"Accept my decision with grace or you won't ever get to go." Luna shot her daughter a pointed look.

Artie rolled her eyes, but Luna let that pass.

"C'mon, Art," Orion said, sounding like a diplomat. "Let's go take an origami lesson at the bookstore. You'll love it. The class starts in ten minutes."

"Enjoy your class and the rest of your afternoon. Meet your grandmother and me right here at six p.m. We'll go for dinner and then you'll join us at the quilting shop for the remainder of the evening."

Artie shot Luna a withering look and followed Orion to park their scooters and head for the bookstore. After the girls disappeared inside A New Chapter, Luna turned away and spied Paul at the far end of the quadrangle tending the abundance of potted plants outside The Yarnery. The plants thrived because of his tender nurturing.

Fingering her bottom lip, she smiled, thinking about how much she'd like to kiss him and see if his lips still held the power to knock her socks off.

He bent over and his khaki cargo shorts stretched tight across his backside. Luna couldn't help tilting her head and staring. He looked just as physically fit as he had at eighteen and he'd always had a great butt.

The door to the chapel opened and Jeanie came out. She looked neither left nor right, all her attention focused on Paul as she made her way toward him.

Anxious, Luna sucked in her breath and put a palm to her chest. What would happen? Luna darted behind a jacaranda tree and peeked around the trunk, watching to see what her mother would do.

"Paul?" Jeanie called.

Paul pivoted toward her.

Luna glimpsed his handsome face unsheltered by his straw Panama hat. Her pulse quickened. He was so gorgeous. An old thrill she hadn't felt in decades ran through her.

Paul set down his gardening shears, peeled off his work gloves, stuck them in his back pocket, and gave Jeanie his full attention.

Worry twisted Luna like a corkscrew. She fought the urge to creep closer so she could hear them. A group of tourists strolled by blocking her view for a couple of minutes. When they'd gone on past, Luna could see Jeanie talking fast and gesturing animatedly, but her mother was partially turned away from her, so Luna couldn't see her face.

Paul listened, head canted, his expression inscrutable.

The sea breeze ruffled Luna's hair. She strained to hear their conversation, but they were simply too far away.

Paul lifted his hat and wiped sweat from his brow with the long sleeve of his sun-protective shirt. He looked so sexy with his thick curly locks spilling from beneath the raised hat. When they'd dated, he kept his hair cut short. She liked this older, more relaxed reiteration. Being a dad suited him, but she'd always known he'd be a good father, even if she didn't agree on his late-night beachcombing policy.

It occurred to her that if they were going to date—were they? She certainly hoped so—they needed a game plan for telling their children about their past. They needed to be deliberate about this and in agreement.

Should they wait to tell the kids until they were sure about resurrecting their romance? Decades had passed. They were virtually strangers after all, and their kids must come first.

*Take it slow.*

They had two months on Hobby Island. Perhaps by then, she and Paul could have figured things out. Wow, she couldn't believe she was thinking about dating Paul Chance.

As Luna watched Jeanie and Paul continue their conversation, almost as if on cue, the outdoor speakers played Cher's "If I Could Turn Back Time."

Jeanie hugged Paul.

He hugged her back. He must have accepted her mother's apology, and everything was sorted between them.

Relief lifted her shoulders. Yes, maybe, maybe . . . *Shh*, she didn't want to jinx it . . . but for the first time in a long while Luna felt hope.

# Chapter 15
## *Artemis*

*"Be like watercolor. Blend, but don't lose yourself."*
—*Eloisa Hobby*

As she lay on the couch in the quilting room of A Stitch in Time at seven that same evening, legs up the wall, head upside down, her hair dragging on the floor, Artie stared at the quilters' choice in footwear.

Gran in her Birkenstocks, Mom in sensible ballet flats, Isabelle in flip-flops, Nanette in sneakers. The only one with any fashion sense was Sharon, who wore gold sandals that showed off her tanned, French-manicured toenails.

Dot, Vivian, and Clare also sat at the table, along with a couple of other women Artie didn't know, but she couldn't see their shoes from her vantage point.

Sighing, Artie texted her brother, Beck, even though she knew the message wouldn't send. Texting made her feel normal in this peculiar world. On my tombstone, write SHE DIED OF BOREDOM.

Okay, fine. The food on this island was bitchin' awesome and the beds were the softest on earth. The sky was bluer here than at home and the night sky took her breath away. But still a snooze-fest.

It was still early in the evening and if she heard one more

word about the many varieties of stitches used in quilting, she was gonna throw back her head and howl at the moon. Why was Mom being so very mean, not letting her go beachcombing with Orion?

Artie texted: I mean c'mon, BUY a freaking quilt at Wally World already and be done with it.

*Could be worse*—she told herself what she knew her brother would say—*could be Julep.*

True enough. Sighing, Artie pocketed her phone, swung her legs to the floor, and sat up. Orion had chores and couldn't hang out with her for now.

Dot put down her sewing and caught Artie's eye. She patted the empty chair beside her. "You're restless. Why don't you join us?"

Artie crinkled her nose. "Not much of a quilter, thanks."

"If you'd like to explore the other craft shops, I'd be happy to accompany you. There's painting, jewelry making, stained glass, baking . . ." Dot checked off activities on her fingers. "And—"

"Yeah, Dot, see, here's the thing, I haven't been into arts and crafts since like third grade when we made pipe cleaner reindeer with googly eyes. I'm over it."

"Bad experience with a glue gun?" Dot chuckled.

"Something like that." Artie couldn't help grinning. An incident involving a glue gun *had* happened. She shot glue at a girl who made fun of her art and it got stuck in the girl's hair and the school nurse had to cut it out. Artie ended up in detention for a week. It wasn't her first—or last—time in detention.

"Don't forget," Dot reminded her, "there's a chance you could win money for your artwork if you enter it in one of the contests."

Artie shook her head. "The money sounds enticing, but I don't have any talent."

"There's a new art category this year," Dot coaxed. "Recycled art."

"Oh, yeah, Eloisa mentioned it in the orientation Gran dragged me to. Not my jam."

"Are you in the habit of shooting down everything before giving it a chance?" Dot asked.

"Now you're catching on." Artie winked at the large woman.

"Artie," Mom said, not even glancing up from her sketchbook. She was working on designing Gran's quilt while Gran sewed practice swatches. "Stop being such a negative Nelly."

Dot raised her eyebrows. "What is your jam if it's not arts or crafts? Music? Animals? Gardening?"

"Animals are all right." Artie ran a hand through her hair.

"Then you'd enjoy the turtle preserve. This time of year, the turtles come in after sunset to lay their eggs." Dot's fingers moved over the piece she was quilting. The woman hand-sewed almost as quickly as Gran.

A nocturnal activity? Now Artie was interested. "Directions to the turtle preserve?"

Dot pointed to a quilted map of Hobby Island hanging on the wall. The turtle preserve was on the western tip of the island, directly opposite Crafters' Corner.

"How far is that?"

"Five point six miles."

"You're not going there alone in the dark," Mom said, shooting her a "cool it" stare.

Artie rolled her eyes and blew out her breath. "Dark is the point. That's when the turtles lay their eggs."

"Turtle preserves at night can be dangerous," Vivian warned and took off her reading glasses.

"Dangerous?" Artie asked. "In what way? Accidentally stepping on turtle eggs?"

"You're not going." Mom put down her pencil and intensified her glare.

"Should I tell them, or do you want the honors, Dot?" Vivian batted her eyelash extensions.

"Be my guest," Dot said.

Vivian spread her arms and motioned everyone to come closer. The quilters leaned in. She lowered her voice as if she was telling a spooky campfire story. "An ancient turtle haunts the beach, and they call her Wicked Martha."

"Ooh," Artie said. "How wicked is she?"

"Martha isn't wicked in a sinister sense, rather, she's more of a mischievous scamp than anything else." Vivian snipped off a piece of thread from the row of stitches she just completed. "Martha loves everything left, specifically left socks."

"Huh?" Artie crinkled her nose. "Whaddya mean?"

"In her younger years, Martha was an ordinary sea turtle, basking in the sun and enjoying the tranquility of island life." Vivian dropped her voice even lower, building the drama. "One fateful day, Martha found a shipwreck submerged beneath the waves. Her curiosity piqued, she ventured inside and found a chest overflowing with knitted socks of all colors, patterns, and sizes."

"No way." Artie snorted, not believing this story for a second. "Who keeps a chest of nothing but socks?"

Ignoring that, Vivian ran fresh thread through the eye of her needle. "Bewildered by the soft textures and vibrant hues, Martha made her choice. One left sock."

"What color?" Artie asked.

"Ocean blue, of course, with a starfish design. Martha was so taken with her newfound treasure that she started collecting left socks from across the seven seas. Nobody knew why she had such an affinity for socks, but theories abound. Some say she's furnishing her underwater abode, but quilters believe she's creating a patchwork quilt for when the seas grow cold."

"But that's ridiculous. There's no difference between left socks and right socks," Artie said.

Vivian's eyes widened as if she believed the kooky fable. "Please *never* let Wicked Martha hear you say that!"

"Why? Will she steal my left sock?" Artie chuckled.

"You laugh, but Martha's cheeky capers are real," Sharon piped up. "Last year when I first visited Hobby Island, I went home with only one sock from each pair I brought."

Artie wasn't buying that for a second, least of all because elegant Sharon was not the sock-wearing type.

"Whenever a single left sock disappears on this island, people know who to blame. Wicked Martha slips ashore under the veil of darkness, pilfering left socks from unsuspecting island guests. To prevent thievery, when you visit the turtle preserve, please take an extra left sock with you as a small offering to the island's quirky guardian," Vivian said, finishing the tall tale.

Artie shot a look at Dot. "Island myth, bullshit or verified?"

A Mona Lisa–style smile settled over Dot's face. "Verified."

"So, if you ever miss a left sock, remember to smile, and say, "Wicked Martha strikes again!" Clare giggled.

"Wicked Martha is the unruly spirit that keeps our hearts filled with joy and our left feet oh so slightly colder at night," Dot added.

"What a charming story!" Gran applauded. "Thank you for sharing it with us."

"Just remember," Vivian said, "the more you embrace our legends, the more Hobby Island reveals her magic."

Magic of what? Making old ladies look foolish? Artie snorted. "That's easy enough to fix. I'll stop wearing socks. Take that, Wicked Martha."

"I have a better idea," Mom said. "Stay away from the beach by yourself late at night."

"Mom, Wicked Martha isn't real," Artie said.

"Maybe not." Her mother's expression told her in no uncertain terms not to go out at night. "But plenty of other dangers lurk in the dark for stubborn young ladies who defy their mothers."

Yeah well, Mom scared easily, but Artie did not. She was almost sixteen. She was capable of making her own choices. She wasn't one to hem and haw like Mom and Gran, weighing pros and cons and analyzing everything to death.

Artie acted. She *did* things.

She was like her father in that regard.

An image of her dad laughing and shooting hoops with her at their house in Dallas popped into her mind, and she felt a hard stab of sorrow. Dammit, she missed him. But she wasn't a bawl baby. Artie hardened her jaw and fisted her hands.

That's when she made her decision that come hell or high water, she was sneaking out of the B&B tonight to go beachcombing with Orion.

*　*　*

After everyone at the Nestled Inn had gone to bed, Artie grabbed her backpack, got out her water bottle, filled it from the sink, and tossed it into the pack. She grabbed the free pretzels and nuts from the welcome basket and put them in too. Spurred by a desperate need for adventure, Artie crept downstairs and sneaked out the front door.

The humid night air wrapped around her, and the thrill of the unknown coursed through her veins.

Hobby Island beckoned.

Her pulse thumped at the promise of what lay beyond the confines of the Nestled Inn and Crafters' Corner. This world was her playground, and nothing was gonna hold her back. The darkness was her ally, concealing Artie as she slipped away from the B&B.

She headed toward the shoreline. So much to explore, experience, and enjoy as she hiked through Crafters' Corner. The heartbeat of the island was quiet. Most everything was closed except the tiki bar, which remained open at the beach, with a few customers on the patio, chatting and laughing. A clock in the town square chimed as she walked toward the beach and counted off each bong until it stopped at eleven.

Burning tiki torches lighted her way from Crafters' Corner to the water's edge. The sand glowed with a silvery light as the moon peeked out again. Artie stopped to pull a map from her pocket. The meeting spot lay three miles up the beach. It was a trek, but Artie ran cross-country. No big whoop for her.

She ducked her head, the wind whipping wilder out here, slapping her hair into her face, but she could handle it. By the time she reached the rendezvous spot, which was near a cave marked Old Turtles Grotto, it was just after midnight.

But there was no sign of Orion. Had she left already? Artie was barely late. Just a couple of minutes. Disappointed, she looked up at the half-moon hanging in the sky. "Orion, where are you?"

The surf washed up to her ankles. Dammit, she should have worn flip-flops instead of her Docs. Artie slipped off her heavy backpack and tossed it up on the beach several feet away. It landed in a clump of sea oats. The waves crashed against the entrance to the cave, sending ocean spray splattering over Artie's face. Sputtering, she wiped her cheeks with the heel of her palm and tasted brine.

Cupping her hands around her mouth, she called out, "Orion!"

The cave echoed back to her, *"Orion! Orion! Orion!"*

Artie waited. No answering call. Maybe her new friend couldn't hear over the wind. Artie called again.

Nothing.

Was Orion screwing with her head? Had she lured Artie into

the dark unknown as a prank? Or maybe she was playing a fun game of hide-and-seek.

Artie liked that thought much better. Perhaps Orion was hiding in the cave. Was she waiting for Artie to come find her? Artie sloshed through the water and winced. Ugh, her Docs! *Oh well, too late to worry about that now*, Artie thought and waded to the mouth of the cave.

It was pitch-black.

If Orion was inside, she was much braver than Artie. She took out her cell phone. On Hobby Island, cell phones were good for only one thing. A flashlight. She shone the narrow beam around the cave entrance.

"Come out, come out, wherever you are."

*"Are, are, are."*

Well, hell. What now? She wouldn't risk going deeper into the cave without confirming Orion was in there.

Feeling punked, Artie tried to pivot and back out of the cave. But her left shoe sank deep into the mud. She gave a grunt, grabbed her knee, and tried to jerk her foot free. But she was already ankle-deep in silt. "Frick!"

*"Frick! Frick! Frick!"*

It was eerie out here, and Artie started worrying . . . just a bit. She was pretty confident in her ability to rescue herself, but the sand pulled at her like wet cement.

That's when she felt *it*.

A slimy cold thing touched her leg. Something big and heavy. Something *moving* . . .

She froze, her blood slamming against her eardrums. Then something firm and wet scraped across her ankle, and she felt that something clamp down on her left sock.

Artie shrieked.

A turtle as big around as Mom's rebounder trampoline tried to pull off Artie's sock with her shoe still on her foot.

Holy shit! Wicked Martha was attacking her!

Martha gave a good hard yank and pulled Artie underneath the water.

*Ulp.*

Dammit, Mom was right. She shouldn't have been alone on the beach at night.

# Chapter 16
## *Luna*

*"Darling, forgiveness is the truest pattern of love one can weave."*
—*Eloisa Hobby*

Luna couldn't sleep despite the supremely comfortable bed and her bone-deep exhaustion.

The events of her busy day dogged her—the truth about what had happened with Paul all those years ago, the mistakes she made, the wrong turns she took, the mother she had to find a way to fully forgive . . .

She and her mother hadn't been alone together since their showdown in the chapel that afternoon, and she dreaded working on the quilt with Jeanie.

And Luna couldn't stop thinking about what it would feel like to kiss Paul again. Which was supremely stupid given her current life circumstances, she knew, but she couldn't stop thinking it.

Gak! She needed some air.

Quietly, so as not to awaken the household, she dressed in yoga pants and a long-tailed T-shirt, shoved her feet into flip-flops, and tiptoed out the back door of the B&B. Once outside, she headed for the beach.

The streets of Crafters' Corner were all but deserted; the only activity was at the tiki bar where she'd eaten tacos with Paul the previous evening. Luna detoured toward the bar, hoping to catch a glimpse of him, but he wasn't there.

Disappointed, she changed direction and walked to the beach. The clouds parted and the receding surf glistened palely in the light of the half-moon. She removed her flip-flops and held them between two fingers as she sank her toes into the damp sand. She took a deep breath and felt her body relax.

It was eerily silent but so very peaceful. She'd never been anywhere so calm and restful.

From the darkness, an approaching golf cart appeared. She watched it draw closer and saw it was one lone person. A man.

Her heart leaped.

Paul.

She stopped walking and he pulled up beside her.

"Good evening, Moonbeam." He grinned.

"Hey," she said. "You're out late."

"Making my nightly rounds. How about you? What's got you out for a solo stroll?"

"Couldn't sleep."

"Yeah," he said. "We scuffed up a lot of old wounds today."

"No kidding."

"I talked to your mom."

"I saw. How did that go? She didn't tell me about it."

"We're good, Jeanie and I." He bobbed his head, and his smile melted her heart into a puddle. "We made our peace."

"You forgave her?"

"I did."

"You're kind of amazing, you know that?"

"Hey, I've worked hard for my peace of mind." His smile softened. "Don't think I haven't had my moments."

"I admire you for it and wish I could get there."

"You're on the path." His kind eyes held her gaze and she had an urge to cry happy tears. Hard to believe they were together again, and it felt . . . *easy.*

Too easy, really. Easy scared her.

"Would you like to go with me to water the plants in the butterfly hatchery? It's my last stop before I head home."

"I would love that."

He leaned over and opened the passenger door. She slid inside, feeling wildly giddy.

Putting the golf cart in gear, he guided the electric vehicle off the beach and onto the cobblestone path. Overhead, a blanket of stars illuminated their way.

"I met Orion today. She's a lovely young woman. It seems our daughters are becoming friends," she said.

"I heard."

Luna exhaled. The question on the end of her tongue had been circling her brain ever since Orion introduced herself in the quadrangle that afternoon. "Do you think we should tell them about us?"

"I already told Orion about you."

"What?" Startled, she stared at him.

"I told her the truth. That you were my first love."

"When was this?"

"A few years back, actually. When we were passing through Julep, I stopped to show her my dad's and my grandparents' gravestones."

"You told her about me, way back then?"

"Yep. I don't keep things from my kid."

That felt like an indictment, even though she knew he didn't mean it that way. "What does she think about me being Artie's mom?"

"I haven't told her that part yet. I was waiting . . ."

"On what?"

He turned his head to look at her. "You."

"Wh-what do you mean?" Luna put a hand to her throat.

"Whether you wanted Artie to know about us or not."

"Oh, I see." Luna felt disappointed but had no idea what she hoped he might say. "I suppose I need to tell her."

"That's up to you, but you are here until the end of July, so maybe sooner rather than later."

Of course, she had to tell Artie about Paul. Especially if she intended on seeing him. *Did* she intend on seeing him?

Then again, considering Artie's recent losses, it seemed kinder not to confuse her with talk of an old flame when Luna's future with Paul was uncertain at best.

"You can't control everything, Moonbeam," Paul said.

"Huh?"

"You're rubbing your knuckles."

"Darn it." She folded her hands in her lap.

They drove past the storybook cottages where the island residents lived, and Paul pointed out his bungalow nestled amid palms and jacaranda trees. Luna tried focusing on the lingering briny ocean scent and hypnotic sound of the receding tide.

Her mind spun scenarios of Artie's reaction, each possibility worse than the previous.

Paul reached over to give her hand a gentle squeeze and steered the cart off the main path, heading toward the butterfly hatchery. He changed the topic and for several minutes, they reminisced about high school.

"Do you remember Mr. Garrison's awful trigonometry tests?" Luna groaned.

"I blocked out most of that trauma," Paul said.

"I haven't forgotten. We spent so many lunch periods in the library studying together, trying to make sense of sines and cosines."

Laughter knitted them together as they shared other memories—bonding over their mutual dislike of study hall, competing to see who could build the best volcanoes in science, vying for top grades in AP Literature.

"I'll never forget our first real date at the county fair. At the top of the Ferris wheel, I worked up the courage to kiss you. I knew then I was falling for you."

"Me too." The sweet and clear memory was vivid in her mind. "And you won me a Kewpie doll at the ring toss. I was *so* impressed."

"Your big smile pumped my ego. I walked on air for a week."

It was fun being with him. Especially now that his secret was out, and he had nothing to hide.

They topped a hill, and the wind blew Luna's hair every which way. She felt youthful and curious, ready to explore.

"I have a question," she said.

"Shoot."

"Do you raise a vegetable garden?"

"We do. In fact, we grow much of our food here."

"No wonder the food tastes so delicious. I haven't had a mediocre meal since I've been here."

"Thanks for the compliment, but I don't do it alone. Dot is a helluva gardener and we also have two employees who come over from Everly."

The butterfly hatchery was a glass greenhouse lit bright from inside. It glowed like a welcome beacon. Paul parked and offered his elbow to her, and they strolled over to the building.

Luna clung to his arm, appreciating his muscled bicep. Gardening had honed his body lean. He opened the outer door and then a second screen door. Classical music played low from a boom box balanced on a metal stool. To the left of the screen door was a table set up with a display of cocoons on it.

One was moving.

"Oh look!" Luna rushed over for a better look. "One's hatching!"

Paul came to stand beside her.

Fascinated, she leaned over, placed her palms on her knees, and watched the butterfly emerge. Over the course of a few minutes, its crinkled wings smoothed and expanded into perfect, colorful fins.

"How amazing." She breathed. "But I suppose this is old hat to you."

"It's still a miracle," he said, moving to a sink in the far corner and filling a watering can from the tap. "I'm awed every day by the magic of Hobby Island."

The butterfly fluttered hesitantly and then lifted off in a wobbly test flight. It zigged and zagged around the room, joining the hundreds of other butterflies in the humid greenhouse filled with water dishes, saucers of fruit slices, and flowering plants.

"Look at that little guy go!" Luna laughed and clapped.

"I love seeing you so happy," he said, his voice husky as if recalling a time when they were happy together.

Her breath caught and their eyes met. They stared into each other. Goose bumps broke out on her arms. Scary stuff, this feeling.

"Here," Paul said, giving Luna one of the two watering cans he'd filled. "You start watering the plants on the left side and I'll start on the right and then we'll meet in the middle. Watch where you step. Butterflies light on the ground sometimes."

Whistling, he went about his work. Careful where she put her feet, Luna moved to water a row of blooming milkweed in potted containers. Roused by her movements, butterflies flew up from the vegetation. It took several minutes, but when she finished, she found herself in the middle of the room, butterflies dancing around the hatchery.

"Good job," he said. "Thank you for your help."

"Thanks for bringing me along. This place is so peaceful."

"It's one of the reasons I save the butterfly hatchery for the last of my gardening chores. Makes for sweet dreams."

"I can see that." She tipped her head back, watching the butterflies swooping and circling.

Paul was so close. Right beside her. Boldly, she leaned against his shoulder.

Then equally bold, he wrapped his arm around her waist. She nuzzled closer, feeling lifted, transformed by this experience. Maybe second chances *were* possible. Maybe broken hearts could learn to fly again.

They were completely alone, just her and Paul.

Luna was in serious trouble.

Not from the incredible majesty of watching butterflies break from their cocoons and pump up their wings to take flight. Not from the place lush with goldenrod, snapdragons, and daylilies. Not from the soothing classical music that had her toes tingling to the vibrating violins in Vivaldi's "Spring."

Those impressive things didn't cause Luna's turmoil.

Rather, it was the gorgeous man beside her, his arms outstretched. Head thrown back, eyes closed, a huge smile on his face. Literally hundreds of butterflies were lighting on him, their wings beating in perfect time to his breathing.

It was such a startling sight, Luna felt hypnotized, mesmerized by his zest for life. She was both envious of and awestruck by Paul Chance. How did he do it?

Not a single butterfly landed on her. The main attraction was too near, how could the creatures do anything else but go to him?

"Show-off," she said.

"What?" he asked, one corner of his mouth quirking up.

"How do you do that?"

"Do what?"

Luna shook her head at Paul's butterfly-attracting powers. "All right, Mr. Butterfly Whisperer, what's your secret?"

"It's my animal magnetism," Paul deadpanned.

"Uh-huh." Luna held out her arms and concentrated, eyes squeezed shut. After a minute, she cracked one eye open. Not a single butterfly. "How come they're not landing on me?"

Paul chuckled. "Here, I'll help."

He moved behind her, his breath tickling her ear. Luna shivered as his hands slid down her arms, positioning them just so.

"You have to relax." His fingers grazed her waist. "Let go, Moonbeam. Let go."

Luna inhaled slowly, trying to ignore the delicious flutter his touch stirred inside her. She focused on loosening her muscles, leaning back into Paul's solid frame.

After a moment, a curious butterfly floated down and landed on her finger. "Oh, oh! Look, look! I did it!"

"See? I knew you had it in you." Humor tinged his voice.

More butterflies swirled around Luna as she stood enveloped in Paul's arms, eyes closed, heart humming, attuned to the gentle brushing of butterflies crawling over her arms.

She opened her eyes to find Paul smiling tenderly at her and she fell in love with him all over again. Even the butterflies adored him, for he was ringed by the colorful creatures.

"Let go. Let life unfold naturally," he whispered.

As if it was that simple.

"We'll get you there," he said, reading her mind. "Step by step . . . if that's what you want."

She searched for her voice. She liked that he said "we" as if he were already committed. "I . . . don't know what I want. My life is a mess. In flux."

"That's okay."

"I don't know who I am anymore."

"You do know." He gently tapped two fingers at her chest right above her heart. "You've just forgotten."

Unerringly, he reached for her, and she let him fold her into his arms. It surprised her how much his touch unraveled her.

An old memory replayed in her mind, Paul tugging a white T-shirt over his head, muscles rippling beneath his tanned skin. Her fingers fumbled with the zipper of his jeans, breathlessly inching it down. She'd been so eager for him, once upon a time.

Honestly, she still was.

Sweat beaded her upper lip. It was sultry in here.

Paul dipped his head, and she was certain he would kiss her. She tensed, waiting, ready.

But he didn't kiss her.

Just peered deeply into her eyes.

Making a noise of frustration, Luna leaned in and rested her palm against his chest. Beneath her hand, she felt his heartbeat. It pounded at the same quick tempo of her own wild ticker.

Paul's lips twitched as if he wanted to say something, but he didn't speak, didn't move.

Luna needed no more encouragement than that. Going up on tiptoe, she gently pressed her lips to his, and the honey-scented world around them fell into oblivion.

His warm angular lips yielded right away. His taste both familiar and new, leaving her scared yet craving more.

"Luna . . ." His voice shook. "What are you doing?"

"No idea." She felt reckless and loved it.

Her arms went around his neck, and his hand went to her waist. He tugged her closer and took over the kiss she started.

A shiver tripped down her spine. She savored the moment and the sweet taste of him on her tongue.

Paul groaned.

Luna threaded her finger through his hair, the strands as silky and thick as ever. He escalated things, his tongue sliding between her parted teeth.

They teleported back two decades and found themselves on the Julep water tower, leaving Hobby Island far behind, and they kissed as if tomorrow didn't exist.

Paul tightened his grip, tipped her head back, and moved his lips from her mouth to the underside of her jaw. He found the erogenous zone that fired her up and nibbled her skin. He remembered what turned her on!

A blazing thrill ran through her.

Kissing Paul felt like coming home after a long absence. Their breaths mingled as he returned to her mouth. His free hand cupped her cheek, his tender touch anchoring them together.

It was too much, too soon, and she knew it.

Why had she started this? She was not impulsive or spontaneous. Quite the opposite. Paul brought out something latent in her. An untamed fierceness that both pleased and scared her.

He broke the kiss and rested his forehead against hers. "Are you all right?"

"No," she whispered.

"Me either. Just making sure we're in sync." He brought his lips to hers again. His taste intoxicated her, dragging Luna deeper under the spell the island had been weaving around her from the moment they'd arrived.

His touch seemed to burn through the fabric of her shirt, and she could feel the heat of his palm spread over her waist. He kissed her like she was his saving grace.

This slow, steady kiss lasted and lasted and lasted as if their lips danced to some long-forgotten tune only the two of them could hear.

The need for air finally drove them apart, their heavy breathing mingling in the breezy night air. Their kisses stirred up feelings she tamped down years ago. Feelings of love and longing, of hurt and betrayal.

Shocked at what she'd done, Luna stepped back, gasping. Her life was a hot mess. She wasn't ready for this.

Wasn't ready for him.

Her heart hammered, lost and uncertain.

Fear, that ever-present emotion that had dogged her since early childhood whenever she woke up in strange campgrounds or on some random person's couch or entered new school classrooms alone, gripped her.

Paul's mouth pulled down in a mournful expression. "You're regretting this."

"Yes. I'm sorry. I shouldn't have kissed you. It was a mistake."

"Moonbeam." He reached for her, but she twirled away.

The genuine emotion in his voice tightened her muscles, kicked her soul. Her heart ached for all they'd lost. But there was no going back. She'd been trying to recapture the past, but it was long gone. They weren't who they used to be. These feelings belonged in the past and she was only confusing herself.

And him.

"It's not . . . I don't mean to sound trite, but we're not the same people we once were. I was foolish for a ridiculous moment and lost my head. Please forgive for me." She took a shuddering breath to calm herself, but the tactic didn't work.

Tangible fear lay like a rock in the pit of her stomach and sent a cold current flowing through her veins.

"It was just a kiss, Luna. Don't build a story around it. Just let it be." He sounded so sensible. He had changed, growing up and calming down. She liked Paul 2.0 even better than the original.

And the original had been pretty darn special.

"Yes, right." She settled a hand on one hip, her feet already pointing toward the door. "I need to go. I need to think. To process everything that's happened."

"Of course." He nodded. "I'll take you back to the Nestled Inn."

# Chapter 17

## *Artemis*

*"The most beautiful mosaics are made from broken pieces."*
—*Eloisa Hobby*

This was how she died.

Drowned by Wicked Martha in the Old Turtles Grotto.

Okay, perhaps she was being a tad overly dramatic, because even though the old sea turtle in question locked a death grip on Artie's sock, they were in shallow water. Still, the whole thing was trippy.

She believed the old ladies at the quilting table were joking about the reptile. She never once considered they were serious about a giant sea turtle who stole left-side socks.

In hindsight, she should have shown more respect.

*Yeah, smart girl. That's what you get for taking off on your own without permission.*

Okay, mistakes were made, point taken, but dissing herself wouldn't solve a thing. Time to fight back.

This thieving sea turtle would rue the night she ever cast the side-eye at Artemis Kathleen Boudreaux's left sock.

With her right foot, Artie kicked as hard as she could, whacking Wicked Martha's thick shell. "Let go, ya bitch."

Wicked Martha dove deeper, swimming at an astounding clip.

"I swear, I'm gonna make turtle soup out of you," Artie warned and tried her best to jerk away.

Who knew a giant sea turtle could be so strong and fast? How had turtles gotten such a slow-paced, plodding reputation?

She slipped on the wet rocks, staggered, fell, and her head went underwater.

Yikes!

Hey, if she could kick out of her shoe, she could let Martha have her sock and swim away.

As if channeling a live-action movie hero, Artie jammed her right foot directly under Martha's chin and then caught the back of her left Doc Martens with the toe of her right shoe.

*Score!*

She kicked off her left shoe and felt it float away on the current. Wicked Martha peeled off Artie's sock and swam to open water.

*Good riddance.*

Freed at last, she paddled back to shore.

Wicked Martha swam to the top, just a few yards away, Artie's left sock dangling from her mouth like a soggy cigarette.

With her adrenaline spent, Artie's limbs went limp as overcooked noodles, and it was all she could do to drag herself back to shore. At last, the tip of her bare foot touched dry land. Like a badass, Artie army-crawled to the sand. She rolled over on her back and stared at the stars, heaving.

She survived.

That's when she heard the slow, echoing clap of applause. Huh? She had an audience.

Artie turned her head and saw Orion approaching.

"Well, that was some kind of entrance." Orion grinned and squatted on the ground beside her. "Are you always such a show-off, Boudreaux?"

Artie lugged herself to a sitting position, dripping wet and shivering in the moonlight, relieved beyond measure to see Orion.

"Hey, you."

Tsking with her tongue, Orion wrestled out of her windbreaker and settled it around Artie's shoulders. The jacket smelled of the girl, her fragrance an intriguing mix of sea spray, caramel, and starlight.

"Thanks." Artie slid her arms through the windbreaker. "I'm freezing."

"You're welcome. I see you met Wicked Martha."

"I thought I was gonna drown." Artie drew her knees into her chest and wrapped her arms around her knees. "I didn't believe Wicked Martha was real."

"And now?" Orion lowered herself to her butt on the beach next to Artie.

Artie planted her bare left foot in the sand and hummed a few bars of the old Monkees' song "I'm a Believer."

Orion threw back her head and let out a cackling laugh.

Goose bumps fled up Artie's arm, and she shivered again. "What's so funny?"

"Look in my windbreaker pocket."

Artie stuck her hand in the pocket and pulled out an ancient iPod that did nothing but play the music already loaded on it.

"Tunes," Orion said. "Turn it on."

Artie started the device and the opening notes of "I'm a Believer" spilled into the night. "How is this song on your playlist?"

"Serendipity," Orion said and started singing the lyrics. The girl had a magnificent voice. Orion hopped up, dancing and snapping her fingers in time to the music. "C'mon, girl. Get up. Dance with me. You're alive!"

Compelled, Artie jumped up, jigging alongside Orion. They danced wildly, kicking up sand.

Next on Orion's playlist came Taylor Swift's "Shake It Off."

"You're a Swiftie?" Artie gasped. "Me too!"

Orion pulled her chin back, gave Artie the side-eye, and wag-gled her head. "Who isn't?"

Giggling, they jumped around in time to the music, moving in perfect unison. It was kind of amazing, actually. Like they'd known each other for years.

They kept dancing, bebopping through Orion's playlist with-out stopping, jamming from "I'm Alive" to "Can't Stop the Feel-ing" to "Try Everything." Every song was positive and upbeat.

As Shakira invited them to try everything, Artie and Orion collapsed on the sand beside each other, spent and breathless, holding their aching sides. As they got their breath back, gig-gling, they turned toward each other. This was so much more therapeutic than sitting in a freaking counselor's office with Mom whining about her feelings.

"I thought Wicked Martha was gonna kill me," Artie con-fessed.

Orion sobered. "Me too. You went right under. Glub, glub."

"Martha didn't scare me," Artie said. "Well, not much. I just kept thinking, damn, I'm gonna die without ever getting kissed."

Orion's eyebrows shot up. "No one ever kissed you?"

"Nope." Artie met Orion's steady gaze. "Not even a peck on the cheek. Except from my parents, brother, and grandmother."

"Well, Wicked Martha didn't kill you, so now you have plenty of time."

"Has anyone ever kissed you?" Artie asked.

Orion grinned. "No. I was the one doing the kissing."

"Oh my," Artie whispered. "I'll try that when the right one comes along."

"Don't rush. It'll happen when it's supposed to." Orion rolled onto her back and stared up at the night sky, and Artie followed suit. Her new friend pointed at the stars. "Look, there's my namesake."

"Do you know the story of Artemis and Orion?" Artie asked.

"*Duh.*" Orion raised her arms, interlaced her fingers, and cupped the back of her head in her palms. She crossed her legs at the ankles. "Why do you think I invited you to come beachcombing with me? Art-te-miss."

"So we can hunt seashells and driftwood together like Greek goddesses?" Artie asked.

"Artemis was the goddess. Orion was a mere mortal."

"But Orion was more gorgeous than any god."

"Yeah, fat lot of good that did him."

"Don't you think it's weird that my name is Artemis, and yours is Orion?"

"No weirder than if your name was Amanda and mine was Ophelia."

"But there's no precedent for Amanda and Ophelia. Artemis and Orion are legendary and branded in the stars." Artie waved her hand at the sky. "I mean, what are the odds of us ever meeting? I mean, both our names are unusual."

Orion replied, "Unusual maybe, but I'm not getting any 'Twilight Zone' vibes unless you tell me your brother's name is Apollo. If that's the case, then I'm bouncing before I have to battle a giant scorpion."

"No." Artie laughed. "His name is Beck."

"Whew." Orion pantomimed wiping sweat from her brow. "My scorpion-battling skills are a little rusty."

"Still, our names feel sort of Alice-in-Wonderland nonsensical, don't you think?"

"Meh, it's Hobby Island. Nonsensical things happen here all the time. Part of the landscape."

"The Greek myths were pretty nonsensical, anyway." Artie

wrinkled her nose at the Scorpius constellation on the opposite side of the sky from hunter Orion. Orion's Belt wasn't visible in the Texas night sky in the summer, but Artie knew where it was. Goddess Artemis had flung the scorpion into the sky as far from her beloved as the heavens allowed. "I mean, seriously, giant scorpions. How did they come up with that stuff?"

"Dunno." Orion jumped to her feet and stuck out her hand to help Artie up. "C'mon, Hopalong, the tide is out. Let's go hunting."

"While we're at it, I need to find my backpack." Artie hobbled beside Orion, her gait thrown off from having lost one shoe. "I tossed it on the sand above the Old Turtles Grotto because it was knocking me off-balance as I climbed the rocks."

"Good thing you did. If you'd been wearing the pack when Wicked Martha attacked, it might have drowned you." Orion put a hand to her throat and made drowning noises. "*Gurgle, gurgle.*"

"Oh, wait, look, my shoe!" Artie skip-hopped down the beach to retrieve her Doc Martens that had washed ashore. She poured the water out and stuck it on; the sole was filled with sand, the wet leather sticking to Artie's skin and making it difficult to get her foot into the shoe. The inside was yucky, but at least she didn't have to hobble back to Crafters' Corner half barefooted. "Okay, let's go."

Orion led the way over a dune and guided her to where she left two woven baskets. She handed one to Artie. "For our treasures."

"First help me find my backpack," Artie said. "I think it's near here somewhere."

It took a few minutes to locate her backpack in the sea oats.

"Wanna power bar?" Artie offered, pulling two bars from the backpack.

"Sure. We might as well have a snack and let the tide go all the way out. The lower the tide, the better the harvest," Orion said, as if they were about to pluck garden vegetables.

After they finished eating, Artie strapped on her backpack. Carrying their woven baskets, she and Orion picked their way through the sea oats down to the Old Turtles Grotto. Artie kept an eye out for Wicked Martha. Mad respect for the old leatherback.

"Martha won't be here during low tide," Orion said, reading Artie's mind. "You can stop worrying."

"Thanks for letting me know."

"Lots of things drift up at the cave's mouth." Orion tiptoed over the mossy rocks Artie had slipped on earlier. The rocks glistened under the moonlight, no longer submerged in water. "The cave sucks things in."

"Do your parents know you spend your nights beachcombing?" Artie asked, following Orion over the rocks. The mouth to the Old Turtles Grotto beckoned them.

"My mom died when I was born," Orion said. "It's just me and my dad."

"Oh, I'm so sorry."

"Why?" Orion tossed over her shoulder. "You had nothing to do with it."

"I just meant I hated that happened to you."

"Bad stuff happens to everyone," Orion said. "Part of life. What matters is that you don't let the shitty stuff define you."

"What about your dad? He doesn't mind you're all alone out here in the middle of the night?"

"I'm not alone." Orion turned and grinned at Artie. "You're with me."

"What about the rest of the time?"

"Dad works until ten most nights, and in the summer, when there's no school, he doesn't mind how late I stay out. Hobby Island is as safe as it gets. Plus, we have walkie-talkies. I can contact him anytime I need him. He encourages my independence."

"Wow, I wish your dad would tell that to my mom."

"She keeps the apron strings tied pretty tight, huh?"

"She tries." Artie laughed.

"Hmm. I'm guessing she doesn't know you're out here right now."

Artie shook her head.

Orion hopped to the sand and started picking up plastic bottles and throwing them in her basket.

"You keep the plastic bottles?"

"Sure, I can use them to make art. And even if I don't have a use for them, I'm a beach steward. How do you think the beaches on Hobby Island stay so pristine?"

"Because you clean them?"

"Yep." Orion tossed a crushed plastic Pepsi bottle into Artie's basket. "And now you do too."

They worked cleaning up the beach, slowly making their way to the cave and chatting as they went. They discussed their favorite movies, podcasts, video games, and books. They talked about pets they'd owned, and vacations they'd taken. They discussed sports and politics and everything under the moon, from their periods to their grades to their hopes for the future. Neither one of them wanted to go to college, both having an entrepreneurial spirit.

"Ooh look!" Orion surged for the cave entrance, her tracks leaving deep footprints in the wet sand. "Creepy dolls!"

"What?" Balancing her basket on her hip, Artie traipsed after her new friend.

Orion crouched, sorting through clumps of debris at the cave's mouth. Artie came to peer over her shoulder. Pulling away seaweed, Orion exposed the face of a toddler-size plastic baby doll, her big blue eyes wide open, her once blond curly hair matted with barnacles. Someone had scribbled on her cheeks in green marker.

Looking at the doll, Artie felt a tug of sadness. A child once loved this toy. How had she gotten discarded?

"Hey! Score! Ariel!" Orion handed the large baby doll to Artie and picked up a Little Mermaid figurine caught in a piece of fishing net. "Wow, she's in decent shape. I'll be able to clean her up and sell her at my market." Orion knocked a big clump of sand off the Little Mermaid and put her in the basket.

"What's that?" Artie gestured toward a porcelain face peeping from the cave. The doll looked old.

"Dope!" Orion leaned over to pick up Artie's find. "Oh, it's just a face. Well, that's disappointing."

"Can I see it?" Artie held out her palm and Orion settled the matte bisque doll face into her hand. It was old, weathered, and yet held a haunting beauty.

Looking at the face, Artie caught her breath, suddenly filled with overwhelming sadness. "You've found dolls like this before?"

"Yeah, fairly often. Several times a month."

"How do they get here?"

"Like most of the trash that washes up on Texas barrier islands. It's caused by a loop current that runs from the Yucatán Peninsula to Florida and swirls rubbish to the Texas Gulf Coast."

"But why so many dolls?"

Orion shrugged, that laid-back gesture of hers intriguing Artie. "My guess is kids leave 'em on the beach, and they get swept out to sea when the tide comes up."

"What do you do with them?"

"I keep the ones that are salvable like Ariel here, clean them up, and resell them. The rest, like the one you're holding and old scribble girl there . . ." She nodded at the baby doll. "I toss out if I can't recycle them."

"You've got more like this?" Artie held up the bisque face.

"Sure, back at our place."

"Would you mind if I take the ones you won't use?"

"You're welcome to them," Orion said. "But why do you want them?"

Artie met her new friend's gaze. "Where you see creepy dolls, I see art."

"Dope! Can't wait to see what you make with them."

The bob of headlights appeared on the beach to the east, and they turned to see one of the Hobby Island golf carts barreling toward them.

Orion and Artie exchanged glances.

"Who's coming?" Artie squinted.

"Dunno. Do you suppose your mom discovered you missing and called the Coast Guard?" Orion asked.

Artie's stomach sank. Knowing her mother, it was a definite possibility.

The golf cart bumped over sand dunes, going far faster than Artie knew golf cars could travel. The clouds shifted, and moonlight shone through, revealing the driver was alone in the cart.

The headlights washed over them, and the driver tooted the ridiculously high-pitched horn.

Dot pulled to a stop beside them, the golf cart tires spinning up sand. "Artie," she said. "Hop in. I've fallen down on my auntie duties, and I've got to get you back to the Nestled Inn before your mother realizes you're missing."

# Chapter 18
## *Luna*

*"Never be afraid to sketch outside the lines."*

—*Eloisa Hobby*

Her night with Paul had been phenomenal—their heart-to-heart chat, the miracle of the hatching butterflies, tending the plants together . . .

*Kissing him.*

All Luna wanted to do was find Paul and hang out with him all day, but of course, she couldn't do that. He had plants to tend, and she had a quilt to design.

*Ugh.*

She was still reeling over what Jeanie had done, even as she chose to forgive her. What she needed was space to give her creativity time to bloom. She couldn't do that if she was elbow-to-elbow at the quilting table with Mom. And from a purely practical standpoint, they had nothing to sew until Luna came up with an award-winning design.

But maybe Artie would come with her. She hadn't spent much time with her daughter, and she felt guilty about that. The poor kid didn't have access to the internet.

To coax Artie from her bed, she descended on the kitchen where Vivian stood at the waffle maker, cooking up waffles as guests served themselves from the buffet. Neither her mother nor daughter were among them.

"Can I borrow a serving tray?" Luna asked. "I want to serve my daughter breakfast in bed."

"Most certainly. Help yourself."

Luna poured two cups of coffee and settled them on the serving tray she gleaned from a stack on the counter. She added two Danishes, one cheese and one cherry, and toted the tray up the stairs to Artie's bedroom. With her hands full, she couldn't knock, so she settled for lightly kicking the door.

"Artie, it's Mom. Open up. I've got breakfast."

No answer.

Luna tapped her foot against the door a second time and in an upbeat singsong voice, she said, "Danishes and coffee for the coolest girl I know."

The door opened. Artie peered out, blinking and yawning, her hair mussed and sticking out from her head. She closed one eye and squinted hard. "What time is it?"

"Twenty minutes to seven. Rise and shine."

"Ugh. You are far too cheerful." Artie left the door hanging open and padded back to bed in her boy shorts and Billie Eilish T-shirt she wore as pajamas. She fell face-first into the covers.

With the blackout curtains drawn, the room was as dark as a cave. Luna placed the tray on the dresser, and then flung open the curtains.

Hissing like a vampire, Artie rolled over, covering her face with her arm. No morning person, this child. Luna had been the same at fifteen.

That's when she saw Artie's scraped knees and a long, shallow scratch running down her right arm.

"What happened?"

"Huh?" Artie blinked.

"Your knees. Your arm."

"Oh, those." She waved her hand. "No biggie."

"Come on, get up. It's a beautiful morning." Concerned about her daughter's wounds but knowing Artie could get testy when pushed, Luna backtracked to the dresser, picked up a coffee mug and the cheese Danish, and plunked into the chair beside Artie's bed.

She took a sip of coffee and then bit through the glossy sheen of the egg-washed pastry.

The warm aroma wafted to her nose as her teeth sank into the crisp buttery dough. The cool softness of the cheese filling contrasted with the crisp flaky pastry. A medley of flavors tingled her tongue—cream cheese, vanilla, and just a hint of lemon. The most delicious Danish she ever put into her mouth. Then again, everything she'd eaten on Hobby Island had been spectacular.

"This is *sooo* good. You better get your Danish before I eat it." Luna pretended to go for the other pastry. "They're addictive."

"Fine." Artie hauled herself off the bed and dove for it.

Luna sipped her coffee, enjoying the hazelnut flavoring. Her gaze fell on Artie's Doc Martens kicked off at the foot of the bed. The shoes looked wet and caked with sand and next to the shoes sat a wicker basket filled with beach debris and broken doll parts.

Ah, the mystery deepened. Artie's wounds were starting to make sense.

"Did you sneak out last night to beachcomb?"

"Don't ask questions you don't want answers to." Artie stirred three packets of sugar into her coffee and guzzled it.

Her maternal instinct pushed her to confront Artie about her midnight escapades, but prudence held her back. Artie was growing up and making her own decisions. Maybe Luna did need to loosen the apron strings a little. She knew she held on too tightly.

Taking in a deep breath, Luna sat with that realization while Artie attacked the Danish with gusto.

"Mmm, delish."

Luna cleared her throat. "I have a request."

"Ask away." Artie noshed her pastry.

"Would you explore the island with me today? I need inspiration for your grandmother's quilt design, and I don't want to go by myself."

"Shooting for an island theme, huh? Classic."

"We have to, it's in the rules."

"Bummer. Rules are restrictive."

"Actually, I think rules enhance creativity. Rules give art shape." Luna was about to say something about how following rules kept you safe, a roundabout way to chastise Artie for sneaking out, but instead she let it go. Some things weren't worth a battle.

"If you say so."

"Remember that mural I painted in the playroom when you and Beck were little?"

"For sure. All the kids in the neighborhood wanted to come hang out in that room. You're a talented artist, Mom."

"You'll come with me to explore the island?" Luna crossed her fingers. It had been ages since they'd done something lighthearted together. "I want to see the turtle preserve."

"No, you don't," Artie said with authority.

"No?"

"Trust me, Wicked Martha is for realz, and you don't want to mess with that old leatherback."

Luna's gaze flicked to Artie's skinned knees. *Don't ask.* Instead, she nodded at the wicker basket on the floor. "What's up with the doll parts?"

"Um, nothing." Artie shrugged.

Luna got up and walked over to the basket. She stared down at the glassy eyes of a toddler-size baby doll covered in barnacles. "Goodness, they're a little creepy."

"They're *a lot* creepy. That's why I like them."

"You're just going to keep them?" Luna had a strong urge to wash her hands after just looking at the sea-roughened dolls.

"Yep."

"And do what with them?"

"What's wrong, Mom? Scared I'm gonna make voodoo dolls?" Artie wriggled her eyebrows for comic effect.

"That hadn't occurred to me." Until now. Artie did enjoy a goth aesthetic.

"Nah, just messin' with you. I had an idea for an art project. I'm gonna enter the recycled art competition with my friend Orion."

Oh boy, maybe this was where she should bring up Orion's dad and Luna's relationship to him, but Artie kept right on talking.

"We're gonna meet up later today and work on our art project together. First, we gotta go to the visitors' center and enter the contest. That's why I can't go exploring with you."

"Well, good luck with your project. I'm excited to see what you create." She leaned over to kiss the top of Artie's head.

"Thanks for the breakfast." Artie hopped off the bed and padded over to draw the blackout curtains closed again. "Now, if you'll excuse me. I'm gonna snag more z's."

Feeling dismissed, Luna gathered up the dishes and went back downstairs.

Back in the kitchen, she asked Vivian if she could have two blueberry muffins. "For a snack," she explained. "I'll be exploring the island on my own today."

"Aah." Vivian nodded. "A pilgrimage. Sometimes being by oneself is exactly what the soul needs."

"Thank you." Luna picked up two muffins, put them in a sand-wich bag, filled her water bottle, and added them to her tote with her sketchbook and pencils. The pressure was on. Time to come up with a design that would blow the contest judges' minds.

Determined to return with something noteworthy, Luna left the B&B and started for Trouble Ridge. No, correction, Oppor-tunity Ridge. This would be a positive day. She decreed it so.

The hike from the Nestled Inn to the top of the ridge was five miles, one way. While Luna ran every morning, and was in de-cent cardiovascular shape, her calves complained about the steep incline. She should add more hills to her regular running routine.

Jacaranda trees lined the road to the top of the ridge, their lovely blossoms decorating her path. Whenever she stepped on a petal, it released a sweet, rich scent into the air and bathed her in lavender. She paused to take pictures.

Two hours later, Luna arrived at the ridge summit and looked down at an amazing view of the valley. The whole island was vis-ible from up here, glistening like a priceless jewel. All purple and pink, surrounded by blue-green water.

For the longest time, she stared, slack-jawed in awe. To the east lay Crafters' Corner. To the west, the turtle preserve. To the south, the lighthouse. In the middle of the island, Prism Pavil-ion, and the butterfly hatchery. For a long while, she absorbed the beauty, integrating it into her body. Her pounding heart matched the rhythm of the ocean waves crashing against the shoreline below.

Luna spied the ferry docking at Marshmallow Landing and watched as people got off, several in uniform. They were shop personnel, she realized, arriving from Everly and headed for Crafters' Corner to begin their workday at ten.

Inhaling the spirit of the island, Luna found a large flat rock to perch on, reached into her tote, and pulled out her sketchbook and pencils. At first, she drew lightly, taking tentative steps on this new journey. It had been so long since she designed anything.

Then she grew more confident and drew bolder lines, swept away by the island's magic. Inspiration flowed from her eyes to her brain to her fingers to the sketchbook. She created sketch after sketch, page after page, refining, revising, reworking. Each picture better than the one before. Possessed by the island's muse, she dropped into the creative zone.

This work was special, certainty stamped on every page.

Together, with her mom's sewing skills and Luna's artistry, they *could* win the quilting contest. Luna felt it in her bones. The sketches would require more detail work, of course, but she nailed the overall concept, and she couldn't wait to show Jeanie. It was as if she channeled some grand master artist—van Gogh, Rembrandt, da Vinci . . . Grandma Moses. Never too late.

That made her laugh.

She took a break, stood up, ate a blueberry muffin, drank some water, and flipped through the sketches. The only thing missing was the focal point that would tie everything together.

Should she use turtles? Or butterflies? Or the lighthouse? Or the jacaranda trees? All four seemed pretty obvious, but she hadn't visited the turtle preserve. Deciding right now was difficult. She still had research to do, but she made a good start. A productive morning.

Slipping back into the creative zone, she plunked back down to elaborate on the initial drawings, adding deeper values, more contrast between light and dark. Luna was so engrossed in her work she didn't hear someone approaching until a shoe snapped a twig on the path behind her.

She whipped around, closing the sketchbook and bringing it to her chest—hiding her drawings, protecting her work. Too much had been taken from her for Luna to let anyone copy her quilt design.

"Oh, hello!" a feminine voice called out. "I see someone else was aiming for a bird's-eye view of the island."

It was Nanette. She wore a festive light green romper with a sunflower print and a wide-brim sun hat, and she carried a sketchbook identical to Luna's.

"Do you mind if I join you?" Nanette didn't wait for her answer. She toddled over, a little breathless, perspiration pearling her upper lip. She smelled like weed and peppermint.

Luna didn't want to offend the woman, but she *did* mind. Her tranquility was broken, and she stood up. "I was just leaving. Have my spot. It's the perfect vantage point."

"Oh please, don't run off. I was hoping we could chat."

Luna had an uneasy feeling that Nanette had followed her, but was that true or was her suspicious nature in overdrive?

"I suppose I could stay a few minutes longer." Forcing herself to soften, Luna sat back down, secured her sketchbook with a rubber band, and settled it in her lap with her hands on top.

"Did you get some good sketching in?" Nanette sat on the rock beside her.

"I did."

"May I see?" Nanette leaned in closer.

Luna shook her head. "I'm not ready to show it. As an artist, I'm sure you understand."

"Say no more." Nanette raised both palms. "I'll be surprised with everyone else when you unveil your prizewinning design at the competition."

Was the woman sincere or sarcastic? Luna didn't know but she'd keep a sharp eye on her. "Why, thank you, Nanette. I appreciate your vote of confidence."

"I already pegged you as my steepest competition." Nanette

turned toward her, shifting her left hip, and angling her legs toward Luna, her knees peeking from underneath the hem of her romper.

Luna reached up to brush a lock of hair from her face. Nanette did the same. The woman was mirroring her body language. Was it instinctive or intentional? Luna couldn't decide. She smiled.

Nanette smiled back. Sincerely friendly or trying to cozy up?

*Reserve judgment.*

What harm would it do to believe her? If the woman had hidden intentions, Luna would handle it if it came up.

"Where are your friends?" Luna asked because she didn't know what else to say.

Nanette blinked. "Friends?"

"Sharon and Isabelle."

"Oh." Nanette shook her head. "We're not *friends* friends. We just know each other from meeting on the island last year. In fact, we hadn't kept in touch at all."

"No? Why's that?"

Nanette shrugged. "No different than a summer romance, I suppose. In a new situation, people can bond quite easily, but you don't really know each other. And when the reality of regular life intrudes, summer feelings evaporate like fantastical illusions."

The way she said it made Luna wonder if she had a falling-out with Sharon and Isabelle. Nanette's words also stirred Luna's own fears.

About Paul . . .

And resurrecting the past.

Were her feelings for him simply nostalgia mixed with novelty and the seductive powers of Hobby Island?

"Don't move," Nanette said, lowering her voice.

"Wh-what?" Luna asked.

"There's a bee on your—"

At the word *bee*, Luna sprang to her feet. She was allergic and hadn't brought an EpiPen. Her sketchbook and pencils fell to the ground as she danced around waving her hands over her shoulders. "Get it off! Get it off me!"

"It's okay, it flew away," Nanette assured her. She picked up Luna's sketchbook and pencil case and dusted them off.

But Luna was too busy looking around for the bee to notice what Nanette was doing. "Is the bee really gone?"

"Yes, yes. You're bee free." Nanette passed the sketchbook to Luna.

"Thank you," Luna said as she glanced from one shoulder to the other. "You're *sure* it's gone."

"Promise."

"I think I'm gonna head out." Clutching her sketchbook to her chest, Luna picked up her tote bag.

"Have a nice rest of your day," Nanette said.

Luna hurried down the trail. Glancing back, she saw Nanette standing there watching her, an inscrutable expression on her face. Luna shivered despite the sunshine. Something felt off about the woman.

But what?

It wasn't until she reached the bottom of the ridge that Luna realized the rubber band around her sketchbook was missing.

# Chapter 19
## *Jeanie*

*"The most profound wisdom can sometimes be found in a simple doodle."*

—*Eloisa Hobby*

Humbled by Luna and Paul's forgiveness, Jeanie spent the morning at the quilting shop, had lunch with Sharon Rooney, and then the two of them hit the beach as Jeanie waited for her daughter to return from her hike.

She let Artie go exploring the island with Orion after Dot promised to watch over them. Luna hadn't left any instructions to the contrary, and Artie was almost sixteen. She deserved some autonomy and Hobby Island was safe.

Jeanie lay on a beach towel beneath a rainbow-colored umbrella, listening to the rhythmic roll of the ocean as Sharon chilled out on a towel next to her. Jeanie hadn't spoken privately to Luna since their confrontation in the chapel. Being unable to communicate by cell phone was giving them some much needed distance from each other and time to think.

In her head, Jeanie circled the salient points that Luna had brought up yesterday.

One, she was codependent. She and Jack had both been addicts. He'd been hopelessly entangled with alcohol, but she'd been just as hooked on their relationship. Her romantic addiction had left her vulnerable to Rex Rhinehart's sweetheart scam.

Two, her addiction to her late husband had led her to betray both Luna and Paul. Her actions were just as harmful as Jack's. She was not virtuous because she sacrificed everything for him. In fact, her actions were worse because she made a calculated decision to manipulate Paul and deceive Luna to keep Jack out of prison.

Three, only she, Jeanie, could break the chains of her addiction. She must learn to be okay on her own. She had to stop depending on others to give her an identity.

*But how?*

This way of seeing herself was hard to accept. She had latched onto Jack when they were in middle school. He became emotional support for a girl with a controlling mother who couldn't love her and a checked-out father who wouldn't protect her.

Had she failed to protect Luna in the same way?

Reality was a sledgehammer bashing away at her. Yes, she let her daughter down in the most fundamental manner and in her selfish addiction, she used Paul for her benefit.

Jeanie had loved intensely and without limits, giving herself away completely to Jack, reserving little emotional energy for her child. Deep down, she suspected all along she was telling herself a fantasy about love, but she had lived happily in her denial, making excuses for Jack, so she never had to deal with her cognitive dissonance.

Or so she thought.

Her cheeks burned, and it wasn't from the sun. The temperature was mild, and she wore sunglasses and sunscreen on top of being under the umbrella.

No, it was hot shame that lay beside her on the beach.

She had to snap out of this dark mood. The quilt she and Luna made together should be filled with joy and wonder. It should encapsulate the magic of Hobby Island. That was where salvation lay—in the optimistic and uplifting power of creativity.

Jeanie's instinct was to draw into herself, slump her shoulders, hide her face, and make herself small to avoid attention. When she was growing up, attention equaled abuse. She passed these self-effacing behaviors down to Luna, but her daughter was stronger. Luna had a stubborn streak, an I-don't-ever-quit-no-matter-how-bad-things-get mentality that Jeanie both lacked and envied.

The big question?

How would she fix her own self-esteem? Keeping their house out of foreclosure was a big step in the right direction, but to do that, she and Luna needed to design the most fantastic quilt this island had ever seen.

"Did you enter the quilting contest last year?" Jeanie asked Sharon.

"Uh-huh." Her voice came out slow and sunbaked lazy.

"Did you win?"

"I did actually."

"Really?" Jeanie turned on her side and looked over at Sharon, who had her straw sun hat resting over her face.

"Just the category contest, not the grand prize."

"But still, that's impressive. Do you have any clue what the judges are looking for? I mean, besides what's in the contest rules?"

Sharon swept her hat off and rolled over to face Jeanie. "Jeanie, can I be frank with you?"

"Yes, please do."

Sharon took a moment before saying anything. "This habit of yours, constantly trying to please others, to adjust yourself to their expectations . . ."

That was odd. Sharon barely knew her. How did she know Jeanie's habit of people-pleasing? "Yes?"

"Have you ever considered that it might actually be a form of manipulation?"

Jeanie sat up, taken aback. "Manipulation? Wh-what do you mean? I'm just trying to make everyone happy and avoid conflict."

Sharon sat up too, facing Jeanie. "I know your intentions are good but think about it. When you're constantly altering who you are, you're essentially trying to control how others perceive you. It's not really about them. It's about your fear—fear of rejection, fear of not being enough, fear of being unloved."

Unloved.

That was it. The knife through her heart. Sharon's words cut deep.

Jeanie's expression softened as she absorbed the blow from a woman she was starting to like. "I . . . I never thought about it like that. I thought I was being selfless, but . . ."

"It's a common misunderstanding," Sharon said. "You want to be liked, to be accepted. That's natural. But in doing so, you're not allowing people to know the real you and that can lead to relationships and situations based on a version of yourself that isn't authentic, and you end up with people you shouldn't be with."

Like Rex Rhinehart.

Although she'd never been with Rex. It had all been limerence on her part and deception on his.

Was she really so transparent that a virtual stranger could peg her so accurately?

Jeanie lay back down, her eyes tracing the clouds drifting across the sky. "So, by trying to be what everyone else wants, I'm actually losing myself?"

"Exactly." Sharon nodded. "It's about finding a balance between being considerate and being true to your own values and desires. It's okay to not always please everyone. It's okay to be you."

Never in her life had Jeanie felt it was okay to be herself. To be dead honest, she had no idea who she was beyond a mother and grandmother.

Something else for her to figure out. Wow, but this summer was chock-full of tough life lessons.

"Is that your daughter?" Sharon asked, shading her eyes with her hand.

"Huh?" Jeanie blinked and struggled to sit up again.

Sure enough, Luna stalked along the road above the beach, a determined set to her shoulders as she headed toward Crafters' Corner.

Jeanie hopped up, waving wildly. "Luna! Hey, hello, wait!"

The wind must have snatched up her voice and tossed it away because Luna kept walking without ever glancing over at the beach.

Jeanie pulled on her cover-up, stuck her feet in her Birkenstocks, and took off after her only child. "Luna!"

At last, Luna turned, saw her, and paused.

"What's up?" Jeanie asked, chugging up to her, a little breathless from her jog up the beach.

"Have you seen Nanette?" Luna asked, her hair blown every which way, her eyes narrowed, and jaw set.

"Yes, Sharon and I saw Nanette as we were coming down to the beach. She was walking on cloud nine. Said she'd been on a hike to Opportunity Ridge and had a creative breakthrough on her quilt design."

"Where is she now?" Luna's tone was brittle and sharp-edged.

"She and Isabelle headed over to the tiki bar to celebrate."

"Thanks." Luna started off again.

"Where are you going?"

"To speak to Nanette."

Jeanie scurried along beside her, the hem of her cover-up swinging against her knees. "What about?"

"She stole my sketchbook." Luna pumped her arms, picking up her pace.

Jeanie trotted to keep up. "What? Are you sure?"

Luna whipped her head around to glare at Jeanie. "Well, I was giving her the benefit of the doubt that she accidentally grabbed my sketchbook instead of her own since ours were identical, but now that you told me she was bragging about her creative breakthrough, I can only assume it was intentional."

"Maybe she had a breakthrough on the ridge too?" Jeanie didn't want to assume the worst, but she felt gut-punched for Luna.

Luna fumbled in her tote bag, still walking, yanked out a sketchbook, and shoved it at her. Jeanie thumbed through it. Each page was empty.

"Oh," Jeanie said. "Maybe it wasn't intentional but once she saw your beautiful sketches, she decided to keep them and say they were hers."

"Whether she intentionally switched our sketchbooks, or it was an accident, she's still taking ownership for *my* work."

"Okay, but give her an out so she can save face."

Luna glared at her again.

"What? I'm all for second chances."

"And thirds and fourths . . . and nine-hundred and ninety-ninths. How many chances did you give Dad?"

"I can see you're upset—"

"You don't get it, Mom. Those illustrations were the best things I've *ever* drawn, no exaggeration."

Cringing, Jeanie made a face. "I'm sorry."

They crested the rise leading to the village. Smoothing a hand over her wind-tousled hair and buttoning her cover-up, Jeanie followed Luna to the tiki bar.

Luna beelined to the table where Isabelle and Nanette sat.

"Good afternoon, ladies!" Jeanie sounded too eager. She could hear it. *Chill pill.* "How are y'all?"

Luna shot Jeanie another dirty look.

Oops, okay, time to zip her lip.

"Hi!" A genuine smile graced Isabelle's face.

Isabelle had told the quilting group that she was originally from Argentina, but she'd been in the US since the 1970s and had become a citizen. She spoke flawless English and had the whitest teeth Jeanie had ever seen.

"Nice to see you, Isabelle," Jeanie said, but her gaze was locked on Luna, who was staring down Nanette like she was a Bond villain.

"Hello." Nanette's tone was cool, distant, and she did not meet Luna's intense glare.

Uh-oh. The hairs on Jeanie's nape lifted.

Luna stepped closer to Nanette. Jeanie hovered a few feet away. The sketchbook, which was identical to the one Luna had handed to Jeanie, lay open on the table in front of Nanette.

"You got my sketchbook by mistake." Luna was standing almost directly over the seated Nanette.

From what Jeanie could see of them, the drawings were amazing, and she could tell from the style they did indeed belong to her daughter. Not that she doubted Luna's veracity for a second. Her daughter was scrupulously honest.

Nanette folded her hands over the sketchbook and leaned forward like a protective mama lion over her cub, and this time she returned Luna's hard, piercing stare.

"Nope, this is *my* sketchbook," Nanette said.

"It's not. I can see the pictures I drew right there on that page."
Luna pointed.

"I drew this." Nanette lifted her chin defiantly. "I don't know
why *you're* trying to take credit for *my* designs. That's a silly way
to cheat."

In the distance thunder rumbled, the afternoon rainstorm
blowing in, and the breeze kicked up, tossing napkins from the
outdoor tables and spinning patio umbrellas. Patrons gasped or
muttered and hurried to secure their belongings.

"She's not lying," Isabelle said. "Nanette brought her sketches
to our brainstorming group and gave us a mini workshop on creativity."

*Now wait just a damn minute.* Jeanie gritted her teeth.

"*After* she swapped her sketchbook with mine." Luna doubled
up her fists and, in that moment, she reminded Jeanie so much of
Artie.

Isabelle clicked her tongue and looked at Luna as if she was a
pathetic loser. A sinking feeling weighted Jeanie's stomach. Her
daughter would not win this. Nanette possessed the sketchbook,
and Luna had no proof it was hers.

"Why would I lie?" Luna asked.

"To win the contest. I showed you my drawings on the ridge
and you said they were amazing. Now you're trying to pretend
I switched sketchbooks." Nanette stuck her haughty nose in the
air. "You're just jealous."

Stunned by the other woman's audacity, Jeanie staggered back.
But Luna stayed rooted in the spot. For a second, she thought
Luna might even deck the woman.

Nanette leaned over to Isabelle and in a snotty tone said, "Can
you believe her? Trying to claim my work as her own. Pathetic."

Isabelle shook her head. "This isn't a good look, Luna."

"Why don't you run along and draw your own sketches." Nanette waggled her fingers. "Cheaters never win."

"Here," Luna said. "I'll prove it." She snatched a napkin from the holder on their table, pulled out a pencil from her tote, quickly doodled a sunflower, and shoved it toward Nanette. "See. My style."

Aha! Luna had her now. Jeanie notched up her chin and rubbed her palms together.

"Or . . ." Nanette said. "You just now copied *my* style."

"Why would I do that?"

"I don't know what your deal is." Nanette wasn't budging in her lie.

Jeanie's jaw dropped. That brazen hussy! How dare she steal Luna's sketches and pass them off as her own!

She thought about snatching the book away from Nanette. But no, that would just make things worse. Jeanie swallowed down the outrage bubbling inside her over what this woman was doing to her daughter.

"Now, if you'll excuse us, we're trying to have a meeting." Nanette waved them away like a gnat.

Luna stood there a moment, looking uncertain and utterly defeated. Then she shook herself and pulled her spine straight. "Fine, the sketches are yours. I give them to you, freely and without reservation, because my mother and I will still beat the pants off you in the contest."

Pivoting on her heel, Luna strode off.

Jeanie knew her daughter was on the verge of tears. Injustice smoldered inside her. She stepped up to Nanette. "Karma will bite you in the ass, Nanette, and I hope I'm there to see it happen."

With that, she turned and went after Luna.

# Chapter 20
## *Eloisa*

*"Art begins by seeing ordinary objects through extraordinary eyes."*
—*Eloisa Hobby*

Eloisa was in her backyard doing a headstand with Felena curled up in a wicker basket beside her when Paul opened her garden gate.

"Knock, knock," he called.

"Halloo!"

He paused. "Oh, I didn't know you were doing yoga. I can return later."

"No, no, come in, come in." Eloisa dropped her feet and righted herself.

He was hatless today, and his thick dark hair curled around his ears. He had on jean shorts and a white, button-down, short-sleeved shirt instead of his gardening clothes, which told her he was working cybersecurity today.

Barefooted, she wore yoga pants and a long T-shirt emblazoned with the Hobby Island logo. Her hat for today was a charming orchid-colored knitted toboggan with orange pom-poms and a pink carnation that stayed put in the weave when she went upside down. She wriggled her toes polished in an aubergine hue on the concrete paver and savored the coolness.

Eloisa cocked her head, trying to decipher the look on Paul's face, but the man kept his emotions close to his vest. Except whenever he spoke of Luna Boudreaux. In those instances, his face would light up and a helpless smile would cross his lips. She enjoyed seeing Paul falling in love. He was a good man and deserved a worthy mate.

Was Luna the one for him?

How nice if that were so and something good would come from this distressing mess over a scammer stealing from her crafters. But Luna and her mother were dealing with a lot. She shouldn't get her hopes up. Eloisa had learned a long time ago not to meddle in the affairs of others.

She wandered over to the cushioned bench beneath the garden waterfall Paul had constructed for her, settled down, and patted the spot next to her.

Paul sat and rested his palms on his knees. A blue-and-black butterfly flitted near his head.

"What have you got for me?" she asked, crossing her legs at her ankles.

Paul inhaled deeply, held his breath, and then slowly let it out. "I caught something on the camera at Opportunity Ridge."

Eloisa rested a palm at the hollow of her throat. "Goodness, that sounds troublesome."

He took his cell phone from his pocket and turned it on to show her the recording he'd pulled from the security camera mounted in the trees at the top of the ridge.

As Eloisa watched, Luna came into view. Oh dear, was Luna up to something? For Paul's sake, she hoped not.

Felena hopped into her lap and Eloisa stroked her soft warm fur and listened to the calico purr. It was such a soothing sound. The sweet creature just seemed to know when Eloisa needed comforting.

On Paul's phone screen, Luna started drawing. Picture after picture of the island unfolded from Luna's deft hand.

"Gracious, she's a wonderful artist," Eloisa said.

Paul bobbed his head. "That's my Luna."

*My.*

Eloisa suppressed a smile.

Paul had spliced the recording and there was a time jump. In the video, Nanette came hiking up the ridge and joined Luna on Outlook Rock. She carried a sketchbook identical to Luna's. As soon as Nanette sat down, Luna closed her notebook and secured it with a large rubber band from around her wrist.

"Nanette's violating Luna's personal space," Eloisa said.

"Keep watching." Paul angled his satellite cell phone, giving her a better view.

Nanette said something and Luna jumped up, dropping her sketchbook and pencil box to swat at her shoulders.

"What's that about?" Eloisa asked.

"I studied Nanette's mouth and I think she said, 'bee.' Luna is allergic to bee stings."

"Does Nanette know that?"

"I have no idea."

"Was there even a bee?"

Paul met Eloisa's gaze. "I don't know but watch what Nanette does next."

As Luna spun and swatted, Nanette bent down to pick up Luna's sketchbook and surreptitiously swapped it with hers.

"Hey!" Eloisa snapped her finger, incensed on Luna's behalf. "She switched sketchbooks."

"Yeah."

"Nanette stole Luna's designs."

"Looks like it."

"Well, sour pickles." Eloisa scratched Felena behind her ears.

"Do you want to confront Nanette with this evidence?" Paul asked.

"No. It very well could be accidental."

"It wasn't."

Eloisa cocked her head. "There's more?"

Paul closed that video and opened another one. It showed Luna and Jeanie in Crafters' Corner confronting Nanette at the tiki bar.

"Oh dear. Do you think Nanette is the scammer?"

"I can't draw that parallel," he said. "But she's definitely a thief. Look at her."

In the video, as Luna and Jeanie walked away from the tiki bar, Nanette took out a pen and, in all caps, wrote NANETTE'S DESIGNS on the front of the sketchbook.

"What about the other two you suspect? Anything on them?"

"Nothing caught on camera."

"It's so sad."

"Sad?" Paul shot her a hard glance.

"That Nanette has so little belief in her own skills she feels forced to steal in order to compete."

"I can intervene and send her packing."

Eloisa leveled Paul a calm look. "I appreciate that she's stolen from someone important to you and it's gotten your emotions involved—"

"My emotions aren't involved."

"No?" Eloisa arched an eyebrow.

Paul surrendered a sheepish grin. "Yes, okay, I feel protective of Luna."

"Nanette has lessons to learn. Luna and Jeanie too for that matter. Let's just keep a close eye on Nanette for now."

"Luna already has trust issues. This thing with Nanette will just worsen it."

"Not your problem to solve, Paul." Eloisa stroked Felena's fur. "If issues arise that demand our attention, be prepared to intervene."

"No worries on that score." Paul switched off his phone and stuck it in his pocket. He was the protective sort and often stepped in when he should have let things work themselves out, but he cared so very much. She'd never known a man with such a pure heart.

"That's comforting."

"I've got eyes all over this island and I'm not about to let Luna get taken advantage of again."

"Ahh." Eloisa clicked her tongue and met his serious eyes. Luna, Jeanie, and Nanette weren't the only ones with lessons to learn.

"Ahh what?" He eyed her suspiciously. He knew her too well. She gave him a sly smile.

"What is it, Auntie Eloisa? What have you got up your sleeve?"

"Why, I think it's time for a healing circle."

"Bringing out the big guns?"

"Don't you know it."

"Okay. I got your back. Always." Chuckling and shaking his head, Paul headed out the garden gate.

Eloisa resumed her yoga, going into crow pose; as she hummed Kelly Clarkson's "Stronger," Felena hopped onto her back and started purring in total agreement.

# Chapter 21
## *Jeanie*

*"The heart craves community the way plants crave rain."*
—*Eloisa Hobby*

One thing was clear to Jeanie after that mess with Nanette: she and Luna had to design their quilt in secret. The other guests couldn't be trusted. No more going to the quilting shop and hanging with the crafters. They'd work at the B&B.

That saddened Jeanie because she had already grown to love Clare, the quaint quilt shop owner, and most of the quilters. She even liked Nanette until the woman stole Luna's design. Then again, Jeanie's main character flaw was jumping too quickly into relationships, Rex Rhinehart a case in point.

Without asking any questions, Vivian gave them permission to use the parlor and put a sign on the French doors that said: PARLOR RESERVED UNTIL FURTHER NOTICE.

Luna granted Artie free rein of the island in daylight hours as long as she stuck with Dot or Orion and didn't go exploring on her own. It was time for Luna to start snipping the apron strings, and Jeanie praised her daughter, hoping to calm Luna's anxiety.

They buckled down, working together to come up with a new quilt design and planning the project to fit the parameters of the contest rules. Each morning Jeanie spread out her fabric swatches and Luna's sketches across the parlor's antique tables, grateful to Vivian for letting them use this space.

As they sketched and planned, laughter and lively discussion replaced the melancholy mood of earlier days. Through their collaboration emerged a design more meaningful than the one they'd lost. One that let Luna's artistic talents shine while also honoring Jeanie's sewing skills.

At one point, they caught Isabelle in the parlor looking over the new designs Luna created. Isabelle didn't act the least bit flustered over having been caught snooping and even told them she wasn't close friends with Nanette, just in case they thought she was on board with what the other woman had done.

After that, they stopped leaving their things in the parlor unattended. Over three days, they talked through different ideas, seamlessly building on each other's inspiration in a way they never had before.

Luna suggested a fairy-tale motif of awestruck travelers entering the magical land of Hobby Island with panels depicting the charming elements of the island, channeling her passion for whimsical mural art in a way that had Jeanie bursting with pride.

"The quilt will be our personal journey," Luna said, "you, me, and Artie."

"I love that idea."

Luna made the sketches and drew up the design. Jeanie showed her the three basic styles of stitches available for hand quilting. The choices were between traditional Western stitching using regular thread and tiny controlled stitches more for texture and subtle design than a bold statement. The more modern big stitch quilting featured larger stitches and heavier-weight thread utilized to make bolder statements or to add more personal touches.

A third option was traditional Eastern stitching, such as kantha and sashiko, which used longer stitches with thicker thread. Mostly these stitches were on solid fabrics for design panels.

After she demonstrated all three stitches, she asked Luna, "Which style best suits your design?"

Luna crinkled her nose. "I don't know. Which is easier for you to sew since you'll be doing all the actual hands-on labor?"

"Don't worry about that. What's best for the quilt?"

Luna studied the swatches Jeanie had sewn. "I really can't decide. All three have pros and cons."

"The design is what we want to spotlight," Jeanie said. "The stitches should honor that."

"So . . . ?"

"We don't want to call attention to the thread. Traditional Western stitching is the way to go." Jeanie loved hand sewing. She found it relaxing.

Luna rubbed her chin in thought. "I have a feeling that's the most challenging of the stitches."

"We're not going to let a challenge stand in the way of winning."

"Or as Eloisa would say, an opportunity."

They grinned at each other.

"I like the way Eloisa reframes difficulties," Jeanie said.

"Me too. She's a special person." Luna tilted her head, studying the sketches.

"Why do you think I belong to her quilting forum? She's so encouraging."

"Well, I'm glad you were part of the group, otherwise you'd never have won a golden ticket, and we wouldn't have come here—"

"And you wouldn't have reconnected with Paul."

Luna blushed.

Jeanie was so happy now that her dark secret had come out and both her daughter and Paul had forgiven her. "How is that going, by the way?"

"I haven't seen him since we started this project." She swept her hand at the table in front of them. "We last talked in the quad on the day I confronted Nanette, and he told me to concentrate on you and getting this project underway."

"I don't want to keep you from spending time with Paul," Jeanie said. "You've already been apart too long because of me."

"Mom, we're taking this slowly. A lot has changed, and we've got children to consider. This pace is just fine. We'll get together once you start the actual quilting since there's nothing I can do on that score."

"Speaking of," Jeanie said, "now that we've settled on the design, it's time to go buy the material."

Luna pulled a sour face. "Which means a trip to the quilt store."

"It does, but maybe Nanette won't be there."

Luna sighed. "It's okay. I'm over it. Truthfully, I feel sorry for her. To have so little confidence in yourself you're willing to steal to win a contest."

"She's not going to win," Jeanie said. "Not with your amazing design."

"The design is nothing without your expertise to take it from concept to finished product."

Jeanie grinned. "Face facts, we're a powerful team."

"That we are." Luna high-fived her.

And these, Jeanie thought, were the moments a mother lived for.

* * *

On the fourth day of working on the quilt design together, they took a golf cart to A Stitch in Time to buy the material needed to complete the quilted lap blanket. Sharon greeted Jeanie like a long-lost loved one, Nanette ignored them, and Isabelle's greeting was a polite "hello" and a nod of her head.

"Have you heard?" Sharon said. "Eloisa is having a healing circle. They're a rare treat. She doesn't do them every year and I missed it last time. I'm so excited."

"What's a healing circle?" Luna asked.

"Why not just go experience it for yourself and find out?" Sharon asked.

"Is Eloisa a doctor? How can she claim to heal someone?" Luna sank her hands on her hips.

"Honey," Jeanie said. "Don't be so contrary. You don't have to go."

"It sounds New Agey and weird."

"Sometimes you have to step outside your comfort zone if you want to grow," Isabelle piped up. "I'm going. I think that's the kind of healing they're talking about. Personal growth."

"Why don't they call it a personal growth circle then?" Luna shot the woman a hard stare.

"It doesn't have the same ring to it as healing circle, now does it?" Sharon tapped her forehead with an index finger.

Clare came into the shop through the back door, just as bubbly as Sharon had been, and delighted in showing them bolts of cloth and spools of threads. Jeanie was glad Clare's appearance derailed Luna's suspiciousness.

"You're just in time for our little speed competition," Clare said. "Would you like to join us? Just a way to help our quilters build up their hand-quilting speed. Finishing a handsewn lap quilt in two months can be a challenge but it's certainly doable."

Jeanie wanted to participate but hesitated. How comfortable would Luna be hanging around Nanette for that long?

"Do it, Mom," Luna encouraged her.

"Are you sure?" Jeanie shot a glance at Nanette.

"I'm not letting her behavior control me," Luna said. She squared her shoulders and tucked back her chin. "You know what, I'm going to resolve this thing right now."

"Oh dear." Jeanie wrung her hands. "Please don't cause a scene."

"No worries, Sainted Mother." Luna laughed. "I'm not gonna get us thrown out of the shop."

Luna walked over to the quilting table. "Do y'all mind if I have a seat?"

"Please," Sharon said. "Join us."

Luna took the chair right next to Nanette, who froze like an opossum. Luna looked the woman right in the eye and said, "Hi."

"H-h-hi," Nanette stammered.

Jeanie nibbled a thumbnail. Everyone at the table had their eyes trained on Luna and Nanette.

Luna offered Nanette a small smile. "I know tensions flared between us the other day. But I don't want bad blood, especially here in my mom's creative refuge."

Jeanie held her breath waiting to see how Nanette would respond.

Nanette bristled slightly, avoiding Luna's eye. "Yes, well . . . but I did not steal your design."

"No, because I give it to you freely. It's yours to use for the contest."

"I don't need your permission."

"Maybe not, but I give it to you anyway," Luna said. "And I choose to extend an olive branch, for my mother's sake and the spirit of this shop. I hope you'll accept it."

Nanette blinked, clearly torn between wanting to cling to self-protection and surprise at Luna's grace. Finally, she gave a tight nod. "Very well."

The tension didn't vanish entirely. But Luna had sewn a first stitch toward possible unity. Gosh, Jeanie was so proud of her daughter and her maturity in the wake of Nanette's wrongdoing.

"Let's get the speed quilting started." Clare clapped her hands. "First prize is a twenty-dollar gift certificate to the store."

Clare passed out hoops while the quilters picked scrap fabrics, needles, and thread from the assortment in the middle of the table.

"Just to kick the competitive atmosphere into high gear, you have an hour to finish your swatch." Clare turned over an hourglass, filled with purple sand, and set it in the middle of the table. "Go!"

Laughing, everyone dove in, including Luna, who didn't even enjoy sewing.

With a running stitch, Jeanie fed the white cotton thread through the crimson flower printed on the scrap of fabric she'd chosen. She was determined to win this thing. That twenty-dollar gift card was much appreciated. Jeanie quickened her pace, jabbing the needle, tugging on the thread, her fingers flying.

She excelled at hand piecing. So many years of altering prom dresses and wedding gowns to make ends meet when Jack was out of a job—which was more often than not—had served her well. Sewing was her superpower.

Pushing herself, she went as fast as her fingers would go, each stitch a mantra in her mind. *You can do this. You can win. You can, you can, you can.*

Jeanie was vaguely aware that the others had stopped sewing and were watching her as if she were Master Yoda.

Even Clare.

Now that Jeanie was working at breakneck speed, she couldn't seem to slow down. She finished stitching the flower and moved on to the leaves. Less than a quarter of the sand had filtered through the hourglass, and she was halfway finished.

In, out, in, out. The stitches grew before her eyes.

And then she jabbed her thumb with the sewing needle.

Hard.

Red blood bloomed on the green leaves.

Why hadn't she used a thimble? She stared at her thumb, felt suddenly dizzy, but kept going, blood dripping all over the square.

That's when the memory hit her.

*Boom!*

Out of the clearest blue.

She was young, six or seven, and her mother, Francine, had finally allowed Jeanie to join her monthly quilting bee after she begged repeatedly to be part of the group. They were in the parlor of the old Victorian in Julep, the furniture pushed against the wall to make room for the quilting frame let down from the ceiling. Settling herself into the chair, her feet barely reached the floor as she wriggled, so excited and anxious to get started. She watched the gathered women with a keen eye, wanting to get everything right and make her mama proud.

Jeanie's small fingers yearned to stroke the fabric scattered on nearby tables, some bolts thick and bumpy, others smooth and cool. Tentatively, her small hand reached out to caress the quilt stretched across the frame, stroking every detail of the intricate star-shaped pattern, and she held her breath. The cloth felt so amazing.

"Get your filthy mitts off the quilt, you stupid, clumsy girl!" Her mother popped her hard across the face with the back of her hand.

Jeanie's nose exploded, spattering blood all over the quilt.

"Get up, get away from the quilt!" Mama's face twisted in outrage. "You're ruining it. *You* ruin everything!"

The quilters gasped and hopped up. One ran for the hydrogen peroxide. Another went to comfort Mama, who'd slung herself sobbing into a chair, railing against her awful child. A third woman picked up her purse and sneaked out the back door.

No one did anything for Jeanie.

Clasping her hands over her nose, she staggered from the parlor, tears mingling with the blood, listening to the women cluck and coo and soothe Mama. It was the first time her mother's slap broke Jeanie's nose, but it wouldn't be the last.

"Mom?" Luna asked, tugging her back into the room. "Are you all right?"

"Huh?" Jeanie blinked. She'd forgotten all about that wretched memory, but now it was as fresh as the day it had happened almost sixty years ago.

Clare pressed a tissue into Jeanie's hand. "Where did you go, honey?"

Jeanie wrapped the tissue around her bleeding thumb, feeling chagrined for causing a scene. "I'm so sorry."

"There's nothing to be sorry for." Clare rested a hand on Jeanie's shoulder. "But maybe you should take a break?"

"No." Jeanie shook her head. "I've got to finish this. I finish what I start."

"All right." Clare gave her a kind smile. "I'll fetch you a Band-Aid and thimble."

Two minutes later, Jeanie was sewing again, her heart still racing from the flashback. Could the others tell how damaged she was? Shame flushed heat up her chest to her neck and on to her cheeks. She ducked her head and kept on sewing.

When she finished, she looked up to see how much sand was left in the hourglass. Well over a fourth of it. She swung her gaze to see how the other quilters were faring, but no one else was quilting. They were all watching her.

Luna, however, looked worried.

Feeling self-conscious, Jeanie hunched her shoulders forward, pulling herself inward, and took the last stitch in the square.

That's when all the women got to their feet, applauding wildly. They were applauding her and a job well done. It was all Jeanie could do not to cry over being recognized. She was stunned by their kindness and overt admiration. It was too much charity to bear.

Clare presented her with the gift card and she and Luna finished their shopping. It wasn't until they were outside in the golf cart that Jeanie broke down sobbing.

# Chapter 22
## *Luna*

*"On this island, threads bind more than fabric; they unite hearts, weaving a tapestry of shared dreams."*

—*Eloisa Hobby*

Luna sat behind the wheel of the golf cart staring out at the ocean where she'd driven when Jeanie broke down crying, clutching her mother's hand in her own.

Silence, except for the sound of waves hitting the shore, stretched between them and for the first time ever, she felt truly united with her mother.

Her mind lingered on the story Mom had just shared with her. A woeful tale of a childhood marred by severe parental abuse, a truth Jeanie had hidden for decades.

Tears blurred Luna's vision as she watched the whitecaps, her heart heavy. She had always seen her mother as fragile, but this revelation cast Jeanie in a whole new light. She was far stronger than Luna imagined. Jeanie's deep attachment to Jack made much more sense now. He'd been a thin lifeline in a hurricane of a childhood.

"Mom," Luna said after Jeanie spilled details about growing up with a cruel and invalidating mother, her voice barely above a whisper.

Jeanie looked over at her, red-rimmed eyes reflecting a mix of vulnerability and fortitude. "Yes?"

"Why didn't you tell me before about Grandmother?" Now the reason Jeanie had barely let Luna be around Francine made sense. Her maternal grandmother had died when Luna was twelve and she didn't remember much about her other than she'd been quite stern.

Jeanie sighed and turned her face into the wind, her long hair streaming over her shoulders. She'd taken down her customary braids and she looked waifish in her timeless beauty. "I thought I was protecting you, but maybe I was just protecting myself."

"I'm not sure I understand."

"Whenever I was around my mother, I subjugated myself to keep the peace."

"Like you did with Dad."

"Yes." Jeanie ducked her head. "I was broken inside, and I attracted a broken man."

"But you have the capacity to change, Mom. You care. You want to do better. Yes, you tend to give yourself away to people who don't deserve your generosity, but that's only because you love so hard and deep."

"You really think so?" Jeanie asked, misty-eyed.

"I know so. I can't speculate why Dad and Grandmother were the way they were. Unable to see beyond their own suffering. Unable to give empathy to others because they were so caught up in trying to supply their own need for control. It's sad for everyone. But *we* can change. We can alter the path for future generations, so the cycle doesn't have to continue. It starts now. With us."

"I'm so sorry I wasn't the mother you needed me to be."

"Life might have been bumpy, and it was hard living with Dad's addiction, but never once did I doubt that you loved me, Mom. Not one single time."

"Oh, Luna." Jeanie started sobbing again. "Thank you so much for your forgiveness."

Luna squeezed her mother's hand. "I'm so sorry you went through that. It explains so much."

Jeanie nodded and wiped away her tears. "It does. But I don't want it to define either of us. Not me, not you, and certainly not Artie."

"It might not define us, but it's shaped us. Because of how your mother treated you, it turned you into a people pleaser and being a people pleaser made you codependent. And because of your codependence with Dad, I went in the opposite direction, keeping people at arm's length. I've often wondered if my avoidance of intimate connections is why Herc turned to gambling for solace."

"Don't put that on yourself. Herc did what he did. It's not your fault."

"Maybe not, but I didn't love him the way he deserved to be loved."

"Because you never really stopped loving Paul."

"Yes," she whispered. "But we're more than our past, Mom. We're this . . ." She gestured to the fabric in the back of the cart. "We're our creativity, our love, our future. We'll mend ourselves with each other's help because healing is the greatest gift we can give Artie."

Jeanie smiled through fresh tears. "You're right. And speaking of our future, this quilt . . . it's more than just a contest entry. It's a symbol of us. Of our journey together. I will sew that into every stitch."

Luna's eyes lit up. "Yes, each panel will represent a challenge we've overcome, a strength we've discovered here on the island."

"It will symbolize our rebirth as we emerge stronger from the ashes of history."

"That's perfect, Mom. The quilt will tell our story of resilience."

"I love that."

"I love *you*."

"I love you too, Luna."

They hugged for a long time, holding each other until their tears dried and the heightened emotions drained away.

"Oh, look." Jeanie pointed to a jacaranda tree on the path into Crafters' Corner several yards from where they sat in the golf cart. "It's Paul."

Sure enough, Paul was on a ladder, wielding pruners to lop off dead branches. Luna hadn't even seen him there when they'd driven up. He'd been hidden by the sheltering tree limbs.

"Would you like to go talk to him?" Jeanie asked.

"I would. Do you mind if I let you take the cart and I'll walk back?"

"Not at all."

"If Artie's around, get her to help you take in our quilting supplies."

"I can handle it," Jeanie said. "You go on and enjoy yourself."

Luna got out of the cart and Jeanie slid over behind the wheel. She started it up and gave a jaunty wave goodbye.

Behind her back, Luna circled her left wrist with her right hand, wandered over to the ladder, and peered up at Paul. "Hi."

He came down the ladder, stopped in front of her, and tilted his sun hat back on his forehead, his eyes crinkling warmly at the corners. "Hey."

Luna's heart skipped. He seemed genuinely happy to see her.

"How you been?" He set the pruners on a ladder rung. He smelled earthy and sweet like the jacaranda blooms.

"Good, good. Mom and I finished the quilt design. Now it's all up to her to sew it."

"I—" he said.

At the same time, she said, "You—"

Their eyes met, and they laughed together.

"You go first." He waved a hand.

"No, no, you."

"I had fun the other night at the butterfly hatchery." He lifted his hat and raked his fingers through his hair.

"Me too."

Silence ensued.

Luna didn't want to say something in case Paul was about to speak, but he just grinned at her as if she were a hundred-dollar bill he found lying on the ground.

"What are you doing tomorrow?" he asked at last.

"No real plans. You?"

"It's my day off."

"Really?" Luna couldn't help smiling.

"Would you like to do something?"

"Together?"

"That's the general idea." Mirth danced in his eyes.

"Just you and me?"

"Unless you want to do something with our girls?" His gaze searched her face.

"We should, I suppose, but I was hoping to wait until we were ready to tell them about us."

"Good idea."

"So tomorrow?" She shifted her weight. "What time?"

"Breakfast at Eggscellence, say nineish, and we'll go from there."

"It's a date."

* * *

After an excellent meal at the eggcentric restaurant overlooking the water, where Luna and Paul laughed and reminisced, they took a golf cart and drove out to the lighthouse.

On a Sunday morning, the place was deserted.

Hand in hand, they hiked up the grassy cliff overlooking the Gulf of Mexico. The majestic white lighthouse stood like a sentinel keeping watch over the island.

Luna gazed out at the hypnotic roll of blue waves stretching endlessly to the horizon. Seabirds floated lazily on updrafts. The salt-kissed air filled her lungs, reminding her of happier, simpler times.

Paul guided her into the tower and told her a bit about the history of the lighthouse built back in the late 1700s. They climbed the spiral staircase to the top, Paul leading the way. The view was even more breathtaking from the widow's walk.

"It's so peaceful here," she murmured. "So quiet. It could still be 1798."

"That's what I love about this island. It's timeless."

"It reminds me of another tower we climbed. Remember?" She peeked at him through lowered lashes.

"I'll never forget that night, Moonbeam. It's forever etched in my brain."

"Mine too." She met his gaze head-on.

"Like old times." His eyes held hers and he reached for her hand. His touch anchored her, as comforting as ever.

Feeling safe with him, Luna tilted her face skyward, eyes closed. She could almost imagine she was seventeen again—young, carefree, believing her whole wonderful future lay ahead next to the boy she loved more than life itself.

Paul reached over to tuck a windblown strand of hair behind her ear, his finger sending electrical pulses sparking heat over her scalp. Luna turned toward him. His handsome face was shadowed, gaze searching hers with poignant longing.

"Luna," he whispered.

"Paul," she whispered back.

Their lips met tentatively, relearning textures and rhythms

grown hazy with years apart. With rising urgency, Paul deepened the kiss into blazing reconnection. He tasted of heat and memories, both poignant and bittersweet.

At last, she pulled away and caressed Paul's cheek, heart brimming. "I can't believe we found each other again."

His eyes clouded. "I never dared hope . . . after everything . . ." He glanced away.

Luna's euphoria dimmed. The past still lay between them like an invisible barrier—so much hurt and misunderstanding yet to work through. Could they truly recapture what was lost? Or were the cracks in their foundation too deep to mend? Doubts and fears she thought long buried emerged to taunt her.

Paul ran a hand through his hair, looking uncharacteristically unsure. "Your life is still in upheaval . . . maybe this is too much complexity added in. You haven't been widowed for very long. Just over a year."

Luna shook her head. "The fact that we met again now, despite the odds . . . it has to mean something."

"Eloisa believes fate brings people together." His tone warmed, but hesitation lingered in his dazzling blue eyes.

"What do *you* believe?"

"I don't want to risk wounding you more."

Joy and yearning battled Luna's misgivings. Was she ready to trust Paul with her battered heart again? Could she handle it if things fell apart once more?

Gulping, she turned, rushed down the stairs, and fled the lighthouse.

"Luna," Paul called after her as she left the lighthouse ahead of him, struggling to get her emotions under control. "Wait."

She stopped beside the golf cart, waiting for her pulse to settle and Paul to catch up.

"Slowing you down, am I?" His teasing grin tickled her heart.

"No, no. I'm just . . ."

"Confused?"

"Yeah, that."

"You've been through a lot lately. Confusion is normal."

Was it? She felt anything but normal.

Paul stopped, turned, leaned against the front of the cart, and held out his arms to her. "Come here."

It was a request, not a command.

And heaven help her, she went.

Straight into his embrace again. Why was she fighting her feelings? Okay, yes. It was too soon. Only thirteen months had passed since her life imploded.

But Paul was here. It was now, and dammit, she still cared about him.

And he cared about her.

Even after the way she treated him. All he'd wanted was to keep her father out of prison. He hadn't been malicious. He'd been thinking of her. She was just so afraid of doing something wrong, of making a huge mistake.

Nothing was scarier than messing this up again.

He pulled her closer, his fingers entangling in the belt loops of her blue jean skirt, put his feet on either side of hers, and snugged their hips together. "*Luna.*"

She shook her head. "Just . . . don't."

He touched her cheek with his knuckle. "Shh."

She wondered if he still had the same skills in bed. "You say my name like it's the most beautiful sound in the world."

"It is," he murmured. "To me."

"I'm confused."

"Join the club, Moonbeam."

She laughed, but it sounded hollow. She kept her eyes squeezed closed and heard seagulls crying as they flew over on their way to the beach. "I don't know what I'm doing."

"No one does. There's no rule book for love."

*Love.*

Was that this wanton, tumultuous feeling? One part of her said, *yes indeedy,* while another part warned that if she kept going down this path, she would crash and burn.

Which perhaps was fine if she weren't a mother, and her fifteen-year-old daughter weren't on the island with her, but Artie was here. Luna wasn't free to follow her heart and ignore all common sense in favor of something irrational.

"We've got kids," she said.

"Who really like each other." He kept smiling as if all was right with the world.

She pulled a palm down her face. "What if we break up?"

"What if we don't?" He sounded so sensible.

Luna shook her head. "I'm far too pessimistic for an optimist like you."

"Let me be the judge of that." His steadfast eyes reassured her.

"We've lost so much time." Okay, she heard it, the fear trembling her voice.

"So let's not lose any more."

"We don't even know each other. Two decades have passed."

"And yet here we are. You and me, feeling the same heady things we felt back then. Take a chance on us," Paul said.

Luna searched his face, wishing so desperately he'd shared his secret with her from the beginning. Wished things could have been different. But wishing changed nothing, and it wasn't healthy to dwell on things she couldn't change.

"And I hope you can understand why I can't rush headlong into the past. It's just really bad timing. Three years from now . . ."

She shrugged. "Who knows? I'm a mess, but you're not. You know what you want. I have no clue."

He nodded. "I do know what I want. And I want you, Luna."

"I have a lot to grieve." So much, in fact, she didn't know where to start.

"I can wait."

"I might never heal."

"You'll get through it. You're the strongest woman I know, and I've known a lot of strong women."

"That's sweet of you to say." She cupped his cheek with her palm and stared into his earnest eyes.

"All right. The ball is in your court. You're in full control."

She liked that he said that. Buffed by circumstance, she'd forgotten what it was like to steer her own fate.

And then he kissed her.

Luna did not resist. She might yearn for control. Her mind might even *crave* it . . . but her body? Oh, her treacherous body!

*It* craved Paul.

He kissed her with abandon, and she kissed him right back, teeth, tongues, and lips enmeshed. This might not be smart. She craved him more than anything, even if it was idiotic.

His mouth ravaged hers thoroughly, and she draped against him, limp and weak with passion. Teenage Luna was in the driver's seat. No looking back. He blazed kisses along her chin, to her jaw, to her throat.

Engulfed, she pushed her fingers through his silky hair, threw back her head, and let out a soft moan. "Paul . . ."

"Yes, yes, I know. You want me to stop." Panting, he tried to pull back, but she kept a tight hold of his hair.

"No," she said. "I want to go to your place."

# Chapter 23

## *Artemis*

*"Let your imagination sail on the canvas of creation, for here, every craft is a voyage of wonder."*

—*Eloisa Hobby*

Artie was on a mission.

For the last four days while Mom and Gran had holed up working on the quilt, Artie and Orion had been racking their brains for an art project they could make with the creepy dolls, but nothing was gelling.

Then last night, Artie had a spectacular dream about the creepy dolls and got a bonkers idea. She couldn't wait to tell Orion about it. In her stunningly lucid dream, the dolls arranged themselves in an artistic way that fired her imagination. Now Artie knew exactly what she and Orion could do to win the recycled art contest.

If they won the category, they'd split the five-thousand-dollar prize. And there was always a chance they could win the hundred-thousand-dollar grand prize. Too bad she had to comb the island to find her new friend instead of texting her.

Stupid lack of cell phone service.

She called Orion's landline from the B&B and got her voicemail. Artie left a message and then got dressed in shorts, a T-shirt, and flip-flops.

At ten thirty, the B&B kitchen was empty. No one around to challenge her. Mom was out, Gran ostensibly off quilting. Neither her fairy godmother, Dot, nor Vivian, the B&B owner, were in sight.

Yay!

Artie loaded up her backpack with water and snacks, borrowed a scooter from the Nestled Inn, and took off. She cruised through Crafters' Corner, stopping to scope out the alley where she first met Orion, but there was no sign of the girl's pop-up shop.

What should she do now?

Up ahead, the path split.

Artie pulled a map of the island from her back pocket. The right fork led to the beach, while the left fork led to the interior of the island, which included Opportunity Ridge, the butterfly hatchery, and Prism Pavilion.

Could Orion be on the beach? Or at the lighthouse? Or in Crafters' Corner? She'd try all three, starting with the farthest location and circling back. Her hair flew out behind her as she sped down the gently sloping hill, jacaranda trees whizzing by in a lavish blur of purple.

Whee! What a blast.

As she sailed along, the scooter tires eating up the ground, Artie's mind toyed with the new direction for the art project. It would certainly be edgy. She doubted whether the older crowd on the island would embrace her rather gothic concept. But she had everything to gain. She risked more by *not* trying.

The scooter's tires made a soft whirring noise against the cobblestones.

The closer she got to the lighthouse, the sweeter the air smelled, like the Bit-O-Honey taffy Gran kept in a ceramic chicken jar on her coffee table. Thick vines with orange trumpetlike flowers covered the white wooden fencing separating the middle of the island from the northern highlands of Opportunity Ridge. She would check the lighthouse, then head inland to the butterfly hatchery and the pavilion. If Orion wasn't at any of those places, she'd tackle the ridge last.

Through the tops of the purple-blossomed trees, the lighthouse pitched upward, and she got excited about seeing the island from that bird's-eye view.

As she rounded a bend, Artie spotted a golf cart parked in the lighthouse parking area. Her mother and Paul were leaning against the front of it.

Kissing.

In broad freaking daylight!

For anyone to see. She knew who he was because she'd met Orion's dad when she and Orion were hanging out together.

Orion's dad was handsome for an old dude, but he had his hands possessively locked around Mom's waist, and they were going at it like horny teenagers.

*Eew!*

Creeped out, Artie gagged and hit the hand brakes. The scooter shuddered to a stop beneath her. She gritted her teeth, whirled the scooter around in a tight circle, and sped off in the opposite direction.

"Adios, mother-jammers." Her voice echoed across the valley, and she half wished her mother heard her.

An odd mix of emotions coursed through Artie's body—anger at her mother, disappointment that she hadn't found Orion, and confusion about what to do next. What would Orion think when she told her their parents were kissing?

Snorting, Artie glanced around for something else to focus on. The higher road led away from the lighthouse and into the interior of the island. She goosed the scooter as fast as it would go and headed toward the tall glass building shining through the foliage.

Had to be Prism Pavilion.

Hopefully, she'd find Orion and forget all about what her mother and Paul had been doing. She knew it was irrational, but she couldn't help feeling like Mom was betraying Dad's memory.

*Eew, eew, eew.*

It took her fifteen minutes to reach the building. Up close, Prism Pavilion was pretty impressive. She pulled her water bottle from her backpack and guzzled it. The twenty-foot glass structure had an archway of glass prisms suspended from the ceiling, creating a kaleidoscope effect of colored light as the sun shone through them, and the whole place just glowed.

Wow!

She stood for a moment, fully present with the lightness of being, and saw what it was she'd been trying to deny. Mom was changing. Artie's life was changing and there was nothing she could do to stop it.

Ack!

Artie's worst fear. Powerlessness. She wanted to punch something. Hard.

"I'm so mad at you, Mom," she muttered. "And I'm mad at Dad and Beck and Gran!"

Artie smacked her fist into her palm. Ouch. She shook it off and stepped into the pavilion.

*Please let Orion be in here.*

Inside it was even more beautiful than the outside.

Everywhere she looked there were intricate designs made of suncatcher prisms—pendulums, chandeliers, orbs, stars, butterflies, and other crystal shapes—all hung from cables and wires stretching across the ceiling like strings of stars.

The multicolored prisms dangled from the ceiling in a rainbow canopy, each reflecting an array of brilliant light throughout the space. It was nothing short of magnificent and Artie was drawn into the spectrum of colors.

She gaped. Gran would *love* it here, and she vowed to return with her grandmother.

At first glance, it seemed no one else was in the building. Head thrown back, staring at the ceiling, she wandered through the empty pavilion, captivated by the light. Why wasn't this sacred space packed with people?

She heard music playing, soft and low, cocked her head and listened. The song was one of Gran's favorites by some old-timey band called the Grateful Dead and the singer was crooning something about glowing like sunshine.

Perfect song for this place.

The tune was really soothing, and Artie felt herself calming. She bumped into a ladder that she hadn't seen because she was busy gawking at the prisms.

"Oops, sorry," she said as she realized she offered an apology to an inanimate object. "Doofus."

That's when she spotted Eloisa Hobby standing on the other side of the ladder, an aurora borealis suncatcher in her hand.

"Welcome to my little home away from home." Eloisa's warm smile lit up her face. "This is my favorite spot on the entire island."

"I can see why."

"I was just about to hang this suncatcher. A guest made it for our rainbow joy. Would you like to hang it for me?"

"Can I really?" Artie grinned.

"Sure." Eloisa handed her the bejeweled suncatcher.

Artie scrambled up the ladder. "Um, how do I hang it?"

"See that cable just above your head?" Eloisa pointed. "It's been strung with hooks. There's a hook without a suncatcher."

"Oh! I see." It was just out of Artie's reach. She leaned forward, extended her hand as far as it would stretch.

The ladder bobbled.

She gasped and threw her weight in the opposite direction, hoping to catch her balance, but she overcorrected, and the ladder tipped sideways on two legs.

It was going over!

Artie stared down at the ground and braced for a fall. The suncatcher was grasped tightly in her hand. Protectively, she brought her hand to her chest.

But Eloisa raced to her rescue. Who knew an elderly woman could move so quickly?

"I'll hold the ladder." Eloisa placed both palms on the sides. "Be careful of leaning over too far."

Artie tried again, reaching for the swivel hook that dangled from the silver cable. This time, she easily caught it between two fingers, and her legs didn't wobble as she opened the lobster clasp of the aurora borealis crystal and looped it around the hook.

"Ta-da." Artie dusted her palms together and scampered down the ladder.

"Thank you so much. Great hanging job." Eloisa tilted her head back, inspecting Artie's handiwork. "I was about to have some tea. Would you like to join me?"

"I'm not much of a hot tea person."

"How about an Arnold Palmer?" Eloisa wriggled her eyebrows comically.

"What's that?"

"Half iced tea, half lemonade."

"Now that's an idea." Artie grinned.

Eloisa crooked a finger, inviting her to a back corner where a round table was set up for tea service with two plates, a teakettle, a teacup, and a glass of half tea and half lemonade, along with cakes and cookies, as if Eloisa had been expecting her.

Artie stared at her. "How did you know I'd be here?"

"I saw you ride up on your scooter and I always bring extra tea supplies in case anyone wanders into the pavilion and wants to join me."

Eloisa escorted her to the table and waved her down into a chair. Artie felt too hot and sweaty for fancy tea, but Eloisa didn't seem to mind. The older woman, however, looked daisy fresh in a summery maxi dress the same color as the jacaranda trees. Today, she had on a lavender pillbox hat with a yellow lily sticking up from the band.

When Artie was small, she and her mom had tea parties on the back patio at the house in Dallas. A stab of nostalgia went through her. They'd never have a tea party there again.

Ack! She wasn't the least bit sentimental. Why did she care?

On the table with the tea things was a bud vase with a bright pink rose in full bloom. It scented the air with its blushing aroma, spring-sweet and floral, both cozy and sophisticated. Almost as if she could taste it, Artie put the tip of her tongue to her lip and inhaled.

"This is quite nice," she said.

Eloisa gave a soft smile. "Isn't it?"

"Do you have tea here often?"

"Sometimes I do, sometimes I don't."

The sun dipped lower in the afternoon sky and the light filtering through the glass building changed, radiating a rainbow-colored halo over the table. Eloisa spread a linen napkin over her lap and nodded that Artie should do the same.

Delicately, Eloisa used a serving spatula to transfer two petits fours to Artie's plate, followed by an almond cookie. Artie's stomach growled.

"Oh my, you must be hungry." Eloisa laughed merrily.

They sat sipping their tea and eating their cakes. The same Grateful Dead song kept looping. The place was surprisingly quiet except for soothing music and clinking dishes. Artie lowered her head for another sip of Arnold Palmer and caught a nose full of the rose bloom. The scent was so strong; she felt a little lightheaded.

It felt weird being here.

Surreal.

As if perhaps, like Alice in Wonderland, she'd fallen down a rabbit hole. Except there was no Mad Hatter at this tea party. Just Eloisa with the kindest of eyes.

"You're going through a tough time," Eloisa said, a statement, not a question.

"How do you know?" Artie asked.

"You're fifteen. The world is topsy-turvy when you're fifteen."

"It's not just that." Artie drew a circle on the tablecloth with her finger.

"Oh?" Eloisa's voice was so light Artie barely heard her.

Artie didn't know what possessed her. Perhaps it was the amazing crystal rainbows shining over Eloisa's face, or the awesomeness of an Arnold Palmer and, frankly, the most delicious cake she ever put in her mouth, but the next thing Artie knew, she was telling Eloisa *everything*.

She spilled her guts. About her dad getting murdered, his gambling addiction that caused them to lose the house in Dallas, her gran being swindled out of her life savings by a sweetheart scam, meeting Orion, getting pulled under the water by Wicked Martha, Mom kissing Orion's dad . . .

All of it came tumbling out.

Eloisa listened and nodded and poured her more Arnold Palmer and gave her another cake.

When finally Artie finished, Eloisa met her gaze with a steady, unfaltering smile as if it would all be okay. "Goodness, you've been through a lot in such a short amount of time."

"I'm sorry," Artie said. "I shouldn't have told you my life story."

"You needed someone to listen."

"You're pretty good at that." Artie ran her hand through her hair, combing out the tangles she got riding on the scooter.

"I've been around a long time, and I've heard lots of stories."

"I'm just so mad, you know? No one thinks about how their actions affect me. I'm supposed to just grin and bear it? That's not me. I'm not a sidelines girl. I enjoy being in the ring."

"I can tell that." Eloisa smoothed her napkin in her lap.

"How do I stop being so pissed off at everyone?"

"That is a big question. Asking for help is a point in your favor." Eloisa canted her head and studied her.

"Okay, so what do I do?" Artie rubbed her palms over the tops of her thighs, nervous that she revealed so much to a stranger.

Eloisa's genuine smile made her feel better. "Anger management is a tricky thing, my dear."

"Tell me about it." Artie exhaled and slumped back in her chair.

"It's important to remember that it's okay to get mad. Anger is an emotion just like any other, so it's neither good nor bad. It just is."

Artie sat with that a moment. "When I get mad, it feels like there are two fists inside me just pounding on my rib cage, trying to bust right out of my chest."

"That's very descriptive, and it's a positive sign that you recognize what anger does to you physically."

"My jaw gets so tight I feel like I could spit nails." Artie cupped her jaw with both palms.

"Anger comes from hurtful experiences, but it's also important to recognize when you're using it as a shield. Like curse
words."

"Yeah, I do have a foul mouth." Artie grinned. "Ticks off my
parents and Gran. Well, not my dad anymore."

"Which perhaps is why you use words you know will upset
people?" The woman sat perfectly still, waiting for Artie to process the question.

"Maybe."

"You might not want to admit this, but do you think you use
anger to keep others at a distance?"

A stranger's question felt like deep insight. Artie would have
gotten huffy if Mom asked the same question. "Could be . . ."

"I'm not saying that anger can't be helpful in some situations,
but if you can't control it, you risk alienating those you love."

"And getting in hot water."

Eloisa's smile deepened. "That too. The trick is to learn how
to control and release that energy productively."

"Yeah? Like how?"

"Like counting to ten—"

"Tried it. Doesn't work."

"Have you tried taking deep breaths while you count? There's
a cool trick to that. Breathe in as you slowly count to four, hold
your breath to the count of seven, and then exhale to the count of
eight." Eloisa demonstrated the technique.

"Never tried it."

"Let's try it now," Eloisa suggested. "Breathe from your abdo-
men, not the top of your lungs. Doing this will focus your mind
on something other than what sparked your upset. Take control
over yourself instead of letting situations control you."

For several minutes, Eloisa and Artie breathed together, and
Artie instantly felt calmer.

Artie liked the technique. She hated being controlled even if it was by her own emotions. "Okay, thanks for the tip. What else you got?"

"You have a thirst for knowledge. That's good." Eloisa looked Artie squarely in the eyes. "Pause before you speak. Think before you act. Pay attention to your triggers so you can recognize them ahead of time and cool off before things get heated."

"Yeah, yeah. Easier said than done."

"It gets easier the more you practice self-control. The fact you're asking for help means you're ready. Remember, it's important to take time out for yourself. Pick a time and place where you're to-tally alone. This is for moments of inward reflection. That way, when the angry feelings rise again, you've got a built-in safe place inside you that will keep you calm and grounded." Eloisa made it sound so simple.

Artie eyed Eloisa and got the strangest feeling this woman held the secrets of the universe inside her. "Like what exactly?"

"Meditation for one."

"Blech. I don't do sitting still well."

"The deep breathing I spoke of . . . and exercise. Whatever you like, running, weight lifting, swimming, any physical activity will do. Exercise takes your focus off your feelings and grounds you in your body."

"I like exercise. Moving sounds more doable than sitting cross-legged with my eyes closed for hours on end."

"And journaling. Try putting your feelings down on paper. It gets them out. You can symbolically let go of the emotions by destroying the writing afterward."

"Thanks for the tips," Artie said and polished off her Arnold Palmer. "That was great."

"I'm so happy you could join me. I hope I helped a little."

"You did." Artie bobbed her head.

Eloisa's smile overtook her entire face. "I'm so very glad."

Feeling immeasurably better than when she walked in, Artie bid Eloisa goodbye and left the pavilion. Outside in the sunlight, she blinked and remembered why she'd come to the building. She'd been looking for Orion to tell her about the creepy doll art project.

Hopping on the scooter, she motored back to Crafters' Corner. The place was livelier now. More guests in shops, restaurants, and at the beach.

And then she saw her friend's beautiful purple hair.

Orion sat at a patio table in front of the ice cream parlor. Beside her was a gorgeous girl wearing pink, heart-shaped sunglasses. Their heads were together as they split one big milkshake with two fat straws, and they were giggling, as if sharing a great joke.

Anger was a sudden fist, punching Artie right in the face. She wanted to hop off the scooter, race over, and demand Orion pick a friend. It was either Artie or the chick with the bad taste in eyewear.

But for the first time, she caught her anger before it overcame her. She touched it. Stayed with it. Counted to ten as she took ten long, slow deep breaths and directed the scooter toward the B&B. She felt her jaw unclench and her muscles relax.

And then she met the feeling that lurked beneath her anger. The thing she desperately tried to cover up with anger and bravado.

Fear of losing control.

# Chapter 24

## *Luna*

*"Ah, the sea and sky. They're like a blank canvas, waiting for you to paint your dreams."*

—*Eloisa Hobby*

Paul parked the golf cart in front of his house, and they tumbled out, grappling for each other, arms and mouths intertwined.

Luna's body boiled for him. She was focused on getting this man naked and into bed. He kissed her. She worked the buttons of his shirt. He pushed his fingers through her hair.

In her peripheral vision, she saw the golf cart was still moving, slowly rolling toward the ocean. "The golf cart!"

"Crap, I forgot to put it in park." He left her side and jumped for the cart, running alongside it as the vehicle picked up speed down the incline headed for the cliff above the ocean. He dove inside and set the brake.

Luna laughed.

He emerged red-faced and grinning. "See what you do to me?"

She beckoned, wiggling a come-hither finger. He looked at her as if she were some forgotten treasure he'd dug up from the sand.

Paul reached Luna, bent, and scooped her into his arms.

"Ooh." A giggle bubbled from her. She wrapped her arms around his neck and hung on.

Muscles bunching, he carried her across the lawn. She rested her head against his shoulder, felt the quick thump-thump of the pulse at his neck.

On the porch, he set her on her feet. She pressed close to him, slipped her arms around his neck again, tilted her chin and stared into his deep blue eyes. "Take me."

Letting out a soft groan, he cupped her face between his strong, calloused palms and kissed her. The smell of honeysuckle, from the vines on the fence, washed over them, filling her nose with sweetness. How she needed to be with this man!

He seemed as desperate for her as his hard body pushed against her pelvis, fully erect. Paul traced his rough but gentle fingertips over her cheek, sending hot electrical tingles straight to her brain.

*I. Want. This. Man.*

Simple and direct. She hungered to explore their full potential. Her body softened everywhere, willing and warm. Eager for him.

Luna parted her lips.

Shadows from the afternoon sun playing peekaboo with the clouds fell across them, enhancing their intimate connection.

Paul lowered his head.

Luna held her breath, waiting, pulse sprinting. Her mind spun with fragments of memories from their past. Freeze-frame snapshots of who they used to be. Sharing nervous laughter and stolen kisses underneath the bleachers at homecoming. Two-stepping at school dances, late-night skinny-dipping at Julep Lake, endless phone conversations, shy glances, and hand-holding. The adrenaline rush when Paul first asked her out. Getting butterflies while waiting for him, wondering if he'd try to kiss her . . .

Luna remembered the way he'd sling his arm around her shoulder at the Julep Diner as they shared a meal. She recalled how he wove their fingers together at the movies, stroking his thumb over her knuckles. Her memory served up the nervous exhilaration of their first time making love on the water tower, tender and tentative. Of Paul whispering how beautiful she was, his eyes shining with awe that she was with him. Of curling up together under the stars, baring their hopes and fears and dreams for the future.

The future they had not had together.

A short-lived romance, ruined by circumstances and misunderstandings. But a love so deep it left an indelible mark that remained even after two long decades.

His smile deepened and he moved closer, inch by tantalizing inch. The years melted away as Paul's mouth claimed hers once more.

Luna marveled at how easily they fell back into each other.

His featherlight touches set her skin sizzling. When he leaned in, Luna fluttered her eyes closed. This time, his kiss was soft as butterfly wings.

He pulled back a smidge.

Luna swayed closer, wanting more but not rushing it. Paul's powerful hands grasped her waist, keeping her steady. His warm breath lingered as he paused, drawing out the thrill.

"You okay?" he asked, his tone thick with feeling.

"I will be if you stop asking if I'm okay and just kiss me." Luna closed the tiny gap, melting against him.

The next kiss exploded like pyrotechnics.

She tangled her fingers in Paul's thick hair as she met his tongue with hers. His groan vibrated through her body. They kissed and kissed and kissed until forced to come up for air.

Panting, they broke apart, her lips buzzing from his zeal.

She opened her eyes and found Paul watching her, the stark need in his eyes plain to see. Her cheeks burned and her nerve endings hummed. She wasn't ready to let go of him and curled her index fingers through his belt loops, holding him in place as he'd done with her earlier.

Paul smiled softly and swept her hair back off her forehead. "We have plenty of time. No need to rush."

Happiness flooded her heart. Paul's thumb brushed her swollen lip. She playfully nibbled the pad and drew a chuckle from him.

That familiar sound delighted her. She wanted to hear him laugh more often. Luna boldly started their next kiss, thrilling to his enthusiastic response.

She tried different pressures, discovering what got Paul's engine running these days. He seemed to prefer medium. Not too light, not too hard. *Just right, Goldilocks.* Gently catching his bottom lip between her teeth, she stroked it with her tongue.

"Careful," he said with gravel in his voice. "You're playing with fire, Moonbeam."

She searched his face.

His blue eyes smoldered, belying his restraint.

Feeling brave, Luna trailed her nails down his neck. The cotton of his shirt slid beneath her fingertips.

Goose bumps rose on his skin, and he shuddered against her. "Luna, you're killing me."

"Good." She pulled him into another deep kiss.

Paul's hands tightened at her waist, but he let Luna keep leading this sweet dance. She loved that he kept his masculine power leashed for her, letting her decide just how far to take things.

Gradually their kisses slowed again, though their lips were still throbbing with passion. When they parted, the ocean breeze cooled her heated skin.

Paul touched his forehead to hers, the simple intimacy swelling her heart. No words needed in this perfect moment.

Whatever this was, it ran soul deep. Paul's eyes made promises she knew he was willing to keep. Was she ready for that? Ready for him? His hand found hers, and he threaded their fingers together.

Yes, she would go wherever their passion led.

"Let's go inside." He opened the door.

"Orion," he called. "You home?"

No answer.

"One of her friends from Everly was coming over on the ferry for a visit. Did Artie tell you about that?"

"Artie was still asleep when I left this morning."

"They're probably together. They've been inseparable since you guys got here." He smiled and let out his breath.

Inside Paul's bungalow, Luna felt awkward. What would he think of her body that had aged twenty-two years since he'd last seen it? Would he see the stretch marks across a belly that had nurtured two children? Would he miss the breasts that had once been high and perky?

"You're gorgeous," he said.

"How did you know I was—" She caught herself rubbing her thumb over her knuckles. "Oh. Am I that easy to read?"

He pressed a finger between her eyebrows, smoothing out the furrow. "Shh," he said. "It's going to be fine."

He dipped his head and kissed her lips, fanning the coals of her simmering sexuality.

She closed her eyes and sighed.

"What is it?" he asked against her lips.

"Is this the right thing to do?"

He stepped back. "Open your eyes, Moonbeam."

Slowly, she lifted her lashes and looked at him.

"It's me. Paul. You used to trust me, remember?"

Yes, but that was before she thought he'd been drinking and driving with her dad in the truck. A lie that caused her to turn on him. Guilt pinched her.

"Do you want to do this?" he asked. "Because if you don't, that's fine. I want you more than I want to breathe, but there's absolutely no pressure. You are in the driver's seat, Luna. You call the shots."

"Should we talk first?"

"Sure, we can do that. Would you like something to drink? I have water, lemonade, coffee, iced tea . . ."

"Water will be fine." She sat down on his comfy couch while Paul got two glasses of ice water from the kitchen and brought them back to the living room.

"Thanks." She took a long gulp, not realizing how thirsty she'd been. When she finished, she lowered her glass and saw Paul studying her.

"What would you like to discuss?" he asked.

"Protection?"

"Oh. Right to business." Amusement lit up his eyes.

"Well, you know, I haven't done this since my husband died. I haven't even gone on a date, and I feel like a fish out of water."

"Please don't feel that way. You're with me, Luna. I'll put your pleasure at the top of the list. You come first." He reached up to cup her cheek and peer into her eyes. "I mean it."

Relief spread through her body. Paul was such a good man. She couldn't believe she ever let herself think otherwise.

"For the record, I haven't had a sexual partner in forever. I've been too busy raising Orion and working to worry about dating. I spent time with an attractive tourist a couple of years ago, but nothing since. Six months ago, I had a full physical and got a clean bill of health and I have a box of condoms in the back of my medicine chest."

"I had an HIV test done after my husband died and I found out he'd gambled away all our money. If he hid a gambling addiction, what else might he have been hiding, right? But I tested negative."

"What about birth control?"

"I had a hysterectomy after Artie was born for medical reasons. No danger there."

"Sounds like everything is copacetic. What else is troubling you?"

Feeling vulnerable, she hauled in a deep breath. The truth was, her life was in disarray and Paul seemed so darned perfect. Too good to be true and Luna was leery of the unbelievable. There had to be something wrong with him. What was she missing?

"I'm afraid of getting in too deep too soon. If we have sex—"

"Make love," Paul corrected.

"If we have *sex*," she emphasized, "it will change things."

"For the better," he said.

"You don't know that."

"It will deepen our connection."

"Which might be a problem."

"Okay." He scooted away from her. "It's too soon. If you've got this much doubt, you're not ready."

"But I want to be with you in that way."

"I know." He got up and held his hand out to her. "Come with me. I have something else in mind."

"Wh-what?" She hesitated, her fears kicking up. In high school she'd been the proverbial good girl. Paul and Herc had been her only lovers. Her experience was limited for a reason. She was a woman who enjoyed her comfort zone.

"Something I longed to do for you, when we were dating, but you were too shy to let me try."

Uh-oh, was he talking about oral sex? Goose bumps danced up her arms.

Herc had never been a fan of going down on her, even though he'd loved getting blow jobs. Her late husband was so bad at oral sex she lied and told him she didn't like it, because with him, she hadn't.

But now? With Paul?

A hard shiver knocked down her spine. She swallowed as she tried to get her breath. His hand was still extended . . . inviting her on an adventure.

"Come along, Moonbeam. It's time for you to relax and let me make you feel good." Goodness, he *was* talking oral sex.

"That's not fair to you."

"Don't you worry about me. I can take care of myself."

That brought a provocative image to her mind, but she shook her head. "It feels too one-sided. Too selfish on my part."

"It's time you were a little selfish and let someone else take care of you for a change." He cooed her name, low and seductive. "Luna, c'mon. It's time for you to get pampered."

Oh gosh, his words were sweet music to her ears. She had carried the world's weight for so long. Letting go of her burdens seemed impossible.

Paul held her gaze. "Yes?"

She nodded, and he led her not to his bedroom as she expected, but outside to a wide lounge chair underneath a cabana on the deck that overlooked the ocean. The view was spectacular. To think he lived here and woke up to this view every day. Jealousy curled inside her stomach. What she wouldn't give to have this lifestyle!

They settled in the middle of the lounge chair, big enough

for them both. He drew the billowy canvas curtains around the cabana closed, sealing them from prying eyes.

Another shiver ran through Luna. She couldn't believe she was doing this. It felt so daring.

Paul tugged her into the crook of his arms and kissed her, slowly warming her up again. The heat of his breath and his spicy cologne made her feel lightheaded, intoxicated.

His hand moved up her side and cupped her breast over her shirt, exploring with his fingertips. She felt as if she were floating in a sea of cotton candy and vanilla ice cream—sweet and soft.

She shared this perfect moment with her first love, no responsibilities, no kids around, no worries about home foreclosures or debt collectors. Her mind buzzed with excitement. What a lovely place to be.

Paul reached up underneath her skirt, took hold of her panties, slid them down her thighs. His warm fingers moved against her, slipping between her legs as he planted hot kisses against her skin.

She closed her eyes tight and grabbed the waterproof fabric of the cushion in both fists. His lips on her inner thigh sent a wildfire blaze burning through her veins. His tongue ignited her, match to gasoline, and she was engulfed before he ever reached the spot where he was headed.

Luna wanted this, even if it was almost unbearable. Wanted him. Yearned for Paul with a deep thirst that twenty-two years away had not extinguished.

His wicked mouth did lovely things to her.

And when at long last she was panting and begging for him, he slid his tongue inside her.

Her body jerked involuntarily, and a startled gasp escaped her lips.

"You like that?"

Her words came out high and faint. "Uh-huh."

"I think I can do better."

"Oh my."

He was all fingers and tongue and suction. And holy cow! What was he doing *now*? She thrashed against the cushion, bucked her hips.

"Ahh, I'm getting warmer," he murmured.

This time, she couldn't push any words over her lips. Had no directions to give. He was unerring. Knowing right where to go and keeping at it until she was breathless and writhing against him. What in the world had he done to her brain? It had simply stopped functioning, shut down, and sent all sensation to her pelvis.

She had never felt this good. Or so she believed, and then he found that sweet button and zoomed her to a whole new level of sensation.

And she was just *gone*, jettisoned into oral sex outer space. Floating. Vibrating with the stars.

Paul turned her inside out and upside down and she wondered where he'd learned those incredible tongue gymnastics. He slipped his hands underneath her hips and lifted her up to his mouth and ate her like she was a Thanksgiving feast.

Luna strained against him, wanting more, aching for everything he had to give. She felt the tension building inside her until she couldn't take it anymore. She moaned his name, and the ocean breeze caught it and threw it out to sea.

*Paul. Paul. Paul.*

She couldn't take it one more second and then he drove her just one millimeter further, pushing her completely over the edge.

Luna let out a yelp of intense pleasure as he stroked her with his tongue, again and again. And then everything dissolved in one hard shuddering orgasm. The likes of which she never experienced.

Total wipeout.

When at last he finished, she lay addled, every muscle in her body quivering.

Tenderly, he slipped her underwear back over her thighs, lifting her hips for her so she didn't even have to make that small effort. He planted sweet kisses on her bare belly, dropping them like gifts, and she shivered again. He smoothed down her skirt, covering the goose bumps spreading over her thighs.

Luna scooted over, making room for him to land beside her, pleasantly exhausted. She looked over at Paul, her high school sweetheart, sprawled out next to her. He looked a bit smug, but he had every right to own his cockiness.

"So it's you," she murmured.

He grinned. "Yep, just little ol' me."

Her expectations had been thoroughly met, leaving her replete and content. She could simply relax in the warm afterglow, drifting mindlessly on a cloud of bliss.

She lost herself in his comforting embrace. This was new. This sweet selfishness on her part. Luna could definitely get used to it.

"You okay?" he asked.

"That was . . . you were . . . spectacular."

"I know," he said without a hint of modesty.

"So . . ." Luna slanted him a coy glance. "Isn't this where you mention something nice about me?"

His chuckle came out low and intimate. "And why's that, darlin'?"

"I threw caution to the wind for you. This was a big step for me. Letting go of my fears, giving you full control."

"You were very brave." He winked.

"Oh, you." Playfully, she swatted his shoulder.

He brushed a strand of hair from her face, his fingers trailing lightly down her jaw. "You're one hell of a woman, Luna Montgomery. Too damn irresistible for your own good."

Montgomery, not Boudreaux. But she wasn't that girl anymore. She'd been married and widowed, and her world was filled with complexity and complications.

"What time is it?" she drawled.

He pulled back the curtains of the cabana and squinted at the sun midway to the western horizon. "I'd say it's around four."

Luna scrambled to her feet, dispelling the sweet laziness. "My gosh! Is it that late? I have dinner plans with Artie and Mom at seven."

He stood up, looking disheveled and impossibly sexy. She blushed, remembering what he'd just done to her.

She ran a hand through her hair and smoothed her clothes. "Would you and Orion like to join us?"

"Really?" He looked pleased to be invited.

"Unless Orion is busy with her friend."

"No, the last ferry to Everly leaves at five. Her friend will be gone."

"We could tell our girls about us at dinner." She paused. "If you're ready for that."

"I was ready from day one. I was just waiting for you to say the word."

"Okay, let's do it," she said, hoping it was okay with Jeanie and Artie. "We've made a reservation at the French restaurant in Crafters' Corner. I can call ahead and add you. See you there?"

"Wouldn't miss it." He dangled the golf cart keys.

"You want me to take your golf cart?"

"It's not mine. The golf cart belongs to Hobby Island."

"How will you get around?"

"Remember, Orion and I maintain the golf carts. There's half a dozen more in the freestanding garage." He pointed to the building in question.

"Oh yes, right. Thanks for today." She leaned over, kissed his cheek, then took the golf cart key. "You were magnificent."

"I aim to please."

"Thank you again," Luna whispered and hurried away, a huge smile spreading across her face. What a day!

# Chapter 25

## *Jeanie*

*"To soothe a troubled mind, quilt, knit, bake, make jewelry. Do something, anything, with your hands."*

—*Eloisa Hobby*

While Artie was having tea with Eloisa and Paul and Luna were reconnecting at his bungalow, Jeanie spent the day alone, quilting in self-reflection.

After hours of hand-stitching, Jeanie's thumb throbbed beneath the Band-Aid where she poked herself with the sewing needle the day before. Her eyes were blurry, a lingering effect of all the crying she'd done in between stitches.

She sat in her cozy room at the Nestled Inn, the familiar solitude providing both comfort and unease. Yesterday had been an emotional roller coaster. She was elated that she and Luna were making progress in their relationship. Their heartfelt conversation brought them closer than they'd been in years.

Yet, despite her newfound joy, a looming shadow cast doubt. The upcoming quilting competition weighed heavily on Jeanie's shoulders. The thought of competing against talented quilters in the island's prestigious event was daunting and the stringent contest rules presented numerous challenges.

*Not challenges*—Eloisa's voice popped into her head—*opportunities.*

That little bit of reframing certainly helped.

In the past, Jeanie had coped with challenges by retreating into herself or by becoming a people pleaser, seeking approval to fill the void left by her traumatic upbringing. But something within her had shifted. Luna's recent openness and vulnerability stirred a longing in Jeanie, a longing for genuine connection with people and the courage to face her past.

Jeanie knew what she needed to do, even though it felt like a monumental step. She couldn't let her past dictate her future anymore. The quilting competition wasn't just about winning. It was an opportunity to break the chains of the past. A chance to embrace the challenges that lay ahead and open herself up to the support of the island's vibrant quilting community.

She glanced at her watch. Four thirty. She still had time before meeting Luna and Artie at the French restaurant they'd been wanting to try.

With a determined sigh, Jeanie pushed herself up from her chair. She wiped away the last of her tears and removed the bloodstained Band-Aid from her thumb and applied a fresh one. She changed her clothes for dinner and slipped on her shoes, her heart racing with a mixture of excitement and trepidation.

Leaving the B&B behind, she walked purposefully toward the soft, inviting hum of Crafters' Corner. With each step, Jeanie felt a weight lift from her shoulders. She was ready to join the circle, to share her passion for quilting, and most importantly, to let go of the painful past that had held her captive for so many years.

Inside the quilt shop Eloisa, Dot, Vivian, and Clare were the only ones around the circular table. They were drinking tea and eating cookies instead of quilting.

"Hello!" Eloisa waved an exuberant hand. "Come join us, Jeanie."

Tentatively, Jeanie took a seat beside the island's owner.

Today, Vivian had draped herself in a pink kimono depicting scarlet dancing dragons, her blond hair styled in a 1960s beehive bouffant. She grinned, revealing the gap between her front teeth, as she poured tea into mismatched teacups.

Dot wore a sunshine-yellow tunic with embroidered daisies over zebra-striped palazzo pants. Her short iron-gray curls were adorned with tiny butterfly clips, and earrings in the shape of lightning bolts nestled in her earlobes.

Clare was outfitted in a paisley print minidress of hot beige, green, and orange over forest-green leggings. Heavy eye makeup gave her an exotic look. These colorful women were delightfully eccentric, and Jeanie wished she could spend more time getting to know them.

Dot studied Jeanie for so long, she had to force herself not to squirm. "Are you all right, dear?"

This was her chance. Her time to open up and tell these kind women what was on her mind.

She hesitated, so afraid of being vulnerable, a lump forming in her throat. "I . . . I've been better," she admitted, her voice barely above a whisper. She felt like a bird with a broken wing, newly healed but unsure if she could fly again.

But the warmth in the women's eyes encouraged her to continue. "I've been struggling . . . with the competition and connecting to people."

Eloisa reached over, her hand a reassuring weight on Jeanie's. "We've all been there, dear. Quilting isn't just about stitches and patterns. It's about mending what's torn inside of us too."

"Oh, for sure," Vivian said. "We've all got stories of missteps and mistakes. We're human after all. Sharing our tales is what sews us together."

Jeanie smiled tentatively, touched by their warmth and camaraderie. "I'd like that," she said, battling back her worry with hope. "To quilt with you and share stories."

The women put up the tea and cookies and took out their quilting materials, and Jeanie's heart fluttered. Yes, she yearned for connection, for friendship, but the scars of her past and the shadow of her strained relationship with her daughter lingered.

Eloisa gave her a knowing look. "Remember, Jeanie, quilting doesn't mean you need to have it all figured out. It's a journey, with ups and downs. We're here for you, in stitches and in hitches."

As they quilted, Jeanie's thoughts drifted to the competition. It loomed over her, a symbol of aspirations and doubt. Could she really stand among these talented quilters? Could she open up to these women, share her inner world that she had so meticulously stitched shut over the years?

Dot, with her keen eye, murmured, "The first stitch is the hardest, Jeanie, but every stitch after that gets a little easier. It's okay to be scared. It's okay to doubt. That's part of the beauty of creating something together, of building friendships."

Their unconditional acceptance of her touched Jeanie's soul and she continued to quilt, her hands slowly finding their rhythm.

Clare told a heartwarming story about her grandson and everyone else joined in with stories of their own. The conversation around Jeanie was a comforting hum, but deep down, she knew she wasn't quite there yet.

She lingered on the threshold, peering into a world of possibility, of healing, and of new connections. But stepping through that door would require more than just a willingness to stitch together pieces of fabric. Bravery needed to be her calling card and speaking up for herself and what she wanted.

This lovely moment with her new friends wasn't a neat conclusion of her struggles, but rather the beginning of a new, complex journey. A journey of self-discovery, of mending old wounds, and maybe, just maybe, of finding true friendship when she least expected it.

# Chapter 26
## *Artemis*

*"Young hearts are like wet clay, easier to shape than to mend. But remember, even a twisted pot can hold a beautiful flower."*
—*Eloisa Hobby*

Artie slouched lower in the wicker chair, glaring at her mother and Paul, who were making googly eyes at each other across the lacquered table. She wanted to grab her butter knife and gouge her own eyes out. This dinner party at Chez Snooty was turning into a total disaster.

Mom and Paul had just broken the news that they'd been high school sweethearts, and they were dating again. Not that Artie hadn't gotten a clue when she'd seen them smooching up a storm in broad daylight.

That cut deep for two reasons. One, Dad had only been dead a little over a year, how could Mom move on so fast? And two, that meant if Paul married her mother, Orion, the betrayer, would be her stepsister.

Artie couldn't just sit by and let that go down without doing something.

Sure, on the surface, Paul seemed like an okay dude—rocking the handsome gardener thing with his tousled hair and awesome tan. But no one could ever replace Artie's dad. She would rather live in a cardboard box underneath a bridge in Julep with nothing but grackles and stray dogs for company than accept this man worming his way into their lives.

Pure burning jealousy motivated her. She wanted her mother—and Orion—all to herself. When she caught her mom sucking face with Paul, it made her want to puke up her guts right on his too-cool-for-school deck shoes. The last thing she needed was more upheaval in her life. Hadn't she been through enough crap this year?

She slid a glance over at Orion, who sat hunched, slathering butter on a chunk of sourdough bread. She hadn't met Artie's gaze since the girl and her dad walked into the restaurant and joined them at their table.

A fresh punch of jealousy hit her. Mom had a boyfriend and Orion apparently had a friend she liked a lot more than she liked Artie.

Where did that leave her?

First her dad was murdered, crushing Artie's world. Then their finances imploded because Dad had gambled away all their money and they lost the house, forcing the move from Dallas to Nowheresville, Texas.

*Great plan, Mom.*

And now, to add flaming insult to already devastating injury, her mom was suddenly all snuggly with her high school sweetheart who'd reappeared out of the woodwork. Heck no. Not on Artie's watch. This train needed derailing ASAP before it ever left the station.

But major conflicts stood in Artie's way, threatening her kinetic plan of romance demolition.

First, Paul and her mom were clearly obsessed with each other, making it nearly impossible to break their tractor-beam connection. They kept gazing into each other's eyes, like they were the leads in some nerdy rom-com, and "accidentally" brushing hands like teenagers. Barf-o-rama.

Heart emojis practically blinked above their heads.

She had to do something fast to smash apart Paul and her mom's disturbing romantic entanglement before Artie needed dental repair from the saccharine sweetness rotting her teeth.

Gran wasn't helping. Tonight, she was distracted and weirdly checked out, staring off into space and giving monosyllabic answers. She was usually Artie's partner in crime, but tonight Gran seemed preoccupied, leaving Artie without a wingwoman.

The waiter brought a plate of escargot drowning in garlic butter. "A complimentary appetizer from the chef."

Artie made a dramatic gagging sound. "Snails? Are you freaking kidding me right now? That's straight-up nasty!"

"Artemis," her mother said and sent her a scathing glare. "Please keep your negative opinions to yourself. We're having a nice dinner."

"Escargot is considered a delicacy in France," said Paul, an encouraging smile on his face.

*Gak.* She didn't need this guy on her side.

"Whatever. It's the same bugs that get squashed by car tires in our driveway." Artie made a show of pushing the escargot as far away from her as her arm would reach, sliding the appetizer plate in front of Orion.

Orion scooped up an escargot with the serving spoon, pulled it from the shell with a tiny fork, and popped it into her mouth. She locked eyes with Artie as if challenging her and chewed. "*Mmm,* snails in garlic butter. Yummy."

Well, that sort of deflated Artie's whole schtick.

The main course arrived, and Paul and Mom were talking about when they were teenagers. Ancient history. Who cared?

"Remember when we went swimming at Miller's Pond in the moonlight?" Mom gazed into Paul's eyes.

From the cat-that-ate-the-canary look on his face, Artie just *knew* they'd gone skinny-dipping. She gagged.

"Honey, are you okay?" Mom asked.

*Hells to the no, woman. You're flaunting this guy in my face.*

Artie shot a look at Gran, who was cutting her chicken into itty-bitty little pieces. What was up with her? She swung her back to Mom, who was staring at Paul like he was crème brûlée and she couldn't wait to devour him.

Stealthily, Artie grabbed the glass saltshaker and dumped a heaping portion onto her mom's food when she wasn't looking.

But as soon as she did it, she felt like a childish brat. Okay, she was mad, but that didn't mean she got to take it out on other people.

Yikes, she needed to stop her mother from eating the overly salted food. What was wrong with her?

Orion caught Artie's gaze. *What did you do?* she mouthed silently across the table, her eyes narrowing.

Artie winced. She hated that Orion seemed peeved with her. But hey, she was peeved with Orion and glared back.

Orion shook her head and curled her lips in disgust.

Artie felt as if the girl had punched her in the stomach. Flummoxed, Artie flung her arm, about to say something profound that needed gestures for effect, but she accidentally knocked her glass of cola off the table.

It hit the floor and exploded in a shower of fizzy caramel liquid, splattering nearby diners.

Orion glared at her.

Artie cringed. Knocking the glass over hadn't been deliberate, but it probably looked that way to Orion.

The couple at the next table, dressed to the nines and clearly fancying themselves the hottest stuff in town, glowered at her too as they dabbed at the soda splashes dotting their designer clothes.

"Artemis Kathleen, what has gotten into you tonight? Apologize this instant, young lady," Mom said.

"I didn't mean to do it," Artie mumbled.

"It doesn't matter. You're amped up and out of control. Apologize to these nice folks . . ." Mom waved at the cola-drenched diners patting themselves dry. "And clean up your mess."

Feeling like the biggest jerk possible, Artie grabbed her napkin and started soaking up the spill while apologizing profusely to the people whose meal she ruined.

Paul leaped into action, asking the server for a roll of paper towels, helping Artie dab away the soda, reassuring her that accidents happened. He was being so nice, which made her feel even worse.

What *was* wrong with her?

Looking embarrassed over Artie's stunt, Mom joined in the cleanup, along with Gran and Orion.

Okay, this hadn't been her intention, but they were working together to fix what Artie had broken as if they were a real family.

She and Orion were underneath the table, wiping sticky liquid off the floor. Orion leaned in and rasped, "Whatever you're up to, knock it off, this isn't cool!"

"You're okay with this?" With her thumb, Artie pointed toward the table.

"What?"

"Your dad and my mom, acting like horny teenagers."

Orion shook her head and looked as if Artie was the most pitiful thing she'd ever seen. "You've got issues, girl. Sort yourself out."

With that, she wadded up the cola-stained paper towels and slid away.

Artie too ducked from beneath the table and hopped to her feet. Everyone else had finished cleaning up and retaken their seats.

They were all staring at Artie.

"Sorry," she said.

Paul smiled. "Let's just enjoy our food."

They went back to their meal. Her mother twirled pasta on her fork. The pasta Artie had laced with salt.

"Mom," she said. "Don't eat that."

Her mother paused, the fork halfway to her mouth. "Why not?"

"I dumped salt all over it when you weren't looking," she confessed.

Everyone stared at her again.

With a pinched expression on her face, her mother set down her fork. "Why would you do that?"

*Because I'm an asshole.*

"She's mad that you guys are dating," Orion said.

Mom studied her. "Artie, is that true?"

"Not mad exactly." Artie shrugged and stared down at her plate, unable to meet her mother's hurt gaze.

"What exactly?" Mom prodded.

*Gak.* She didn't want to discuss this in front of everyone.

"Artie?"

She raised her head to see Paul lightly put his hand on Mom's shoulder.

"Maybe now's not the time, Moon—er . . . Luna," he said.

Oh great! They had pet names for each other already.

"It's all right." Artie lifted her chin and met Paul's gaze with a challenging stare. "I can speak for myself."

"Please do," he said, looking amused.

His amusement raised her hackles. Then she remembered what Eloisa had told her in Prism Pavilion and breathed the way the quirky older woman had taught her. Almost immediately, she felt her anger ebb. Dang, she should have tried that sooner.

Everyone at the table waited, watching her.

Okay, she started this. Time to finish it.

"Things are changing too fast," Artie said. "I mean my dad died, we lost all our money, had to sell the house and move in with Gran, now Gran's about to lose her house and we ended up on this weird purple island where Mom runs into her high school sweetheart. It's surreal."

Paul and Mom exchanged glances. Artie couldn't read the expression they passed to each other, but it was an identical look. As if they could read each other's thoughts.

"It feels like nothing lasts. You know?" To Artie's horror, her voice cracked with raw emotion.

"Nothing does last," Orion said, her bleak words blunt as a hammer. "The sooner you realize that and be grateful for what you do have, the happier you'll be."

Well, she didn't need a lecture from Miss Holier Than Thou Orion, thank you very much.

"Orion," Paul said. "Artie's hurting. Let's give her some emotional support."

"Whatever," Orion said. "I have to use the bathroom." She got up and left the dining area.

Artie didn't miss seeing Paul reach for her mother's hand underneath the table and she gave it to him. Comforting each other over their ornery kids?

"May I be excused?" Artie asked.

"Yes," Mom said. "I want you to know I'm so proud of you for opening up and making yourself emotionally vulnerable. That's a challenging thing to do, even for grown-ups."

"Thanks," she mumbled. Her mother's soothing words warmed her, but being vulnerable was hard work. Ducking her head, Artie hopped up and followed Orion into the restroom.

\* \* \*

Orion stood rigid at the sink, her arms crossed tightly over her chest, shoulders tense, eyes narrowed to slits. "What do you want?"

"Can we talk?" Artie shifted her weight and stared at the floor, struggling to put her conflicted feelings into words. She didn't do vulnerability and yet that's what this required.

"Free country. I can't control your mouth."

"I'm confused," Artie said, being honest and putting her feelings out there. This wasn't easy for her.

Music piped in through the sound system playing on a low volume. It was the same Grateful Dead song that had been playing in Prism Pavilion about tossing pebbles into still waters and causing ripples.

Was it a sign she should drop this line of questioning and just leave Orion alone? The weird song was both uplifting and sad at once.

"About?"

"You."

"What about me?" Orion's eyebrow quirked up as she stared Artie down.

"Why the whiplash? One day you're running hot and the next day cold. One day you like me and the next . . ." Artie trailed off with a shrug.

"Like *you're* not running hot and cold?" Orion threw her

hands in the air and looked exasperated. "It's a little psychotic. What gives?"

Artie exhaled. They were at the truth of it now. Scary as quicksand. "I like the idea of us being sisters, but since I saw them kissing at the lighthouse, I freaked out. I've never seen my mom kiss anyone but my dad."

Orion's face softened. She uncrossed her arms and stepped closer. "I understand. You're still grieving your father."

"I know." Artie hung her head. "But I'm supposed to be the strong one in the family."

"Being strong means being brave enough to admit when you're not okay. Give your mom a chance, doofus."

Artie angled Orion a sidelong glance. "How did you get so smart?"

Orion quirked up one corner of her mouth. "Being raised on Hobby Island with a bevy of aunties. I have privileges most people don't, and I'm darn grateful for them."

"If being brave means admitting you're struggling and can't deal, there's something I need to tell you."

"What's that?"

Artie wanted to tell Orion about being jealous over Heart-Shaped Eyewear Girl, but she didn't think the women's restroom at La Maison du Chat Noir was the place.

*Or you're just too cowardly to come right out and say it.*

"You don't have to tell me anything, Artie, unless you really want to." Orion didn't pressure her. She just waited.

*No more pussyfooting. Just spit it out.*

"I saw you with that girl."

Orion frowned in thought. "Um, okay. What girl was that?"

"How many girls do you share milkshakes with?"

"Ahh, you saw me with Suki." Orion nodded.

"I got jealous. It was stupid. I know it. But we had such an immediate connection and when I saw you looking so cozy with that girl . . . I just . . . well, my feelings got hurt."

Orion rubbed a palm over her mouth. "You really want to know why *I* didn't want my dad to date your mom?"

Artie nodded and watched the muscles in Orion's jaw clench. Her friend was struggling with something too. "You don't have to tell me anything you don't want to."

Having her advice reflected back to her brought a brief smile to Orion's face. "You were brave enough to be honest with me, so here goes." She took a deep breath and locked gazes with Artie. "I didn't want my dad to hook up with your mom because if things work out and they get married, we'd be sisters."

"I know! You don't think that would be wonderful?"

"No."

"Why not?"

"Because I have feelings for you."

Earnestness pushed through Artie. "I have feelings for you too."

Orion shook her head. "Not these kinds of feelings. Not sisterly friendship feelings."

"Oh . . ." Artie felt her eyes widen as it dawned on her what Orion was saying. "*Oh.*"

"Yeah." Orion studied her, gauging Artie's reaction.

"Wow. Um . . ." Artie pressed her palm to her forehead. "I'm not . . . I don't . . . I like guys."

"I know." Orion sounded resigned and looked a little sad. "That's why I called Suki. I needed someone to talk to who understood."

"Does your dad know you're . . ." Artie caught her breath.

"Gay? It's okay to say the word."

"I know, I know. I just . . . um . . ."

"Of course my dad knows. I tell him everything."

"So, he's cool?"

"My dad loves me, no matter what, and he accepts me for who I am."

"That's good. That's great." Artie's voice came out too high. She was blowing this. The last thing in the world she wanted was to hurt Orion.

"So, you see, I hoped I might be your first kiss." Orion shrugged sheepishly. "Just a little fantasy that got dispelled, that's all. I'm over it."

"Orion?"

"Yeah?"

"I don't know what's going to happen between our parents, but I can tell you one thing."

"What's that?"

"Having you as my sister? I should be so lucky. It would be a dream come true."

"Guess we'll just have to wait and see how things shake out between the folks, huh?"

"Yeah."

"So maybe no more sabotage, okay? Let them figure out their own romance."

"Agreed."

"Come on, let's get back before they get nosy and stick their heads in here." Then Orion draped an arm across Artie's shoulders and led her back to the dining room.

# Chapter 27

## *Luna*

*"In each stitch, a healing; in every thread, a connection. Our circle crafts wholeness from brokenness."*

—*Eloisa Hobby*

The following day, as the sun dipped in the sky, it cast a golden glow over the quad where Luna found herself wandering, lost in thought. Jeanie was quilting at the quilt shop and Artie was working on her art project with Orion. The air was filled with the mingled scents of sea salt and blooming flowers, typical of the island's enchanting aroma.

"Are you going to the healing circle tonight?" Paul's voice cut through her reverie as he approached, pulling off his gloves stained with soil from his afternoon in the gardens.

Luna raised an eyebrow. "Oh, please don't tell me you believe in that too."

"Of course I do. It's amazing. And Eloisa doesn't put the healing circle on very often," Paul said.

"What's the occasion?" she asked, more to satisfy her curiosity than actual interest.

"Whenever we get guests who seem to need a little extra help, she'll have a circle. The island talks to Eloisa and tells her what's best for the collective," he explained, reaching over to brush a drifting jacaranda flower from her hair.

Her scalp tingled from his touch. "Now that sounds really woo-woo."

"Hey, I don't question Eloisa's methods. I've seen too many good things come from this island."

"Do you attend the healing circles?"

"Absolutely. I never miss one if I can help it. I feel so good afterward. It's like a magical tonic. Orion will be there too, and I think Artie plans on going."

"Really?"

"Yeah. You should come."

"It's not really my thing." Luna stuck her hands in her pants pockets.

"Okay, suit yourself. But if you change your mind, we'll be in Prism Pavilion at nine. Wear something loose and comfortable." He leaned in, planting a kiss on her cheek that left a lingering warmth, then turned back to his gardening.

*  *  *

Luna hesitated in the dark outside Prism Pavilion, watching people go inside, many wearing pajamas and most carrying pillows and blankets. This was getting weirder by the minute.

She was right. This wasn't her thing.

But Paul endorsed it.

The ocean breeze gusted over her, and although Luna wrapped her arms tightly around herself, there was a palpable warmth emanating from the group that intrigued her. The soft glow of lanterns hung from the trees, casting a gentle light over the faces of the attendees as they entered, their expressions a blend of serenity and anticipation.

She was both intrigued and put off.

Creeping closer, she peered through the glass walls, watching as people made pallets on the floor with their pillows and blankets. Paul had told her to wear comfy clothes and she'd come in loose-fitting lounge pants and a T-shirt, but he'd said nothing about bringing bed linens.

The silvery light of the moon cast a tranquil glow over the proceedings.

"Are you coming in, my dear?" Eloisa's sweet voice came out of the darkness behind her.

Luna jumped.

"Goodness, I didn't mean to startle you. We're about to begin if you want to come in."

"Um . . . I don't know." Luna backed up and tightened her grip around herself.

Eloisa held out a hand. "You can always leave if it doesn't suit you."

For so many years she felt isolated, alone, but now, here was someone reaching out to her, and she was isolating herself by holding back.

"Your mother and daughter are inside." Eloisa's smile was tender, welcoming as always.

Eloisa gestured and Luna peered through the glass, saw the backs of Jeanie's and Artie's heads. "Paul and Orion too."

"All right," she said. "I'll give it a try."

Eloisa ushered her inside and Luna took an empty spot beside her mother, who was sitting cross-legged on a cushion, snuggled with Artie in the quilt Jeanie had brought from home. Candles flickered in the room, casting long shadows.

Some people lay in the center of the circle on a bed of pillows, their faces tranquil, almost ethereal, under the celestial tapestry in the moonlight spilling through the windows and reflecting off the prisms hanging from the ceiling. There were a few whispers from the attendees, but most people were quiet, settling in.

In a rainbow-colored caftan, Eloisa took a seat on the outside of the circle.

Someone sat beside Luna, and she turned to see Paul.

"Hey," he whispered. "Glad you could make it."

"What have you gotten me into?" she whispered back.

"It's not what you think." His presence was a comfort. His eyes, bright with a faith she didn't yet understand, encouraging her to open her heart to the experience.

The air seemed to strum with a powerful energy, as if the very atmosphere of the island was alive with ancient wisdom. Luna felt a stir of curiosity, mingling with her reluctance.

Eloisa welcomed everyone and thanked them for coming. "A healing circle," she explained, "is when a group of people gather with a clear intention of personal healing. We form a circle because it represents life's continuation with no beginning and no end. This space has been purified with sage. Thank you, Paul, and Orion, for doing that."

People murmured thank-yous and Paul reached over to take Luna's hand and squeeze it. She smiled at him.

"Those of us sitting on the outside of the circle will chant a blessing to those on the inside of the circle. Those inside the circle, when you are filled up with blessings, come out of the circle and tag someone to take your place. We'll continue until everyone has been blessed with the energy of the group."

Luna shot Paul a panicked look.

"It's okay," he said. "You're safe. Trust that."

"This is a huge leap of faith for me."

"I know." His smile filled with pride for her bravery.

"Paul," Eloisa said. "Would you like to start the chant?"

Paul nodded. "Everyone seated in the circle join hands. Those lying inside, close your eyes and relax."

Jeanie took Luna's hand on her other side. Her skin was cool and soft.

Paul's deep voice rang out in the glass room. "May the light within you awaken. May your heart find peace. May your spirit be renewed, and your burdens released."

Eloisa joined in with him and soon the others did too, forming a steady looping chorus of "May the light within you awaken. May your heart find peace. May your spirit be renewed, and your burdens released."

As they chanted, people inside the circle started coming out. Touching people on the outside of the circle and switching places with them. Orion, who'd been in the center of the circle, touched Artie, who skipped into the middle.

Sharon touched Jeanie.

Nanette touched Isabelle.

The blessings continued. One by one people came and went. At first, Luna was anxious about going in, but as more time passed with no one touching her shoulder, she started to feel left out.

Dot got up and tapped Paul's shoulder and he went in.

Clare came out and Eloisa went in.

Gosh, wasn't anyone going to pick her?

Finally, Artie left the inner circle and tapped Luna's shoulder. "It's awesome, Mom," she whispered.

Silently, Luna stepped forward with grace, her footsteps light. Lying down on the soft pillows next to Paul, she closed her eyes as the murmur of blessings swirled around her, enveloping her in a cocoon of sound and warmth.

At first, she felt nothing but the slight pressure of the night air and the distant echo of waves against the shore. But slowly, as the words of blessing grew louder and more heartfelt, a warmth began to spread through her. It was as if each word were a droplet of light, seeping into her pores, easing the knots of her doubts and fears.

Tears welled up unbidden in Luna's eyes. The emotions caught her by surprise—a mix of relief, joy, and a profound sense of connection to something larger than herself. She opened her eyes to the sky above the transparent ceiling, where the stars seemed to dance in approval, their light reflecting in her tear-filled eyes.

The chanted blessings went on and on. Paul left the circle and Vivian took his place. Feeling filled up, Luna left the center with a newfound lightness. It was as if a weight had been lifted from her shoulders. She reached out, almost instinctively, to tap a young man on the shoulder, inviting him to experience the healing she had just felt. Her touch was gentle.

She rejoined the circle and caught Paul's eye, a wordless *thank you* in her gaze. His smile was knowing, a silent acknowledgment of the journey she had just undertaken.

Eloisa's voice, a soothing balm, continued to guide the ceremony, but Luna was already transformed, her skepticism replaced with an inner tranquility she couldn't quite explain. The night air, once cool, now embraced her with a warm, comforting hug.

It might be weird. It might be awkward. But darn it, this healing circle was transformative.

In that moment, Luna understood the true magic of the island. It wasn't just in the healing circle or the ritual chant. It was in the connection of hearts and souls, gathered beneath the moonlit prisms, bonded in a moment of peace and unity.

# Chapter 28
## *Luna*

*"Love is the golden thread in life's loom, making every tapestry a masterpiece."*

—*Eloisa Hobby*

After the healing circle, everything shifted for Luna and a contentment settled over her unlike anything she ever experienced. The next six weeks skipped by, strung together by one joyous moment after another. Not just for her but for Jeanie and Artie too.

Artie and Orion hung out together as often as possible, working on their art project. The dustup at the restaurant was forgiven and forgotten.

At Paul's urging, Luna loosened her rules and allowed her daughter to go night beachcombing with Orion, just as long as they both had walkie-talkies to keep in contact with Paul.

The girls grew as close as sisters, confiding their secrets in each other and reveling in summer activities. They went surfing and parasailing and scuba diving and kayaking. Each night, Artie recounted her day to Luna and Jeanie, concluding with "Best day ever!"

Jeanie spent her days at the quilt shop, working on Luna's design and hanging out with the quilters. Whenever she took a break from quilting, she and Sharon grew closer over spa treatments, mojitos at the tiki bar, and trips to the island's attractions.

Luna no longer missed cell phones, and, in fact, she was enjoying the peacefulness of being disconnected from constant streams of information. She grew more relaxed and felt herself slowing down to the island's natural rhythms. There was nowhere to rush off to. Nothing to do. Nowhere to be except on this laid-back island.

While Paul worked, she spent her days sketching, resurrecting the art skills she thought long buried. Paul would show up with a picnic lunch or they'd eat at the tiki bar and watch the ocean. They met in the mornings for coffee and pastries at Breaking Bread and took a leisurely beach stroll hand in hand most nights. Often, he surprised Luna with bouquets of exotic island flowers, and they would sneak kisses whenever they could.

Once, Paul cooked a spaghetti dinner for Luna, Jeanie, and the girls, making his mother's secret marinara recipe. They ate alfresco while sharing their day with one another. Later, they played charades until the sun dipped low and then watched a movie on Paul's outdoor screen.

Together, Paul and Luna took things one step at a time and did not rush physical intimacy—although there was lots of hugging and kissing, teasing and laughing. Twice, on Paul's day off, they read books in side-by-side hammocks on the beach. Afterward, they wandered to the dock to watch the sunset with other lovebirds.

In the circle of Paul's strong arms, Luna felt her fears of being abandoned and left without support that had dogged her since childhood slowly start to melt.

Her heart opened to him the way it hadn't been open when they were teens. She didn't know what was different. Perhaps it was the magic of Hobby Island. Perhaps it was Paul's laid-back ease, a man now comfortable in his own skin. Perhaps she was healing her old wounds and making space for new love in her life.

Most likely all three.

She couldn't shake the feeling that their meeting on Hobby Island was fated somehow. He'd appeared in her life again, right when she needed him most. Not that she wanted him to rescue her. Far from it. She wanted them to be on equal footing, each helping the other, but responsible for their individual growth. No, what Paul gave her was the gift of self-forgiveness and she owed him a deep debt of gratitude. Making amends with him was part of her healing journey, but she had to walk the path alone.

Then on Saturday night, the last weekend before the competition, Vivian, Clare, and Dot threw a bon voyage slumber party for the teenage girls on the island. Orion and Artie chattered about it nonstop. Neither had ever attended a big slumber party, and they eagerly awaited the planned activities—from Truth or Dare to campfire s'mores to pillow fights.

Paul dropped Orion off at the Nestled Inn and picked Luna up for dinner.

"I fear I won't get a wink of sleep with all that giggling and karaoke going on at the Nestled Inn." Laughing, Luna shook her head as she climbed into his golf cart.

"Spend the night at my house," Paul said.

Luna lost her breath. "Are you suggesting . . ."

"Only if you're ready. You can sleep in Orion's room if you're not."

"Oh, I can't begin to tell you how ready I am."

His eyes lit up. "Do you want to skip the dinner reservation? I have sandwich fixings at the house."

"Yes, please. Let me run and get an overnight bag."

"Are you going to tell Artie where you'll be?"

"She'll be so busy with the slumber party that I doubt she'll know I'm gone. If she asks, I won't lie, but there's no reason to volunteer information about my love life. Having boundaries is a good thing. And Mom will be there if she needs anything."

"Hot dog," Paul said. "I feel like the luckiest man alive!"

* * *

She went back for her bag. Artie was having a blast with the others, too busy to realize Luna wouldn't be sleeping at the B&B that night. When Luna told her goodbye, Artie barely let her kiss her cheek.

"Bye, Mom. Later." Artie took off.

"I'll run interference," Jeanie whispered. "Don't worry about a thing. You go enjoy your night with Paul."

"Thanks, Mom." She gave Jeanie a hug. Things had improved enormously between them since their shared cry at the beach. It was Luna's greatest hope that they could solidify the foundation of their relationship and keep growing and healing together.

A grin spread across Luna's face in the darkness, pulse picking up speed. Reuniting with Paul, her long-lost high school sweetheart, after twenty-two years apart, kicked her anticipation into overdrive. She was so ready for whatever magic this night held in store.

One thing was certain. The man still gave her Olympic-worthy butterflies. She hadn't felt this giddy and breathless since that day in his cabana.

Luna fanned herself, inner temperature rising. Whether the night brought fireworks or a deepening of their connection, she planned to savor every second with Paul. It wasn't every day a woman got a second chance to rewrite history. She hoped she didn't ruin it.

As they got out of the golf cart, Paul took her hand and led her to his cozy bungalow cottage. The white wooden porch swing swayed in the breeze, chain creaking softly, and the honeysuckle growing along the fence filled the air with sweetness.

At the front door, Luna hesitated. No turning back once she crossed this threshold.

Paul waited, his eyes trained on her face, still holding on to her hand. "No rush, Moonbeam. No pressure. I'll wait a lifetime for you if necessary. Do you want to return to the B&B?"

"No."

The moment hung suspended, shimmering like moonbeams dancing on the water. Luna shimmered too, swaying in the soft glow, lost in the mojo magic.

It was straight out of a dreamy movie montage—a seaside storybook love scene on their own personal island paradise. For this one perfect instant, nothing existed except tranquility and togetherness.

It was her first time having sex with Paul in over two decades. She didn't know where this thrill ride was headed next. She tried not to project into the future. Right now, who cared? All that mattered was the way he pulled her close, kissed her like a starving man, and then smiled like she was the most beautiful creature he'd ever seen.

Welcome to make-out city, population: two. Woo! This night had taken a delightful turn from PG to NC-17. And Luna planned to enjoy every steamy second of this blissful pit stop with her sexy flame before life got real again.

Inside the house, though, she had another attack of awkwardness, just as she had the first time he'd brought her here. She felt a lot less emotionally messy now than she had then, but she was still a work in progress. Paul just seemed so very perfect. Was she good enough for him?

"Hungry?" he asked, heading for the kitchen area. "I've got turkey, ham, or roast beef."

"Wow, lots of choices."

"What can I say? We're a sandwich family. Or if you're in a veggie mood, I can make us caprese sandwiches."

"Caprese sounds great."

"On it."

"Can I help?"

"No, you're the guest." He got out the panini press from underneath the counter and plugged it in to heat. He gathered the sandwich ingredients and nodded at the barstool. "Have a seat."

Luna perched on the barstool and watched Paul drizzle the thick sourdough with extra-virgin olive oil. She felt like a virgin with him again. Was that silly? She propped her cheek in her palm and admired his strong wrists so muscular from gardening.

"What was the first plant you ever grew?" she asked.

"Gosh, that was ages ago, but I do happen to remember it because I won a Green Thumb award."

"Get out. Really? You never told me that."

"It was Mrs. Steph's second-grade class," he said, slicing a big beefsteak tomato with a serrated knife. "It was in the spring, and she had us plant seeds in tiny clay pots and grow them in the windowsill."

"What did you grow?" she asked.

He made a face. "Lima beans."

"But you don't like lima beans."

"Yuck." He stuck out his tongue. "No."

She shivered, thinking about what he might do to her with that fabulous tongue. "If you didn't like lima beans, why did you grow them?"

"Mom had a package of seeds in the drawer, and she told me to use them. I wanted to grow corn. She said I had to give up my pipe dreams. People like us had to accept whatever life handed us."

"Oh, Paul, I'm sorry that she didn't believe in you."

He shrugged and stacked mozzarella on top of the tomatoes, drizzling it with balsamic vinegar glaze. "She didn't believe in herself. How could she believe in me?"

"For all her flaws, Jeanie's always been my biggest cheerleader," Luna said. "I need to tell her how much I appreciate her support. Except for what she did to you and then pushing me toward marrying Herc. That was huge betrayal."

"She thought you'd be better off with Herc. Looking at it through her lens, I see why she believed that."

"She was wrong," Luna said, watching the steam rise from the panini press as Paul cooked their sandwiches.

"I think she knows that now."

Luna got up and walked around the bar to wrap her arms around his waist.

"Hold up," he said. "I'm manning a hot instrument."

"Mmm. I like the sound of that." She pulled his head down for a kiss.

He kissed her until the timer on the panini press dinged. "Dinner is served."

They sat side by side at the bar, eating the tangy, cheesy caprese sandwich, crunching potato chips, and washing it down with iced tea.

"Where do you see yourself in ten years?" Why had she asked? She was inviting trouble. She told herself she was just going to enjoy the evening, no expectations.

"Gardening on Hobby Island," he said. "If Eloisa will still have me."

"Even after Orion is gone? No plans of resurrecting old dreams?"

"No. Not for a second. You couldn't pay me enough to rejoin the rat race. I have it made here. I love what I do. I want for nothing. My bank account is healthy. Julie had a large life insurance policy, and I invested the money well. While I loved the military, I honestly love gardening more."

"Wow," Luna said. "I'm jealous. You're set."

"What will your future look like?" he asked. "Back to Dallas?"

"Oh no. I'm over that."

"Julep?"

"No, no. Julep is temporary until I get my life sorted."

He traced his finger over her hand and stared deeply into her eyes. "Where then?"

"Honestly, I don't know. Maybe one of my kids will get married and raise babies and I can live near them and babysit."

"That sounds nice." His voice was low. "No big art career dreams for you?"

Luna gave a little laugh. "Oh, Paul, I have no money. No credit. I'm lucky if I can buy a candy bar on what I have left after Herc lost our life savings." She paused. "If I did have the money to pursue my art, what would you think about that?"

"Me?" His gaze never left her face. "I would be thrilled for you."

"Would it—" She broke off, hopped off the barstool, and started clearing their plates.

"Would it what?"

"It's moot." She hunched her shoulders and walked around the counter to rinse the dishes in the sink. "I can't afford to go after my art dreams. I've still got Artie in high school for another two years."

He came to stand beside her at the sink and put his hand on her wrist. "Luna."

She looked up at him, heart pounding. "Yes?"

"I'm going to go brush my teeth now," he said. "You might want to do the same."

"Hmm, are you saying . . ."

"The night is young."

"What if we're not compatible anymore?"

His gaze searched her face. "After those red-hot kisses we've shared these past weeks? I'm not the least bit worried."

"I just don't want you to feel obligated."

"Obligated? For what?" One corner of his mouth quirked up in an endearing grin.

"A future together."

"What if that's what I want?"

She bit her bottom lip. "Then maybe we shouldn't do this."

"Moonbeam, are you telling me the feelings I'm having for you are one-sided? Because that's not the message I've been getting from you."

She shook her head. "No, they're not one-sided."

"All right then." His curls flopped rakishly across his forehead. "Just gonna brush the old chompers and I'll be right back."

\* \* \*

They ended up in the cabana again, curtains drawn back so they could stare up at the stars. Luna smiled, remembering her previous visit to the cabana.

Curled up next to each other, their legs entwined, her head on his chest, they named the constellations the same way they'd done in the back of Paul's truck the last time they had made love twenty-two years ago.

Nothing felt righter than this moment.

"There's the Big Dipper." Luna pointed.

"Ah," Paul said. "Ursa Major."

"The bear." She growled and laughed. "Too bad we can't see Orion this late at night in the summer sky."

"There's Cassiopeia."

"We considered that as our children's names, remember?"

"I do." Paul's voice came out husky. He tucked her closer to him and kissed her forehead. "But Artemis and Orion just felt right."

"They're wonderful young women," Luna said. "We both got lucky."

"That we did." His fingers toyed with her hair. "There's Hercules, rich and bright, high up, hogging the night sky."

*Hercules. Hercule. Herc.*

Luna tensed, wondering why Paul had pointed out that constellation. "Are you jealous?"

"Of Herc Boudreaux? Hell yes!"

"Don't be." She drew a heart with her fingertip over his sternum.

"He got two decades with you that I missed."

"Herc and I never had the connection that you and I do. But I made the best of our marriage. We raised two great kids. I can't regret that."

"No, you can't."

"There was a stark difference between the two of you," she said.

"What was that?" Paul asked. "Besides the fact that Herc was rich and I was poor?"

"I remember when I knew I wanted you to be more than just my friend."

"When was that?" he asked. "I wanted to be more than your friend all along, but I was too afraid to say it, so I held back and waited for you to catch up."

"Really?"

"Oh yeah." His velvet voice caressed her in the star-studded night. "So when did you want more? Was it the night I wore a tight pair of jeans? Because that was on purpose."

"Don't think I didn't notice the jeans." She laughed and rolled on her side to face him. She peered into his eyes. "But that wasn't the moment I knew."

"Are you gonna keep me ignorant of my charms that got the girl?" His smile widened to his twinkling eyes.

"It was the night our astronomy class came back from the Stephen F. Austin Observatory in Nacogdoches. The school bus didn't get back to Julep until two in the morning. Everyone else just walked off the bus, got into their vehicles, and took off. But not you."

Paul frowned thoughtfully. "What did I do that so impressed you?"

"You stayed behind. You helped the driver unload the bus, and you cleaned up the debris. No one asked you. You just did it. That's when I thought, here's a guy I can count on."

"Really?"

"Yes. I thought of you every time Herc and I came home from family vacation, and he left the unpacking of the car for later. Later was always when *I* did it. I'd think, *If I were with Paul, we would do it together as soon as we got home.* No putting things off like Herc or my father."

"Oh, Moonbeam." He looked so sad it tore her heart in two pieces. "You were alone in that marriage, weren't you?"

Mutely, she nodded, but it didn't matter now. "How were things between you and Julie?"

"They were good. Then again, we were married less than two years. She was a sweet, unassuming person and I loved her." He paused, his gaze never leaving her face. "Not in the same way I loved you, but we had something."

"I'm so deeply sorry you lost her. I hate that for you and Orion."

"I was wrecked when she died. You think I've got it all together? You should have seen me back then. Single dad, changing diapers on my own. I had help, don't get me wrong, but I spiraled.

I went wild. I took care of my responsibilities but on the nights I had a babysitter?" He clenched his teeth. "I was out drinking and whoring around."

"That's understandable. You lost your wife so young." She rubbed his shoulder.

"Believe me, I was a hot mess."

She moved her hand from his shoulder to cup his cheek. "But look how you rebounded."

"Only because of Eloisa. She's a saint."

Luna felt a tug of unexpected jealousy she wasn't proud of. She pulled her hand back, curled it under her chin. Her insecurity asked, "How different am I than Julie?"

He stroked her cheek with his knuckle. "Julie didn't challenge me the way you do. She was uncomplicated."

"Oh, so I'm complicated, am I?" She smiled, trying for light-hearted. She had no right to be jealous of his late wife. None at all.

"Yes, ma'am," he said. "And I wouldn't have it any other way."

"You sure about that? I can be a handful."

"Lucky for you, I'm good with my hands." He gave a soft laugh.

She sobered, locked gazes with him. "These past few weeks have been so special to me, Paul. I can't begin to tell you how much."

"Ditto, Moonbeam." Then he drew her closer and kissed her long and sweet.

She absorbed his heat, but instead of firing her up, his kisses stoked her melancholia. "We've both lost so much."

"All the more reason to celebrate our reunion." He nibbled her bottom lip.

"I want this," she whispered.

"Me too."

Softly, she started crying.

"Wait, whoa, what's all this about?" He encircled her with both arms and kissed away her tears.

"Life's just so fleeting and precious."

"Yes, but look how much we've gained."

"I regret everything I did that hurt you."

"Shh, shh, stop beating yourself up. Just let it go." Then he scooped her to his chest, got to his feet, and carried her into the house.

They made love, not like the red-hot, randy teens they'd once been, but like mature adults who knew they'd found a precious thing to hold on to.

And their intimacy was better than ever.

# Chapter 29
## *Jeanie*

*"Trust your craft, it will never lead you astray."*

—*Eloisa Hobby*

I can't believe the summer season at Hobby Island is drawing to a close," Sharon said as she and Jeanie sat in lawn chairs watching the teens play an evening game of pool volleyball underneath the string lights at the Nestled Inn. "Next Saturday is the competition and then we all leave on the thirty-first."

They were drinking the pineapple punch Vivian had made for the sleepover, but Sharon had tipped a bit of rum into their glasses from a flask she drew from her tote.

Because of Jack's struggle with alcohol, Jeanie had never been much of a drinker, but she was on holiday and Sharon twisted her arm, saying she didn't want to drink alone. Jeanie had more drinks this summer with Sharon than she had in the whole of the past ten years. While she enjoyed relaxing with Sharon, she wouldn't continue the habit once she returned home.

But tonight, she was still on vacation and feeling mellow.

"Will you have your quilt ready for the competition in time?" Jeanie asked, watching the lightning bugs twinkle in the night.

"I think so. You?"

"All I have left is finishing the binding."

"Oh, you'll be done in no time. I'm still layering."

"If you need any help, I can pitch in when I'm done with mine."

Sharon shook her head. "I couldn't impose on you like that, Jeanie. Besides, I'm not sure it's allowed for one contestant to help another."

"There's nothing against it in the rules."

A rogue volleyball arced through the air, heading straight for them. Sharon ducked and blocked the ball before it could knock over her drink. Jeanie's reflexes kicked in. She jumped up, catching the ball in a smooth arc. With a gentle toss, she sent it spiraling back to the cheering teens in the pool.

"Thanks, Gran," Artie said, her face shiny with water droplets.

"Easy, girls. You almost beaned Sharon."

Jeanie settled back into her chair, feeling the pleasant warmth from the rum-enhanced punch. "Artie's really taken to the island, hasn't she?"

Sharon nodded, her face illuminated by the soft glow of the lights. "She's much more relaxed than when we first arrived on the island."

"We all are."

"That's Hobby Island for you."

Jeanie took another sip of her punch, the sweetness of the pineapple mixing with the slight kick of the rum.

"It's been quite a summer, hasn't it?"

"Uh-huh." Jeanie's thoughts drifted to the quilt, a symbol of her family's summer journey. "It's been an incredible experience. I feel like I've learned so much about myself, about letting go of the past and being true to who I am."

Sharon smiled, lifting her glass in a toast. "To finding ourselves."

Jeanie echoed the toast, feeling a surge of gratitude for Sharon's friendship. She had come to value their talks and Sharon's insights, even if they sometimes hit a little too close to home. Her mind flickered back to a moment earlier that summer when Sharon found her crying quietly at the beach. Without a word, Sharon had simply sat beside her, offering silent company that spoke louder than any words of comfort.

"You've been a big part of that journey for me, Sharon," Jeanie said, her voice thick with unshed tears. "I can't thank you enough."

Sharon gave an odd smile that seemed to hold a deeper meaning, but Jeanie couldn't quite read what that was. "We all need someone to help us see things in a new light. I'm glad I could be here for you."

The conversation drifted to other topics, and they continued to enjoy the evening as contentment mixed with the inevitable sadness of summer's end. Jeanie glanced at Sharon, who was now watching the volleyball game, her expression thoughtful.

Jeanie caught herself studying Sharon's profile, the soft glow of the lights casting shadows that added to her enigma. Despite their growing closeness, Sharon reminded her of a puzzle with a few key pieces missing—you could see the overall picture, but the details remained elusive.

"I just realized something," Jeanie said.

"What's that?" Sharon asked, her voice dreamy as she took another sip of rum punch.

"Even after almost two months, I don't know anything about your personal life." Whenever she asked Sharon about the past, the other woman would distract her or just ask Jeanie questions about her situation. There must be something painful there she didn't want to talk about.

Sharon shrugged. "That's because there's nothing to tell."

"Of course there is. I'm assuming you're not married since you've never mentioned a husband and you don't wear a wedding ring."

Sharon waggled her ring finger. "Free as a bird."

"Ever been married?"

"Once or twice." Sharon took a long pull of her drink.

"Which was it? Once or twice?"

Sharon laughed. "Three times. None of them stuck."

Now Jeanie was even more intrigued. "Children?"

"Nope."

"Did you ever want any?"

"Never had the opportunity."

Boy, this was like pulling teeth. "Siblings?"

"Only child."

"Like me and Luna."

"Uh-huh." The ice clinked in Sharon's glass.

"It's lonely, isn't it. Growing up without siblings."

"Never much thought about it."

Jeanie waited but Sharon didn't expound. "Are your parents still living?"

"They died when I was six. Airplane crash."

"Oh my, you're an orphan!" Jeanie's heart went out to her. No wonder she hadn't wanted to talk about her past.

"That was almost sixty years ago. I've long forgotten them."

Jeanie didn't know what was worse. Losing your parents at an early age or having abusive parents. "So you grew up in foster care?"

"Old-fashioned orphanage."

Jeanie caught her bottom lip between her teeth. "And you never got adopted?"

"I did, but it didn't take." Sharon's tone turned brittle.

"Sorry about all these questions," Jeanie said. "I didn't mean to pry. Just trying to get to know you better."

"It's fine." Sharon waved a hand, not quite meeting Jeanie's eyes. "I'm just a private person."

They sat without speaking as laughter and lively chatter flowed around them. Jeanie studied Sharon's troubled expression, realizing how little she truly knew this woman who had become her closest friend this summer.

"'Scuse me, Jeanie." Sharon got to her feet, swaying slightly. "I gotta pee."

Jeanie sipped her rum punch gone watery from the melting ice and gazed out over the shimmering pool to the spot where Sharon had disappeared inside the inn. Her friend's abrupt departure left Jeanie feeling oddly unsettled.

What had she said to cast that shadow over Sharon's face and the quaver in her voice when she excused herself?

*You and your clumsy questions*, Jeanie scolded herself. Probing into Sharon's tragic past, no wonder she made a quick exit. Some wounds never fully healed, even with time. Jeanie knew that well enough.

She pictured a young Sharon, suddenly orphaned and alone, facing a harsh world without parents to shield her. The image brought an ache to Jeanie's throat. Her own childhood had come with difficulties, but at least she had family, no matter how dysfunctional they'd been.

Jeanie longed to embrace Sharon and whisper that she didn't have to be self-reliant anymore. Not when there were those who cared deeply for her. Those who knew from experience that burdens were lighter when carried together.

She'd tell Sharon this when she returned. If only she could find the right words to help her wounded friend let down her guard. To convince Sharon that this connection they'd found was one built to last far longer than a season.

"Hey, Gran, watch this," Artie hollered from the diving board. Apparently, the volleyball game was over.

"Be care—"

She didn't get the word out before Artie did a gainer off the diving board. Jeanie sucked in her breath, overwhelmed by her granddaughter's fearlessness.

Artie broke through the water beaming.

"Amazing!" Jeanie applauded. "Good job, Art."

Sharon returned from the restroom, her steps a bit unsteady. She seemed lost in thought as she sank back into the lawn chair.

"Is everything okay?" Jeanie asked.

Sharon glanced over, flashing a faint smile that didn't reach her eyes. "Of course. Must be the rum hitting me harder than expected."

Jeanie studied her friend's pensive profile, wishing she could ease the sadness she sensed lingering beneath Sharon's usual vivaciousness. What sorrows haunted her from that childhood tragedy?

"It means so much to have a friend like you in my life," Jeanie said, leaning over to give Sharon's hand an affectionate pat. "I want you to know you never have to pretend with me."

She turned to meet Jeanie's earnest gaze, eyes glistening. She opened her mouth as if to speak but seemed to think better of it. Instead she managed a shaky smile.

"We all have chapters we'd rather keep closed," Sharon said. "But your friendship helps me see the past through gentler eyes."

Jeanie gave Sharon a hug, hoping her fierce embrace could convey what words could not—that the present was a gift not to be squandered. That judgment could be set aside for understanding.

"I'm here whenever you need me," Jeanie whispered, and she meant it with all her heart.

# Chapter 30

## *Luna*

*"Sometimes you have to unravel the yarn and start again."*
—*Eloisa Hobby*

Golden rays of sunshine peeked through the bedroom window, bathing Luna in a warm glow. After a night in Paul's loving arms, Luna felt fundamentally changed. Picking up where they left off made everything seem possible.

Smiling, she opened her eyes and strolled her fingers across the sheet to touch him. She could scarcely believe she was here.

Or their memorable night together.

"Mornin', Moonbeam." He lay on his side, facing her, his hands tucked underneath his cheek.

"Hey there, handsome."

His smile deepened as his eyes softened. "That was worth the twenty-two years' wait."

"Amen to that."

"Mint?" He reached for a tin of Altoids on the bedside table.

"Are you saying I need fresh breath?"

"Kissing *is* on my agenda."

She propped up on her pillow and took the Altoid he offered, popping the potent cinnamon mint into her mouth, not the least bit embarrassed to be naked in his bed. "How do you suppose the slumber party went?"

"My guess is that they had a terrific time and they're still slumbering."

"What time is it?" She craned her neck to see the clock on the dresser.

"Seven thirty."

"Oh yeah, they're still conked out."

"Not missing us at all . . ." He lowered his lashes and reached for her.

The landline phone next to Paul's bed jangled, startling Luna. Paul checked the caller ID. "It's Orion, so obviously we've misjudged the sleeping capacity of our teens."

She clasped a hand to her chest and reflexively started worrying. Had something happened? Were the girls okay? *Calm down. Stop imagining the worst.*

Paul answered the phone. "How's it going, Ry?"

Luna couldn't understand what Orion was saying, but she could hear the girl's excited voice. "Are they okay? Where's Artie?" Luna asked.

He shook his head and held up a finger, asking her to hold on a minute while he listened to his daughter. "That sounds like a lot of fun."

Whew. If it was fun, that meant everything was okay. Luna relaxed and sank back against the pillow. She was getting better at letting go of her fears more easily. Baby steps.

"Hang on, let me ask her." Paul put his palm against the receiver so Orion couldn't overhear their conversation.

Luna mouthed, *Me?* If Orion knew she was there, Artie had to know too. How would she handle this?

"Orion and Artie want to go rock climbing. All the girls from the slumber party are going. One of their dads is a Boy Scout troop leader and a former marine. He's got the supplies and equipment."

It showed a great deal of personal growth on Luna's part that she didn't give a knee-jerk negative reaction. "What do you think?"

"I know the girl and her father," Paul said. "They're from Everly, and the girl is in Orion's class at school."

Luna's instinct was to say no. Rock climbing sounded dangerous. "Um . . ."

"Gotta loosen the apron strings sometime, Mama Hen."

He was right, but still. "Where will this rock climbing take place? On a climbing wall in Everly?"

"Opportunity Ridge."

Outdoors. Eek. Even worse. "You mean Trouble Ridge?"

Paul put the receiver to his ear. "Artie's mom isn't sure about this."

He listened while Orion talked, then put his hand over the receiver again. "She says Dot's going along to help. How dangerous can it be if Dot can do it?"

"Dot looks like she could wrestle an alligator and tie it up in a red Christmas ribbon," Luna said. "But it does make me feel better that another adult will be there as well."

"So yes?" He sent her a coaxing grin. He lowered his tone. "Gives you and me more time alone."

She sent him a sidelong glance and playfully licked her lips.

"Besides," he said. "Dot has a satellite phone. She can call us straight from the ridge if anything goes sideways."

"Just had to say that last part, huh?"

"Honey, odds are ninety percent the worst that happens is a few skinned knees. Artie's tough. Let her have a little freedom."

It went against Luna's parenting instincts, but she didn't want her daughter to grow up fearful the way she had. If they'd been back in the real world, her automatic answer would be a solid *Over my dead body*. But this was Hobby Island, a safe and magical place. Artie would be with Orion, Dot, and a host of other people. Letting Artie be independent was so hard, but here, with Paul smiling at her confidently, it was a little easier.

"Let her go," he whispered.

"Okay, okay. Just tell them to be careful, put on sunscreen, and hydrate, hydrate, hydrate," she said.

Paul relayed the message to their daughters and Luna could hear their whoops of happiness through the phone lines. He turned to her. "They'll have a fun time. You'll see."

"Yeah?" Luna shook her head and teased, "If anything happens, I'm holding you responsible."

He dangled the phone out to her. "Wanna talk to Artie?"

"Yes." She took the phone. "Hello, kid."

"So," Artie said, "you spent the night with Paul."

Wow, they were getting right into it. "You had a sleepover. So did I."

"I think that's great." Artie giggled.

"Do you really?"

"Yeah. Paul's good for you." Artie's voice sounded a little husky. Luna hoped she wasn't coming down with something. "You smile all the time when you're with him."

"Do I?" She grinned at Paul, who leaned over to nibble her thigh.

"You do. And I know he's the only reason I'm getting to go rock climbing."

"Just be careful, okay? Wear sunscreen, watch for snakes, and—"

"I know, I know, hydrate, hydrate, hydrate."

"Love you."

"Love you too, Mom." Then she was gone, leaving the dial tone in Luna's ear.

Luna cradled the receiver in its dock and turned back to Paul, who'd draped himself artfully over the sheets, stretched out fully naked . . .

And fully erect.

*Holy firecracker!* The man was smoking hot.

"Are you—"

She didn't let him finish his sentence, covering the short distance between them and pouncing on him like they were eighteen.

"Whoa-ho!" He laughed, wrapped his arms around her, and kissed her until Luna's head spun.

If last night had been slow, sweet, and solicitous, this morning was fast-paced, spicy, and passionate.

Quickly, their desire mounted. Hearts pounded, blood heated, lust stirred. *Wow!* Fingers tickled. Pillows flew. Sheets twisted and Luna got to explore those rock-hard gardener muscles of his all over again. *Wow, wow!*

Then Paul backed off. "We better slow down if we want this to last all morning."

"Oh, yes."

He slipped under the covers and went down to her feet. Lightly, he sucked at her toes.

She giggled and wriggled away.

"Still ticklish around your toes?"

"Uh-huh."

He moved up to her ankles, licking swirly little circles with his tongue.

"So, what's your favorite flower?" she asked as Paul pressed sizzling kisses up her shin.

"Huh?" Glassy-eyed, Paul raised his head to peer at her, grinning.

"Your favorite flower. What is it?"

"That's a hard question for a gardener to answer," he said, "but I'm partial to lunaria, for obvious reasons."

"You're making that up. There's no plant called lunaria."

"What do you think all those purple flowers in the Crafters' Corner quadrangle are?" His mouth was at her knee now and she flashed back to that glorious day in the cabana when his mouth had completely wiped away her senses.

"Seriously? Those flowers are called lunaria? I thought they were called honesty plants."

"That's the common name. The scientific name is *Lunaria annua*. I think of you whenever I collect the moon-shaped seedpods for planting the next season."

"No." She couldn't believe that. "Really? You planted those flowers for me?"

"Not just you," he said. "They're purple and purple is Eloisa's favorite color and honesty is her favorite trait. By a happy coincidence, we have the same favorite flower."

"Oh, Paul." She felt her emotions overflowing again. "Tell me about the *Lunaria annua*."

"Hmm," he said, moving his mouth up her belly, planting kisses in between his words. "Because the seeds are the size of silver dollars, they've come to symbolize money, honesty, and sincerity."

She shivered against the tickle of his lips vibrating against her skin. "You don't say."

"In witchcraft, the lunaria is considered protective and keeps monsters away." His mouth went up one thigh, but instead of going where she was throbbing, he veered up to her hip bone.

Eek, he was teasing her. Dragging things out. "Well, since the plants are everywhere on Hobby Island, I think we're very safe and protected."

His body moved over hers as his wicked mouth inched to her breasts. He kneaded her breast gently, teasing the nipple with his thumb. She arched her back and closed her eyes as her body gave in to the sensations. His body was hard and tight, like a steel beam, his skin hot, and heavenly soft.

He smelled of honeysuckle and jacaranda flowers. The scent of her own arousal stalked her senses, the musky smell of love.

Paul tugged her head down for a kiss. He tasted like cinnamon Altoids and the flowers of the island, sweet as nectar. His taste was the last thing she remembered, his mouth warm and soft, like a sponge, drawing her soul into it.

"Tell me more about the lunaria," she whispered.

"When the seedpods are dried and ready to pop open, they rattle softly in the wind. It's such a soothing sound, like a lullaby. I hear them whisper *Luna, Luna, Luna*."

"So how do you plant them?" she asked, mesmerized by his voice.

"Oh, I see what you're getting at. You want a blow-by-blow account." He pressed his mouth against her belly and blew a soft raspberry.

She giggled again.

"Well," he said, "they come back from seed every year. I only had to plant them that one year."

"Just once?"

"They seed the second year. If you have the right soil and weather, which Hobby Island does. They're called biennials."

"You don't say."

He reached her breasts and tenderly touched his tongue to her.

She shuddered against him and threaded her fingers through his hair.

"These plants, they're easy to grow?"

"They're like love. The more you plant, the more they grow."

Luna's heart was pounding so hard. What Paul was doing to her nipple was driving her straight out of her mind.

He sucked lightly, then let go to speak again. "They grow thick, bushy, and healthy. It's fun for me to watch them thrive. I love watching the seeds wiggle in the wind."

"Like this?" She wiggled her hips and widened her legs. She was so ready for him. Luna pressed into his pelvis to let him know exactly how much.

"Moonbeam," he whispered.

She grasped his shoulders, sank her mouth against his neck, and nibbled. He tasted so damn good.

"That's it." His hands found her hot spot, traced her.

She let out a gasp. "More!"

He moved over her, his hardness against her softness, and then he was there. Inside of her. Her breath came out in a hot hiss.

"Oh yeah." His lips roamed freely, a cartographer mapping unknown territories. Curiosity was his compass, and she had to admit, he knew how to navigate her body.

He gently turned her onto her back, giving her a master class in the art of cultivating desire. Their gazes intertwined, a silent conversation between souls while their bodies danced in harmony. A web of sensations washed over Luna—waves of pleasure, bursts of happiness, flares of exhilaration, and peaks of bliss.

In this moment, with Paul inside her, she felt an unshakable serenity. No turmoil, no issues. She was fully present and connected to him, attuned to herself, and in sync with their mutual rhythm.

Luna wrapped her legs around Paul's waist and pulled him more deeply into her. "Now that's what I'm talking about."

In a sweaty tangle of arms and legs, they pushed each other into places they'd never touched before and when they came together, shuddered together, trembled as one, they stayed locked until they both fell sound asleep.

The sound of the phone ringing woke them up, broke them apart. Groggy, Luna pushed her bangs from her forehead, her gaze going to the clock on the dresser.

One thirty in the afternoon. How long had they been asleep, wrapped in the bliss of each other's arms?

Paul rolled over and reached for the phone.

Humming under her breath, Luna got up, the braided rug welcoming her feet in the quiet. The gentle rhythm of the ocean waves outside the open window whispered through the air, merging with the serenity of her contented hum. Everything felt so right, so perfectly aligned, as if the island affirmed her choices.

Stepping through what she assumed was the door to the bathroom, Luna halted, her heart skipping a beat. Instead of the bathroom, she was staring into a small, dimly lit cubicle. Rows of monitors flickered in the semidarkness, each screen a window into various parts of the island—Crafters' Corner, the row of B&Bs, the beach, the lighthouse, the butterfly hatchery . . .

The sight struck her like a physical blow, realization dawning painfully—Paul held secrets far deeper than she had imagined.

What was going on?

Luna turned back to him. He'd just hung up the phone and looked stunned. She was stunned too. "Paul, what is this?"

His face that before was relaxed and open was now guarded, serious. "Luna, I should have told you earlier. This is part of my work. I'm responsible for the island security. That's my primary job. I'm not just the gardener and maintenance man."

The room felt colder to Luna, the screens an invasive presence. "All this time . . . you've been watching everyone? How could you keep this from me?"

"It's complicated."

She raised both palms. She needed space and time to process this new, unsettling layer of the man she thought she knew. "I need to go."

Turning, she searched for her clothes, finding them scattered all over his bedroom. She put on her bra, concentrating on the hooks so she didn't have to think about Paul's secrecy. They'd been on the island almost two months and he'd kept this information from her.

"Luna, you need to listen to me."

"I can't. I . . . please. I need to get away from you."

"This isn't about the cameras, my job, or even you and me."

She looked up from yanking on her panties. His face was so dear, but her emotions were in free fall. He'd withheld information from her now just as he had twenty-two years ago. Vital information that changed how she thought of him.

"What is it, Paul? What's so important?"

"That phone call—"

"Yes?"

"It's about Artie." The usual steadiness in Paul's voice gave way to a tremor, a raw note of fear that Luna had never heard before. His face, usually sun-kissed and reassuring, was now pale, his forehead creased with worry.

"What's happened?" Luna's question tumbled out, her composure starting to fracture.

"She's fallen into a crevice."

The news hit Luna like a rogue wave. While her mind, honed by years of living with an alcoholic father, snapped into efficient planning, her heart, fragile and exposed, teetered dangerously close to despair.

"Is she—" She couldn't bring herself to say the awful word that flashed in her mind.

"She's alive, Luna, that's all I know." Paul stepped closer, his presence shifting from betrayer to beacon in this dark storm.

A whirlpool of emotions churned in Luna. The betrayal and hurt she felt toward Paul were distant, secondary to the piercing terror for her daughter. She nodded, her resolve as a mother overshadowing her personal turmoil.

"Take me to her. But Paul . . ." Her voice was steady, but inside she was wrecked. "This isn't over. Your secrets, everything I've just uncovered . . . we're coming back to this."

"All right." He pulled on his jeans and wrestled into his shirt. "Let's go get your girl."

# Chapter 31

## *Artemis*

*"Sometimes, the best way to be found is to hide in plain sight."*
—*Eloisa Hobby*

Well, crap-a-doodle-do," Artie muttered under her breath. Not exactly what she imagined for this day.

After a fantastic slumber party, rock climbing seemed the perfect topper to a terrific weekend, and she'd been so excited to scale Opportunity Ridge.

Turns out, not so much.

She was in a fix of her own making with no idea how to fix it. Yes, she had people around her . . . or rather, above her . . . but they seemed powerless. Not that she was blaming them. Far from it. Facts were facts.

Her happy ass was stuck between a rock and another rock.

If she hadn't been showing off her athletic skills, she wouldn't be here. Apparently, she was a natural at rock climbing, scrambling up the rock face with an amazing agility that surprised even her. The problem came when they reached a plateau. If she hadn't sprung like a spider monkey over the crevice, she wouldn't be in this fix.

She almost made the jump too. Everyone else was too scared to take it, even Orion. Artie thought the jump across the crevice was simple, as she had broad jumped almost seven feet in her PE class, doing as well as many of the boys.

But the second she was airborne, an *uh-oh* feeling came over her. She landed on her toes on the other side, at the very edge of the crevice. But gravity, that Debbie Downer, pulled at her backpack and she lost her purchase.

Orion, who was tethered to her, hollered, "Falling! Falling!" Just as the Scout leader dad had taught them to do in his tutorial. The other girls took up the cry. "Falling! Falling!"

Artie, unfortunately, couldn't stop her fall.

Orion tugged on her end of the rope and tried to yank Artie across the divide before she tumbled all the way in, but Orion simply was no match for downward momentum and Artie's heavier body weight. While Orion was able to set herself and keep from falling in, she couldn't prevent Artie from going down.

The Scout leader dad and the other girls helped anchor Orion.

Now Artie was wedged like a canned sardine, her backpack smashed hard against her back, acting as a stopper.

Which was lucky. It kept her from a full-on crash to the bottom.

Another bit of positive news. The crevice wasn't too deep. If she managed to dislodge herself and fell farther, she would only tumble about eight feet. Alarming, but survivable as long as she didn't land on her noggin. Although she could end up with broken bones.

Eh, it wouldn't be the first time she broke something.

She was a good six feet from the top and from that distance, no one could grab her hand.

Thirty minutes had passed since her descent. Artie begged them not to call her mother, but Dot, she of the satellite cell phone, insisted.

The traitor.

She was also miffed that Dot had been holding out on her about the satellite cell phone. The woman was a self-proclaimed Luddite. The hypocrite.

Dot also had the audacity to yell down at her, "See why I call it Trouble Ridge?"

*Yeah, got it.*

The sun beat down, and Artie was pretty darn thirsty, but her water bottle was in her backpack, which she could not reach, pinned in as she was.

*Sorry, Mom, can't hydrate.*

"C'mon, guys, get me out of here before my mother shows up! She'll have a literal cow." To be fair, they had tried but their efforts so far had only led to a tighter wedge.

"Too late," Orion said. "Here she comes."

Artie grimaced and braced herself.

"She's got my dad, your gran, and Eloisa with her too."

*Ahh, the circus had come to town.*

"Artie!" Her mother's panicked voice sounded above her.

"Hi, Mom."

"Are you all right?"

Well, her legs were numb, but she wouldn't bring that up. "Hunky-dory."

"How did this happen?" Mom's voice echoed through the crevice.

A shadow fell over Artie, and she craned her neck as much as she could under the circumstances and saw her mother leaning over her. "Long story. Doesn't matter. Let's work on the fix, 'kay?"

"Luna," Paul said in a kindly tone. "Please come back from the ledge. We don't want you tumbling down there with her."

The shadow disappeared and to Artie's surprise, she felt a little orphaned. Her mom would never leave her, but being trapped was freaking her out. Right now, she'd be happy as grape punch to have her mother squeeze the stuffing out of her.

"How are you doing, Pumpkin Pie?" It was Jeanie now, peering down at her. Her forward lean didn't go as far over as Mom's.

"Just hanging out, Gran. What's going on up there?"

"They've got a huddle. Don't worry, they'll get you out of there," her grandmother said.

"Could they hurry? I gotta pee."

"They have to do some figuring. Something about lines, angles, and pulleys. You know, geometry." Gran put a cheery note in her voice.

"My dad is good at mathy stuff," Orion reassured Artie.

Several minutes passed.

"Hello up there. How's the escape plan coming?" Artie asked, her legs prickling pins and needles. Her chest felt tight, and she was sick to her stomach. Ack. The last thing she needed was to barf on herself.

Her mother's face appeared again. "Hang on, sweetheart. They're figuring the best way to pull you out, don't worry!"

"Um, okay." Breathing was becoming a chore, but panic? Nah, not Artie's style. "Mom?"

"Uh-huh?"

"Can someone be afraid of depths?"

"Oh, baby. I know how that anxiety feels. We're going to get you out of there. I promise. Can you take some slow, deep breaths?"

Mom sounded calm. Too calm, really. That freaked Artie out a little. Mom got supercalm when things turned serious.

"I'm . . . tr-trying. The backpack is pressing on my lungs kinda hard."

Mom stood up and moved from the crevice. Artie heard her murmuring something urgent to someone Artie couldn't see.

More time passed.

Artie eyed the sliver of sky she could see. She'd been down here at least an hour.

Finally, Paul appeared. "We've got enough people now and we've worked things out. We're going to start pulling the rope now. Give a holler if anything feels wonky on your end."

Artie gave a half-hearted thumbs-up. Her arms were achy and so was her neck from staring up. This was nerve-racking. They tugged, and gradually she started to move, and for a glorious moment the pressure on her backpack eased.

*Yay!*

They tugged her up a few inches. It was working! Until the rope caught on a tree root growing out of the crevice wall.

"What's happened?" Paul called down.

"Tree root," Artie said. "But keep going." She wanted out of here before she had a complete meltdown.

They yanked.

The rope sawed against the tree root.

"Harder!" she yelled.

They heaved, and the rope bumped past the tree root, but then it gave a sickening crack and Artie gasped as she watched the fraying strands break. "Hurry!"

They tugged even more forcefully.

She swung wildly and tilted upside down.

"Holy shit!" she screamed, struggling to right herself. If she landed on her head, she was screwed. Squeezing her eyes tightly shut, she braced for impact.

Air whooshed past her body as she fell, and she heard her voice echoing through the crevice. "Ayeeeeeee!"

A bone-jarring crash abruptly halted her fall as pain exploded through her body. Far above, faint panicked voices called her name.

But Artie couldn't respond, the wind was knocked out of her. She focused on breathing through the agony. Now came the real test of her grit.

# Chapter 32
## *Luna*

*"In the darkest of night, a single flicker of inner light can guide you to the dawn."*

—*Eloisa Hobby*

For the first time since she lost her husband, Luna wished for Herc. If the man excelled at anything, it was emergency medicine.

She paced the emergency department waiting room. The doctor and nurses had asked her to leave the room so they could prep Artie for surgery.

For over two harrowing hours, the search and rescue team had worked to extract her tough daughter from the dark chasm. Finally, they extracted her and airlifted Artie to Everly General Hospital.

The instant Artie fell, her screams echoing from the crevice, Luna had dropped to her knees in utter agony and shouted desperately into the void. "Artie! Baby, can you hear me? It's Mom! Talk to me!"

Luna's brain was short-circuiting with a million horrible scenarios. Had she just watched her daughter fall to her death? How could she bear it? She brought her knees to her chest and rocked on her tailbone, chanting a one-word mantra.

*Please.*

Paul approached her, fear in his eyes, but she waved him away and growled, "Go back to your daughter."

Drawing a line. Yours and mine.

She was typically more sympathetic, but the situation was too overwhelming for her to avoid being harsh. If her baby was alive down in the deep, dark hole, Artie needed for her to hold it together. If Paul were to wrap comforting arms around her, she would disintegrate.

"Artie! Answer me if you can!" Luna strained to make out the faint reply that drifted up.

"M-Mom! I'm okay."

Although her daughter sounded weak, it sent waves of relief rippling through Luna. Artie was alive!

"But my leg. It hurts really bad!" Pain and fear quivered Artie's voice. "I can't move it. I . . . I think it's broken."

"Try not to move. Stay right where you are."

"There's nowhere to go."

"Just hang on, sweetie. Help is coming! The rescue team is on the way. You're going to be okay!"

Luna kept shouting encouragement, doing her best to comfort Artie throughout the long, excruciating wait. She told her daughter brave stories of rescues she heard about, making light jokes, anything she could think of to keep her daughter's spirits up.

After a while, Artie fell silent.

"You still there?" Luna asked.

"I'm here, Mom. Just tired. I need to rest."

It occurred to her then that Artie might have a concussion. She needed to stay awake. "Honey, you can't go to sleep. Stay awake, okay?"

"I'm trying."

"You're being so brave right now, sweetie. Do you remember

when you climbed the big oak tree in our backyard when you were little? How proud of yourself you were when you reached the top?"

"Yeah."

"But then you were scared to come down? I told you to take it slow, branch by branch. Despite being eight years old, you made it down all by yourself."

"I miss our house."

"I do too, honey, but it's just a place to live. Home is in your heart. And we're each other's home. Along with Gran. Wherever we are together, it's home. A house doesn't matter."

"What about Paul?"

"Don't worry about him. You hang on. We're gonna get you out of there."

"I want to be brave . . ." Artie trailed off.

"You've always been my tough girl. Just think about how we'll celebrate when you're safe. Your favorite ice cream, a movie marathon, anything you want!" Luna kept up the one-sided conversation, refusing to let her daughter feel alone down there. Artie called back periodically, her voice growing weaker.

Luna clung fiercely to the sound, letting it anchor her sanity amid the unbearable waiting. Jeanie approached her twice, but she waved off her mother's offers of water and blankets, her eyes locked on the crevice. Comfort did not exist for her now. Getting Artie out was her only priority.

Then Jeanie softly touched Luna's shoulder, and she instinctively recoiled. "Please, just go wait with the others, Mother." She didn't want to hurt Jeanie's feelings, but she simply couldn't tolerate anyone trying to make her feel better.

From the corner of her eye, she saw Paul watching her with empathetic eyes. He raised a hand and gave a sad smile. She knew he was only trying to help, but his presence made her feel crowded, almost claustrophobic, and she turned away from him. He was the one who'd convinced her to let Artie go rock climbing. She wasn't blaming him. No, she blamed herself for not listening to her gut, for letting down her guard.

For trusting him.

She knew better, and yet she'd listened to him, anyway. Damn her hide for believing in happily ever after. She'd known all along it was a stupid dream and she'd allowed herself to become enchanted by Paul and this whimsical island.

Why had she been so willing to abandon the defense mechanism that had kept her safe for forty years?

When the rescue team arrived via chopper, adrenaline coursed through Luna's veins as they rappelled down to get Artie. She wanted to jump into the crevice with them, to be with her child and comfort her.

But the rescuers told her to get out of their way, and they would handle it. Part of her thrilled to their authority, that someone in charge would take care of things, while another part of her, which found it almost impossible to trust, questioned their every move.

During the extraction process, Luna could do nothing but agonize over her daughter's terror and pain, feeling utterly helpless.

Finally, the team emerged with Artie strapped onto the litter, and Luna wept. Seeing her daughter's ashen face and the awkward angle of her leg, she knew Artie's ordeal was far from over. The rescue team allowed Luna to go on the helicopter with them and she held Artie's hand the entire way, repeatedly whispering words of love to her.

Now Artie was knocked out, loaded up with morphine, and prepped for emergency surgery to repair the leg that was fractured in three places.

Luna paced the corridor, arms wrapped around herself, chilled to the bone with worry. She wore yesterday's clothes and she smelled of Trouble Ridge and fear.

Then Paul walked through the pneumatic doors.

At the sight of him, her heart leaped, and her first instinct was to throw herself into his arms, but she held back. She wouldn't depend on him. Couldn't allow it.

He came closer, his mouth twitching. He looked as if he wanted to say something but suppressed the urge. Questions hung in his eyes, but he said nothing.

"She's going to be okay," Luna said.

He exhaled audibly and the lines of concern etching his handsome face eased. "That's great news."

"She's got a compound fracture of her right leg, but they can repair it. Nothing else appears to be wrong beyond some scrapes and bruises."

"Thank god."

"They're prepping her for surgery right now."

"Orion wanted to come with me, but I told her to wait until Artie's feeling better. She did have me swing by the souvenir shop in Crafters' Corner to pick these up for Artie before we took the ferry over."

From his pocket, he pulled out a pair of new gripper socks in Artie's favorite color, black, and handed them to Luna. She examined the package. In white lettering, the grippy material spelled out RIGHT on both socks.

"I don't get it." She raised her head and met his gaze.

"So Wicked Martha won't steal her left sock."

"This was sweet of her. I'm so glad Orion was there when it happened, and Artie wasn't all alone." Of course, Artie would never have been there in the first place without her partner in crime, but Luna wouldn't say that. She didn't blame Orion.

"Orion feels terrible."

"It's not her fault."

"That's what I told her."

"Where is she now?"

"Her grandparents who live in Everly met us at the landing. She's spending the night with them, so I can be here with you."

"No." Luna shook her head, hugged herself again while holding the socks in her fist, and stepped back from him.

"No?"

"You can't be here."

"Is there a rule?" He studied her as if she were a time bomb that he expected would explode at any moment.

"Yes, my rule." Her knees wobbled, and she lifted her chin to bolster her resolve.

All expression left his face, and Paul inclined his head toward a row of chairs. "Do you want to sit?"

She nodded, even though she wanted him to leave. She hated that she couldn't just tell him to go.

He escorted her to the seating area. "Coffee?"

She stomach ached, but the caffeine would help her stay alert throughout this ordeal. "Uh-huh."

He wandered to the coffee station and came back with two paper cups of steaming coffee. He'd made hers just the way she liked it—two sugars, one cream. His thoughtfulness stirred her wretchedness over what she must do.

Paul sat on the edge of his chair and angled his body toward hers. She could tell he wanted to touch her but didn't.

She was glad. Her courage to speak her mind would be lost if he touched her.

His gaze searched her face, waiting, as if he already knew somehow.

Luna crossed her legs and took a sip of hot coffee, steeling herself. She could not meet his kind eyes.

"I'm glad Artie will be okay. She's tough." Paul's patient voice jarred her. "Like her mom."

Luna gave a jerky nod, her throat constricting. Every scrap of her focus was needed to resist her pull toward him. She concentrated on the muted TV on the wall tuned to the news. Headlines scrolled about the latest political scandal.

"Thank you for coming to the hospital. You didn't need to do that." There was a tremor in her hands. She desperately hoped he wouldn't notice. She rested the socks in her lap, heard the plastic crinkle.

"Of course." He leaned forward, and she caught a whiff of his outdoorsy, windblown scent.

A heavy silence fell between them. A woman crying in the corner dabbed her eyes. The man beside her spoke into his phone. They both looked exhausted. The couple had Luna's sympathy.

Paul said nothing more. Sensing the tempest behind her stillness?

At last she forced herself to speak what was on her mind. "I can't do this. I thought we . . . no, I was wrong. This was a mistake."

There. She said it. Luna felt no relief, just weary regret at causing him pain yet again. But she had made up her mind as she rocked on that precipice, waiting for the rescue team to bring her daughter out of the crevice.

She would break things off with Paul.

Paul let out an audible exhale. He set his coffee cup on the table. She clutched her own cup, terrified he would try to take her hand. If he touched her, she was toast.

When he finally spoke, his voice held no accusation, only patient concern. "What is a mistake?"

"You. Me. Us. It was too much, too soon."

"Moonbeam—"

"No, don't call me that." She felt emotion clog her throat.

"Okay." His eyes were shiny. "But I think this is just fear talking."

"It might be, but my fear is warranted."

"You've been through so much, Luna. You've been emotion-ally alone much of your life, but you don't have to do this by yourself. There are people who love you and want to help. I—"

"No," she said, heading him off at the pass, shutting him down before he told her he loved her.

"You've been so brave and strong, carrying the world on your shoulders for so long, and if you let me, I'd like to help shoulder your burdens."

She shook her head. Meeting his eyes at last, she willed him to understand. To make this easier for them both, and just let her go.

"It was foolish to think we could recapture the past. I'm not the girl you knew back then. Too much has changed." She forced steadiness into her voice.

"Luna . . ."

"We followed a lovely fantasy these past weeks, and we found the closure we needed, but it's time I put my child first again."

Paul leaned forward, compassion emanating from his eyes. "You can do that. I'll support you however you need."

"Good. I need you to back off."

"For how long?"

"Why, forever."

He looked shocked to the depths of his being. "You don't mean that."

She bit the inside of her cheek. She would not cry. "I've been foolish. Rash. You convinced me to drop my guard, to believe that there was hope. That I could finally find peace. I wanted that so much I went against everything I knew to be true. That the world is a dangerous place."

"That belief is all the more reason why you need people you can trust." He stared at her as if she was speaking total nonsense. "Shutting me out will only deepen your wounds. Healing takes openness, Luna. And courage. When you withdraw, it keeps you shut down. If it's because I didn't tell you about working security on the island, I had my reasons for staying silent. Reasons I can't yet share. You have to trust me that I have your best interests at heart."

Something in his words pierced her armor, threatening to breach the walls she had rebuilt. This was always his gift—seeing past the barricades to her core. She nearly wavered but sitting here in the emergency waiting area reminded her of the price she'd paid for letting pipe dreams distract her.

Luna looked away, retreating into her doggedness. "My mind is set, Paul. I can only say that I'm sorry if I've hurt you, and I hope you'll honor my wishes."

The finality of her last words sounded cruel in this stark environment, already filled with so much hurt and pain.

He put his hand on her wrist. "Luna, give this some time. You're suffering and not thinking straight."

Every instinct screamed for her to turn into his warmth and let the pretense fall away. But if she let the boulder she carried roll loose, who then would she be? She pulled away, avoiding his pained expression.

"What do I tell Orion?"

"Thank her for being Artie's friend."

"No, what do I tell her about us?"

"Tell her life got in our way."

A side door leading into the hallway between the emergency department and the surgical suites opened, and the doctor, dressed in scrubs, surgical cap, and booties, appeared. "Mrs. Boudreaux?"

Saved by the surgeon.

"Yes." She moved toward the doctor.

"We've got your daughter in preop holding if you want to see her one last time before she goes under. She's pretty groggy from the morphine, but she can still hear you."

"Yes, yes." Gripping the socks in her hand, she hoisted her purse higher on her shoulder. "Take me to her."

Her steps felt impossibly heavy crossing the tiled floor. Reaching the door, she dared to look back, and immediately regretted it.

Paul stood alone in the middle of the waiting room, hands in his pockets, shoulders curved in defeat.

Their eyes met across the short distance.

A hundred unspoken words exchanged in silence, but her choice was made. She would do what was needed—straighten her spine, dry her tears, and carry on for her child. Even if it meant locking up her heart forever.

She tore her gaze from his and followed the surgeon.

\* \* \*

Ten minutes later, Luna moved to the surgical waiting area. Artie had been so groggy, she didn't even rouse when Luna kissed her forehead and told her she loved her.

The attendants rolled Artie away and Luna was left alone.

There was no one else in the surgical waiting area either. Just rows of empty chairs and stale coffee smells lingering in the air. Luna sank onto one of the seats, feeling the heavy weight of exhaustion now that the adrenaline drained away.

She shifted, trying to get comfortable, but comfort eluded her.

The chair's rigid edges dug into her back. The four walls felt like a cell. In the past, she would've welcomed this aloneness, sought it even. When the world hurt too much, she retreated deep within herself for safety.

But something inside her had shifted these past weeks with Paul. She had let down her guard, allowed true joy back into her heart. And though it terrified her, part of her mourned the loss of that refuge she'd found with him.

Still, she was reluctant to venture out to the rest of the hospital in search of food. Here, at least, she could break down in private. Plus, what if something happened in surgery and they needed her immediately?

Luna wrapped her arms tightly around herself, as if holding her body together physically would keep her from emotional collapse. Her knees bounced and hands trembled. Interlacing her fingers, she clutched her hands to her heart. The ticking clock on the wall pounded in her ears like an ominous heartbeat.

She thought of Paul again, the man encroaching into her mind when she should be one hundred percent focused on Artie.

"You did the right thing," she told herself, even as doubts needled in. She wished she had someone to talk to, someone who would just listen without judgment, but she'd pushed everyone away.

The empty waiting room seemed to echo with everything she tried not to feel—fear, grief, regret. She needed noise to drown out the thoughts shouting in her head. Luna escaped to the restroom and splashed cool water on her face. The person staring back from the mirror looked hollow, haunted.

She went back to the waiting room and sank into a chair, clasping the socks Orion had bought for Artie to her chest, and finally she let the tears fall. She didn't care who saw. Sobs racked her body as she hunched inward. She thought about young Luna, shy and sensitive, finding solace in books and her artwork. She could see now that retreating from the world had never been the answer. Even animals stayed with their pack for safety. Withdrawal only led to more isolation and grief.

Footsteps approached, but Luna didn't look up, too lost in sadness. A gentle hand rested on her shoulder.

"Oh, sweetheart . . ."

Luna's breath caught. She looked up into her mother's compassionate face. Jeanie sat beside her and wrapped an arm around her shoulder, saying nothing more.

The dam broke. Luna collapsed into her embrace. "Mom . . . I . . ."

"Shhh, just let it out," Jeanie soothed and patted her back.

When her tears subsided, Luna realized they were not alone. Dot, Clare, Vivian, and Eloisa stood nearby, concern radiating from their kind faces.

"We didn't want to disturb you," Dot said. "We just wanted to offer our sympathies."

"And to let you know we care," said Vivian.

"And to bring you snacks and a change of clothes," Clare added.

"Thank you all so much." Luna gave them a quivering smile. "You didn't have to do that."

"Of course we did, dear," said Eloisa. "We stick together through thick and thin. That's the Hobby Island way."

"You're part of our community now," Clare said. "And you always will be."

Their enduring compassion opened Luna's heart and eased some long-forgotten ache she hadn't realized was still there—the need to belong. She'd never had a community before and thought she hadn't needed it, but now she saw the value in belonging and understood what she'd missed by insisting on going it alone.

The women sat beside her and soon they took out quilting

projects, their needles gliding in soothing, rhythmic stitches. They talked, smiled, and doled out the food they'd brought, offering Luna the best kind of support—comradery.

And there, in the comfort of her loving friends, Luna felt her body relax in connection with these women.

While dreadful things did happen, living in a state of constant alert wasn't the answer. Hypervigilance had stolen her joy and robbed her of closeness with others. She could either stay guarded and alone or open herself to people and trust that everything would be all right.

The startling realization told her how wrong she'd been to turn Paul away. Once Artie was better, she'd reach out to him and hope that he could understand her turmoil and forgive her. But for now, Artie was her sole priority.

# Chapter 33
## *Jeanie*

*"Even the sharpest scissors can't cut open a closed heart."*
—*Eloisa Hobby*

Jeanie bustled into Artie's hospital room, carrying a tote bag with the lap quilt she'd finished just in time for the contest this weekend, along with a box of snickerdoodles from Breaking Bread bakery.

Things were looking up for her family. Artie was on the mend. The doctors were amazed at the progress she'd made, and they planned to discharge her tomorrow. Artie would be back on Hobby Island in time for the competition. Luna seemed more relaxed and open than she'd been in . . . well, forever.

Jeanie didn't know what had caused the shift, but her daughter had changed for the better. Laughing more, smiling often, worrying less, and not letting the little bumps ruin her day. And Jeanie was convinced that the quilt she and Luna had created together and finished in the wee hours of the morning would win the grand prize. She couldn't wait to show it to her daughter and granddaughter.

"How's my brave girl today?" Jeanie beamed at Artie, who was sitting up in bed with her leg encased in a black cast signed by the nurses in white marker.

"Gran!" Artie grinned as Jeanie leaned over to kiss her forehead and settled the box of cookies in her lap. "I've been texting up a storm. I sure have missed social media!"

"Glad you're back in the saddle, Pumpkin Pie." Jeanie turned to Luna, who stood up from her chair beside Artie's bed and gave her a big hug. "How are you holding up?"

"Much better now that the worst is over. The nurses are saints. They brought me pillows and blankets and showed me how to turn this lounger into a bed."

"I can stay the night," Jeanie offered, as she had every night.

"No need. It's only one more night. This one is healing at lightning speed." Luna leaned over to ruffle Artie's hair. Her kid was busy thumbing the keyboard on her phone and didn't look up.

"Will you be able to attend the art competition on Saturday?" Jeanie asked.

"We'll have to see if she's up to it," Luna said, giving Artie a soft smile.

"I'll be up to it," Artie said. "Orion put the final additions on our project. I'd show you guys the pic she just sent me, but I want it to be a surprise."

"We're looking forward to seeing it." Luna opened the cookie box, took out two snickerdoodles, gave one to Artie, and kept one for herself. "Mom, you want a cookie?"

"I had two on the ferry over. You enjoy. I finished our quilt, and I'd love to get your opinion on it," Jeanie said.

"Yes." Luna's eyes lit up. "Let's see."

Jeanie pulled out the small quilt in the coastal palette required by the rules. "Here it is . . . our Hobby Island quilt. What do you think?" Jeanie watched Luna for her reaction.

"Oh, Mom!" Luna gave a little gasp. "This is absolutely perfect. You took my design and ran with it."

Jeanie nodded. In the center square, she'd re-created the chapel in Crafters' Corner where she and Luna had their showdown. From fabric scraps, she'd crafted a mother and daughter sitting in a pew, holding hands and talking.

Around the focal panel Luna had designed, she'd sewn four smaller squares on each side, depicting the journey the three of them had taken together. The squares along the top featured their arrival—the ferry, Marshmallow Landing, the jacaranda trees, and Eloisa knitting atop her unicycle.

"Ooh, Gran. Smart move. Sucking up to Eloisa." Artie let out a laugh.

"That doesn't help us," Jeanie said. "Eloisa's not judging. Besides, I was simply following your mother's design and cataloging our time on Hobby Island. Eloisa's been a big part of our journey."

The east side of the quilt represented their first week on the island—the quilt shop, the Nestled Inn, and scooters with names. Along the bottom of the quilt, the panels contained places and sights they'd seen—the beach, the butterfly hatchery, the turtle preserve, and Prism Pavilion.

On the west side of the quilt was the deepest part of their pilgrimage—dinner at the French restaurant, the lighthouse, and a collage of Dot, Vivian, and Clare sewing around the table.

Emotion misted Luna's eyes. "Mom, you outdid yourself. Your sewing skills are spectacular. It looks three-dimensional!"

Goose bumps of happiness spread up Jeanie's arms. "I couldn't have done it without your amazing design."

"Yeah." Artie dusted cookie crumbs from her fingers. "The center square leaps right out at you."

"I want to touch it so badly, but I don't want to get the oil from my fingers on the material." Luna clasped her hands behind her back to resist temptation. "It's stunning. I can't stop staring at it."

Jeanie flushed, absurdly pleased. She had poured all her hope, joy, and hard-won wisdom into every stitch. After a lifetime of shrinking herself small, her craft reflected her expanding spirit.

Even if she didn't win, she'd already gained so much. A new closeness with her daughter and granddaughter and all the friends she'd made on Hobby Island. By starting over and pushing herself, she'd produced the best work of her life, and it was all thanks to Luna.

Of course, she still wanted to win, and she was pretty confident they could do it. Jeanie felt much gratitude that she'd been awarded that golden ticket. How lucky she was!

After visiting Luna and Artie a little longer and eating more of those yummy cookies, Jeanie carefully tucked their quilted masterpiece back into her tote bag and headed to catch the return ferry to Hobby Island. Saturday was the big day—their chance to win the prize money that would save their home.

*      *      *

The sun's rays bounced off Prism Pavilion's glitzy glass walls, casting rainbow snippets everywhere. Jeanie took a second to appreciate the hypnotic prisms before heading into the quilting exhibition area, carrying her entry carefully wrapped in brown paper and nestled in her tote bag.

The space looked a lot different than it had during the healing circle, but it was just as powerful in the daylight, if not more so with all the prisms alight and casting rainbows.

Practically everyone from Crafters' Corner was there. People waved and greeted her, giving wings to her already high spirits. Jeanie soaked up their good vibrations. She needed all the positivity she could get.

It was Saturday, the big day. The day she'd been working toward ever since she accepted the golden ticket. And with Luna's invaluable help, she'd gotten here.

One hundred thousand dollars—and the fate of her ancestral home—were on the line. Her family legacy hung in the balance. No pressure, huh?

Win or lose, Jeanie was proud of stepping outside her comfort zone. She'd put her soul into every stitch. Sewn herself into the seams. Just as Luna had put her heart and soul into the design. And if they lost, she felt confident that together, she, Luna, and Artie could move forward, with or without the house. Because that's what families did.

That thought freed her.

But—Jeanie couldn't suppress her grin—she was certain she and Luna *would* win. She hadn't survived this long by thinking negatively. She fully planned on bringing in that cash. Vision board goals!

"There's Gran!" Artie waved from her wheelchair near the entrance, her leg encased in the black cast that had now been artfully decorated by everyone who'd been present at her rescue.

Luna stood beside her, looking relaxed and happy.

Jeanie's heart swelled at having her family here. "I'm so thrilled we're doing this together."

So much had changed in two short months. It was hard to believe how much.

Two men who'd arrived on the ferry from Everly that morning wore JUDGE buttons on their lapels and were walking around, hands clasped behind their backs, studying the quilts as contestants hung them from display frames.

"Oh goodness, I'm so nervous," Jeanie said. "Oh my gosh! The taller one is Michael Smith. He's an icon in the quilting community! He's a celeb."

"Dot's one of the judges too," Artie pointed out. Indeed, Auntie Dot wandered behind the two men with a judge badge of her own.

"You and Mom are gonna be shoo-ins, Gran," Artie said. "You got this."

"Come on, Luna, let's go register." Jeanie beckoned her daughter to join her at the registration table to check in.

The brisk clerk checked their entry off the list and handed Jeanie a Tyvek number and a safety pin. "You'll be displaying at station 137. Pin your entry number to your quilt." The clerk pointed to their station. "Good luck!"

Jeanie's eyes widened and she whipped her head around to shoot Luna jazz hands. "Did you hear that? Number 137! The same number that was on my golden ticket. It's our lucky number! The universe has spoken. We're going to win."

"Would you like me to carry the quilt, Mom?" Luna offered.

"No, no, I've got it." Clutching the quilt in the giant tote bag, Jeanie navigated their way through milling artists and spectators to station 137 tucked in a far corner. Jeanie stopped to study the milling throng.

"You okay?" Luna asked, touching her elbow.

"Oh my, it's so overwhelming." Jeanie splayed a palm to her chest.

"Here, let me unwrap the quilt."

"I can do it. You go get Artie settled and then come back for the judging."

"Are you sure?"

Jeanie nodded and held her breath, savoring the suspense of unwrapping the quilt for all to see. This was it. Time to share their creative vision with the world.

Winning the grand prize would solve everything. Her palms were slick with anticipation, and her heart fluttered. She rubbed her hands together, trying to dispel her case of nerves.

She took the quilt from the tote bag and slowly unwrapped

the brown butcher paper. Finally, the last of the paper fell away and . . .

It took a few seconds for Jeanie's brain to register the carnage. It looked like something out of a horror movie—weeks of work gutted without mercy.

Jeanie staggered back with a strangled cry, hands flying to her mouth.

No . . . it couldn't be. Their beautiful quilt—the one she and Luna had poured their hearts and souls into—was utterly destroyed.

Jeanie couldn't comprehend it. Her mouth dropped open, and she couldn't get her breath.

The material was slashed to ribbons, batting erupting from numerous vicious gashes. Jeanie fell to her knees, her hands grasping helplessly at the tattered remains scattered on the ground. Weeks of meticulous hand-stitching had been shredded by hateful sabotage.

Hot tears flooded Jeanie's eyes, but she blinked them back, desperate not to make a scene. How could someone be so cruel? Who would do such a thing?

Footsteps approached, and a lilting voice exclaimed, "Oh my stars! What's happened to your lovely quilt?"

Through a watery film, Jeanie looked up to see Eloisa Hobby standing over her. She wore a powder blue caftan and a matching top hat with a white carnation anchored to the brim. Shock and dismay were written large on her gentle features.

"I-I-I don't know," Jeanie stammered. "It was fine when I wrapped it up after I came back from visiting Artie in the hospital. Now it's just . . . *savaged*."

Eloisa knelt down and placed a comforting hand on Jeanie's shoulder. "This wasn't an accident, my dear. Someone did this intentionally." Her normally musical voice hardened.

"But why?" Jeanie asked, her heart breaking. "Why would someone destroy all my hard work?"

"Jealousy can drive people to cruelty," Eloisa said, sorrow in her voice. "I fear it might be one of your competitors. But don't despair. We'll find who's responsible and make sure they don't profit from this malicious act."

Jeanie could only nod mutely, the glittering pavilion swimming around her. Eloisa helped her to her feet. Could one of her fellow quilters, the women she'd sat around a table with and shared laughter, food, and stories for weeks on end, actually have ruined her quilt to take her out of the running?

She hated to believe it, but who else would have done it?

"Let's take this away from prying eyes," Eloisa said. With great care, she wrapped up the shredded quilt and guided Jeanie out the side door.

As the kind woman tended to her, Jeanie's fog of shock lifted enough for red-hot fury to break through. For the first time in her life, she felt an urge to confront and punish whoever had callously demolished her quilt.

Hands curling into fists, she turned to Eloisa. "I need to find who did this. Please, will you help me?"

Eloisa nodded, her eyes flashing like an avenging goddess. "Of course, my dear. You have my word. This won't go unpunished."

"But we can't prove anything."

"You leave that to me." With an encouraging wink, Eloisa disappeared into the crowd.

# Chapter 34

## *Luna*

*"Some threads are destined to be snipped away, allowing for a new pattern to emerge."*

—*Eloisa Hobby*

While Jeanie went to set up their quilt for judging, Luna wheeled Artie over to the registration table so her daughter could check in for the recycled art category.

"Orion should be here any minute," Artie said after she'd signed up and been given their station number. "Do you see her?"

"It's pretty crowded in here. I've even lost sight of your grandmother."

"Orion is hard to miss," Artie said. "Look for the purple hair."

Luna and Artie glanced around the crowded pavilion for Orion. Or at least Artie did. Luna searched for Paul.

After she and Artie arrived back in Hobby Island, she'd been so busy taking care of Artie's post-op needs, they hadn't been out of the B&B until Dot drove them over to the pavilion in a golf cart. Luna had insisted Artie rest as long as possible before the event.

She hadn't seen Paul since the day of Artie's accident when she'd sent him away. How would he react when he saw her? She prayed he would give her a second chance.

There was so much she wanted to tell him about the metamorphosis she'd gone through since that day. The epiphany she'd had as she sat with the quilters in the waiting room.

She owed him an apology, and she planned to grovel. Big-time. But she wanted to do it right. She needed a grand gesture to prove to him that this time, she wouldn't flake at the first sign of trouble.

"Mom, something's wrong with Gran." From her wheelchair, Artie tugged on Luna's sleeve. "Look."

Luna's alert eyes tracked to where Artie pointed.

Eloisa and her mother were coming in the side door from outside. Jeanie looked visibly shaken and Eloisa had her arm around Jeanie's waist, supporting her. The hairs on Luna's nape lifted and her guard went up.

"Will you be okay on your own for a sec?" Luna said.

"Sure. I'll go over to our station. If you see Orion, tell her we're at number fifteen."

"I'll be right back." Luna rushed to her mother, dodging contestants and spectators alike. "What's happened?"

Eloisa stepped back, giving them space. Jeanie opened the tote bag she carried and held it out.

Luna peered inside and saw the beautiful quilt depicting their family journey on Hobby Island sliced to ribbons. "What in the world happened?"

Her mother pressed a palm to her forehead. "After showing you the quilt at the hospital, I didn't look at it again. I stuck it in my bedroom closet. Just now, I unwrapped the protective paper to hang it from the frame and discovered this."

The anguish in Jeanie's voice was palpable and Luna too felt dismayed and saddened about the destruction of so many hours of hard, dedicated work. "But who?"

"Eloisa thinks it could be a fellow quilter who was jealous of my skills."

Luna cast a glance at the quilters standing before their quilts. She spied Sharon, Isabelle, and Nanette displaying the design she'd stolen from Luna. "My money is on Nanette."

"We shouldn't assume," Jeanie said. "And what does it really matter? Bringing the culprit to justice won't change anything."

"Oh, Mom." Luna held her arms wide. "I'm so sorry."

Jeanie sank into her embrace, rested her head on Luna's shoulder, and just sobbed her heart out. "I feel so bad, baby. I won't be able to win the money and save our home."

"Shh, shh." Luna patted her back, comforting her. "It'll be all right. We'll find a solution together."

"But the house has been in our family for four generations. It's a Vincent tradition."

Luna took a tissue from her pocket and passed it to her mother. "Mom, do you know what tradition is?"

"N-no." Jeanie sniffled.

"Peer pressure from dead people."

That drew a chuckle from her. "There are some things I won't miss about that old house. It's drafty."

"And the floorboards creak. *Loudly.*"

"It's expensive to heat and cool." Jeanie forced a smile.

"The plumbing squeals when you take a shower."

"Zero storage space."

"The roof has storm damage." There'd been tornadic winds in Julep a few days after Luna and Artie had arrived.

"Why were we trying to save that old monstrosity in the first place?" Jeanie asked and circled a finger at her temple to indicate they'd been out of their minds.

Luna sobered. "Because it was ours."

"Not anymore."

Their eyes met.

"Life is about change," Luna said.

"And learning how to let go." Jeanie dropped the tote bag.

"It's about facing your fears." Luna wasn't talking about the house anymore.

"And trusting you'll get past the challenges."

Luna held out her hand to her mother. "We'll be okay."

Jeanie smiled. "I know, with you and Artie by my side."

They hugged again as people streamed around them. Over Jeanie's shoulder, Luna saw Eloisa step up to a small podium, a microphone in her hand.

"Looks like Eloisa is about to make an announcement." Luna put her arm around her mother's shoulder and in unison, they turned toward their hostess.

"Contestants, please take your places beside your works of art." Eloisa's voice boomed out across the pavilion. The soft-spoken woman's voice came out so loud it was unnerving. "Judges, it's your time to shine."

Luna put her mouth to Jeanie's ear. "Since we can't compete, let's go over to Artie's station and cheer her on."

Jeanie nodded and Luna took her hand, and they made their way over to the recycled displays.

Eloisa doffed her top hat. "My dear friends, crafting brought you here today in search of connection, creativity, and healing. Like colors of thread woven into a quilt, each of you has added your own bright spirit to our island's tapestry."

She gestured expansively with her top hat. "Art is the magic that binds our hearts together! Be it sewing, writing, painting, quilting, knitting, or bedazzling, any act of creation builds bridges."

As Luna and Jeanie approached, they saw Orion standing beside Artie in her wheelchair. On the display stand, their art was covered by a canvas. Artie had been secretive about their project and Luna was curious to see what she and Orion had created.

The girls spied them and waved madly.

"Crafting turns strangers into friends," Eloisa continued, "wounds into wisdom, scraps into beauty. With needle and brush, we stitch the rips in our society and darn the holes in our souls."

Luna looked for Paul, but he wasn't with the girls.

From the podium, Eloisa glowed as brightly as the prism lights. "The world can be uplifted by the power of arts, don't let anyone diminish it. Whether you win a prize today or not, take pride in having touched lives through your gifts and unique self-expression."

The room erupted into applause as Eloisa took a sweeping bow. "And now, what we came for. Competition! Unveil your creations, if you haven't already, and let the games begin!"

"You want to do the honors?" Orion asked Artie. "Since the project was your idea."

Beaming, Artie reached over to whisk the canvas off their art, revealing the mosaic beneath. Gasps echoed around the hall, the haunting art stopping spectators in their tracks.

Shards of shattered dolls, resurrected into something surreal and provocative. Each fragment a discarded relic, now seamlessly reimagined into hypnotic visages.

Artie's and Orion's talent glowed brighter than the constellations Luna had admired with Paul so long ago. She was so enormously proud of their daughters!

"Your vision is extraordinary," Luna said, getting choked up by their artwork. Out of heartbreak, Artie and Orion had crafted beauty. In luminous faces with mosaic eyes, Luna saw her own reflection—piecing back together that which life had fractured.

Perhaps she could do the same with Paul. Fear was a thief. She had to be brave and rekindle what they'd lost.

Jeanie squeezed her hand, pride misting her gaze. In her mother's gentle strength, Luna found courage. She would reach for happiness once more. Life shattered everyone eventually, but she had a choice—create art from the shards and get on with living or stay broken. Luna knew she would take that leap of faith. Where others might only see broken pieces, she and Artie and Jeanie had found beauty.

The air buzzed with tension as the contestants waited for the judging results.

"Mom," Artie asked, "do you think we have a chance?"

"I do. I really do." Luna leaned down to give Artie a side hug in the wheelchair.

"We got this in the bag." Orion nudged Artie with her elbow. "Have a little self-confidence."

"Is your dad coming?" Luna asked, hoping to sound casual, but fearing she sounded desperate.

Orion glanced over her shoulder. "Yeah, he was supposed to be here, but there was something he had to take care of first."

"So he's not coming?" Now she did sound desperate for sure.

Orion shrugged. "Your guess is as good as mine."

"Girls, the mosaic is stunning." Vivian came over to admire the art. To Luna she said, "You must be so proud of them."

Luna met the pink-clad innkeeper's effervescent smile. "So proud I could pop."

"Very creative. This is the best in show if you ask me," someone else murmured and then soon a crowd was encircling Artie and Orion's art.

Luna stepped back, letting her daughter and Orion have their time in the spotlight. A current of anticipation coursed through the glittering hall. Luna turned to see Dot and the two male judges walk to the podium to confab with Eloisa. Around them, the artists and crafters whispered and wondered.

When Eloisa stepped up to the microphone, a hush fell.

One by one, Eloisa called off the categories and the winners—knitting, woodworking, jewelry making. Amid erupting cheers and applause, the winners went up to receive their five-thousand-dollar checks.

"First place in the quilting category . . ." Eloisa made a drum-roll noise. "Nanette Marston, for her dreamy quilt called 'In a Summer Meadow.'"

Nanette squealed and grabbed Isabelle's hands and they jumped around together in celebration. Sharon, who was standing next to her own quilt, looked disappointed.

Luna gritted her teeth. Nanette had won with her design. But she wasn't concerned for herself. She glanced over at Jeanie. "Mom, are you all right?"

Jeanie's mouth twisted tight. "Fine. I'm fine."

"You don't look fine," Luna said.

"Yeah, Gran. If you were a cartoon, you'd have steam coming out of your ears right now." Artie giggled.

"Nanette won with your mother's design," Jeanie said to Artie. "She should be disqualified."

"If you recall, Mother, I gave her the design with my blessings. She only won because our quilt was sabotaged." Luna settled a hand on Jeanie's shoulder to calm her. "Let it go."

Eloisa cleared her throat, drawing their attention back to the stage. "And for the last category, recycled art, the winner is—'Creepy Dolls Redeemed,' created by Artemis Boudreaux and our very own Orion Chance. Give it up for our youngest winners ever!"

Amid raucous applause, Orion wheeled Artie to the podium to get their honor. Luna looked again for Paul, hoping he'd been able to witness this, but she didn't see him. Too bad. He'd missed an important moment.

Artie beamed with so much joy. The happiest Luna had seen

her since Herc died. How proud she was of her talented daughter! What a wonderful summer this had been, despite all the troubles they'd navigated. How much they'd all grown.

After the excitement died down, Orion and Artie headed back toward them, and Eloisa had one more announcement.

"For the Best in Show event, our attendees will decide who wins the grand prize of one hundred thousand dollars. Please cast your vote for one of the category winners. The judges are going through the assembly passing out ballots. Once you've cast your vote, deposit it in this red box on the podium. The judges will tally the votes and then I'll return to announce the grand prize winner. In the meantime, please enjoy the refreshments. You have twenty minutes to vote." With that, Eloisa strolled offstage.

# Chapter 35
## *Jeanie*

*"Sometimes life frays us, but it's up to us to mend and make something beautiful from the threads that remain."*

—*Eloisa Hobby*

Jeanie cast her ballot for "Creepy Dolls Redeemed" and not just because it was her granddaughter's project. She genuinely thought the mosaic was the best artwork of them all.

Eloisa had promised to help Jeanie bring the culprit to justice, but she'd wandered off somewhere and Jeanie couldn't help thinking she'd slipped the whimsical woman's mind. Was Luna right? Was Nanette the one who'd destroyed their quilt?

What did it really matter? What was done was done. Time to be a good sport and congratulate Nanette. She'd prove to Luna and herself she could let go of grudges.

Jeanie navigated through the bustling art show, her eyes briefly lingering on the vibrant displays and the lively faces of attendees. The air was thick with excitement and the subtle hum of shared appreciation for the arts.

As she approached Nanette, who stood proudly beside her winning quilt, a swirl of dark emotions tugged at Jeanie's heart.

When Nanette saw her, she looked scared and backed up. She raised her palms. "I won fair and square!"

Jeanie mustered a smile over gritted teeth. "Yes, I saw. Congratulations, Nanette. Your quilt is something special."

Nanette's eyes widened in surprise. "You . . . you're not mad?"

"I'm not a sore loser. You deserve your prize."

"Thank you! I still can't believe it. But I heard about your quilt . . . I'm so sorry, Jeanie. It's just awful what happened."

The words, meant to be comforting, stung, but Jeanie held on to her composure. "Yes, it was unfortunate. But today is about celebrating the winning artists and their talents."

Nanette embraced her quilt still hanging from the frame, hugging it tight. "It was my original design. I didn't steal it from your daughter."

Obviously, the woman was feeling guilty. Jeanie had to bite her tongue to keep from saying something that would cause a scene. She wouldn't spoil this day for Artie. "Enjoy your time in the spotlight."

Jeanie turned to see Sharon hovering nearby. Her friend reached out and gave Jeanie a quick hug. "You're a class act. Nanette doesn't deserve your compassion."

"I'm sorry your quilt didn't win," Jeanie said.

"It's okay. I'll be coming away from this summer with your friendship. That's enough for me."

"Aww, what a sweet thing to say."

Sharon's mouth twitched but she didn't quite smile and gave Jeanie another hug.

Pulling back, Jeanie said, "Well, I better get back to my family."

"Maybe we could have dinner later?"

"Luna is planning on taking the girls out to celebrate their blue ribbon."

Sharon looked disappointed. "Oh, yes, you're right. Sure. Have fun."

Jeanie gave a small wave and went to find Luna.

Near the ballot box, her daughter was talking to Clare while Artie and Orion were posing for pictures with their artwork.

Just then, Eloisa returned, and she had Paul with her.

Luna's head immediately whipped around to track Paul's movements. His face was solemn, and Jeanie noticed he didn't make eye contact with her daughter. Was he angry with Luna, or did he have something on his mind?

Eloisa stepped up to the microphone. "Folks, one of our category winners has been disqualified. Any votes cast for 'In a Summer Meadow' by Nanette Marston will not be counted and the quilting category will not be eligible for the grand prize. The runner-up, Sharon Rooney, will collect the five-thousand-dollar category prize."

Someone gasped, and murmurs ran through the crowd. Sharon squealed, "Oh my heaven!"

"Nanette Marston," Eloisa said in a stern voice. "Please return the check you were given."

"Hey!" Nanette said. "Disqualified? For what? It was my design! I swear it!"

Eloisa's tone brooked no argument. "Please go with Paul Chance. He'll explain everything to you."

Nanette whipped her head around to where Paul was coming up behind her. "What's going on? Just tell me."

"Not in front of everyone, Nanette. Please come with me," Paul said.

Nanette looked panic-stricken, her gaze frantically darting a look at the exits.

"This way," Paul said kindly and extended his arm.

Eyes wide, Nanette reluctantly took his elbow, and he escorted her from the pavilion.

The pavilion swelled with whispers as Eloisa clapped her hands and raised her voice to be heard above the private conversations speculating about what had disqualified Nanette.

"The votes have been counted by the judges and we have a hundred thousand dollars to give away." Eloisa motioned to Dot. "The envelope, please."

Dot walked up the steps to hand it to her.

Eloisa opened the envelope. "Well, isn't this just the bee's knees! The moment you've been waiting for, our grand prize winner!"

Folks hushed up quiet as church mice. Jeanie, still reeling from the hullabaloo, took several long, slow, deep breaths and crossed her fingers. *Please let it be Orion and Artie.*

"And the winner is . . ." Eloisa paused for an exaggerated wink. "'Creepy Dolls Redeemed' by Artie Boudreaux and Orion Chance!"

The crowd erupted in raucous cheers for the girls. Artie's eyes went wide, and her mouth dropped open as Orion let out a loud "Woo-wee!"

Luna applauded madly and Jeanie joined in.

The girls hurried up to the stage, Orion pushing Artie up the ramp again. Eloisa presented them with a four-foot check. "Your doll mosaic takes the cake! Congratulations!"

Eloisa handed the microphone down to Artie.

Artie beamed at the crowd. "I wanna thank my mom and Gran for always believing in me. And my best gal pal, Orion." She smiled shyly. "You saved me out there on Opportunity Ridge and I'll never forget it."

Then she passed the mic to Orion, who gave a speech of her own thanking her father for letting her beachcomb to her heart's content and Artie for being her friend.

Jeanie was so proud of them. Overcoming challenges had brought the girls closer.

As people rallied around the girls offering a fresh round of congratulations, Eloisa walked off the stage and came over to Jeanie.

In a soft voice, Eloisa said, "Please follow me."

# Chapter 36
## *Luna*

*"Sometimes, the best way to mend a broken heart is with a needle and thread."*

—*Eloisa Hobby*

Y our kid is pretty amazing," Luna said.

Luna and Paul watched their daughters adroitly glad-hand the well-wishers at the reception toasting them on their prizewinning artwork. She and Paul stood side by side at the refreshment table, munching canapes, feeling each other out, getting the lay of the land and seeing where they stood.

"So is yours." He smiled a smile so deep it cut through Luna's doubts.

"They're even more amazing together."

"*We're* more amazing together." Paul's voice deepened, husky with meaning.

She turned to look at him and lowered her lashes. "Are you saying we need to get together so they can be sisters?"

"It's a thought." He grinned. "I mean, come on, they're teen-agers and already worth fifty grand apiece. We can't wrangle them alone."

"Good point." She moved infinitesimally closer to him.

He laughed.

"What's so funny?"

"I'm staying right over here. I'm not crossing any more boundaries with you, Moonbeam. You want me, you gotta ask."

"I'll take that under advisement." Her cheeks burned from the heat of his stare. The air crackled electric between them. She lowered her lashes and sent him a sultry look.

The crowd thinned, many people heading back to Crafters' Corner after the art show. The sun was sliding toward the horizon, casting rainbow light everywhere.

"Paul?"

"Uh-huh?"

"I shouldn't have treated you the way I did at the hospital."

"No need to apologize. I get it. I've got a daughter too."

She studied his arms. Licked her lips at how muscular they were flexed against the sleeves of his T-shirt. "This is twice I let my fear push you away."

"I noticed."

"But you don't hold it against me. Why not?"

"Moonbeam, it would be like holding it against the sun for setting in the west."

"Yikes. That sounds bad."

"Bad is a value judgment. I try not to make those if I can help it."

"I've been working really hard to be less distrustful."

"I know. You are who you are, Luna. You're cautious, prepared, and suspicious. Those are neither bad nor good qualities, they're just traits. The problem is, we've all got a set of traits that kept us safe in our lives, but those traits, when overused, become our flaw. It happens to every single one of us. The key is recognizing those traits and taking corrective action when they get in our way."

"My distrustful trait gets in my way all the time."

"That's because you're afraid that if you put your trust in

someone, they'll let you down like Jack and Jeanie did when you were a child. Not throwing shade on your parents. This isn't about blaming your parents for their traits. It's about recognizing where our upbringing came up short and taking steps to plug the gaps."

"Wow, look at you. Gardener. Cybersecurity ninja. Philosopher. Be still, my heart."

He let his palm hover at her chest, right above her heart. "May I?"

"Touch me?"

He nodded.

She cracked a grin. "Please do."

He settled his palm on her chest. "It's steady. True."

She softened her smile. "What are your traits that have a tendency to get out of balance?"

Paul moved his hand, his calloused thumb brushing her wrist and sending tingles up her arm. "Feeling compelled to always do the right thing."

"That sounds like a lot better trait than being cautious."

"Just like any other trait, it can go either way, depends on if you keep it in bounds or not."

"Okay, give me an example."

"You said you fell for me because I helped clean up the bus after our school field trip. You said I reminded you of what your dad was not, diligent, disciplined, principled. But when I depend on those traits too much, take it too far, I become rigid, rule-bound, and yes, even self-righteous."

"Ooh, you're right. I've seen that in you a time or two."

"See? None of us are perfect."

"But you've done a lot of healing. You've had a head start."

He held his arms wide. "Hey, I live on Hobby Island. Healing is inevitable here. We're a mixed bag, us humans. But I am steady.

I'm loyal. I'm trustworthy and I do love you, Luna. If you give me a chance, I think we can work this thing out."

"Take a chance on Chance?"

"You got it."

That sounded absolutely beautiful and after all that had happened, Luna wasn't a bit scared. This man had always had her best interests at heart. She just hadn't been able to see it for her fear of abandonment. Paradoxically, she'd pushed him away to keep from being abandoned.

"I'm not going anywhere, Luna. Go back to Julep, sort your life out. When you're ready, I'll be here."

"Waiting on me?"

"I've already waited twenty-two years. I'd wait twenty-two more because you're worth it."

"What if I'm ready now?"

"No need to rush, I want you to be certain."

"I am." Luna's heart skittered as Paul's kind eyes met hers. "You're right. You're steadfast and true. I'm ready to start our life together now, no more waiting."

Paul searched her face for any wavering and his smile spread like sunshine after rain.

"Moonbeam," he rumbled, voice gravelly with emotion. "You've gone and made me the happiest man alive."

Calloused hands framing her face, he drew her close. As his lips claimed hers, warmth rushed through Luna, quick as a flash fire.

She clung to his broad shoulders, dizzy with the rightness of it, the power of a love they'd danced around for so long. Now she could fall into it wholly, without fear of landing too hard.

When their lips parted, Paul touched his forehead to hers. "Partners for life's adventures?"

"With you? Forever, my love."

# Chapter 37
## *Jeanie*

*"Forgiveness mends torn hearts, weaving together what was once broken with grace and understanding."*

—*Eloisa Hobby*

In the quiet confines of Eloisa's delightful cottage filled with curios and collectables of all sorts, the air was thick with tension. Jeanie and Eloisa were in chairs facing the couch where Nanette sat on the sofa, clutching a tissue. Eloisa's calico cat was curled up in her lap.

Eloisa cleared her throat, her voice calm yet carrying an undercurrent of sternness. "Nanette, we know you destroyed Jeanie's quilt."

"I didn't—"

"Don't even try to deny it." Eloisa reached for a tablet computer, turned it on, angled it so Nanette and Jeanie could see it, and hit the play button. "Paul has security cameras in the hallways of all the B&Bs."

As they watched, a video of an empty corridor at the Nestled Inn came into view. It was time-stamped the previous day.

Jeanie's room was the first door on the left.

A woman appeared in the corridor, her back to the camera, but then she glanced around, making sure the coast was clear, and when she turned, her face was plainly visible.

No mistake. It was Nanette.

"That's not me!" Nanette hopped up.

"Sit back down," Eloisa commanded and pointed at the screen.

On tiptoe, Nanette went straight for Jeanie's room. That's when Jeanie saw she had two things in her hands. A key and a pair of scissors. Nanette let herself into Jeanie's room. She stayed five minutes and slipped back out, unnoticed by anyone except the security camera.

Stunned, Jeanie couldn't believe what she was watching. "Where did you get a key?"

"Vivian keeps a master key in the kitchen drawer," Nanette said, her head down, giving up on her denial. "I noticed it when I was here last year."

"But why did you do it?" Jeanie asked. "What did I ever do to you?"

"You're so lucky." Nanette sneered. "I've got so little, and you've got so much. A daughter and granddaughter who love you. Not everyone has your advantages." Nanette's voice held threads of bitterness and envy entwining every word. "You walk into a room and simply . . . *shine*. Your quilt would have taken the prize. You don't even realize how it feels not to be fairy-dusted."

Jeanie's hands clenched into fists, the anger mixing with a profound sense of betrayal. "You think ruining my work will make *you* shine? Is that your way of standing out?"

Eloisa's gaze flicked between Jeanie and Nanette, her fingers absently stroking the calico's fur. She let out a weary sigh. "Nanette, Jeanie's loving family is no excuse for you committing a savage act."

The tissue in Nanette's hands was shredded now, much like

the remains of Jeanie's quilt. She raised her head, eyes glinting with unshed tears or perhaps the cold sheen of desperation. "I thought . . . I thought if I could win this competition, finally someone would notice. It was supposed to validate me."

"With a design you stole from my daughter." Jeanie softened her voice despite her anger. "Stepping over others, destroying what they love . . . it's no ticket to success, Nanette. It's a one-way path to loneliness."

Nanette's lips trembled, and her face crumbled at the magnitude of her actions. "I just . . . I felt I needed to do something drastic to change my fate."

Eloisa sighed with a sense of finality. "You've changed more than just your fate. You've altered how everyone on Hobby Island will see you. And you've torn the very fabric of our community. It's more than a quilt that needs mending—it's trust."

Jeanie looked at the pathetic woman. "You've left a scar, Nanette, on all of us."

"Big deal." Nanette's face went ugly. "Scars are part of life."

Eloisa turned off the tablet, the screen's glow dying as the finality settled in the room. "My quilting group was built on respect, on community. I don't know how we go forward from this, but it won't be the same."

Jeanie searched Nanette's face for any sign of true remorse. "Is it worth it, Nanette? The title, the ribbon—is it worth losing friends over, being alone?"

The tissue twisted further in Nanette's hands, now a knotted mess. "I didn't think about that. All I wanted was to be seen, to be admired like you." The admittance sounded sour—a confession laced with bitterness.

Jeanie felt her anger dissolve into pity. There before her was not a rival but a person consumed by her inadequacies, by an invisible competition that had grown to unhealthy proportions. "Admiration that comes at the cost of other people is hollow, Nanette. It's not admiration at all."

"You need to make this right, Nanette. But some things, once torn, can't be patched up the same way," Eloisa said.

Jeanie watched as Nanette stood, her movements unsteady. There was no righteous vindication at this moment, only the profound sadness that accompanied shattered trust.

"You'll resign from the quilting group immediately, and you'll have a lifetime ban from the forums," Eloisa said, meting out Nanette's punishment. Both she and Jeanie stood at once.

Nanette winced. A lifetime ban from Eloisa's vibrant quilting community felt too harsh. Jeanie physically felt the other woman's pain, the ache a hard knot in her own belly. She too had made mistakes and done foolish things, and her instinct was to rush to forgiveness. But she quelled her codependent urges to excuse the woman's behavior as she thought of all the times she'd forgiven a falsely contrite Jack just to keep the peace.

"Yeah, well, it was a stupid group anyway." Nanette tossed her head. "Who cares? You're all a bunch of losers anyway. I'm outta here on the next ferry to Everly."

With a childish flounce, she stormed out, slamming the front door behind her.

Years of putting up with Jack's drunken behavior had Jeanie yearning to chase after Nanette to smooth things over and take the blame for the woman's turmoil. It was all she could do to stay rooted in place, taking deep breaths and thinking of the healing circle that had brought her so much peace.

This wasn't her mental health issue. She wasn't to blame for the lens through which Nanette viewed the world. In fact, she was the injured party here and entitled to her hurt. She didn't have to turn herself into a pretzel to keep others happy. Other people's happiness was not her responsibility. All she could control was herself.

Eloisa turned to Jeanie. The warmth that had drained from the room in the wake of Nanette's emotional storm slowly seeped back in under the strength of Eloisa's steady, comforting gaze.

"Let's sit back down," Eloisa invited.

Jeanie sat, her fists slowly uncurling as she let out a measured breath. The adrenaline from the confrontation still hummed through her veins, an uncomfortable reminder of the chaos that had just unfolded.

Eloisa settled onto the couch beside her. "You handled that with grace, Jeanie. It's hard not to get swept up in the tempest of someone else's making. Not giving in to Nanette's petulance shows the strength of your character and your personal growth."

Jeanie managed a weak smile, her emotions a tangle of relief and sorrow. "I could have easily been the one to lash out," she admitted, "but what would that have solved?"

"Nothing at all," Eloisa agreed. "It's easy to return anger with anger, but you chose to hold your ground without stooping to that level. That's something to be proud of."

"Thank you, Eloisa. It wasn't an easy thing to witness," Jeanie said, finding some solace in the older woman's understanding. "Or to endure."

"Nanette made her choices," Eloisa mused, her own disappointment a subtle undercurrent in her voice. "Now she must live with the consequences. But we will move forward. Our group will heal. It's what we do."

Jeanie nodded, feeling the truth in Eloisa's words. The road might be rocky, but she had Luna and Artie and the crafting community—and that meant everything.

"Yes, we will," Jeanie agreed, comforted by the sense of unity between them. "One stitch at a time."

"Indeed," Eloisa said, smiling. "Now, shall we have some tea?"

\* \* \*

The delicate clink of china and the soothing aroma of Earl Grey filled Eloisa's quaint living room. Jeanie felt the weight of Nanette's crimes ebb as she savored the warmth of the teacup in her hands. They sipped in companionable silence, the hum of mutual understanding enveloping them, and just as her heart rate returned to normal, a rap on the cottage door sliced through the tranquility.

She and Eloisa shared a glance, the corners of Eloisa's mouth tipping into a gentle smile. "My, who could that be? Everyone but us should be out celebrating their last weekend on the island."

"Perhaps it's Luna and Artie come looking for me." Jeanie settled her cup into its saucer. "I did go off without an explanation."

Eloisa got up to answer the door. "Oh, hello, Sharon, come on in."

A gust of fresh island air accompanied Sharon Rooney as she edged into the living room. She seemed somber and downcast, unlike her usual confident self.

"Would you like some tea?" Eloisa invited.

"No, I can't stay. Th-there . . . there's something I need to get off my chest," she stammered.

"Are you all right, dear?" Eloisa's brow furrowed, her hospitable nature kicking in despite Sharon's obvious distress. "You look as if you've seen a ghost."

Sharon shook her head. The normally polished woman's clothes were rumpled, her hair mussed as if she'd been repeatedly raking her fingers through it.

"Please, sit." Eloisa made space on the couch, scooting over to give Sharon enough room to nestle in between her and Jeanie.

But Sharon didn't sit. She stayed standing, facing Jeanie. Felena took advantage and hopped into the spot Eloisa vacated and curled into a ball.

"I saw Nanette as she was headed out to the ferry. All she had to say was ugly things about you when she was the one who hurt you, Jeanie. She made my skin crawl because it hit home how much she hurt you . . . and how like her I am."

"What do you mean?" Jeanie asked, confused. "You didn't steal Luna's design or shred our quilt."

"No," Sharon said. "I did something far worse."

Jeanie went perfectly still as she braced herself.

"I have something to confess, and well, I-I just can't bear the guilt any longer."

Jeanie's heart hitched, unsure if she was ready to face another betrayal, but she said nothing, allowing Sharon to continue.

"I am the person who catfished you, Jeanie."

"What?" She blinked, uncertain if she heard her correctly.

"I'm Rex Rhinehart. Or I was. I created him. It was me who . . . who you talked to, who . . . who asked for money."

Jeanie's gasp echoed in the cozy room, her mind struggling to process Sharon's words. "You?" she echoed, disbelief etching her features as sharply as the pain when she learned she'd been swindled of her life savings. "You're Rex Rhinehart?"

Sharon's head bowed, and she knotted her hands into white-knuckled fists. "I was desperate, drowning in debt, and I couldn't see past it. Then there you were on the quilting forums, kind and trusting, offering support to others. Talking about Jack and how much you wanted to meet a new soulmate. I took advantage, and it's something I've not been able to live with, not since I've truly gotten to know you."

There it was. The raw, naked truth laid bare. Jeanie's mind raced, her initial instinct to console, to forgive. But she steeled herself, remembering the forgiveness she'd wanted to extend Nanette, a mistake not to be repeated out of mere habit.

Jeanie shot a glance at Eloisa, who sat quietly, watching, letting them sort out their issues.

The silence was stiff, layered with the thick residue of violated trust. Jeanie stroked Felena, searching for comfort in the cat's soft fur. Eloisa reached across and squeezed Jeanie's forearm, signaling her support.

"You listened to Nanette deny her guilt, deflect her blame, and that's what brought you here?" Jeanie's words were a whisper, not meant to wound but to understand.

Sharon nodded, small but deliberate. "Seeing her indignation, seeing you hurt . . . it held up a mirror to my misdeeds. I don't want to be that person, Jeanie. I can't be her."

Jeanie weighed Sharon's gaze, seeking sincerity in the moist eyes that met her own. "You're here now," she finally said, "facing the pain you've caused. That counts for something."

"I'll return the money. Every last dollar." Sharon blinked away fresh tears. "It might not undo the harm, but I hope it's a start. I hope it's proof I'm not like Nanette. I'm not running from this."

"You betrayed my trust," Jeanie said, her voice even, her gaze unflinching. "You played on my emotions and my loneliness."

Eloisa leaned forward. "It takes a strong soul to bare their sins."

Jeanie was uncertain how to respond. She was hurt beyond measure. Two betrayals in one day. She thought of how much she'd betrayed Luna and Paul. Perhaps this was her comeuppance.

"I don't deserve your forgiveness. I know that, and if you can't give it to me, I understand. What I did was inexcusable, but I vow to make amends. I will make this right. I'll give everything back to you, every last penny. It's all I can think about." A tear spilled over Sharon's lower lashes.

Jeanie studied her, detecting none of Nanette's defiance or self-absorption. Sharon's remorse was palpable, her shame a shroud that she couldn't shrug off. Jeanie felt the sincerity of the apology, the genuine repentance.

"It takes a lot of courage to admit your wrongs so openly," Jeanie noted, surprising herself with the calmness of her voice. "You didn't double down on your mistakes. You owned them, and that counts for something."

Eloisa gave an affirming nod, her approval clear. "There's remorse, and then there's redemption, Sharon. You're taking the first step."

Jeanie could see the path forward, where forgiveness was a choice made from strength rather than a knee-jerk reaction to appease. "Returning what you've taken is a start." Her heart felt lighter as she spoke. "And it's more than some are willing to do. You confessed when you didn't have to do so. That's something as well."

"I should have confessed sooner. I hurt you badly, and there is no making up for it. While I can't pay you back the money immediately, I swear I will pay it back. I don't know how to save our friendship."

"I'm not sure it can be saved."

Sharon grimaced. "I don't blame you."

Jeanie's heart thundered as she regarded Sharon, her body stiff with tension yet. Only Felena's soft purring punctuated the room.

"You caused this," Jeanie said, each word carrying the weight of her disillusionment. "How could you do such a thing?"

*And how could you have let Paul take the fall for Jack?* Her hypocrisy ate Jeanie up.

Sharon's face crumpled; her glossy veneer shattered. "I know, and I've hated myself every day. I tried so many times to tell you and couldn't get the words out because I knew it would ruin our connection. But when I saw Nanette, angry and defiant, and blaming you for her deceit—it was like looking in a mirror. I saw how ugly my soul was."

Eloisa sat like a sentinel as Sharon's confession unfolded. "You'll return the money?"

"It will take time. I spent the money getting out of debt, but I will find a way to pay you back, every single cent." Sharon's gaze fixed firmly on Jeanie, her eyes swimming with regret. "It was about more than the money, it was also about escaping my lonely life, but I ended up trapping myself and hurting you."

Jeanie exhaled, her anger giving way to an aching sort of empathy. She could see Sharon for who she truly was. A woman driven by desperation, her actions a reflection of her inner turmoil.

"And you think returning the money will fix what you've broken?" Jeanie asked, feeling little more than bone-deep weariness.

"I know it's a small start," Sharon said. "It doesn't consider the pain and suffering. I desperately need to make amends. To prove I'm nothing like Nanette. To prove I'm worth a second chance. Even if you can't find it in your heart to forgive me, I need to be able to forgive myself."

Eloisa's voice cut through the tension in the room, her tone calm but firm. "Jeanie, the road to forgiveness isn't about forgetting or pretending the hurt never happened. It's about deciding whether there is more good in someone than bad, whether they can learn and grow from their mistakes. Nanette couldn't, but maybe Sharon can if we give her the opportunity."

Jeanie locked eyes with Sharon, the woman she'd considered a friend, reading the earnest plea written across her face. There were echoes of Nanette's betrayal, of Jack's false promises, and of her own missteps with Luna and Paul.

The web of deception and repentance was complex, but Sharon's next steps were crucial, as were Jeanie's.

"Forgiveness is a gift, Sharon, not an entitlement," Jeanie said with newfound clarity. "I can give you the chance to redeem yourself, but trust . . . that will take time. More than money, I need to see you change."

Sharon nodded vigorously. "You will. I swear it."

Jeanie got up from the couch, standing tall amid the damage. "Then go. Start making things right. But remember, redemption isn't a single act. It's a journey. Just never do that to anyone else again."

"I won't! I've learned my lesson." Gratitude lifted Sharon's shoulders.

"Please go to your accommodations, Sharon, and we'll sort out the details of your rehabilitation later." Eloisa stood up.

As Sharon scurried away, Eloisa turned to Jeanie. "You've been so profoundly wronged, and yet you showed her grace. I'm proud of you for valuing kindness over vengeance."

"I had to show mercy so I can have compassion for myself and my own misdemeanors." Jeanie let out a shaky breath.

Eloisa wrapped an arm around Jeanie's shoulder. "Oh, my friend. That may feel true now but have faith. Your light is too bright for this darkness to extinguish."

Jeanie managed a small, tentative smile, still reeling. She had a long road ahead to process this pain and betrayal. But here, now, she let herself feel a flicker of hope.

Eloisa went on, "I'll make certain you get the money back that Sharon took. I'll pay you myself so you can save your home, and she can repay me. It's the least I can do since my laxness led to this swindle. I got complacent, and *I* need to make amends."

"Thank you," Jeanie said, relieved they wouldn't lose the house after all. "It's a hard lesson."

Eloisa gave her a heartfelt hug. "And you don't have to walk that path alone, Jeanie. We're here for you. Me, Paul, Dot, Vivian, and Clare."

Jeanie had come through the crucible and passed the test. She was bruised but not beaten, wiser, and filled with resolve. She'd been tried and risen above her flaws. Overcoming her codependency was a process, but she was on the right path.

All thanks to Eloisa and the ordinary magic of crafting, community, and Hobby Island.

# Epilogue
## *Eloisa*

*"Life's a craft. You can master it, but never stop being a student."*
—*Eloisa Hobby*

*One Year Later . . .*

This morning, as she had for the last sixteen years, Eloisa dined on a breakfast of fresh-picked berries, homemade scones, clotted cream, and peppermint tea. She fed her sweet calico, Felena; donned a festive hat that didn't match her outfit; detoured into the flower garden; and plucked a bright bloom and stuck it in her hatband.

But she did not gather her knitting and ride her unicycle through Crafters' Corner, because today was blessed.

There was a wedding on Hobby Island. The church bells rang in the chapel, sending peals of joy throughout the land. In all honesty, today smelled like roses from Paul's flower garden—sweet and delightful.

Because her dear Paul was marrying his beloved Luna.

"Happy wedding day!" she called to everyone dressed in their finest as she marched down from her cottage to the village.

"Happy wedding day!" they echoed, raising hands and sending sunny smiles in greeting.

"Great day to get married." She laughed merrily and marched on.

Auntie Dot came out of her house to join Eloisa on her mission. "I'm nervous."

"Whatever for?"

"I've never officiated a wedding before." Dot had just gotten ordained online for this momentous occasion.

"Fiddlesticks. When have you ever been shy about anything? You'll do fine."

"I'm so happy for them. I thought it might not happen after that terrible incident on Trouble Ridge."

"Oh, my dear friend, do you mean that lovely opportunity that brought Artie and her mother closer together?"

"Must you always insist on seeing the glass half full?" Dot grumbled.

"Always." Eloisa laughed and held her head high.

As they drew close to Crafters' Corner, Vivian popped out of the Nestled Inn looking like a creamy confection in pink.

"Hold up, ladies," she called, and they waited for her.

"Happy wedding day!" Eloisa greeted her. "Are you going to march in those shoes?"

Vivian looked down at her elegant pumps. "Indeed. March on. I'll deal with the blisters if they come."

"*When* they come," Dot muttered.

The three of them—tall Dot in red, short Eloisa in purple, and vibrant Vivian in pink—cut quite a glorious sight, or at least Eloisa liked to think so.

Clare, who had a small cottage at the back of the quilt shop, hurried to catch up with them when they went by. She was dressed in a glorious shade of butter yellow.

"We look like Easter eggs," Vivian said. "I love it."

"Did you see the dress that Jeanie sewed for Luna?" Clare asked. "Jeanie missed her calling. She should have been a wedding dress maker instead of a quilter. It's far more lucrative."

"Ahh, but Jeanie is a quilter deep in her heart. And one must always follow her heart," Eloisa said.

"I for one am thrilled to hear Jeanie has a beau. A nice man she met in person at a square-dancing club," Clare said. "She's bringing him to the wedding. We can check him out to see if he's good enough for her."

Vivian high-fived Clare and almost stumbled on a cobblestone but managed to catch herself. "Don't say a word about my shoes," she warned.

"Our lips are forever zipped on the topic of your footwear," Eloisa said. "Who am I to comment on someone's attire considering my own glorious hats."

The church bells chimed louder now that they were so near. Outside the chapel, where Orion and Artie, Luna's maids of honor, clutched wildflower bouquets filled with honesty plants.

Luna's son, Beck, was standing up as Paul's best man. Home on summer break from his sophomore year at OU, Beck had really bonded with Paul throughout the engagement when they both came to visit Luna, Jeanie, and Artie in Julep.

Paul told Eloisa he considered Beck the son he never had. Their shared love of fishing and sports brought them closer.

"Happy wedding day!" Eloisa called to the girls as she and her posse marched up to the chapel.

"Happy wedding day!" the girls said in unison.

"I'm off to the altar," Dot announced. "Must rehearse." She entered the chapel, the door creaking quaintly on its hinges.

Eloisa turned her attention to Artie. Luna, Jeanie, and Artie had been wrapping up their lives in Julep for the past year. They would all soon be moving to Hobby Island after the wedding. "I saw an article with your mother in the *Houston Chronicle* about the mural she painted for the governor of Texas."

"Yes." Artie beamed. "Her career as a muralist is really taking off. She's had to turn down offers because she wants a good work-life balance."

"Good for her! I'm so happy she's able to pursue her calling." Eloisa turned to Orion. "Are you excited to officially become sisters?"

"Yes!" Orion and Artie said in unison.

"Oh, this is indeed a happy wedding day." Eloisa crooked a finger. "Come on, ladies, let's take our seats before it gets crowded."

"As if you couldn't sit wherever you wanted, Auntie Eloisa." Orion laughed.

"'Tis true." Eloisa laughed and led the way into the chapel.

Inside, Dot was at the altar going over her notes. Sharon was busy affixing white satin bows to the pew.

Eloisa's eyes met Sharon's.

Almost shyly, Sharon smiled and nodded and kept on with her work. The woman had owned up to her flaws, made amends, and turned her life around. Moved by Jeanie's mercy, Sharon took responsibility and worked for Eloisa to pay off her debts.

She turned out to be a fine employee and Eloisa was happy they'd given her a second chance. Through these acts of service, Sharon experienced the power of forgiveness. Though she had acted wrongly, the townsfolk saw her for more than her worst mistake. She vowed to live honorably. The grace she was shown now extended to others.

Eloisa, Vivian, and Clare chose their spots and settled in to wait.

Not long after, Dot hollered, "Places, everyone! It's showtime!"

The music started and Artie and Orion lined up under the

flowered archway entwined with trumpet vines. Paul took his place, looking dapper in a light linen suit with a purple jacaranda flower pinned to his lapel.

After the bridesmaids came down the aisle, Luna, joyously radiant, appeared on Jeanie's arm as the "Wedding March" played.

The simple ceremony flew by in a blur of meaningful, heartfelt vows, the brightest smiles, happy tears, and cheers.

After Dot pronounced Paul and Luna husband and wife, Artie and Orion whooped louder than anyone. They were now officially a family!

Eloisa's heart filled to overflowing for the man who was like a nephew to her and the woman who completed him.

The outdoor reception in the quadrangle at Crafters' Corner passed in a vibrant whirlwind of laughter, dancing, celebration, and feasting. A long buffet table was loaded with a mouthwatering smorgasbord and every morsel was delicious.

Then, when the music started, Artie grabbed Eloisa's hand to lead an impromptu conga line, weaving enthusiastically between the tables and tiki torches to kick off the after-dinner dancing.

Paul and Luna's choreographed first dance as newlyweds drew exuberant cheers and applause. The groom couldn't seem to stop grinning as he effortlessly dipped and spun his bride across the wooden dance floor before the dramatic final lift that had everyone hooting.

After their showstopping number, other couples flooded the dance floor, showing off moves from suave to silly to spastic.

Even Jeanie and her date busted out some shockingly good salsa steps, inciting another round of cheers as they twirled across the floor. The electric celebration raged on as the golden sky shifted to twilight.

Strings of lights and tiki torches set aglow illuminated the beach reception area as laughter and pure joy bubbled over endlessly like the foamy waves. The presentation of an extravagant five-tier tropical fruitcake topped with artistic fondant sculptures of the bride and groom garnered thunderous applause.

\* \* \*

Just as Eloisa was about to call it a night, a woman approached her from the shadows. When Eloisa saw her face, her heart almost stopped. Once upon a time, that woman had saved her life back when Eloisa was married to Charles.

She went to her old friend, arms wide open in welcome. "Demetra, it's so good to see you."

But the woman shook her head and backed up. "No, Eloisa. It's not good. Not good at all."

Eloisa linked her arm through Demetra's, her mind racing with concern. Her old friend looked gaunt, haggard.

"What is it?" she asked, guiding her away from the revelry. "What's wrong?"

"I don't want to spoil your evening with my sad tale of woe."

"Please." Eloisa made a chiding noise. "You know all my tales of woe. What do you need?"

"I'm dying, Eloisa."

"Oh no!" Eloisa's heart trembled.

"It's okay. It's all right. I've made peace with it. What I haven't made peace with are my daughters. And I have a huge favor to ask."

"Name it," Eloisa said. "And I will move heaven and earth to make it happen."

# About the Author

LORI WILDE is the *New York Times*, *USA Today*, and *Publishers Weekly* bestselling author of ninety-nine works of romantic fiction. She's a three-time Romance Writers of America RITA Award finalist and has four times been nominated for the Romantic Times Reviewers' Choice Award. She has won numerous other awards as well. Her books have been translated into twenty-six languages, with more than eight million copies sold worldwide. Her breakout novel, *The First Love Cookie Club*, was made into a Hallmark movie titled *A Kismet Christmas*.

Lori is a registered nurse with a BSN and an MLA from Texas Christian University. She holds a certificate in forensics and is also a certified yoga instructor.

A sixth-generation Texan, Lori lives with her husband, Bill, in the Cutting Horse Capital of the World.

## Discover more from
# LORI WILDE

---

The Summer
That Shaped Us

The Undercover
Cowboy

How the Cowboy
Was Won

---

### JUBILEE, TEXAS

A Cowboy for Christmas

The Cowboy and the Princess

The Cowboy Takes a Bride

### TWILIGHT, TEXAS

The Christmas Brides of Twilight

The Cowboy Cookie Challenge

Second Chance Christmas

The Christmas Backup Plan

The Christmas Dare

The Christmas Key

Cowboy, It's Cold Outside

A Wedding for Christmas

I'll Be Home for Christmas

Christmas at Twilight

The Valentine's Day Disaster

The Welcome Home Garden Club

The First Love Cookie Club

The True Love Quilting Club

The Sweethearts' Knitting Club

### MOONGLOW BAY

The Wedding at Moonglow Bay

The Lighthouse on Moonglow Bay

The Keepsake Sisters

The Moonglow Sisters

---